DECROMANCER

by Ken Warner

© 2024 by Kenneth H Warner, II

All rights reserved.

Maps by Zenta Brice

CONTENTS

CHAPTER ONE: LOOKOUT 1

CHAPTER TWO: COUNCIL 13

CHAPTER THREE: SPANBROOK 33

CHAPTER FOUR: THE SWORD 45

CHAPTER FIVE: SHADOW 59

CHAPTER SIX: UNLEASHED 71

CHAPTER SEVEN: PRINCESS MIRANDA 85

CHAPTER EIGHT: ESCAPE ATTEMPT 103

CHAPTER NINE: SHAPESHIFTING...115

CHAPTER TEN: MAGES GALORE 127

CHAPTER ELEVEN: FALLOUT 139

CHAPTER TWELVE: MISSING 151

CHAPTER THIRTEEN: THE RITE OF BINDING 161

CHAPTER FOURTEEN: RESCUE 173

CHAPTER FIFTEEN: BAIT 185

CHAPTER SIXTEEN: CLOSE CALL 195

CHAPTER SEVENTEEN: FOREIGN EMISSARY 207

CHAPTER EIGHTEEN: ANGUISH 221

CHAPTER NINETEEN: RESISTANCE LEADERS 235

CHAPTER TWENTY: ICE FORTRESS 247

CHAPTER TWENTY-ONE: LAYING PLANS 259

CHAPTER TWENTY-TWO: LURING THE ENEMY 271

CHAPTER TWENTY-THREE: SPRINGING THE TRAP 283

CHAPTER TWENTY-FOUR: FALLING BACK 293

CHAPTER TWENTY-FIVE: TRUE NAME 311

CHAPTER TWENTY-SIX: THE BATTLE OF HIGHGATE 327

CHAPTER TWENTY-SEVEN: TACTICAL WITHDRAWAL ... 339

CHAPTER TWENTY-EIGHT: BAYFAST 349

CHAPTER TWENTY-NINE: PLAGUE 361

CHAPTER THIRTY: LEVERAGE 371

CHAPTER THIRTY-ONE: CHANGE OF PLANS 381

CHAPTER THIRTY-TWO: SACRIFICE 391

CHAPTER THIRTY-THREE: GOING HOME 401

CHAPTER THIRTY-FOUR: THE RETURN OF THE QUEEN 413

EPILOGUE 421

NECROMANCER

CHAPTER ONE
LOOKOUT

amilla had camped in the woods to the east of Spanbrook Town, not far from the fields where the wayfarers always set up their tents. This kept her close enough to the town and Castle Barclay to keep a lookout, but not so close that she was likely to attract attention. Since the princesses had left with their armies, not a single elf had come near her little camp. She was close enough to the road to see their patrols passing back and forth, but they didn't seem to be searching for stragglers. Camilla kept her camp invisible and cast the spells to prevent anyone from hearing her.

Most of the elves had departed for the battle in Stoutwall, but they'd left a few companies behind to guard the castle. Now they were all back, their numbers diminished in the fighting. It had been three days since their arrival. Camilla had awoken the morning after the battle to find their army camped in the fields to the east of Castle Barclay. She'd caught a brief glimpse of Nyro walking among her troops, but lost track of her. After moving to a better vantage point, she spotted her again moving into an enormous tent they'd erected that seemed to be their command center.

At that point, Camilla had contacted Princess Jezebel by mirror to let her know Nyro had returned with her army. And though she'd spent the entire day watching that tent, she'd never seen Nyro emerge. She had no idea if she was still inside, or if she'd created a portal to return to the elven continent. And try as she might, she couldn't find a position that afforded her much of a view inside the tent.

The center half of its front end was open to the elements, but for most of the day, she could see only a few feet into the tent. As sunset approached, more of the interior was illuminated, but not enough to tell if Nyro was in there. And there was no way to get any closer without moving through the camp—something Camilla was not about to risk.

Camilla had a feeling Nyro had returned to her island in the elven kingdom of Drengrvollr. Jezebel had told her they'd seen Nyro taking Emma there through a portal. Nyro could have secured her there, then returned to move her army back to Spanbrook before going back to Drengrvollr.

Or she could have taken up residence inside the castle.

Camilla knew about two secret passageways leading into Castle Barclay. They'd taken the one that led to the Barclay farm when they evacuated. The safety walls had been lowered, but she could call air to raise them to their original positions. Or she could try the one that came out behind the smithy in town.

Of course, if Nyro *were* in the castle, going in herself would be extremely dangerous. Camilla knew the castle, though, and felt confident she could move about without being detected. Establishing Nyro's whereabouts could be crucial to the war effort. It could help Princess Jezebel plan an assassination if Nyro were here in Spanbrook—or a surprise attack on her troops if she were not.

One way or another, Camilla was determined to help her princess recover Emma and defeat Nyro. Learning her sister's fate after all these years had ignited a fire in her bosom that only revenge would extinguish. Camilla had accepted long ago that Gemma must be dead. She would have found some way to get word to her if she'd been alive. But learning that Nyro had killed her reopened old wounds, rekindling her grief.

Camilla and Gemma had lost their parents to the plague when they were very young. Their mother's sister had raised them along with her own four children, but the girls always knew she didn't relish the task. When their magic first manifested, it made matters that much worse. Their aunt considered them freaks and was only too happy to be rid of them when they came of age and went off to the university.

Gemma had been her sole confidant for as long as she could remember. Their adoptive family had provided food, shelter, and safety, but life on that farm hadn't brought much in the way of love or joy. The sisters had made the trek from western Dorshire to the university on their own, going on foot the entire way. The journey had taken many weeks, and they'd become closer than ever. They promised each other that they'd stay together always, and upon graduating, would only accept an assignment *together*.

As it happened, the governors assigned Gemma to Spanbrook and Camilla to a princedom in southern Maeda. Camilla had pleaded with them to reconsider, but they wouldn't hear of it. So she defied them, traveling with her sister to Castle Spanbrook and begging Prince Aldo to accept her service along with Gemma's.

Aldo had agreed. Witches and wizards enjoyed more freedom than sorcerers when it came to life choices like this. Camilla could have turned down the governors' assignment and gone off on her own wherever she pleased. In the worst case, she would have made a life for herself in Spanbrook Town, independent of the prince. But Aldo had pleaded her case to the governors, and they finally acquiesced, approving her formal assignment to Spanbrook.

Gemma and Camilla had served the Barclay family their entire adult lives. And Aldo, Jezebel, and Allison had treated them with love and respect at all times, earning their loyalty. So in addition to avenging Gemma's murder, Camilla wanted to do whatever she could to ensure their princedom's victory.

Camilla decided to try the entrance behind the smithy. After the evacuation, the elves had killed the town's remaining population, closed the gates, and posted guards. Camilla didn't know a way inside. She could get into Castle Barclay, but that had been built *outside* the town. Spanbrook town had grown beyond its walls over the years. Princess Jezebel had commissioned repairs to sections of the wall that had fallen into disrepair, but some areas of the town still lay beyond them, especially on the west end.

Making herself invisible, Camilla left camp and set out through the woods. With the elven army camped outside the castle to the east, going that way would be hazardous. Moving around the city to the north meant crossing the river, but that would be far safer. She'd have to swim, but the Ember wasn't that deep, and the current wasn't very strong.

Camilla reached the river without encountering a soul. Stripping out of her robes, she waved her wand to tuck them into the void. Invisible or not, she had no way to hide her splashing from observers, so she checked the surrounding area before moving into the water. She didn't see anyone and heard nothing but chirping birds, so she waded into the river. Clutching her wand in her teeth, she swam the rest of the way across, worrying the whole way that someone would see her. But she made it to the opposite shore without incident.

Calling air to dry herself off, then removing her robes from the void, she dressed as quickly as she could and set off again. As she neared the western end of town, she heard metallic clinking noises coming from the general direction of the smithy. Drawing closer, she could hear voices, too. Emerging from the woods, she darted from one alley to the next, peering around corners before proceeding. She thought the noises had to be coming from the smithy, though the way they echoed off the buildings made it impossible to pinpoint the source.

It felt so strange to see the town empty. Spanbrook was small compared to cities like Arthos or Highgate, but even in the dead of night, there tended to be at least a few people about. And it was always bustling with activity during the day. Seeing it abandoned like this filled her with sorrow.

Sure enough, when Camilla reached an intersection that afforded her a view of her destination, she spotted several elves. They were hard at work on something, but she couldn't tell what. Moving around the block, Camilla approached the smithy from the opposite direction. And from here, she could tell that they were crafting armor. In the alley behind the smithy, she spotted wooden stalls piled high with breastplates and helmets. This struck her as strange. Why would they need this much armor? The elves had arrived in Anoria well-equipped for battle, with armor and weapons aplenty. If anything, after losing so many soldiers in battle, she figured they'd probably have a surplus.

Looking closer, it struck her that the new armor was too small for elves. Their kind towered over the humans, and this equipment would never fit them. What was going on here? This was only a small smithy, and if they were working here, she had to believe they'd have other teams using the larger facilities inside the walls, too. She'd need to tell Jezebel about this for sure.

The hidden entrance to the secret tunnel was in the little alley behind the smithy, and there was no way Camilla could get there unnoticed. With those stalls there, even if she tried climbing her way across, the noise of her passage was sure to alert the elves.

Camilla went back the way she'd come. She'd have to try the passage from the Barclay farm. It took her a couple of hours to make her way back across the river and out along the path running parallel to the road. She saw a couple of elven patrols go by, but they gave no indication that they'd spotted her.

This route took her out near Rockhedge, which she always did her best to avoid, but it couldn't be helped. It was daytime, so the spirits that dwelled there were unlikely to be active. A shiver still ran down her spine as the giant stones came into view, and she hurried onward.

Reaching the edge of the forest, Camilla scanned the road in both directions to make sure the coast was clear. Even invisible, her crossing here would kick up dust and dirt that might alert anyone nearby to her presence. Holding her breath in suspense, she hurried to the other side, breathing a sigh of relief when she reached the grass. She scanned the road again, but there was no sign of any witnesses.

Camilla reached the farm and made her way cautiously toward the barn. The house looked unmolested, and there was no exterior damage to any of the other structures. Reaching the barn, Camilla crept inside.

"Shit," she muttered. The trapdoor leading to the tunnel was gone. Beyond the first couple of steps, the passage was filled with dirt, and judging by the ditch leading toward the back of the barn, someone had collapsed the tunnel. She could try calling air to remove the dirt and clear a path, but there was a good chance that whoever had done this had sealed off the tunnel at other points as well. This wasn't going to work.

Leaving the barn, she headed back toward her camp. She'd have to contact Jezebel by mirror and ask about other secret entries. Camilla knew there were more, but had no idea where they might be.

As she reached the road, she got a bad feeling someone was watching her. She was invisible and checked her spells to be sure, but she couldn't shake the sense that watchful eyes were about. She decided not to try crossing the road just yet. There were only fields on this side, leaving her more exposed, but at least her progress across the grass would betray no sign of her presence.

Camilla spotted a cloud of dust in the distance and froze. It was a patrol heading toward her from town. Creeping farther from the road, she crouched, wand at the ready. She could make out the individual elves as they came nearer. There were six of them, all soldiers, based on their armor and weapons. Good thing. A mage among them might have sensed her invisibility spell. She held her breath as they went by, her heartbeat pounding in her ears.

They didn't detect her. Camilla breathed a sigh of relief, standing upright and keeping an eye on them as they faded into the distance. She didn't feel like anyone was watching her anymore, and there shouldn't be another patrol for a while, so she hurried across the road, glad to move into the cover of the trees.

Camilla wasn't certain of the route back to her camp from here but knew the general direction she needed to go. After forging ahead for several minutes, she reached a clearing and had to get her bearings before deciding which way to continue. She was pretty sure she still needed to move farther west.

"Halt!" a voice cried out before she'd taken more than a few steps. A soldier had stepped out from behind a tree, standing on the path she needed to take, brandishing a spear. He was human—thank the stars, he was human. Several others appeared from other paths, and

Camilla was surrounded. "We can't see you, but we know you're there!" the first soldier said. "Show yourself or I'll order my men to cut you down!"

Camilla knew most of the elves could call only the four basic forces—only the mages could cast illusions. And as far as she knew, they hadn't encountered elves masquerading as humans. Playing it safe, she held out her wand and cast the spell to cancel illusions. Nothing happened, which meant they were human. She removed her invisibility spell. Holding both hands overhead and pointing her wand toward the sky, she said, "I'm on your side! My name is Camilla, one of Princess Jezebel's witches. I'm here on her orders, doing reconnaissance."

"I know her," the lead soldier said, lowering his spear. Camilla recognized him, but couldn't place him—or remember his name. "She's telling the truth."

"She *looks* like Camilla, there's no denying that," one of the others said. He had an arrow nocked in his bow, aimed at her. "But how do we know it's not one of their mages masquerading as her, eh?"

"He's got a point," the lead soldier said with a frown, but Camilla noted that he didn't raise his spear. "Their Highnesses held a celebration in the private hall right before the invasion. What was the occasion?"

"Princess Jezebel's pregnancy," Camilla said.

"And what did Princess Jezebel wear that night?"

"A white dress," Camilla said. "Quite revealing, as I recall."

"What about Princess Allison?"

"Identical dress in black," she said. "They always dress the same, one in black and the other in white."

"Satisfied?" he called out to the other soldier.

"How could I be? I wasn't there!"

"Well, I was, and she's right," the lead soldier said. "I was in the royal guard before the battle and on duty that night," he added to Camilla.

"Ah, yes," she said. "I knew I recognized you. Lance, isn't it?"

"Yes, my lady. It's good to see you again, despite the circumstances. We'd better get you to our camp."

"Your camp? How many of you are there?"

"Not many, I'm afraid," he said. "Couple of dozen, not nearly enough for a proper company. And no mages until now. Our captain will be glad you're here."

"And who's your captain?"

"Mobo from the Eagle Company. Well, that wasn't his rank, I don't think, but he's taken on the role for our little group. Doing a good job of it, too."

"All right," Camilla said. "Lead the way." She still wanted to find a way inside the castle. Doing it with an armed guard wouldn't make her any safer if Nyro were there, but it would put her mind at ease a bit.

Lance led them through the forest, and they walked in silence. Their camp was in a clearing by the base of a rocky escarpment. Lance introduced her to Mobo when they arrived, and as predicted, he seemed thrilled to welcome a mage to their band.

"How did you come to be here?" Camilla asked. "The rest of the Eagle Company evacuated with Their Highnesses."

"I was probably left for dead," he said. Mobo was tall even for a Shifari, lighter-skinned than most. "Took a blow to the head that knocked me out despite my helmet, and by the time I woke up, the battle was over, and everyone was gone. Most of these men have a similar story. We haven't been able to do much, but maybe with you here, we can inflict some damage."

"On the elven army?" Camilla asked. Mobo nodded. "No, I don't think so. That would be suicide. Nyro's Sacred Circle is gone, but they still have plenty of mages, all of whom are much more powerful than I."

"What do you mean the Sacred Circle is gone?" he asked skeptically. She told him about the battle in Stoutwall. "That's incredible," he said, shaking his head when she was done. "So what's Nyro doing now?"

"That's what I'd like to know," Camilla said. She told him about what she'd seen so far and her attempts to get inside the castle.

"What would she be doing in there?" Mobo asked.

"Don't know," Camilla said with a shrug. "I haven't seen any signs of life, but if she *is* there, our sorcerers may be able to take her out.

And if she's gone back to the elven realm, our forces could launch a sneak attack. We could inflict some heavy damage on that army if they don't know we're coming."

"I like it," Mobo said with a nod. "So how do we get into the castle? Or inside the town, for that matter—the castle might be empty, but they've got guards posted all along the city wall."

"I'll need to contact Princess Jezebel," Camilla said.

"And how do you plan on doing that?" he said with a chuckle. "Stoutwall's a long way from here."

Camilla held out one hand, waving her wand with the other and casting the spell to remove her mirror from the void. "With this," she said with a grin, showing it to Mobo.

"Oh, I've heard about these," he said, his eyes wide. "Her Highness has one as well, then? You can speak to her this way?"

"Yes, and I should do so now," she said. "If you'll excuse me?"

Mobo nodded, and Camilla moved off to get a little privacy. It took a few tries, but she finally found the princess staring back at her in the glass. She could hear the girls in the background and smiled.

"Camilla," Jezebel said. "Is everything all right?"

She told her about the soldiers she'd joined and her efforts to get inside the castle.

"It sounds like they're making armor for humans," the princess said with a frown.

"That would be my guess, too."

"This doesn't make any sense. Have you seen any prisoners in their camp?"

"No, Your Highness. I'm wondering if they're keeping them in the castle somewhere. The dungeons, perhaps? But neither these soldiers nor I have seen any evidence of activity in the castle."

Jezebel told her where to find a couple of the other hidden tunnels. "Glean what you can, but don't take any great risks. If you do find Nyro in there, get out as quickly as you can."

Camilla conferred with Mobo again, and they decided to wait until nightfall before executing their mission. She'd make them invisible, but they'd need to move uncomfortably close to the enemy camp to get through the city wall, and that would be safer under the cover of darkness.

She ate with the soldiers—they'd raided some of the stores the army had left behind. It was the same kind of fare she'd been getting by on since she'd been here, dried meat and fruit. But it was nice not to eat alone for once.

After dark, she set out with Mobo and Lance, making the three of them invisible. Stealth would be the key to their success, not strength in numbers. There was an entire army out there, so a larger force would be no help. Mobo led the way through the forest. The elves had a heavy guard stationed at the city gates, so they crossed the road about a mile out and then moved in closer.

Camilla took the lead after that. South of the gates, but still well north of the army camp, she took them right up to the city wall. This section had fallen into extreme disrepair prior to Princess Jezebel's reign, and she'd had it rebuilt. A stone walkway surrounded the wall, and Jezebel had told her how to locate a slab that covered the entrance to a secret tunnel. It was slow going—they had only the moons to light their way, making it tough to see very much.

Finally, she found it. A flower marking etched into the corner of one of the slabs. Calling air, she lifted the stone off the ground, sliding it over on top of the next one. Sure enough, this revealed a hidden stairway underneath. Mobo led the way, Lance right behind him, and Camilla last. She called air again to slide the stone back into place, plunging them into utter darkness.

Camilla called a small flame to light their way, and they continued down the steps. At the bottom, they found a tunnel leading under the city wall. They followed that, eventually reaching another set of steps. Moving up those, they found a trapdoor at the top. Camilla extinguished her flame, waited a minute for her eyes to adjust, then inched the door open. Peering into the space above them, she could see only a faint light within. Moving to the top of the steps, she risked a small flame.

As Jezebel had told her, it was a storage room in the back of a bakery. She beckoned the two soldiers to follow her. She closed the trapdoor behind them, and they moved through the space. Mobo led them out of the shop and into the city. Again, the emptiness struck Camilla. In all the years she'd lived here, she'd never seen the streets of Spanbrook Town so lifeless.

Halfway across town, they reached the potter's shop they were seeking. Jezebel had told her there was a false wall in the back. Pressing the right stone would activate the mechanism to move that aside, revealing a hidden stairway leading down to the secret tunnel into the castle. Camilla called a small flame again, but they had trouble finding the right stone—it wasn't where Jezebel had said it would be.

Finally, they found it. Three stones from the left, not from the right as she'd been told. Mobo and Lance moved into the stairway, and Camilla closed the wall behind them. Down the steps, through a long tunnel, and they reached another stairway delving even deeper. The light of Camilla's flame didn't reach the bottom—she knew they'd have to cross under the moat, so this wasn't surprising.

On the other side, they reached another long stairway leading up. And at the top, they reached the movable section of the wall leading into the castle. This time, they found the stone they needed to press exactly where it was supposed to be. Moving through the entry and closing the false wall behind them, they found themselves in a seldom-used area of the undercroft.

Camilla led the way across the castle. They passed through the dungeons, which were empty, much to her surprise. After seeing the armor the elves were making, she felt sure they'd find it full of people.

They reached the stairway to the main level, stopping to listen for a moment. It was utterly silent. They crept up the steps, emerging in the main entry hall. There were no signs of life here. Camilla led them through the castle, checking the administrative area, the great hall, the private dining room, and the princesses' chambers, but they found no one. Nor any evidence that anyone had been here since the evacuation.

"No Nyro," Mobo said. "I'm not sure if I should feel relieved or disappointed."

Camilla had to chuckle. "Both, I think. Come with me—I want to check one more thing."

She led them up to the ramparts, moving around to the east side, overlooking the army camp. From this vantage point, she could see that there was a huge opening on this end of the command center tent, too. There was a flickering light inside, but from this angle, she couldn't see much beyond the entrance. If Nyro were in there, she'd have no way to know it.

"That's the tent you told us about?" Lance said. "Where you saw Nyro go?"

"Yes, but I can't imagine she's still in there," Camilla said with a sigh.

"Might be," Mobo said. "Could be smart to keep a watch around the clock. Both here and somewhere with a view of the other end. In case she comes out."

"I know the perfect spot," Camilla said. "I'll contact—"

At that moment, a blinding light erupted inside the tent, and Camilla had to shield her eyes. It was as if someone had captured the sun and brought it to earth.

"What the hell is that?" Lance said, turning his head away from the light.

Everything went dark again, and Camilla couldn't see a thing. Once her eyes had adjusted, she spotted two figures moving through the camp, out beyond the tent, illuminated only by the campfires. Both were female elves, tall, black, and naked. They were too far away to get a good look at their faces, so Camilla couldn't tell if either of them had a scar running down one cheek. But of all the elves they'd encountered so far, only Nyro and some of her Sacred Circle had gone about in the nude.

For the next hour, the elves moved through the army, stopping to talk with various soldiers. A core group followed them around like sheep, and Camilla figured they had to be her top generals and mages. After that, the pair led their entourage back into the command tent. As before, a brilliant light erupted from within, disappearing again only seconds later. Camilla stayed on the ramparts with Mobo and Lance for the rest of the night, but the two elves did not make another appearance.

CHAPTER TWO
COUNCIL

llison knew she was dreaming but couldn't wake up. She was walking through a castle undercroft, but it was nowhere she recognized. It was dark, the small flame she'd called providing the only light. Jezebel was calling out to her, but Allison didn't know where she was. She was trying to follow the sound of her voice, but it kept echoing off the stone walls, making it impossible to find the source.

I'm dreaming. This isn't real, she told herself. But it didn't help. For some reason, she was terrified.

"Jezebel?" she cried. "Where are you?"

Her own voice echoed off the stone, and it didn't seem that Jezebel had heard her. She kept calling Allison's name, too. Finally, Allison spotted her wife in the distance, far across the undercroft—it seemed like it went on for miles. She called out to her again, but Jezebel didn't see her.

Allison ran toward her, the sound of her footfalls multiplied a million times, and finally Jezebel spotted her. Allison smiled, but Jezebel screamed, her expression one of horror. Allison didn't understand, until suddenly she realized she herself was on fire.

Waking with a start, Allison sat up in bed, throwing the covers off of her. It was only a dream. There were no flames, only moonlight streaming in through the window. Jezebel lay beside her, sound asleep. They were inside the castle in Stoutwall, where they'd been staying since the battle. Allison breathed a sigh of relief. Despite knowing it was a dream, it had seemed so *real*.

Slipping out of bed, Allison padded over to the door connecting their room to their daughters'. She opened it, careful not to make any noise. Peering into the other room, she could see Leda and Alanna lying in bed, breathing softly. Leda was curled up in a ball, Alanna spread eagle beside her, one arm lying on Leda's head. Allison had to stifle a giggle.

She returned to her own chamber, closing the door softly behind her. Gazing out the window, she saw the moonlight reflecting off the lake. Dawn was approaching, and she doubted she'd get back to sleep, so she decided to start her day. Slipping out of her nightgown, she donned her armor, the leather like a second skin.

Allison walked through the castle and into the courtyard, pulling her carpet out of the void and unfurling it on the ground. Sitting in the center she took off, startling a couple of the dragons. They'd taken to roosting on the castle walls at night, like a flock of giant, serpentine birds. Allison had to laugh.

Shooting over the waterfall, she circled the lake a couple of times, flying at top speed for the pure joy of it. After that, she spiraled outward from the castle, on the lookout for any unwelcome intruders below. All was quiet and peaceful, though, the landscape betraying no evidence of the violence that had taken place here only a few days earlier.

The sun had cracked the horizon by the time she returned to the castle. She spotted some of their soldiers stirring in the army camp outside the walls. It was staggering how many troops they'd assembled here—and how many they'd lost. And for what? Nyro was still at large, undoubtedly preparing for her next attack.

This peace and quiet was a lie. Anoria was on the brink of apocalypse. The elf they'd captured in Spanbrook told them Nyro wanted to exterminate their people. The entire continent. And Syllith had confirmed Nyro's intentions. They'd managed to deal her an unexpected blow here, but this respite wouldn't last much longer. She'd regroup and formulate a new plan that was sure to unleash horrors they would never see coming.

Landing in the courtyard, Allison rolled up her carpet and tucked it into the void. The dragons were waking up, stretching and roaring to announce the sunrise like so many roosters before taking off to hunt for their breakfast. Allison could only hope they'd forego the local livestock in favor of wild game in the forest surrounding most of the lake.

Heading into the great hall, Allison spotted Shatter sitting near the head table. Only a handful of people were here this early, and it didn't look like the staff was serving breakfast yet. Except that Shatter had several platters of meat and eggs in front of him—enough food for three or four people.

"Good morning," Allison said with a smile, sitting down next to him. She'd agreed to an early training session with him, Imani, and Battleaxe, and they'd decided to meet here.

Shatter grunted a reply as he scarfed down his food. Allison couldn't stand to eat before training. The mere thought of it nauseated her. Battleaxe showed up a few minutes later, sitting down next to Allison.

"That does look good," she said, eyeing Shatter's feast, "but I think I'll eat after we're done."

"My thought exactly," Allison said.

Shatter belched.

"I could use some coffee, though," Battleaxe said, gazing around the hall. "I'm going to go find some."

She strode off toward the kitchen, returning a minute later with a flagon and four mugs on a big tray. Setting it all down on the table, she poured herself some. "Coffee?"

"Yes, please," Allison said.

Shatter grunted and nodded. Battleaxe poured them each a mug. She and Allison drank their coffee and chatted while Shatter finished his meal.

"Where the hell is Imani?" Battleaxe said, getting to her feet when Shatter was done.

"I haven't seen her," Allison said, standing up and pushing in her chair. "I'll run upstairs and see if I can find her. I think I know which room she's in."

"Never mind," said Battleaxe, nodding toward the door.

Allison turned to see Imani striding over to them. "I'm not late, am I?"

"You? Never," Battleaxe said, her voice deadpan.

"Shatter just finished his breakfast," Allison said with a grin, "so you're right on time."

"Let's do this," Shatter said, belching again.

He led them out of the castle, across the moat, and onto the grounds, between the army camp and the lake. Like Allison, Battleaxe had already donned her leather armor. They found Shatter and Imani's squires waiting for them, each standing guard over a pile of plate armor. It was going to take those two a while to get suited up, so Allison and Battleaxe squared off.

They'd agreed not to use magic against each other in these sessions—Imani was no mage, so that wouldn't be fair. And they wanted to focus on their fighting skills. They could, however, use void magic to switch weapons.

In recent times, Allison had been fighting primarily with her two longswords. But those had been damaged beyond repair in the recent battle. She actually had more experience with her two-handed sword, though, and decided to use that today.

She pulled her blade out of oblivion, and Battleaxe her axes. They circled each other for a few moments until Battleaxe charged, swinging both weapons. Allison evaded one axe, parrying the other with her blade, spinning around for a vicious overhead stroke. Back and forth they fought, neither able to gain any advantage. Allison managed to knock one axe out of her hand at one point, but Battleaxe pulled another out of the void and kept fighting.

After twenty minutes of this, they decided to call it a draw. Battleaxe tucked her weapons into the void, giving Allison a one-armed hug and patting her back. Allison was soaked in sweat but felt good. She'd spent most of the time since the battle trying to imagine what Nyro's next move might be, and the vigorous exercise finally got her mind off that.

Shatter and Imani were ready, so they faced each other next. They were of a similar height, but Imani was thin and muscular, while Shatter was built like a mountain, much more massive than the Shifari woman. Like Allison, Imani wielded a two-handed great sword, and Shatter used his long-handled sword with the spike on the back end.

Allison was quite familiar with Imani's fighting style, so she paid close attention to Shatter, analyzing his tactics. His method was simple and direct, relying on his brute strength more often than not. But he was fast, too, much more so than Allison would have expected for someone so huge. And efficient—he moved no more than necessary, expending as little energy as possible.

Imani was agile and flexible, and Allison knew only too well how difficult it could be to land a solid blow on her. Shatter seemed to grow frustrated by this and started overcommitting on some of his attacks. Only slightly, but it was enough for Imani to unbalance him. After one such exchange, she tried kicking him in the ribs to knock him down, but it had no effect; she bounced off of him.

In the end, Shatter's greater size and weight proved too much for the Shifari. He disarmed her, throwing her to the ground and planting the spike on the joint between her helmet and breastplate.

"Yield!" he shouted. Imani laughed, trying to dislodge his weapon, but couldn't move it. Shatter growled at her.

"All right, all right—you win," she said.

Several people from the army camp had wandered over to watch, and they cheered for Shatter.

"Good fight," Battleaxe said, nodding appreciatively. "Great focus," she added to Shatter. "Didn't let her distract you."

"Why would I be distracted?" he said with a frown.

"She's got that same energy as Allure," Allison told him. "Don't you feel it?"

"Sympathetic magic does not affect me," Shatter said.

"No kidding?" Battleaxe said. "So Allure can't read you?"

"She's tried, but no," he confirmed.

"How do *you* do it?" Battleaxe asked Allison. "I hear you two spar all the time. Her sex magic doesn't distract you?"

Imani chuckled.

"One gets used to it, I suppose," Allison said, catching Imani's gaze and smiling.

"My 'sex magic' stopped working on Her Highness once we'd slept together a couple of times," Imani said with a grin.

Battleaxe's jaw dropped. "Damn. I had no idea you two were involved. Does Princess Jezebel know?" she added.

Allison felt herself blushing. "Yes, she knows—she condoned it. But it was only a fling. Very short-lived."

"You've got a bit of that sex magic, too, you know," Battleaxe said to Allison.

"Oh, please," she said, shaking her head. "You're imagining things."

"No, I don't think so," said Battleaxe. "Not as strong as Imani or Allure perhaps, but it's there." Allison had been told this before but thought it was ridiculous.

Battleaxe and Imani agreed to go next. Battleaxe offered to give her a few minutes to catch her breath, but Imani hardly seemed winded. She told her she needed no rest. They fought, and at first, it seemed like Imani might overwhelm her old schoolmate.

"Damn sex magic," Battleaxe muttered, and Allison realized she must have been distracted.

Battleaxe disarmed the Shifari woman after that, but still couldn't land a killing blow with her axes. She managed to keep Imani from recovering her sword, and once the Shifari disarmed *her*, they fought empty-handed. Imani's longer reach proved too great an advantage to overcome, so Battleaxe finally tackled her, and they wrestled until Battleaxe put her in a chokehold. Imani struggled to escape but ultimately yielded.

The crowd had grown during the match, and they had a couple of dozen spectators now. They cheered for both women.

Allison faced off with Shatter next. She chose double sabers instead of her usual two-handed sword. Shatter's reach with that nightmare weapon of his would exceed her own regardless of what she used, negating any advantage of the longsword. And the two sabers would improve her defense against the power of his swing.

The fight started, and Allison took the initiative. Charging her opponent before he could swing his blade, she sliced at his neck with both sabers, one after the other. Shatter was incredibly nimble for such a large man, and slipped out of the way, countering with an attack of his own. Allison kept him on defense after that, going at him with every conceivable attack, but Shatter evaded them all.

Tucking her sabers into the void and swapping them for daggers, she tried a new strategy. Shatter's weapon was too large for close-quarters fighting, so she stayed close, trying to slip her blades into the joints in his armor. He grunted in frustration, lifting her by the neck with one hand and tossing her away from him.

Allison hit the ground hard, the impact knocking the wind out of her. His unconventional move had taken her by surprise. She scrambled to her feet as he pursued her, swinging his blade over and over again. The daggers were useless at this range, so she switched them out for her two-handed sword.

For several minutes, they fought hard, each pressing the attack against the other. Allison was most proficient with this blade, but it didn't matter. Shatter was too fast and strong. She misjudged his swing one time, and the force of the blow when she tried to parry broke her sword in two. He swept out her legs with the butt end of his weapon, placing the blade against her throat as she hit the ground.

"Yield!" he shouted. Allison thought about producing another weapon and trying to get out of this, but it was no use. He was pressing his blade into her neck, and while the spells she'd woven into her armor stopped it from piercing the leather, the blunt force might collapse her windpipe. "YIELD!" Shatter repeated.

"I yield!" Allison screamed.

Shatter grinned at her, withdrawing his blade and holding out one hand to help her up. "You fight well," he said as she regained her feet. "I had to work for that."

Allison realized then that their audience had continued growing, and there were at least a hundred soldiers now, men and women, all cheering for Shatter. It seemed like most of them were from Stoutwall.

"You're saying it wasn't any work to beat me?" Imani said with a grin.

Shatter only shrugged.

"That council meeting is starting soon," Battleaxe said, "but this was fun. We should do it again."

"Agreed," said Allison. "It'll help me sharpen my skills." Shatter was the toughest fighter she'd ever faced, and the best way to improve was to practice against someone better.

"Sounds like a plan," Imani agreed, as her squire helped her out of her armor. "But right now, I'm sweating like a pig, and I can't stand my own stink." She stripped out of her undergarments, going completely nude, and striding off across the grounds. Her squire watched her with a grin. Much of the crowd had gone back to the camp, but the stragglers cheered and whistled for Imani.

"Uh... where is she going?" Battleaxe said.

"The lake, I think," Allison said, following her. "Come on!"

Battleaxe went with her, but Shatter stayed behind. Sure enough, Imani jumped into the water. "Much better," she called out to them. "Come on!"

Battleaxe gave Allison a frown. "Public nudity's not my thing."

Some of the spectators from their sparring session had followed them, and more were coming.

"Mine neither," Allison said with a shrug. "But that does look refreshing." She started removing her armor, and the gathering crowd cheered her on.

"Fuck it," Battleaxe said as Allison finished stripping, tucked her armor into the void, and ran toward the water. She took off her armor and joined the other two in the lake. Before Allison knew it, half of the watching soldiers had jumped in as well.

The swim in the cold water was invigorating, and Allison felt clean by the time she returned to dry land. Dozens of soldiers had joined them in the lake, but Allison, Imani, and Battleaxe needed to get ready for their council meeting. Allison called air to dry off Imani and herself, and Battleaxe cast her own spell.

Imani strode off toward the camp with no thought for her lack of clothing. Bathing nude was one thing, but Allison was not about to traipse through the castle that way, and her armor was wet and smelly. She and Battleaxe both cast illusion spells to make it look like they were wearing clothes, then headed back to the castle together.

Jezebel greeted Allison with a kiss when she reached their chambers. "Swimming in the nude?" she asked. "I saw you from the window and wished I could have joined you."

"It wouldn't do to have the ruling princess so exposed," Allison replied with a grin, canceling her illusion spell. Jezebel looked her up and down, flashing her a sultry smile. "I'm only a princess *consort*, so I can get away with it."

"You're probably right," Jezebel said with a sigh.

"Why couldn't you have joined us, though? Other than the impropriety?"

"I just finished speaking with Camilla," she said with a meaningful look.

"What's happening?"

"I'll fill you in at the meeting," Jezebel said. "Come on—we'd better go before we're late."

Allison threw on some clothes, and the two of them headed down to Augustine's private dining hall. His council chambers were too small for all the extra attendees. In addition to his usual staff, Prince Carlo and his daughter, Princess Yolanda, from Blackstone were present, as well as Allison, Jezebel, Khaldun, Mira, Gregor, Amari, and Imani from Spanbrook, Allure, Sage, Battleaxe, and Mist from the university, Prince Leto from Keepstone, and Commandant Bishop from the Bastion. Allison had flown Governor Amelia back to the university the previous day.

Prince Augustine called the meeting to order, and said, "I believe Princess Jezebel has some news for us this morning."

"Yes," Jezebel said, clearing her throat. "I just spoke with our witch, Camilla, by mirror. She's in Spanbrook, keeping an eye on things for us, as you all know." She spent several minutes explaining everything Camilla had seen and done the previous day.

"They're crafting armor for humans?" Allison said. "But Camilla found no evidence of human prisoners in the castle or the camp?"

Jezebel shrugged. "I can't explain it."

"We diminished her forces," said Augustine. "If she is holding prisoners somewhere, it would make sense to arm and equip them to fight against us. She could use magic to compel them into service. We'll have to keep an eye out for this."

"Camilla also suggested Nyro's absence might make this a good time for a surprise attack on her army," said Jezebel.

"Surely Nyro can communicate with her commanders via mirror, just like we do," said Khaldun. "By opening a portal, she could join the battle within minutes if we were to attack."

"So Nyro's not residing in your castle," Leto said.

"Nor anywhere in Anoria," Jezebel said. "The light of the sun inside that tent? That must be Nyro opening a portal back to the elven continent. It would be daylight there when it's night here. She took Emma there, and that must be where she's staying."

"Literally the light of the sun, then," Prince Carlo observed. "Shining through her portal."

"Yes," Jezebel agreed.

"Would mirrors work over such a large distance?" asked Battleaxe.

"We've never tried it," said Sage. "But there's no reason to believe they wouldn't."

"Assuming one of the visiting elves is Nyro," said Allure, "who's her companion? An elf mage reanimated by a new demon, perhaps?"

"That's my guess," Jezebel said.

"We need to find out for sure," Allison said. "I should fly there today. Observe her camp from the castle night and day until she returns."

"You won't be able to tell if it's a normal elf mage or a demon reanimating an elf body," Khaldun pointed out. "Mira should go with you. She'll know the difference if she gets them inside her null."

"Fair enough," Allison agreed. "But I was thinking it could be Emma."

"That's a good point," said Sage. "Leaving Syllith behind last time turned out to be her undoing. I doubt she'd risk that again. She's probably taking Emma with her everywhere. It would be simple enough to keep her under an illusion spell."

"Or perhaps Nyro's companion is an elf mage, and she's keeping Emma tucked into the void," said Gregor.

"Not possible," said Allure. "Nothing in the void can move through a portal."

"One way or another, it would be best to find out who it is," said Jezebel. "Doing so will give us an idea of what Nyro's doing. And if it *is* Emma, we may be able to rescue her."

"Forgive me for my ignorance," said Carlo, "but we've never been assigned a sorcerer in Blacksand, much less a necromancer. Could we perhaps spend a few minutes discussing how all of that works—both in general, and how it happened for Nyro? I understand things are different for her now as a demon, but I'm not entirely clear on the mechanics of it."

"Governor Allure?" said Augustine. "Shatter's been with me for years, so I have a rudimentary understanding of these matters, but I'm sure your explanation would be most enlightening. And reviewing all of this might spark an idea that could help us defeat our mortal foe."

"Yes, of course," Allure said, taking a moment to collect her thoughts. "I suppose it starts with one's heredity. Only someone with a history of magic in their family can become a mage. And to become a sorcerer, one must inherit the talent from *both* parents. Not everyone with magic in their blood will become a witch or wizard, and similarly, only a small percentage of those with a double inheritance will become a sorcerer.

"Anyone with magic can choose to become a mage or not. The basic talent typically manifests itself at a young age, but will not develop without an instrument—a wand or staff—and a teacher.

"Becoming a sorcerer, however, is not a matter of choice. Either one transforms or not. The metamorphosis changes the body—you're all familiar with the outward signs."

"Golden skin and red eyes," Carlo said. "Chiseled features."

"Exactly," Allure said with a nod. "But more importantly, the change opens the mage's channels of power. His or her own body becomes the conduit for the magical force, so no instrument is necessary."

"Dredmort used the rite of binding to create the wraiths," Jezebel said. "That's what happens when you try to use it on a normal mage."

"Yes, that's right," Allure said with a nod. "Nyro created many wraiths during her reign, and they were not seen in Anoria again until Dredmort.

"Nyro and her Sacred Circle all started out as sorcerers. It has been our practice for all of recorded history to bind every sorcerer to a conjurnor. In essence, the mage's soul is tethered to the conjurnor's, and they can do that person no harm. Moreover, during the rite, the conjurnor learns the mage's true name. Uttering that in the naming rite destroys the mage, body and soul."

"So they cannot become a demon," Augustine said. "They're just… gone."

"Yes, that's correct," Allure said. "In recent times, that's what happened to Myrddin of Spanbrook as well as Enigma and Syllith from the university. Those mages can never return as demons."

"And what about necromancers?" asked Yolanda. "They're physically different, too, aren't they? My understanding is that Myrddin's irises turned white."

"They did," said Allure. "And his skin became translucent. Those are the only outward changes when a sorcerer becomes a necromancer. In theory, any sorcerer can use most of the spells that involve necromancy. Summoning ghouls and demons, for example. In reality, few have an affinity for the spirit realm. Princess Allison and I both do, but it's fairly rare.

"Becoming a necromancer is different. To do so requires a rite of binding similar to the one a sorcerer undergoes. Only this one binds a sorcerer's soul to a demon. In essence, the two are merged as one. The rite for binding a demon was lost for centuries after Nyro's downfall."

"Until we found it in Spanbrook," said Khaldun. "Nyro wrote it down on a scroll she hid in a concealed cavity in the mage's tower, along with the pyramid artifact she's using now to create her portals."

"Dredmort found a copy of the spell in Fosland before that," Allure said. "One of the ancient governors retired there and recorded it in one of the books he wrote. We recovered those tomes along with Dredmort's notes after Henry was defeated.

"Historically, the university has never assigned more than one sorcerer to any princedom," Allure continued, "or kingdom in the old days. They assigned Nyro to King Saliman of Pytha. And unbeknownst to the governors, those two began abducting unbound sorcerers before they could be taken to the university. Nyro bound them all to Saliman.

"Nyro also had a strong affinity to the spirit world. She bound a demon and became a necromancer. Over time, every Pythan sorcerer became a necromancer. And by the time Saliman revealed what he had done, it was too late. Commanding the power of so many necromancers, he overran the entire continent.

"Nyro was the most powerful mage in the history of Anoria. She found a way to reverse her bond to Saliman, effectively making her *his* conjurnor. In so doing, she retook her true name."

"What does that mean, exactly?" Khaldun said. "I remember Raphael telling Princess Jezebel and me about that. But I'm not sure I ever understood it. Saliman *knew* Nyro's true name. Did he just forget it when she reversed the bond?"

Allure took a deep breath. "It's tough to explain. When someone becomes a conjurnor, no one *tells* them the sorcerer's true name. They just know it. The rite of binding plants that information in their consciousness."

"Yes, that's exactly how it happened for me," Jezebel said. "Both times."

"When Nyro reversed that bond, the magic she used would have revealed Saliman's true name to her the same way," Allure said. "And taken knowledge of *her* true name away from him. So he wouldn't have known it anymore."

"Saliman wasn't a sorcerer, though," said Imani. "How could he have a true name?"

"Before Nyro, it was believed only sorcerers had one," said Sage. "But her ability to learn Saliman's changed that. He wasn't even a mage, and he had one, so the thinking now is that everyone must have a true name. Unfortunately, there's no way to test the theory. Other than Nyro's reversal, the rite of binding is the only known method of exposing someone's true name."

"Dredmort invoked the wraiths' true names to end them," Allure said, "providing further evidence that everyone has one. They were witches and wizards before they were transformed, not sorcerers."

"Long ago, when Raphael first told Khaldun and me about true names, he said that any sorcerer who learned their own could use it to live forever," Jezebel said. "Yet they were able to kill Nyro after she learned her own true name. How is that possible?"

"Learning your own true name would make you immortal, that much is true," Sage said. "In theory, at least. As far as we know, Nyro's the only one who ever gained such knowledge—and she might well have lived forever were it not for the elves. But learning your true name doesn't prevent you from being killed."

"There might be an opportunity there," Khaldun said. "Saliman knew Nyro's true name for years, right?" Sage nodded. "He could have written it down somewhere. Or revealed it to his heir. The knowledge could be out there somewhere. And if it is, and we can find it, that could be the answer. Using the rite of naming on Nyro would destroy her for good."

"They must have searched for that during the war with the elves," Leto said. "Surely if it had been recorded somewhere, they would have found it."

"We should contact Azure," Mira said. "His people were going to translate the tome we found in Ostland—maybe there's some mention of this in there."

"I'm sorry, but what are you talking about?" said Augustine. "What tome?"

Mira told them all about the historian from Blacksand and the book he'd hidden in Ostland. "Highgate's translators provided us with a summary of the important points, but the invasion started before we ever got a chance to see the full translation."

"It's worth investigating," said Allure. "Acquiring Nyro's true name would change everything."

"Is it possible to cancel the magic when someone invokes your true name?" Khaldun asked.

"No," said Allure. "It's not like other spells. The true name captures a person's most fundamental essence. Invoking it acts directly upon the mage's being, without using any of the forces as a medium, so there is nothing to cancel."

"So we could invoke Nyro's true name even from within Mira's null?" he asked.

"Probably not," said Sage. "Remember, the null works differently. Cancelling a spell negates it. The presence of the null prevents the magic from ever forming in the first place. That's the only thing that could protect against the invocation of a true name."

"So Nyro couldn't counteract it somehow if we were to invoke hers?" Khaldun asked.

Allure and Sage exchanged a glance, and Allure said, "We don't think so. But again, Nyro is unique. For any other sorcerer or necromancer, it would be impossible, but Nyro is the only one who's ever retaken her own true name. We don't believe that would prevent the invocation from working against her, but this is completely untested."

"And Nyro's just a demon now?" said Carlo. "If I've got this right, the elves killed Nyro and the rest of her necromancers, but only their bodies died. Their souls were trapped in Pytha?"

"You've got it right," Allure said with a nod. "When Nyro reversed her bond with Saliman, she took over as emperor. And because the other necromancers were bound to Saliman, she gained control over them *through him*. They became her Sacred Circle, as we refer to them now. For generations, Saliman's direct descendants inherited both his bond to Nyro and the other necromancers' bonds to him.

"When the elves killed them, only their bodies died—dissolving their bonds to Saliman's heir—and their souls continued as demons.

Their souls had merged with their demons when they became necromancers, so each of them existed as a single entity in the spirit realm from that day forward. And as demons, they could possess living beings. That's how Nyro controlled Syllith at first. Once she was liberated from Pytha, she possessed Syllith's body and took over completely.

"Once she reached the elven continent, Nyro killed an elf mage named Estrid, left Syllith's body, and reanimated Estrid's. She's stuck in that body until it dies. As it turns out, a human sorcerer can be bound to her in that form. That's why Nyro abducted the witch, Gemma, from Spanbrook. She forced her to bind Syllith to her. Once that was done, she forced Syllith to bind each member of her Sacred Circle, becoming a necromancer in the process. And each of them reanimated a dead elf, just as Nyro had done with Estrid."

"Which means that like she had done through Saliman and his descendants, Nyro controlled her Sacred Circle through Syllith," Carlo said. "They were bound to Syllith, and she was bound to Nyro."

"Yes," Allure said with a nod. "When Syllith finally escaped and came here, we performed the rite of binding to reassign her bond to Gregor. Her soul became tethered to his instead of Nyro's."

"And then Gregor spoke her true name, destroying Syllith body and soul, and in the process, destroying every member of the Sacred Circle, because each of them had merged with her soul," said Carlo. "Do I have that right?"

"You do," Allure said with a smile. "And that is the whole story."

"Only it's not," said Prince Augustine, "because Nyro has taken Emma Barclay, giving her the ability to start over. She can trigger Emma's transformation into a sorcerer, force someone to bind her, making Nyro her conjurnor, and then force Emma to bind a new crop of demons. They won't be as powerful as her Sacred Circle, but they will still make her formidable."

Jezebel gasped. "I didn't think about this—Nyro needs another mage to bind Emma to her. Emma can't perform the rite of binding on herself. And as a reanimated elf, Nyro is incapable of performing that spell because it works with someone's soul."

"That's correct," said Sage. "She needs a human mage to perform the rite of binding for her."

"Has anyone here gone missing since the battle?" Allison asked. "Any mages?"

None of them were aware of any.

"I wonder what she's waiting for," Carlo said.

"She could take a mage from anywhere," said Khaldun. "It's possible she's done so already."

"Knowing Nyro, I'd expect her to try taking one from Stoutwall," Jezebel said. "If only to demoralize and intimidate us."

"She'll need time to regroup, though," Allure said. "Destroying the Sacred Circle was a major blow—she could not have been expecting that, or she wouldn't have left Syllith behind."

"And due to my presence, she couldn't have foreseen it," said Mira. "My null prevents prophetic visions from getting through."

"Yes," Allure said. "Nyro will need some time to formulate a new plan, and she must be moving very cautiously, taking great care to plot her next steps in a way that prevents us from stopping her."

"Lady Mira, perhaps it would be best for you to protect the castle with your null for the time being," Augustine suggested. "Nyro could acquire a mage from anywhere in Anoria, but at least this will impede her from taking any of ours."

"That would be a wise precaution, Your Highness," Allure agreed. "If we need to use any spells or communicate by mirror, we can do so outside the castle."

Mira focused for a moment. Allison felt her magic die—she hated this feeling. "It's done, Your Highness. I'll leave my null in place at all times until instructed otherwise."

"Thank you," Augustine said with a nod.

Not long after Mira's transformation into a sorcerer, they learned that her null would prevent a demon from entering or leaving the spirit realm. It also made it impossible for a demon to possess someone or leave a body it had previously possessed. Over the years, they had discovered that no demon could enter or leave her null, either. Any demon nearby when she expanded her null would be trapped there until she extinguished it.

As a demon, not even Nyro could penetrate Mira's null from the outside. In her reanimated elvish body, however, she had no such trouble. Like any elf or human, she could come or go as she pleased. But she still couldn't use her magic in the null, and wouldn't be able to enter the castle through a portal as long as that was in place.

"Do we know for sure Nyro can force Emma to become a sorcerer?" Carlo asked. "How would she know if she inherited magic from both parents?"

"Emma and I both did," said Jezebel. "Allure gave me a reading many years ago, and did not find the potential for the transformation in me. But Syllith did not possess that potential, either, and Nyro was able to trigger her metamorphosis anyway."

"Nyro can read people the same way I can," said Allure. "She would have sensed the dual inheritance in Emma and known she could force her to transform."

"It would seem her ability to read people exceeds yours," Allison said. "When she was here looking for Syllith, she learned of the seven-sided tower by reading Prince Augustine's thoughts."

"That would explain how her demons found us," said Sage. "You're sure about this?"

"No, I'm not," Allison said. She'd been on her way to the university with Sage and the others at the time, but Jezebel told her about their encounter with Nyro. "Your Highness?"

Augustine frowned. "Yes, I do believe she's correct. I told Nyro that Syllith was not here, but I was thinking about our plan. She stared at me, and it felt like she was boring into my mind with her eyes. I don't understand how that's possible."

"Sympathetic magic is usually more limited," said Allure. "I can sense someone's magical potential and what drives them. Intuit was able to read someone's intentions and sense whether they were telling the truth or not. But it may be that Nyro's power goes further."

"Shit—does that mean she could learn Allison's and my true names by reading Princess Jezebel?" Khaldun asked.

"Quite possibly," said Allure. "It wouldn't matter though. This is not common knowledge, but only the conjurnor can destroy a living mage by invoking their true name. The bond between their souls must exist for that to work. If I or anyone else but Princess Jezebel were to invoke your true name, nothing would happen."

"I had no idea," said Jezebel. "I was under the impression anyone could use it that way."

"As are most people who know anything about this subject," Allure said.

"But that means learning Nyro's true name wouldn't help us destroy her after all," Khaldun said.

"She's no longer a living mage," Allure said, "and she has no conjurnor. Anyone can destroy a demon by invoking their true name."

"As long as that demon isn't bound by a necromancer," Sage added. "When Aldo invoked Myrddin's true name, that act destroyed both the necromancer *and* his demon. When a necromancer binds a demon, their soul merges with it, and their own true name supersedes the demon's."

"If Nyro can read minds, that's going to make it impossible to defeat her in single combat," Allison observed.

"Is that how she defeated Shatter?" Augustine asked, meeting his sorcerer's gaze.

"No, Your Highness," Shatter said. "Sympathetic magic does not affect me. Nyro is a better fighter."

"Do we understand how that works?" Allison asked Allure. "Is there a way we could make ourselves unreadable to Nyro?"

Allure turned to Sage, who shrugged.

"We'll have to think about that," said Sage. "The fact that Shatter can't be read that way proves it's possible. It may be something we can duplicate."

"That could prove critical if we are to defeat her," Augustine said. "In the meantime, I do agree with Camilla that we may have an opportunity here. Without Nyro or her Sacred Circle on the field, we may be able to score a decisive blow against her army.

"But first it would be wise to establish the identity of Nyro's companion. Or at least, that being's nature—elf mage or demon in elf form."

"Or Emma under an illusion spell," Jezebel said.

"I can depart for Spanbrook immediately," said Allison. "If Lady Mira is ready?"

"I don't see why not," Mira said.

"This mission is for reconnaissance only," Allure said. "No heroic acts. You're not ready to face Nyro."

"Agreed," said Allison. "You have my word."

"Allure and I will put our heads together regarding ways to block sympathetic magic," Sage said. "That could get you one step closer to being ready."

"I have one more matter I need to address," Jezebel said. "Emma is still in my line of succession."

"That's not good," Khaldun said. "I should have thought of that. If something happens to you, our bonds will pass to Emma," he added, nodding to Allison. They'd kept Emma first in line until their daughters came of age.

"Or to anyone Nyro puts in *Emma's* line of succession once she becomes a sorcerer," Allison said. "I could take care of this, but our potions are back in Spanbrook."

"I can do it," said Shatter. "Come with me to my tower after this. We'll need Lady Mira to extinguish her null until the rite is complete."

"Yes, of course," Mira said. "I'll do it now—we'll lose that protection here once I leave for Spanbrook anyway."

Allison felt her magic return and breathed a sigh of relief.

"Very well," said Augustine, getting to his feet. "Let us adjourn for today. We'll meet again when Princess Allison and Lady Mira return."

CHAPTER THREE
SPANBROOK

llison and Jezebel left with Khaldun and Mira, Shatter right behind them.

"Let me go change into my armor and I'll meet you back here," Mira said as they walked into the courtyard.

"You two will need to take my carpet," Khaldun said.

"I always forget about that," said Allison. Only Khaldun's had the straps Mira needed to keep from falling off. "It might be better if you join us. I'm unaccustomed to flying with Mira on board." Things were different when she could use magic to keep her passengers in place. Not having that would throw off her flying instincts.

"Yes, you should go with them," Jezebel said to Khaldun. "We've still got plenty of other mages here."

"We'll meet you here," Khaldun said with a nod. He took off with Mira, and Allison and Jezebel followed Shatter up to his tower.

The sorcerer's potion cabinet was smaller than Khaldun's, but Allison had never had the impression that potions were his forte. Of course, Khaldun had inherited his from Myrddin, who had long favored potions before becoming a necromancer. Shatter started preparing his concoction.

Jezebel had placed Emma first in her line of succession when she came of age, followed by their parents. They wanted to wait until the girls were older before adding them and agreed it still wasn't time.

"Leda could probably handle it," Allison said.

"Not with Alanna around to influence her," Jezebel said with a grin. "No, for now, I think we should go back to my parents and my uncle, Treynor."

Allison agreed. Shatter finished his work and said, "Names?"

Jezebel gave him the information and he handed her a vial. She drank the potion and Shatter performed the necessary magic.

Allison returned to her chambers with her after that. She called air to dry her armor, then changed into that. There were pockets sewn into the material to hold her mirror, leather helmet, and facemask, as well as leg sheaths for two daggers. Normally, she kept those items tucked into the void. But if Mira was going to be keeping her null extended from now on, it might be best to keep them in her armor instead.

Once she'd taken care of that, she pulled the rest of her weapons out of the void, laying them out on the floor. Two sabers, a second set of daggers, and a short sword. She missed her longsword, but these would do. She tucked the blades back into oblivion along with her carpet, then bade Jezebel farewell with a hug and a kiss.

"No unnecessary risks," Jezebel said. "You promised."

"You have my word," Allison said. "If there's any opportunity to rescue Emma, I'll consult with you first."

Allison ran down to the courtyard where Khaldun and Mira were waiting for her. Someone else was with them, and it took Allison a moment to register who it was.

"Lord Asterly," she said as she approached them.

"Your Highness," the young man said with a bow. "I apologize for intruding, but I was inquiring after Emma. Lord Khaldun and Lady Mira were just explaining what happened." He paused to wipe a tear from his cheek. "I-I'm sorry to hear she's in so much danger."

"I don't yet know how or when, but you have my word we'll get her back safely," Allison said, her throat burning. "You *will* have her hand in marriage."

"Thank you, Your Highness," he said, forcing a smile and bowing again before hurrying off.

"We have to get her back," Allison said.

Khaldun and Mira had changed into their armor, too, and Mira had donned her sword belt and strapped a dagger to each leg. Allison knew Khaldun kept his own weapon tucked into the void like she did. He unfurled his carpet on the ground, and Mira sat down and started strapping herself in. Allison took her seat by the front edge, Khaldun at the rear.

Once Mira was ready, they took off, shooting into the sky. No thaumaturgic magic could work on Mira. As long as she kept her channels of power closed, spells would work in her presence, but they could never affect her directly. Khaldun's magic kept the carpet aloft, drove it forward, and shielded them from the wind—but none of those spells had to act on Mira.

As they flew over the lake, Allison spotted a dragon in the distance matching their course. It moved closer and she realized it was Magna, Mira's steed. The beast flew alongside them for a minute before roaring and circling back toward the castle. Allison knew Mira must have told him what was going on—he was sure to be concerned about her leaving without him. The dragons used sympathetic magic to communicate with their riders, otherwise it never would have worked with Mira.

Allison called air, adding her own power to Khaldun's to double their speed. It still took half the day to make it to Spanbrook, and Allison's joints were stiff by the time they reached Castle Barclay. She'd contacted Camilla by mirror during the flight, and they'd agreed to meet there. Khaldun had made them invisible before reaching the princedom, but to be safe, he kept them high above the enemy camp. Once past the castle, he dove, moving toward the keep from the west.

They landed on the roof, and he canceled the invisibility spell. The three of them got to their feet and stretched, and Khaldun tucked his carpet into the void. Camilla emerged from one of the towers, two soldiers in tow. Allison recognized Lance from their royal guard, but the other was unfamiliar. The witch embraced each of them in turn and introduced the second man as Mobo from the Eagle Company.

Allison headed toward the ramparts with Khaldun and Mira, making the three of them invisible. The enemy camp stretched across the fields to the east, their tents arranged in perfectly straight rows and columns. Allison made an estimate of their numbers.

"I count sixty thousand or so," she said. "No change." The troops who'd appeared outside of Highgate before the battle had joined the rest of their army not long after the main force arrived.

"I get the same number," said Khaldun.

The combined armies of Spanbrook, Blacksand, Keepstone, the Bastion, and Stoutwall had numbered fifty thousand going into the Battle of Stoutwall. Only twenty thousand had survived. Princess Salerna had another twenty-five thousand in Highgate. If they transported every soldier here, they'd still be outnumbered. And the elvish soldiers were bigger, stronger, and faster than their own.

Their sorcerers were all stronger than the elf mages, though the elves outnumbered them. And they had the dragons now. But Nyro could get here very quickly. And even without her Sacred Circle, she alone might neutralize their entire cadre of thaumaturges.

They had Mira, and Nyro had nothing that could counter her null. At best, though, she could take magic off the table, and they'd be facing combat of arms against a vastly superior force. Surprise or not, Allison didn't see how they could prevail. And on top of that, there was no telling what Nyro might be doing back in Drengrvollr to prepare for the next phase of this war.

With her Sacred Circle intact, Nyro could have crushed them in Stoutwall. They were fighting a losing battle, even with the dragons, and they all knew it. It was only Syllith's bold move that had spared them their fate. And forced Nyro to regroup. Allison felt sure she'd want to be guaranteed a sweeping victory before making her next attempt.

"Nyro could be preparing to transport more troops," Allison said out loud.

"That may be," Khaldun agreed. "It would take weeks to get them here, though."

They'd make the journey by ship, like the first wave. Even Nyro lacked the power to keep her portal open anywhere near long enough for an entire army to cross. Tucking them into the void wouldn't help, because nothing could move through the portal that way. And making an ocean crossing by carpet was impossible, even for Nyro.

The three of them moved away from the parapet and Allison canceled the invisibility spell. Lance returned to the ramparts to keep watch, and the others followed Camilla inside, making their way down to the great hall. Camilla served them food from the castle's provisions.

"We believe it must be Nyro you saw here that night," Allison said. "And the light you reported had to be sunlight streaming through the portal from Drengrvollr. We're unsure about the second elf, though."

"They came again last night," Camilla told them. "About the same time—around midnight or so. I'm not sure why they're making their visits, and they don't stay long. Only minutes."

"Could be for morale," Mira said. "Making sure her troops know she hasn't abandoned them."

"That may be," Allison said. "Hopefully they'll show up again tonight, and we'll do our best to identify the second elf."

Allison walked through the castle and she had to fight back the tears. They'd always known Nyro would return one day, and this building and its fortifications had been a big part of their preparations against that certain attack. But they'd made their home here, too. Raised their daughters within these walls. She'd always tried to focus on a future beyond Nyro, and this place had been an intrinsic part of that vision.

Now, seeing it abandoned like this, knowing they'd surrendered it to that force waiting outside for them, she wondered if they'd ever reclaim it. She tried to tell herself that they would. Even Nyro would meet her end eventually. But Allison could no longer visualize that future. The image simply refused to form in her mind.

There had been no sign of Nyro or her companion by nightfall. Allison, Khaldun, and Mira joined Camilla, Lance, and Mobo on the keep roof. It was a beautiful, clear night, and they lay there gazing at the stars, taking turns keeping an eye on the enemy camp. Khaldun cast an invisibility spell that encompassed the entire roof, just to be safe.

Sure enough, around midnight, Mira called over to the others, though it was hardly necessary. Allison could see the sunlight shining on the towers even from flat on her back. She got to her feet, hurrying over to the parapet.

"There," Mira said, pointing toward the two naked elves who'd emerged from the command tent. "That must be them."

The others joined them, and Camilla said, "Those are the same ones I saw the last two nights."

"They'll fall within my null if I extend it to its full size," Mira said. "I'll be able to tell what they are."

"Not yet," said Allison. "They're too far away to see clearly. I want to move in closer and see if we recognize them."

"By carpet?" Khaldun asked. Allison nodded. He pulled his out of the void and unfurled it on the roof. The three sorcerers took their seats, Mira strapped herself in, and they lifted off. Once Allison had cast an invisibility spell around them, Khaldun took them out over the camp.

They flew beyond the newcomers, turning to face back toward the castle. Khaldun took them in low enough to get a good look at the elves' faces, but not too close, in case they needed to flee in a hurry. The pair moved into the light of a campfire, and Allison got a good look. One of them was Nyro, all right, still in Estrid's body. She could clearly see the scar running down one side of her face.

Allison didn't recognize the other elf. But from this distance, she could sense the illusion spell concealing her true appearance. With a wave she canceled it.

"Emma," Mira whispered.

Nyro hadn't triggered her transformation yet. She was nude, the light of the campfire flickering on her pale skin. Judging from her blank expression, Allison figured Nyro must be using compliance spells to keep her in line. That kind of magic could cause madness, but there was nothing she could do about that now.

At that moment, Nyro gazed up at the sky—she must have sensed Allison's cancellation spell. She swept one hand over her head, and Allison could feel her magic. Nyro was trying to cancel invisibility.

Khaldun took them higher, shooting away from the camp and over the adjacent fields, circling back to the castle.

"It's Nyro and Emma," Allison told Camilla and the two soldiers once they'd landed on the keep roof and she'd removed their invisibility spell. "Emma's still a witch—Nyro hasn't triggered her transformation yet."

"I wonder what she's waiting for," Khaldun said as they got to their feet.

Daylight erupted from the camp, illuminating the towers again.

"They must have gone back to Drengrvollr," Allison said, hurrying over to the parapet. The others followed. She couldn't see Nyro or Emma anywhere.

"I don't see any way we can rescue Emma," Mira said. "We could neutralize Nyro's magic with my null, but then you'd have to fight Nyro and sixty thousand elves to get her out of there."

"Staying invisible, we might be able to get close enough to her portal to follow them through it," Khaldun said. "We wouldn't have to face an army, but we'd still have to fight Nyro to get Emma out of there. And we'd have no way to get back to Anoria."

"We'd have to travel by ship," Allison said with a sigh. "No, this isn't going to work. I need to bind a demon and become a necromancer. Then we can use our pyramid to mount a proper rescue mission."

Allison didn't want to stay in Spanbrook a minute longer. She contacted Jezebel by mirror to give her the news, then asked Khaldun and Mira if they'd be willing to fly back to Stoutwall right away. They agreed, so the three of them bade Camilla and the soldiers farewell and set out on their return journey.

Nyro sensed a cancellation spell but couldn't determine its source. The illusion she'd cast over the girl disappeared, revealing her frail human form. No harm done—it didn't matter if her people knew the girl's true identity. Opening her senses, she thought she caught a whiff of magic overhead, but saw nothing. She cast the spell to cancel invisibility across a swath of sky, but it was too late. Whoever had been there was gone.

It had to be one of their sorcerers on a flying carpet. Their objective must have been identifying her companion. They might even be planning to attempt a rescue. Nyro doubted it—any such effort would end in their death. Not only was she surrounded by the most formidable army Anoria had seen in centuries, but Nyro herself could still overpower all of their sorcerers combined. She might have lost her Sacred Circle, but her own might had not diminished in the slightest.

She almost hoped they'd try it. At least then, she could exact a sliver of revenge for what they'd done to her in Stoutwall. What that bitch Syllith had done. It wasn't worth it, though. She had the girl, and when the time came, she could be transformed. Having to replace her would only hinder her progress.

Returning to the command tent, Nyro removed the artifact from the void, opened a portal back to her island in Drengrvollr, and walked through it with the girl. Closing the portal behind them, she tucked the pyramid back into oblivion.

After her foolish mistake with Syllith, Nyro had beefed up her island's defenses. She'd constructed a protective dome identical to the one they used at the university. Well, almost identical. She'd added a special touch all her own. There was reason to believe the university had in its possession a pyramid artifact, like the one she used to create her portals. None of their people were strong enough to use it like she did, but that could change. So she'd woven spells into the barrier that would prevent anyone but her from penetrating it with portal magic.

And she'd also stationed four of her elf mages here. They were the ones she trusted the most, but she'd also used spells to enforce their total obedience. And she'd shared the spell to open a gateway through the island's protective barrier with only one of them—Gorm, the most powerful one.

Gorm now acted as her steward here in Drengrvollr. They still needed to keep the castle fully stocked with food and supplies, and Gorm could manage that. When the supply boat arrived, he would create an opening in the barrier long enough for their staff to move the goods inside. Gorm stood guard the entire time, along with the other three mages, ready to eliminate any intruders.

Perhaps these precautions were unnecessary. Nyro wasn't letting the girl out of her sight this time. But she wasn't taking any chances.

Nyro kept the girl fully compliant with a powerful spell whenever she took her out of the castle. Now that they'd returned, though, she canceled the magic. The girl gasped, taking in her surroundings, seemingly surprised to find herself sitting at the table in the great hall, a feast laid out for them. Nyro hadn't allowed her clothes, and she'd finally given up trying to cover herself.

"Where did we go?" she asked. The spell sometimes caused memory problems for the weak-minded. It hadn't affected Syllith that way, but this one wasn't as strong. In time, her tolerance would build up and she'd remember more. Especially once she became a sorcerer. In the meantime, she had at least figured out that anytime Nyro used that spell, they had gone somewhere.

"Spanbrook again," Nyro told her. "One of your people showed up this time. They canceled the illusion spell."

"Who was it?" the girl said, leaning forward with excitement in her eyes. "Allison? Khaldun?"

Nyro knew she was harboring hopes they might rescue her. "I don't know. And it doesn't matter. They're not getting you back. You should eat."

The girl stared at the table in silence. Nyro drank some wine and feasted on the food. The girl had refused meals the first day or two, but that hadn't lasted long. She filled her plate and scarfed down her food.

It might be time to trigger her metamorphosis. She wasn't ready for the girl to bind any demons yet, so she'd been holding off. The trouble was that her Sacred Circle had been unique. Nyro had developed spells to help them retain as much of themselves as possible in the spirit realm. Most demons lost more of their identities, their personalities, their knowledge and memories, even, the longer they'd been dead. Reaper had succumbed to this decline, despite the preventative magic. He'd bound more demons than most of the others combined, and Nyro suspected that had been the cause.

Her dilemma now was that there were no others like her Circle. The most recently deceased sorcerers had all been loyal to the other side. She had many means at her disposal to compel them to obey. But always she would have to force them to carry out her orders. Some of the older ones she'd contacted were far more willing to support her cause, but they'd decayed worse than Reaper.

Nyro knew what she'd have to do, but wasn't willing to accept it yet. She hoped by delaying the decision a little longer, some other option might present itself.

There was more to it, though. Losing her Sacred Circle had shaken her to the core. She had not foreseen this possibility, which had to be because of the null. Never had any vision shown her this outcome. They'd endured centuries of hell together and she'd been certain they'd be by her side for centuries to come, reigning over their new empire.

Fate was a fickle bitch.

If she'd had any inkling of this possible future, maybe she would have taken greater precautions in safeguarding Syllith. She could have erected the protective dome before leaving Drengrvollr. Or stationed more mages to support Reaper. It hadn't seemed necessary at the time. She'd covered her tracks well enough, and even now, none of the remaining senators had any idea she was anyone but Estrid. Unlike her prophetic visions, her sympathetic magic remained reliable. She could read these elves as easily as she could the humans.

And her readings hadn't caused the breakdown in her plans. The senators weren't involved in freeing Syllith. It had been an elf mage from the resistance movement. Nyro had underestimated the rate of Reaper's decline. It had accelerated after her departure, to the point that the mage was able to overpower him. And he was no one she had ever encountered. If she had, she knew for sure she could have read his intentions. And she would have eliminated him before he could cause her any trouble.

No, her sympathetic magic had never failed her. But Nyro had learned to distrust prophecy. She'd foreseen her downfall at the hands of the elves and launched her invasion of their kingdoms to *prevent* it. Yet in the end, that campaign had *precipitated* her demise. If only she'd ignored the prophecy, her empire could have lasted thousands of years. The elves never would have had any interest in Anoria.

She refused to make such a mistake again. Yet once more, she'd prophesied her own downfall—and this time, it was her ultimate death. Complete removal from existence. As if someone had invoked her true name. But that was impossible now. She'd retaken her own true name, and her bodily death had severed her bond to Saliman's heir. No one could ever use that name against her.

This new augury was the last prophetic vision she'd had. Not long before breaking out of their Pythan prison. She'd foreseen the foe who would terminate her existence, and then she'd shown up in the flesh. In that cursed watchtower with the boy from the tower and the oaf who'd taken up residence there. Nyro had been unable to read her from inside that prison, but she'd *seen* her. And she'd never forget.

Nyro saw her again when the boy summoned her in his tower. The doom from Spanbrook. Ironic that they came from the same town. She'd read her then and knew for sure she was the one from her prophecy. How could one so weak ever bring about the eternal destruction of one so powerful? It defied all logic, and though Nyro had spent years pondering this question, still it made no sense, and she could puzzle out no solution.

When she was alive, she would have sought this witch and destroyed her to ensure the prophecy could never be fulfilled. Now she knew better. Seeking out this lowly witch could prove to be the very action that brought the augury to fruition. She could not allow that.

Yet now she had her sister sitting at her dinner table. Two normal mages there had been in that castle with the dual inheritance of magic, and this one with powers fully developed. Nyro's choice had been made easy.

"Why am I here?" the girl demanded, shaking in fear, but summoning the courage to speak regardless. Nyro admired that. "We've done nothing but sit here for days. If you don't need me, let me return to my people! My family!"

It was true. They *hadn't* done anything. Perhaps it was time to change that. Initially, Nyro had thought only of reclaiming her empire in Anoria. Over time, that plan had changed. She wanted revenge. Against both the humans and elves. The elves were superior to the humans in every way, and their continent possessed riches beyond any Anorian's imagination.

So, instead of reclaiming her empire in Anoria, she decided to establish her new reign over the elven continent and exterminate the humans. Elvendom was hers, but unfortunately, the means of extermination she'd chosen was no longer available to her. She believed there was a way to get it back, but she had much research to do.

Yes, she had wallowed in her indecision long enough. It was time to get back to work.

CHAPTER FOUR
THE SWORD

It was dawn by the time Allison made it back to Stoutwall with Mira and Khaldun. Jezebel was awake, but Alanna and Leda were still sound asleep. Mira had already extended her null around the castle—meaning there was no way to cast the spell to block sound—so Allison and Jezebel kept their voices down as they discussed the night's events.

"This is so frustrating," Allison said. "Emma was right there—she's not even a sorcerer yet—and there was nothing I could do. Nyro's only showing up in the midst of her army, but even without that, I'm not strong enough to confront her."

"There may not be a way to get her back," Jezebel said. "I want to rescue her as badly as anyone, but if it's not possible, what can we do?"

"If I were stronger, I could use our pyramid to go to Drengrvollr myself and take Emma back," Allison said. "But to do that, I need to become a necromancer. I have to bind Shadow."

"The demon in the seven-sided tower at the university," Jezebel said.

"Yes. I need to talk to Allure. It's time to make this happen."

Allison went to Allure's chambers, knocking on the door. There was no answer, and it was quiet inside. She knew Allure often tended to sleep in, and she felt bad about disturbing her, but she was anxious to get this process started. She pounded on the door, but still, there was no answer.

Maybe she was up early today? Allison headed down to the great hall. Sure enough, Allure was there for breakfast with Battleaxe and Mist. Allison realized she was famished after staying up all night, so she sat down to eat with them.

Battleaxe asked Allison how it went in Spanbrook, so she spent a few minutes telling them what they'd seen outside Castle Barclay. "It's infuriating," she said when she was done. "I want to rescue Emma, but I can't. I feel so helpless."

"You need to unwind, Princess," Battleaxe said. Allison glared at her. She detested the honorific. "You're under a lot of pressure, and I understand how you feel. But you need a break. Mist and I are going to that tavern with Imani tonight. You should join us."

"That does sound like fun," Allison said with a grin.

"Allure?" Battleaxe said. "Wouldn't hurt to get your mind off of things for a while." Allison knew losing Semblant had hit her hard.

"I don't think so," Allure said. "Another time, maybe."

Once they were done, Allison pulled Allure aside. "I need to become a necromancer so I can wield the pyramid and rescue Emma," she told her. "How do we go about doing this?"

Allure met her gaze for a moment, taking a deep breath. "I'll contact Shadow. You have to understand, this is up to her, not me. So I'll let you know what she says."

"What about the pyramid? Does Shadow have that?"

"Yes," Allure confirmed. "I'll get that from her so we have it once you're ready."

Allison had been hoping for a more definite plan of action, but that would have to do.

The thought of binding a demon terrified her. After the ordeal she'd endured in the old castle with Myrddin's demon, it had taken her a long time to overcome her fear when working with ghouls and demons. Her stomach still fluttered a bit, even after all these years.

But merging her soul with a demon was a whole other matter. This would change her. Permanently. She was committed to this course of action—it was the only way they could get Emma back, and it might make her powerful enough to go head-to-head with Nyro. But there was no going back.

Allison had questions, too. She didn't understand how the relationship with her demon would work or what it would feel like. Her soul would merge with the demon, she'd heard that enough times. But what did that mean? Growing up with Myrddin, she understood that he and the demon could still operate independently. It had never seemed like Myrddin exerted *constant* control.

And she knew that demons could go anywhere almost instantly by moving through the spirit realm, though they didn't typically travel very far. Most demons remained attached to places they had frequented in life, whether they were consciously aware of it or not. But they could also latch onto living beings in the case of hauntings and follow them wherever they went.

In summoning a demon, she had the power to command it to go anywhere she wanted. Normally, once it moved into the spirit realm, it could free itself of her will. It was almost impossible to force a demon to do one's bidding once it had moved into that plane. So, generally, she could only control demons within her visual range once she'd summoned them from the spirit realm. Allure had told her this was one of the key differences in *binding* a demon. Once that happened, it didn't matter how far away they were.

Unfortunately, demons were incapable of taking anything with them when they moved through the spirit realm. They could not use void magic, either, and it wasn't possible to tether anything in the void to them, so there was no way to send people or things with them.

Allison ran into Mira and Khaldun in the courtyard, Jezebel and the girls right behind them. She was about to ask where they were going when a dragon roared, startling her so badly she stumbled. Turning, she spotted Magna swooping over the walls, circling the courtyard once and landing in the middle.

"Alanna and Leda wanted to meet him," Mira said, flashing Allison a grin.

The dragon waddled over to them, and being this close gave Allison a new appreciation of his true size. She understood that they were all enormous, and Magna was the largest of them all, but seeing one at this range drove the point home in a way that seeing them from the air could not. Magna was at least as big as Jezebel's parents' farmhouse.

The dragon lowered his head as Mira approached, almost as if he were bowing to her. She placed her hands on his snout, touching her forehead to his nose. Allison couldn't sense it, but knew she must be using her sympathetic magic to communicate with him.

"You can approach," Mira said, turning to the others and smiling. "He understands that you're friends and won't do him any harm."

Allison had to stifle a giggle. Them do *him* any harm? That was hardly likely. Conversely, Magna could incinerate them all in a single breath. Standing so close to such a powerful beast was intimidating, to say the least.

Alanna strode forward, fearless as always, and touched Magna's snout. Leda approached more cautiously, and Allison could tell she was equal parts terrified and intrigued. Her curiosity won out, and she tentatively placed a finger on the dragon's nose. He snorted and she screamed, backpedaling and falling over.

Alanna had jumped but managed to stay on her feet. "Don't be such a chicken!" she said to her sister. "He won't hurt you!"

"Be nice," Jezebel admonished her. "He startled you, too."

"Hmph," Alanna said, turning her attention back to the dragon.

Leda recovered her courage and in no time was stroking Magna's neck, smiling from ear to ear. Alanna turned to say something to Khaldun, and Magna bumped her with his snout, sending her sprawling. Alanna regained her feet, giggling as she tried to push Magna's nose away from her. He knocked her over again, so she got up and ran, and the dragon waddled after her.

Before long, the girls and the dragon were chasing each other around the courtyard, making a game of it. Passersby scrambled to get out of their way, and the next thing Allison knew, they had the courtyard to themselves. Mira hurried after her dragon at first, calling out to him, seemingly nervous that he'd hurt the girls, but she gave up after a while and watched in amusement, Khaldun at her side.

"A part of me wishes we could run away somewhere with Khaldun, Mira, and the girls, and leave the war behind," Allison said with a sigh, embracing Jezebel. "Once we rescue Emma, of course."

"I know what you mean," Jezebel said, smiling at her. "Unfortunately, there's no place we could run where Nyro wouldn't catch up with us eventually."

"Always the pragmatist," Allison said, shaking her head. She knew she was right, though. Maybe they could escape to Ostland. Nyro might not have any interest in an uninhabited island. Then again, with Okset establishing a settlement there, even that island might not provide safe harbor.

Another dragon roar snapped Allison out of her reverie. She thought it was Magna, but the second roar came from the opposite direction. Gazing skyward, she spotted another dragon swooping over the castle wall, landing in the courtyard and roaring again. It was much smaller than Magna, and Allison had a feeling this was one of the younger ones.

Magna answered its roar, startling the girls again, who stopped their chase and covered their ears. The newcomer strutted over to the sire, bowing its head, before turning its attention to the girls. Leda backed away, staying close to Magna, but Alanna approached the younger one.

"Alanna, no," Jezebel called out. "Its rider's not here—this might not be safe!"

Alanna ignored her, moving right up to the dragon. Allison took off at a run, intending to grab her daughter and get her out of there, but Mira said, "It's all right—she won't hurt her. This is Sigrid—she hasn't taken a rider yet."

Allison pulled up short, watching nervously despite Mira's words. She had no idea this dragon was female, and wasn't sure how to tell the difference. The dragon lowered her head, nuzzling Alana with her snout. She giggled, stroking her nose. Allison started to relax, but then Alanna screamed, her eyes going wide as she scurried away from the beast, tripping and landing on her backside.

"What's wrong?!" Allison called, running over to her.

Alanna gazed up at her and gasped as Allison squatted next to her. Jezebel, Mira, and Khaldun had run over, too, and they stood around them, concern in their eyes. "She spoke to me!"

"In your mind?" Mira asked, sounding excited.

Alanna nodded vigorously. "She showed me an image of her flying over some mountains with a whole bunch of other dragons!"

Sigrid squawked at them, and Allison breathed a sigh of relief. Alanna got to her feet, going back to the dragon and stoking her long neck. The beast purred. "I'm showing her Castle Barclay," she told them with a grin, "and all of us eating in the great hall."

Mira chuckled. The adults moved out of the way, gathering by the keep as the girls resumed their game, chasing *both* dragons around the courtyard.

"That's truly something," Mira said. "They don't typically open up to a human like that unless they're going to claim them as a rider."

"I'm not sure Alanna's ready for that," Jezebel said. "She's wild enough with both feet planted firmly on the ground."

Allison had to agree.

She and Jezebel spent a few minutes chatting with Mira and Khaldun about recent events, until Leda yelled, "Alanna, *NO!*"

Allison scanned the courtyard for the source of Leda's alarm and gasped. Sigrid had lowered his head and one wing and Alanna was climbing onto his back.

"Alanna, get down this instant!" Jezebel shouted.

It was too late. Sigrid took off at a run, flapping her giant wings and going airborne. She swooped around the courtyard once to gain some height, then flew over the castle wall, Alanna on her back, screaming her head off.

"Oh, shit," Allison muttered. Mira extinguished her null to allow her to pull her carpet out of the void. She unfurled it on the ground, stood in the center, and took off in pursuit. Clearing the castle wall, she spotted Khaldun right behind her.

Sigrid had soared across the lake, and Allison caught up to her in no time. "I'll move in closer and you climb onto the carpet!" she called out to Alanna. For once in her life, Alanna looked terrified.

Allison moved in closer, ready to grab her daughter, but Sigrid had other ideas. She went into a dive, wings flat against her sides, and for a moment, it looked like she was going into the water. Alanna screamed, and Allison had to stifle a scream of her own, but the dragon pulled up at the last instant, climbing again.

Khaldun and Allison spent the next several minutes trying to rescue Alanna, but it seemed like the dragon wanted to play. Or show off, perhaps—she kept doing barrel rolls and steep dives, evading their every attempt to get close. Alanna seemed to have recovered from her terror, screaming for joy now instead of fear, but Allison hadn't. She couldn't understand how her daughter had managed to stay on the beast's back, given the extreme maneuvers she was doing.

An earsplitting roar caught Allison's attention, and turning, she saw Mira swooping in on Magna's back. Her dragon flew directly over Sigrid, cuffing the younger dragon on the snout with his wing. Sigrid squawked in response. Magna roared again, and Sigrid turned for home.

They all landed in the courtyard, and the dragons lowered their heads and wings to let their riders off. Once they were clear, Magna roared at Sigrid, who cowered away from her sire. Jezebel ran over to Alanna, hugging her tight and closing her eyes against her tears.

"Mother, I'm fine," Alanna said. "That was the most—"

Jezebel gripped her by the shoulders, holding her at arm's length. "Don't you *ever* do something so reckless again! You could have been killed!" She escorted her daughter toward the keep, disappearing inside.

Allison caught Leda's gaze.

"I told her not to do it," Leda said with a shrug.

"I know," Allison said. "Let's give them a little time, shall we?" Leda nodded.

"That was truly remarkable," Mira said. "Sigrid seems to have chosen Alanna as her rider. That's how it works, from what I understand—the dragon always chooses the rider."

"How much danger was Alanna in up there?" Allison asked.

"To be honest, not much," Mira said. "The others claim no dragon has ever dropped a rider. I don't know if that's true, but the beasts do have an amazing sense of balance."

"I guess that's a relief," Allison said. "Can the dragon be convinced to choose someone else?"

"I don't think so," Mira said. "But I'll see what I can find out." She put her null in place, and Allison sighed, ruing the loss of her magic.

Allison spent most of the day with Leda, giving Jezebel and Alanna some space. But the four of them ate dinner together in the great hall. After that, Allison went to meet Imani, Mist, and Battleaxe in the courtyard. Imani was late as usual, but once she'd arrived, they set out on foot. They could have gone by carpet, but it was such a beautiful night, it felt good to walk. Unlike many other princedoms, Stoutwall's castle was a few miles away from the city. Allison breathed a sigh of relief as she felt her magic return outside of Mira's null.

"What was up with Allure this morning?" Battleaxe asked her. "You seemed pretty upset when you were talking to her."

"Oh, no," Allison said. "We were just discussing the next steps for me to become a necromancer. She said it's up to Shadow."

"Shadow," Mist repeated. "It's so weird that there's a demon at the university, pulling the strings from some secret tower."

"I know, right?" Battleaxe said. "Mist and I are governors and we never heard of this until right after the battle."

"That is very strange," Imani said. "Here we are fighting against a demon reborn, and meanwhile, we've got one running the university."

"I've encountered Shadow before," Allison said. "But I don't remember it very well. They say she's a demon, but she's not like any demon I've ever seen. She appeared to Jezebel long ago, too. As a spark of light."

"A spark of light?" Battleaxe repeated incredulously. "You're right, that doesn't sound like a demon at all."

"Can demons take things with them through the spirit realm?" Mist asked. "Like one of us? That might be a way to get to Drengrvollr."

"Unfortunately not," Allison said.

"Just like you," Battleaxe said. "You can't take anything with you as mist."

"No, but I *can* if I tuck it into the void first," Mist said.

"You can?" Allison said. "I guess that makes sense, I just never thought about it before."

"I hadn't either before my first carpet," she said. "Azure didn't make one for me till after the last Battle of Highgate. I would have been a lot more useful if I'd known I could do that back then. I ended up realizing it by accident. The first time I transformed after I started keeping the carpet in the void, it was still with me when I changed back."

"I wonder what it's like in the void," Allison said. "We've started moving entire armies that way, but I've never been."

"I haven't either, but I'm told it's… well, a void," Mist said with a chuckle. "Endless darkness in every direction."

"Yes, that's it exactly," said Imani. "Not pleasant at all."

"Oh, that's right," said Battleaxe. "You traveled that way on the way to Stoutwall. I forgot. Khaldun tucked me into the void once, but only briefly."

"I could turn to mist and take you the rest of the way to the tavern in the void if you want," Mist said. "We'll get there faster that way."

"No, thank you," Imani said. "It's not an experience I wish to repeat."

"Oh, come on," said Battleaxe. "Let's do it."

"Yes, I'd like to see what this is like, too," said Allison.

"All right," Imani said with a sigh. "Fine."

"Your wish is my command," Mist said with a grin before turning to mist. She surrounded them, and suddenly, Allison found herself standing in the void.

"I'll be damned," Battleaxe said, gazing around them.

Allison, Battleaxe, and Imani were glowing slightly, so they could see each other, but everywhere else was only blackness. This reminded Allison of being inside Shadow's tower at the university, only that place had a stone floor that extended as far as the eye could see in every direction. She wondered if they'd created it using a form of void magic.

"I can walk, but I don't feel anything beneath my feet," Battleaxe said, taking a few steps away from them. "Try it!"

Allison moved to her side, and she was right. It was a very strange feeling to walk on nothing. Imani leaped, shooting over their heads, and coming to rest several feet above them.

"Neat trick," Battleaxe said. She jumped, too, stopping right next to her.

Allison joined them. "I wonder if it's possible to get ourselves out of here."

"One way to find out," Battleaxe said. She disappeared with a popping sound.

"Apparently so," Imani said with a wry smile. "For you magical types, at least."

Allison was about to try moving them back to the real world when suddenly it happened of its own accord. She found herself standing in Stoutwall City, right in front of the tavern, with Imani and Battleaxe. The mist around them coalesced, turning into Mist.

"So, how'd you like it?" she asked them with a grin.

"It wouldn't be my first choice if I had to travel somewhere," Allison said.

"Sure was interesting, though," Battleaxe said.

They went inside and grabbed a table. There were only a dozen or so people here—most of the city had been evacuated before the battle—but it was quite the crowd compared to the last time they'd come here together. A minstrel in the opposite corner was singing and playing a lute.

A man hustled over and served them ales. Allison took a swig and sighed. It was good ale.

"Has Khaldun made any progress with his shapeshifting?" Battleaxe asked.

"I don't think so, but I'm not sure," Allison said.

"How's it going with Mira and the dragons?" Imani asked.

"Hah," Allison said, taking another drink. She told them about Alanna's incident with Sigrid.

"That's amazing, actually," Mist said. "I'd love to have my own dragon."

"How does Leda feel about this?" Battleaxe asked with a knowing grin. "I don't imagine she's going to be too happy that her twin sister gets one and she doesn't."

Allison hadn't thought about that, but Battleaxe was right. "Well, I'm not prepared to allow Alanna to become a rider. She's too much of a wild child. There's no telling what kind of trouble she'd get into."

"I'm not sure you have any say in the matter," Mist said. "I was talking to a couple of the riders the other day, and they explained that the dragon chooses the rider, not the other way around."

"Yes, that's my understanding as well," Allison said, taking another swig of ale. "Mira's going to talk to them. See if there's a way around that."

The others chatted for a while, and Allison listened to the minstrel. He was quite good. But as she paid attention to his song, she realized it was quite familiar. It was about a girl journeying across the continent with a wayfarer boy, seeking a renowned sorcerer.

She gazed at the minstrel, and he made eye contact. Smiling at her when he sang about the two travelers making love in an inn.

"I don't believe it," Allison muttered to herself. He was singing about Khaldun and Jezebel. And he was familiar with intimate details of their story that he shouldn't have any way of knowing.

When he was done, Allison went over to talk to him.

"Princess Allison," he said, getting to his feet and putting down his lute. He was only a little taller than her, rather stout, with light red hair and a bushy beard. "It's a pleasure to meet you," he added, shaking her hand.

"I'm afraid you have me at a disadvantage," she said.

"Thomas Broadpaunch, traveling minstrel, at your service," he said with a little bow. The barkeep hurried over, handing him a mug of ale. Thomas took a long drink and smacked his lips. "Excellent ale they brew here," he said. "Have you tried it?"

"Yes, I—"

"The food is quite good, too. I recommend the mutton."

"I'll have to try it," she said. "I wanted to ask you about that song you were singing."

"Sounds familiar to your ears, I'm guessing?" he said with a grin.

"A little too familiar, I'm afraid. Where did you hear that story?"

"From the Lord Khaldun himself," he said. "He was here with the lady Mira the other night. Enjoyed the ale almost as much as I do," he added with a belch and finished his mug. "I did ask his permission to turn it into a song and changed the names as promised. He asked me to leave Your Highness out of the tale, as well, and I honored his request. I hope it was to your liking?"

"Yes, yes, it was very good," she said. The barkeep brought him another ale. "Might I ask for one little adjustment?"

"You may ask," he said, taking a swig of his drink. Allison frowned. "I jest, Your Highness. What would you like me to change?"

"Could you leave out the bit about the travelers becoming, ah, intimate?"

"Consider it done," he said, bowing slightly.

Allison had forgiven Jezebel her transgressions long ago but hated to think of them being forever memorialized in song. She thanked the minstrel and returned to her companions.

"What was that about?" Battleaxe asked.

"Oh, nothing," Allison said, drinking some of her ale. "I was complimenting him on his performance."

"He is very good," Mist said as the minstrel started his next song. Allison was relieved that this one recounted no familiar events.

They stayed late into the night, and Allison enjoyed talking and laughing with her friends. Battleaxe had been right—it did feel good to forget their troubles for a while. She drank several ales and felt the alcohol going to her head. The crowd grew as the night wore on, and Thomas Broadpaunch entertained them all. But at last, it was time to return to the castle.

Allison bade the others goodnight when they reached the courtyard and headed for the keep. She noticed light flickering in the windows of the mage's tower and wondered what Shatter was doing up so late.

She found her chambers awash in the moonlight streaming through the window and Jezebel sound asleep in bed. She stripped out of her clothes and was about to slide under the covers with her wife when she spotted a long, wooden box standing in the corner. It was painted black with gold and red runes along its surface.

Grabbing the box, she placed it on the table and unclasped the lid. Opening it, she gasped. There was a two-handed longsword inside, the most beautiful blade she'd ever seen. The hilt was fashioned to look like a dragon's body, its cross-guard forming the wings, and the blade protruding from its jaws.

"Hey, you're back," Jezebel said. Allison turned to see her sitting up in bed and yawning.

"Where did this come from?" Allison asked.

"A courier brought it a few hours ago," she said. "Said that Shatter sent it for you."

Allison picked up the sword, holding it in both hands. It was too long for her but surprisingly light and perfectly balanced. "This is amazing. I love it." She'd thought about talking to Augustine's blacksmith at some point about replacing her broken blade but hadn't gotten around to it. "I want to go thank Shatter for this," she said, moving to the bed and kissing Jezebel. "I'll be right back."

"It's the middle of the night—surely he's asleep."

"There was a light in his tower," she said with a shrug. She considered that she probably would have waited till morning were it not for the alcohol—she was feeling rather uninhibited. "I won't be long."

Allison hurried out of their chambers and over to the tower, sword in hand. She swung it a few times as she crossed the courtyard, and couldn't get over how good it felt in her hands. If only it were a little shorter. Shatter answered the door when she knocked and let her inside.

"I'm sorry to disturb you," she said, staring up at him. Gods, he was tall. "I just wanted to thank you for the sword." She held it up to admire it in the light. "It's terrific!"

"I felt bad for breaking yours," he said. "Our blacksmith was already working on this for me, but your need is greater."

"Oh, I cannot accept this if it was supposed to be yours," she said, trying to give it back to him.

Shatter wouldn't take it, raising his hands as if in surrender. "No, no, it's yours. We might have to take it back to the smith to have it shortened a bit, though."

"You're sure?" she said, still holding it out to him.

"Certain," he said. "I rarely fight with anything but my long-handled sword. And I can always have another longsword made."

"Very well, thank you," she said again. "I think I'll try it out in practice first before having it altered. It might work just like this."

"It's made from Stoutwall steel," Shatter told her. "Just like my weapon—that's the only reason it broke yours."

"Oh?"

"It's stronger than any other steel on the continent," he said. "The fabrication method was handed down from ancient times—predating the Old Kingdoms—and it's a closely guarded secret. Only our smiths know how to make it."

"Impressive," Allison said, gazing at the sword with newfound appreciation. "I will take good care of it. Thank you again!"

She returned to her chambers, placing the sword back in its box and closing the lid. Jezebel cuddled with her when she slid into bed, falling asleep again almost immediately. It didn't take long for Allison to doze off, too.

But she woke with a start. It was still dark out, and she wasn't sure what had awakened her. Someone knocked. Allison slid out of bed, donning her robe, and answered the door to find Allure standing there.

"I'm sorry to wake you, Your Highness," she said, "but it's time to go see Shadow."

CHAPTER FIVE
SHADOW

Allison gaped at her for a moment, finally registering what she'd said as the sleep receded from her mind. "Oh, yes—come in for a moment. I'll need to get dressed."

Allure came into the room and Allison closed the door behind her. She dropped her robe and put on her leather armor. She wanted to take her new sword with her but would have to wait until they left Mira's null to tuck it into the void.

"What's going on?" Jezebel said, sitting up in bed.

"My apologies for the late hour, Your Highness," Allure said. "Shadow has asked me to bring Allison to the university to meet with her."

Jezebel started awake all the way. "For the binding? They're doing that now? I should go with you—"

"No, Your Highness," Allure said. "This is only a preliminary meeting. There is some work to do first before Her Highness will be ready."

Allison's heart sank—she'd been hoping they'd do the binding tonight. "I'll return as soon as I can," she said, kissing Jezebel. "Go back to sleep."

Once they were outside the castle, Allison tucked her new sword into the void, and Allure removed her carpet, spreading it out on the ground. She sat at the rear edge, and Allison took the front, and they launched into the sky. The university was much closer to Stoutwall than Spanbrook was, so with the two of them calling air, it took very little time to get there. Allison opened a portal through the protective barrier, closing it again behind them, and Allure set them down by the seven-sided tower.

Allison got to her feet and stretched as Allure rolled up her carpet and tucked it into the void. The effects of the alcohol had faded, thankfully, but she had a bit of a headache. And butterflies in her stomach. She'd been inside the tower before, but never to meet Shadow.

"Ready?" Allure asked with a grin. Allison nodded. She held her arms to her side and spoke an incantation. Allison followed her through the brick wall. Like last time, the blackness extended forever in all directions with only the stone floor visible.

Allison spotted a spark of light darting around in the distance, but then realized she couldn't tell how far away it was. The spark started growing, quickly reaching the size and shape of a human female, but only her outline, glowing brightly.

"Welcome, Allison," a voice said, seeming to come from all directions at once. "Long have I awaited this day."

"Shadow," Allison said, bowing her head. She could feel her pulsating with power, more than she'd ever felt before.

"You may call me that," she said. "But most have known me as… Blaze."

"*Blaze?*" Allison repeated, stunned. "From Nyro's Sacred Circle?"

"The very same."

"I don't understand," Allison said, seeking Allure's gaze, but the sorcerer wouldn't look at her. "How can you be Blaze? You served our enemy!"

"I did. But I have not in many long years. I believe you've heard the story of Nyro's downfall at the hands of the elves?"

"Yes."

"So you know that there was a traitor who betrayed Nyro to them?"

"That was you?" Allison remembered the story, and the details started falling into place. They'd suspected the traitor had to be someone very high up in the imperial infrastructure, possibly one of the Sacred Circle.

"It was. I taught Nyro when she was a student here at the university. I was a necromancer then. And the only one who'd already bound a demon before entering Nyro's service. Nyro and I became intimate when she studied here. We had to keep our affair a secret, of course. I was a governor, in addition to being a professor, and the relationship was completely inappropriate.

"Nyro was the most powerful sorcerer we'd trained in generations—perhaps ever. I pleaded with the others to assign her *here*. To continue developing her magic and teach one day. I was in love with her, too, and wanted to keep her close. But the others overruled me. King Saliman of Pytha was overdue for a new sorcerer—his last one had finally passed away after serving his family for over two hundred years.

"I stayed in touch with her for many years after that. We'd linked two mirrors together to facilitate our ongoing communication. But one day, Nyro stopped talking to me. I didn't understand what had happened. We'd discussed finding ways to meet in person, and I thought she'd changed her mind.

"Then we got word that Saliman and Nyro had been abducting unbound sorcerers. Nyro was binding them to him. And then she and the others became necromancers and Saliman openly revealed what they'd done. It was too late to stop them by then. They conquered the entire continent, and the rest is history."

"How did you end up joining them?" Allison asked.

"I didn't at first," she said. "That didn't come until later. The university resisted Saliman. It didn't fall until after he subverted the other kingdoms. I had to flee with the rest of the governors. There were a handful of princedoms in Kong that managed to remain independent, and we went into hiding there.

"I'd kept my mirror that whole time. Sentimental, I know, but I was still in love with Nyro, even if I didn't condone what they were doing. I never expected to hear from her again, but one day, she contacted me. She told me she'd found a way to reverse her bond with Saliman. I told her that was impossible—she had to be wrong. But she insisted she could do it. And then she did."

"How?" Allison said.

"I never did find out," Shadow said. "I tried piecing it together, but I couldn't figure it out and she refused to tell me. But once she took over, everything changed.

"Saliman was the worst kind of tyrant. He ordered his people to commit unspeakable acts of barbarism, slaughtering entire cities—men, women, and children—in his quest for total domination of Anoria. He enslaved millions. It was one of the darkest times in the continent's history. Until then anyway.

"Nyro turned it around. She freed the slaves, restored people's basic freedoms, and rebuilt cities. Anoria thrived under her rule like never before. The governors returned to the university, and Nyro didn't interfere. The education of the continent's mages resumed, and she provided the workforce that constructed the buildings we use to this day. She even contributed most of the books we house in our library from her personal collection.

"When Nyro invited me to join her Sacred Circle and live with her in the capital, I accepted. We resumed our love affair, and I was in heaven. The years I spent by her side at the height of her reign were the happiest of my life."

"But then she had her prophetic vision of the elves coming to destroy her empire," Allison said.

"She had that vision over and over again. Those events reverberated through time, assaulting her mind with their power. Nyro always told me she'd never before experienced a prophecy so powerful. She was certain it would come true and she dedicated her life—and the resources of a continent—to preventing it.

"I worried that it could become self-fulfilling. We had no evidence that the elves had *ever* taken an interest in the affairs of Anoria. It made no sense. I tried to convince Nyro to send a delegation to the elves to establish diplomatic relations. Or at the very least, to send spies.

"She refused to do the former and agreed to the latter. Her spies could find nothing. No sign that the elves were preparing to attack. Nyro remained convinced that the elves had identified her spies and fed them false information. Or that the preparations for their invasion had not yet begun, and she needed to act preemptively.

"No matter what I did, she remained committed to her plans. She became obsessed with preventing her vision from coming true. I found out only later that she'd foreseen our deaths—all of us. Her and every member of the Sacred Circle."

"And all of it *did* come true," Allison said, "but only because she brought it on?"

"Yes. I was terrified of what might happen if we invaded the elven kingdoms. So I reached out to the human resistance movement. And I started providing them with intelligence. If I couldn't stop Nyro from the inside, perhaps they could do it from the outside. But it was no use. The humans tried to warn the elves, too, but they refused to listen. And Nyro eventually crushed any meaningful resistance. She pressed ahead with her plans for invasion, and you know the rest."

"How did you escape the prison in Pytha?" Allison asked.

"I passed information to the elves myself when they came here," Shadow said. "Helped them defeat Nyro and the rest of the Circle. When the time came, they refused to spare my life. They said I had done too much to help Nyro to deserve a pardon. But they agreed to show me some mercy. They allowed me to leave Pytha when they incarcerated the others there."

"So you were in charge of the university after that?" Allison asked.

"I wouldn't put it that way. The governors have always had that authority. I advised and guided certain among them over the centuries. They heeded my counsel. I exist now only in spirit form, so there is only so much I can do. I created the space you see here using spells that would keep me hidden from Nyro and her demons should she ever escape. I can still travel anywhere through the spirit realm, but now that Nyro is at large once more, I must never get too close. The protection I established here does not extend beyond this building."

"Will that be true after I bind you?" Allison asked.

"No. The danger now is that she could force a human sorcerer to bind me. Once you do so yourself, that threat will be removed."

"Why did you allow the guard to lapse at the watchtowers? If those spells had been properly maintained, Nyro might never have escaped."

"She would have broken free regardless. Even if we'd maintained the watchtowers, we never would have known what she was doing with that temple. Or that she'd left the pyramid in Spanbrook. Or any number of other machinations she might have put in place before her downfall that we never uncovered.

"We *did* maintain the watchtowers in the beginning. We set a perpetual watch. And after a hundred years, there was absolutely no sign that Nyro or her demons were affecting the elves' barrier in any way. And what could we have done if they *did* discover something? The elves never gave us the spells they used to erect the barrier. Our only hope would have been to seek their aid to repair them for us. And as history has shown, they have no interest in our affairs. Even when we warned them that Nyro was plotting an invasion, they refused to listen. No, there would have been no help there.

"The barrier was solid. Impenetrable. I knew the most important safeguard was to make sure no one else could ever follow in Nyro's footsteps."

"So you initiated the purge," Allison said. "You instructed the governors to destroy any record that could possibly lead to someone becoming a necromancer."

"Exactly. Sorcerers can only grow so powerful. They can be defeated. Becoming a necromancer provides the potential for limitless power. By harnessing demons, someone with Nyro's innate talent can become like a god. We could not allow that to happen ever again."

"Only now, you're going to allow me to become one."

"I am. Only because I believe this is the sole path to defeating Nyro. And your heart is pure, Allison Barclay. Nyro's was too, in the beginning. But where she turned, I believe you would stay the course. Learn from her mistakes and never do what she did. Never blindly chase phantom prophecies."

"Phantom prophecies?" Allison repeated.

"Nyro's vision was true only because she made it so. She was so afraid of losing everything she'd built that she started seeing threats everywhere. No one could have contested her at the height of her power, but it didn't matter. She believed with her entire being that it could all be destroyed. And so it was."

"But how can you know I wouldn't go down the same path? If we defeat Nyro, it's entirely likely that Jezebel will become the queen of Dorshire—and I her queen consort. With two more sorcerers in our service, not to mention an entire crash of dragons, we could easily conquer Anoria and establish an empire of our own. And I'll be a necromancer with the potential for unlimited power. Wouldn't I fear losing it all exactly like Nyro did? What's to stop me from doing what she did?"

"*I* would stop you," Shadow said, and Allison felt waves of power emanating from her. "You will bind *me* to become a necromancer, so you and I will merge, sharing a single soul. Yet we will remain separate in every other way. Our minds and our emotions will be our own. I couldn't stop Nyro. But should you take even the first steps down the same path, I *will* stop you."

"Wait," Allison said, her heartbeat suddenly pounding in her ears. "You're more powerful than I am. What's to prevent you from taking me over completely? I watched what Myrddin's demon did to him, and his power was a shade greater than the demon's. There's no way I will suffer the same fate. I would refuse the rite of binding before I would do that."

"No, child, that is not our way forward. First, we must unleash your full power. We will take care of that tonight. But also, there is a way to perform the rite of binding that ensures that you will stay in control. I must be the one to initiate it. And for that, I must prepare. It will take some time. But you'll need to grow into your power before we can proceed regardless."

"Is that true?" Allison asked Allure. She didn't know if she could trust Shadow. If she wanted to use Allison as a way to regain a body, that would certainly constitute an ulterior motive. But Allure had been her mentor. She had earned Allison's trust long ago and only strengthened that bond over these long years.

"It is," Allure said, meeting her gaze. "Sage and I were able to verify that independently in the tomes we confiscated from

Dredmort's library after the victory over Fosland. And I'll be able to tell if she's following that rite."

Allison took a deep breath. "All right. In that case, if you'd be unable to take over my body, how would you stop me from doing what Nyro did?"

"By refusing to do your bidding," Shadow said. "Nyro discovered ways to save us from the decline most demons experience over time. We were able to retain our identity and our will in this form thanks to her research. Without those precautions, even the most powerful demons would lose themselves over time.

"Resisting your will would cost me. The pain would be excruciating and not something any normal demon would be able to endure. Nor would it be something I would be able to undertake lightly. Only if I saw you going down the same path as Nyro could I summon the strength to resist. But I promise you, resist I would if it should become necessary."

Allison nodded. "I can agree to that." It wasn't time to bind her yet—she'd need to think on this long and hard. And discuss it with Jezebel, Khaldun, and Mira. But she had no objections to this plan, should she decide to go through with the binding.

"Very well, sorcerer," Shadow said, and Allison could swear she heard tinkling bells. The demon seemed amused. "Come with me and let's see what you can do."

Shadow's human form shrank down to a spark and she darted around a few times before disappearing. Allison could sense that she'd left the tower, and she followed Allure out. The sky was already starting to lighten in the east—how long had they been in there? It must have been hours, though it felt like only twenty or thirty minutes had passed.

"Where did she go?" Allison asked, gazing around but not seeing the spark anywhere.

"This way," Allure said, taking her by the hand and leading her along the path that led behind the quad. "She's putting a lot of faith in you. I know she had some doubts, but it would seem you've allayed those."

"Do you trust her?" Allison asked. "She was a member of the Sacred Circle—could this all be a ploy to get me to join Nyro?"

"I don't believe so. She was behind the university's purge of any information pertaining to necromancy. And you heard what she said—she will do whatever it takes to stop you from going down the same path as Nyro. She doesn't want to see anyone do that to Anoria again."

"Could she just be making sure no one else can ever challenge Nyro?" Allison said. "I'm sorry for being so skeptical, but I was shocked to learn that she was Blaze. After what we've been through, it's hard for me to imagine one of Nyro's Sacred Circle betraying her like this."

"I don't blame you," Allure said. "It's wise to be cautious. And I felt the same way when she first revealed herself to me. But she allowed me to read her. I may not have truth sense like Intuit did, but protecting Anoria from tyranny—Nyro's or anyone else's—does drive her. To the point of being an obsession."

"That's good to know," Allison said. "I want time to think about this before I bind her. This is a big decision, and if I do it, there's no going back."

"No, there's not," Allure said.

They walked in silence for a few minutes, Allison lost in thought. This was a lot to take in and she would need a while to process it all. Allure stopped, and she realized they were in the cemetery. A chill ran down her spine.

"She's here," Allure said.

Allison spotted the spark of fire darting about only a moment before it grew, taking on the outline of a human female form again. "Summon me a demon, Princess," she said.

Allison fingered the ring on her right hand, as she always did before doing a summoning. Its presence reassured her. All sorcerers wore one; it helped protect them from demonic possession. With her channels of power open, as they had to be to project the magical force, she was vulnerable to spectral attack. The ring couldn't stop it, but would prevent most demons from finding her. And woven into the magic she would use to call the demon were elements that would prevent it from attacking *her*.

Channeling her magic, Allison held out one hand and opened her mind to the spirit realm. She found a demon, average in power, and called it forth. It erupted out of the earth, first as a shadow, then turning to smoke, quickly taking on the shape of a human, towering over them. Allison could sense its displeasure at being summoned against its will. It roared, and she felt it more than heard it as a low rumble shaking the earth.

"Very good," Shadow said. "Now banish it."

Allison did so, and the demon turned to smoke once more, dissipating on the breeze.

"Now, prepare yourself," Shadow said.

"For what?" Allison said, her heart jumping into her throat.

An enormous shadow oozed out of the ground, dwarfing the monster she'd called, taking human form and reaching out for her. Allison cast the spell to banish it, but nothing happened—this one was too strong. She fired off more spells and lightning and fire danced inside the demon as it backed away, screaming in pain.

Allison tried banishing it again, thinking maybe now it would work with the monster distracted. But it was no use. She kept up her attacks, but the demon neutralized her spells. Reaching out with one hand, he hit her with an air spell, lifting her off the ground. Allison screamed as the magic carried her high above the cemetery.

Pulling her carpet out of the void, she canceled the air spell and flew a circle around the demon, hitting him with fire spells again. He was ready for her this time and canceled her magic. Suddenly, he turned to smoke, engulfing her.

Allison screamed again as the demon hit her with fire and lightning. She tried to cancel the spells, but the demon was too strong. It was agony—as if her insides were cooking. Projecting her full power, she summoned a dozen smaller demons, sending them after the monster. He screamed as the lesser ones tried to consume him, blowing holes in the smoke, and allowing Allison to see her surroundings.

The demon turned its attention to its assailants, dropping Allison. She was high above the earth, and she'd lost her carpet. Falling like a stone, she summoned air to cushion the impact, but still hit hard, falling and rolling several times before regaining her feet.

Allison stood her ground, ready for another attack, as high overhead, the demon banished its foes and came at her again.

"Enough," Shadow said, and the demon disappeared before it reached her. "Your power has grown more than I thought."

"You could have given me some warning," Allison said, dropping her guard and approaching Shadow and Allure.

"I'm going to unlock your latent talent, Princess," Shadow said. Allison glared at her. "It will take some time for you to reach your full potential. And by then, my preparations should be complete. Are you ready?"

Allison took a deep breath and nodded.

Shadow held one hand to her cheek, and she was hot to the touch. Allison felt nothing at first, but then her entire body began tingling. After a few moments, her vision started going dark around the edges, and she thought she might swoon. Her knees gave out, but Allure caught her, supporting her weight. Allison's head cleared the moment Shadow withdrew her hand.

"It is done," she told her.

Allison didn't feel any different, but that wasn't surprising. It would take time. "What you did—is that similar to the magic Nyro used to trigger Syllith's transformation?"

"Yes, in essence, it's the same. She used spells like that on all of us to help us reach our full potential."

"Did she take power from you when she did that?" Allison asked, standing without Allure's help now. "I watched her destroy Castle Spanbrook with an earthquake, but I thought only Xythor possessed that ability."

"Nyro can do that, too," Shadow said. "I'm not sure if she possessed such latent power from the beginning and used her own spells to bring it forth, or took the abilities from others. It would be extraordinarily rare for one mage to possess so many latent talents.

But she was extraordinary in many ways. If she took the power from the others, however, then I don't know how that might have worked. Never have I encountered spells that could do that."

"Which other talents did she share with the Sacred Circle?" Allure asked.

"I'm not certain. She could create earthquakes like Xythor and perform weather magic like Typhoon. Her command of fire rivaled my own. On the other hand, she was no shapeshifter, and could not create plagues. She didn't bind as many demons as Reaper, but necromancy was her forte, perhaps even more than his. Beyond those, I cannot say.

"I will leave you now, sorcerer," Shadow concluded. "Practice, and I shall be in touch again soon." She diminished to a spark of fire and vanished.

CHAPTER SIX
UNLEASHED

llison recovered her carpet and flew back to Stoutwall with Allure. It was full daylight by the time they reached the castle.

"Join me for breakfast?" Allure said once they'd landed on the grounds and she'd tucked her carpet into the void.

"Yes, I'm famished," Allison said. "Let me go see if Jezebel would like to come."

"I'll see you in the great hall," Allure said with a smile.

Allison ran up to her chambers. Jezebel greeted her with a kiss, but something seemed amiss. "You're nervous—what's wrong?"

"It's probably nothing," Jezebel said. "The girls went out for a walk at sunrise, and they should have been back by now."

"The only part of that I find strange is that they were up at sunrise," Allison said with a grin. "I'm sure they're fine. Augustine's got his people patrolling the entire area, and we'd hear from Camilla if the troops in Spanbrook were preparing to move out. Right?"

"Camilla says there's been no change," Jezebel said with a sigh. "I worry, though. You know how Alanna gets."

"I'll tell you what," Allison said. "Join me for breakfast—I'm starving. If they haven't turned up by the time we're done, I'll go out looking for them."

"All right," Jezebel said with a sigh.

They ran into Khaldun and Mira on their way downstairs, and they accompanied them to the great hall. Allure was sitting at one of the larger tables with Battleaxe, Mist, and Imani.

"There you are," Battleaxe said as the four of them sat down. "You missed an intense training session this morning. Shatter kicked our asses."

"When are you training next?" Allison asked.

"Tomorrow at dawn."

"I'll be there." She was eager to try out her new sword.

Their food was served, so they ate in silence for a few minutes. As they finished, Allison told the others about the developments in Spanbrook and her encounter with Shadow. They were as shocked as she had been to find out that Shadow was Blaze.

"This changes everything," Khaldun said. "She was part of the Sacred Circle, for heaven's sake. I don't understand how we can possibly trust her. And not only that but what's in it for her? Why would she willingly give up her autonomy by letting Allison bind her?"

Allure explained her reasons for trusting her. "And as for allowing herself to be bound, it's the only way forward. She wants to see Nyro defeated, whatever the cost. And neither she nor Allison is powerful enough to do that alone. She's the last of the Sacred Circle—there are no other demons out there with anywhere near as much power. Binding Shadow is the only way Allison can grow strong enough to defeat Nyro before it's too late. And joining with Allison is Shadow's only remaining path, too. She cannot face Nyro in her current form. And demons cannot bind other demons. So the only other way she could increase her power would be to do what Nyro did. Reanimate an elf, bind a human sorcerer, and force that mage to bind demons. She is unwilling to go that route."

"I don't blame her," Jezebel muttered.

"Why hasn't Nyro transformed Emma yet?" Mira asked.

"There's no way to know for sure," Allure said. "I would guess that she's not ready to bind any new demons yet. And she won't want to transform Emma until she has someone available to bind her."

"Because it would be dangerous to have Emma running around as an unbound sorcerer," said Khaldun.

"Yes, exactly," Allure said. "And there wouldn't be any reason to complete the rite of binding until she's ready to bind some demons. That's the only reason she needs Emma in the first place."

"Why couldn't she start binding demons right away?" Battleaxe asked.

"I'm sure she could," said Allure. "But the situation has changed. The Sacred Circle possessed vastly greater power than any other specters, but more than that, they took steps to ensure they didn't lose themselves. Most demons are more like animals. Nyro will want to find the strongest ones she can, but also ones that will be pliable to her will. No normal demon could defy her outright, but some are more cooperative than others."

"Do you think Nyro's new demons will reanimate elvish bodies?" Jezebel asked.

"It's possible, but I doubt it," said Allure. "That worked for the Sacred Circle because they'd retained their ability to function autonomously. It would probably work to Nyro's advantage to keep the new ones free to possess her enemies."

"Great," Battleaxe muttered.

"Do you think Shadow could bring out my shapeshifting abilities?" Khaldun asked. "I've not been able to make any progress."

"Certainly not for lack of trying," Mira said with a grin. "He's become obsessed."

"What are you able to do?" Mist asked.

"I can change my features at will, and those of others," he said. "But I can't change my shape."

"Let me see something," Mist said.

"I can't inside of the null," he reminded her.

"We should be safe without the null for a few moments," Jezebel said, nodding to Mira.

Mira collapsed her null. Khaldun focused for a moment, and his skin turned from golden to brown, as it had been before his transformation.

"And that's not an illusion?" Mist asked.

"Try canceling it."

She did, but nothing happened. "Wow. That's legitimate. Do something to me." He furrowed his brow in concentration for a moment, and Mist's skin turned purple, including her bald head. The others chuckled. She stared at her hands wide-eyed for a moment, and said, "This is terrible! Change me back!"

Khaldun reversed the magic, returning himself to his normal appearance, and Mira restored her null. "I'm afraid that's about all I can do. I can change people's hair, skin, or eye color—or my own. And I can do minor cosmetic changes, like fuller lips or a smaller nose, that sort of thing. I haven't been able to transform myself or anyone else in any other way. In addition to trying to shift my form to that of a bear or a dragon, I've tried simpler things, like making myself taller or stronger, and none of it works."

"Only appearance modifications," Mist said. "Interesting. But not all that useful if you can already cast illusions."

"Right, exactly," he said. "Being able to disguise my nature as a sorcerer came in handy back when we were fighting Henry. But it doesn't serve much purpose now."

"Could be fun in bed, though," Battleaxe said with a grin. "I mean if you can change the size of your nose or lips…" She finished with a shrug.

"It *is* fun," Mira said, giggling and turning a darker shade of gold.

"I'll talk to Shadow," Allure said. "She'll probably be willing to help."

"What about the rest of us?" Battleaxe said. "Can she bring out other talents in us?"

"That's not how it works," said Allure. "She can't give you powers you don't already possess. All she can do is unlock those you already have that have yet to manifest. I've done readings for all of you, and I'm afraid Allison and Khaldun are the only two with unrealized power."

"Damn," said Battleaxe. "I was kind of hoping maybe she could give me some of that sex magic you have. I haven't been laid in ages now, and my fingers get tired if you know what I mean."

The others laughed, and Mist said, "There are thousands of men camped right outside these walls, and I'm sure most of them would give their right arm to take a sorcerer to bed."

"Women too," Allure said with a grin.

"That's fair," Battleaxe said with a shrug. "I'll stick to the men. I've been trying to flirt with Shatter, to tell you the truth. He's kind of oblivious, though."

Allison and Jezebel bade the others farewell and headed back to their chambers. Alanna and Leda still hadn't turned up, so Allison agreed to go out looking for them. She left the castle and pulled her carpet out of the void when she heard giggling. The girls ran up from the lake, saw her, and stopped short.

"I was about to go out looking for you," Allison said, tucking her carpet back into oblivion. "Where were you?"

They looked at each other and burst out laughing again. "We went for a walk around the lake," Alanna said. "It's a lot bigger than we thought, so we had to turn around and come back the way we went."

She was lying. Allison wasn't sure how she could tell, but she was certain of it. A vision came to her of Alanna riding that dragon—Sigrid—around the lake. "Leda, please go up to our chambers," she said, hugging her. "I need to talk to your sister in private."

"Yes, Mother," she said with a sigh before hurrying off.

"What did I do now?" Alanna said, pouting.

There were people about, and Allison did want this conversation to be private. "Come with me." She led her away from the castle and took the path up to the top of the waterfall. There was a bench there, and they each took a seat.

"You lied to me," Allison said. "You did *not* go for a walk around the lake."

"Yes, we did!"

"You rode that dragon again."

Alanna gaped at her. "You have people spying on us?!"

"No."

"How else could you know that?" She gasped. "Wait—can you read minds now?"

Allison chuckled. "I don't think so. Don't worry about how I know. You were told to stay away from the dragons."

"It's not fair—Sigrid was *pining* for me! She came to visit us and I could tell she wanted to fly. And besides, no dragon has ever dropped a rider. I'm perfectly safe!"

Allison knew she was lying again. "You're not being truthful."

"I swear I am!"

"Who told you no dragon has ever dropped a rider?" She'd left with Jezebel the other day before Mira told them that.

Allison saw Alanna and Leda leaving the castle at dawn, heading over to the camp where the dragon riders were staying. They met a boy there, probably a little older than them, and he took them to see the dragons. They were hunting in the forest along the lake's northern shore. Sigrid spotted them and waddled over to greet Alanna. She kissed the boy—a very *adult* kiss—before climbing onto the beast's back and flying off.

"It's common knowledge, Mother," Alanna said, rolling her eyes.

"Did that boy tell you that?"

"What boy?" Alanna said, narrowing her eyes.

"The one you kissed before you took off on your dragon."

Alanna gasped. "You ARE spying on us! I knew it!"

Allison didn't understand how she was seeing these visions, but that would have to wait. "I am not. Who is the boy?"

Alanna sighed. "This is *so* unfair. His name is Soren. He's a good person, Mother. He's the one who told me no dragon has ever dropped its rider."

"And how old is Soren?"

Alanna glared at her.

"He looks much too old for you."

"He's *seventeen*."

"I want you to stay away from him—and from the dragons. And I'll know it if you disobey me."

"I'm *fourteen*! The same age you and Mother were when you made love for the first time."

Allison gasped. "You did *not*!"

"I only *kissed* him," she said, and Allison knew she was telling the truth this time. "At least it's only *one* boy. It's not like I took two people to bed at the same time."

Allison's eyes went wide. "You are such a brat!"

"I'm not doing anything you and Mother didn't do at my age."

"We didn't ride dragons."

"You know what I mean."

Allison sighed. "All right. You listen to me. I'm going to keep this to myself for now—the dragon *and* the boy."

"You won't tell Mother Jezebel?" she asked hopefully.

"I have a couple of conditions."

"Ugh."

"Number one. You will stay away from that dragon until we hear back from Mira."

"About what?"

"She's going to find out if there's a way to convince Sigrid to choose another rider."

"NO!" Alanna said, her eyes welling up with tears. "She's *mine*! How can you do this to me?"

"Let me finish. I don't think there's going to be any way to change the dragon's mind. And if that proves to be true, I will plead your case. But *only* if you stay away from her until Mira gets back to us!"

"Agreed," Alanna said with a smile, wiping her tears away.

"Number two. You will tell me before you take this boy to bed."

"Mother! That's my personal business!"

"Yes, I'm aware, and that's why I'll allow you to continue seeing him. When I was only a little older than you are now, my father tried to force me—"

"I know, I know. Grandfather tried to force you into marriage. But you didn't even like boys."

"Right, and I promised myself then I would never do anything like that to my own children. So I won't interfere with you and Soren. But we do *not* want you to become pregnant at this age. So you will promise me that you will tell me before you take him to bed."

"Is there some magic you can do to prevent pregnancy?"

"It's a potion. I'll need a little time to prepare it."

"Oh. Well, don't worry, I'm not planning on that anytime soon. Mostly I'm using him to get to Sigrid."

Allison snorted. "I'll prepare the potion anyway, just in case. You promise to come to me before taking him to bed?"

"Yes, Mother," she said, rolling her eyes.

Allison would have to tell Jezebel about all of this soon. Hopefully Mira wouldn't take long getting back to them. And if she was right about the dragon's decision being final, she was pretty sure she could talk Jezebel into allowing Alanna to ride her.

The situation with the boy might be another matter. But Jezebel *was* the pragmatist. She'd know as well as Allison did there would be no stopping Alanna from doing as she pleased where boys were concerned. Teaching her to avoid pregnancy until she was older was the best they could hope for.

Once she'd brought Alanna back to their chambers, she went to see Shatter in his tower.

"Princess Allison," he said. "Please, come in."

"I need to brew a potion, and of course, I lack the supplies and equipment."

"I'd be happy to take care of it for you," he said. "What do you need?"

"If you don't mind, I think I'd prefer to do this myself," she said, "if you'd be willing to let me raid your stores."

"As you wish," he said. "What ingredients do you need."

She gave him the list.

Shatter froze, meeting her gaze. "Understood. Your secret is safe with me."

"Oh, no," Allison said, feeling herself blush. Of course he'd know what she was making with those ingredients. "It's not for *me*. I'm not remotely attracted to men."

"Princess Jezebel, then?"

"No, she's already pregnant. It's for someone else, and I'd rather not identify them. You know, on second thought, perhaps it would be best if you were to take care of brewing this for me, after all." She worried he'd continue prying if she stayed here to do it herself.

"Of course, Your Highness," he said with a little bow. "I'll let you know when it's ready."

"Discreetly, please," she said. "I'd prefer that no one else know I'm having this prepared."

"You have my word."

Allison hurried out of the tower. She wished she had a way to take care of this herself, but she'd have to make do with Shatter's help.

Jezebel asked her where she'd gone off to, and she said she asked Shatter about the possibility of having her sword shortened a bit. In truth, she still wanted to try it out first, but Jezebel bought her story.

That evening, they dined with Prince Augustine and his family in the private dining hall. Allison had seen his wife, Princess Audrey, from a distance, but had never met her before. Their children, Oliver, Peter, and Jane, were there as well. Oliver was a couple of years younger than their girls, Peter a year younger than him, and Jane only seven. They were very well-behaved, more like Leda than Alanna in that regard.

Augustine told them that Princess Salerna had requested a conference. She was eager to hear any news they had of Nyro's activities and to formulate their battle plans against her return. Augustine was reluctant to leave the castle with the armies gathered there, so Jezebel and Allison agreed to fly to Highgate and meet with Salerna the next day.

They ran into Battleaxe, Mist, and Imani on their way out of the keep. The three of them were headed to the tavern again and invited Allison and Jezebel. Allison didn't feel like it though, so she returned to their chambers with Jezebel.

They turned in early—Allison hadn't slept in a couple of nights, and it was catching up with her. Jezebel didn't have sleep on her mind, though. She kissed Allison, taking off her dress and kissing her all over her body. Allison's arousal flared immediately. Their passion for each other remained strong after all these years, but since the invasion, their lovemaking had fallen off. Allison hadn't realized how much pent-up desire she'd had.

After a couple of hours, they were finally spent. Allison fell asleep in Jezebel's arms and slept soundly.

Waking before dawn, she slipped out of bed and put on her armor. She met Shatter and Battleaxe in the great hall. The sorcerer was eating his usual meal-for-three, and Battleaxe was drinking her coffee. Allison sat down and poured herself a cup. Imani walked in only moments later, so once they'd all finished, they headed out to the grounds. Word of their morning practice sessions must have spread because a large crowd had already gathered to watch them train.

Like last time, Imani and Shatter needed some time to put on their plate armor, so Allison fought Battleaxe first. She felt a little clumsy with the new sword at first. It definitely seemed like it was too long—she even managed to get it stuck in the ground once. The others laughed at her. Battleaxe was off, too, though, and Allison had no trouble besting her despite the difficulties with the new blade.

"Looks like we're both having an off day," Allison said when they were done.

"Sorry, I wasn't ready for the extra sex magic," Battleaxe said, shaking her head. "Felt like I was fighting Allure."

"What?" Allison said.

"Shadow must have unleashed more of that energy when she augmented your spirit powers," Battleaxe said. "I'm not even into women, but damn."

"She's right," Imani told her. "I can feel it, too."

"That makes no sense," Allison said, waving one hand dismissively. "I don't see why unlocking my latent power would have that effect. You must be mistaken."

They both shrugged.

Shatter fought Imani next. Allison was intimately familiar with her abilities, and thought she was in prime form. Her loss was a testament to Shatter's incredible skill. Allison didn't know if she would have been able to best Imani that time, but Shatter made it look easy.

Battleaxe had recovered from her distraction and gave Imani a hell of a fight. After almost a half hour, they decided to call it a draw.

Allison squared off with Shatter. Her bout with Battleaxe had allowed her to grow a little more accustomed to the new blade, and she didn't struggle with the extra length as much this time. Sparks flew every time her sword met Shatter's weapon, and she figured it had to be because of the special steel. This sword was faster than her old one, and she almost thought she'd win this time. Until Shatter lifted her off her feet with one hand again. She kept trying to fight, but couldn't escape his grip. He knocked the weapon out of her hands with his blade, and she surrendered. Their audience cheered.

"I thought you had me this time," he said with a grin once he'd put her down.

"So did I," she said, recovering her sword. "Your greater size and strength are too much to overcome, I'm afraid."

She'd have to put some thought into how she might neutralize those advantages. Or discuss it with Imani and Battleaxe at some point. They both had more experience than she did.

They took off their armor and underclothing and went for a swim in the lake again. Shatter even joined this time, along with most of the crowd that had gathered to watch. Allison had felt unclean even before the training session, and the cold water felt refreshing.

She called air to dry off her armor, then donned that and tucked her sword into the void before returning to her chambers. Jezebel and the girls weren't there, so she figured they'd probably gone downstairs for breakfast. She went to check, and sure enough, they were in the great hall. Jezebel was sitting with Khaldun, Mira, and Allure; the girls were at the head table with the royal family. Allison hoped they wouldn't corrupt the younger ones; they seemed so innocent.

"How was your session?" Jezebel asked as Allison sat down next to her.

Allison told them about her progress as they ate. Her food had arrived by the time she was done.

"I don't see how someone our size could ever beat Shatter," Allure said. "It must be like fighting a mountain."

"A *fast* mountain," Allison said with a chuckle.

"Mira talked to the dragon riders," Jezebel said with a frown.

"Oh?"

"I'm sorry, Your Highness," Mira said, "but they say once a dragon has chosen a rider, there's no changing their mind. Alanna can avoid her all she wants, but she'll never leave her alone. I'm afraid you're stuck with her."

Allison tried to stifle a grin.

"I guess we have no choice," Jezebel said with a sigh. "You're sure it's safe?"

"You're remembering *our* first experience with a dragon," Khaldun said with a knowing grin.

"How could I forget?" Jezebel said. "He tried to kill us—and he almost succeeded."

"That dragon you faced all those years ago was only a danger to you because he didn't know you," Mira said. "And Sigrid would never harm Alanna. Quite the contrary. She'll never let her fall and will forever be her fierce protector. Dragons are extremely loyal to their riders."

"All right," Jezebel said, sighing again. "I'll give Alanna the good news."

"Let me do it," Allison said, pushing her chair back and getting to her feet. She went over to the head table, wishing Augustine and Audrey a good morning. They made small talk for a minute, then she asked Alanna to step aside with her for a moment.

Alanna squealed with delight when Allison gave her the news. "Let's not mention your transgression the other morning to Mother Jezebel, though, all right?"

"It'll be our secret," she said, smiling ear to ear. "I promise."

Allison returned to her table as the other were getting ready to leave. "She's thrilled," Allison told Jezebel.

"I hope I don't live to regret this," Jezebel said. "Well, we'd better get going. We have a long ride to Highgate."

"Give me a moment; I want to talk to Allure briefly."

Allison asked the sorcerer if she could speak to her privately, and they headed outside. They walked to the lake, and Allison told her about the visions she'd had when Alanna lied to her about the boy and the dragon.

"Shadow's spell must have unlocked more sympathetic magic," she said. "I'm not too surprised."

"Why not?"

"I didn't sense it in you, and I'm not sure I can. I've only ever been able to read thaumaturgic abilities. But that's how our sexual magnetism works, so I always knew you had it in you to some degree."

"You did?"

"Since I first met you. There's no other explanation for the 'sex magic,' as Battleaxe calls it. Imani has it, too, but she's never manifested any ability to read people."

"So, it seems like my talent is similar to Intuit's. I could tell Alanna was lying to me, and I saw what really happened."

"Your ability goes further than his," Allure said. "He could sense whether someone was telling the truth or not but didn't see visions like that. You'll have to experiment with this new magic—it may be closer to what Nyro can do."

"Reading someone's thoughts, essentially?"

"Yes. And if you can do that, you might be able to block Nyro from doing it to you. I could lie to Intuit without him knowing it if I wanted, for example."

"I'm not sure how I would practice that without confronting Nyro."

"Come and find me when you return from Highgate," Allure said. "Blocking sympathetic magic should work the same regardless of the specific nature of someone's talent. So if we can train you to block me, you should be able to close your mind to Nyro, too."

"That would be terrific," Allison said.

"That reminds me," said Allure. She pulled a scroll out of the void. Unrolling it, she showed it to Allison. "These are the spells you'll use to bind Shadow. You can take this with you when the time comes, but it might be best to commit them to memory in the meantime."

"Yes, I will do that," Allison said, reading the spells before rolling up the scroll and tucking it into the void. "Thank you!"

CHAPTER SEVEN
PRINCESS MIRANDA

llison met Jezebel outside the castle gates. They took their seats on Allison's carpet, Jezebel at the front and Allison at the rear, and shot into the sky. Highgate was roughly the same distance from Stoutwall as the university, but due east. They would both call air, but Jezebel was nowhere near as powerful as Allure, so this trip would take quite a bit longer than the one to the university had.

Some movement off to their left caught her eye, and Allison spotted a dragon flying toward them. A moment later, a second one flew into view, chasing the first. They soared across the carpet's path and Allison realized Alanna was riding the first one, her hair streaming behind her. The second rider was male. She figured this was probably Alanna's friend, Soren, but didn't get a look at his face.

The two dragons matched their course for a while, crisscrossing their path and doing barrel rolls around them, before finally turning back. Allison increased their speed after that. A few hours later, Highgate came into view, the crystal tower gleaming in the sunshine. This mighty city looked like it had grown from the very bones of the earth.

Allison took them over the city, soaring once around the castle before landing on the keep roof. Azure was there to greet them. Allison tucked her carpet into the void and they followed the diminutive sorcerer into the castle. Salerna was waiting for them in her council chambers. Her son, Albert, heir apparent to the throne, was there as well, and the two of them got to their feet to greet Allison and Jezebel.

Allison couldn't get over how much Salerna had aged. Her hair was white now, her skin far more wrinkled than the last time she'd seen her, and she seemed somewhat diminished in stature. Albert, on the other hand, looked as strong and healthy as ever. He towered over the rest of them, stout in build and broad in shoulder. His brown hair hung below his ears, and he wore a short beard.

Azure cast the spells to prevent anyone from observing their conversation from afar. "Thank you both for coming," Salerna said as they took their seats. She sat at the head of the table, her son and sorcerer to her left, and Jezebel and Allison sat to her right. "Augustine's people have been sending us updates by mirror, of course, but it's helpful sometimes to discuss such weighty matters in person and lay everything on the table."

"I couldn't agree more," Jezebel said. "And it's our pleasure to come to your great city."

"I've invited my son to attend our meeting today," Salerna said. "I want him fully involved in our plans so he can take over should anything happen to me." Allison sensed that she was holding something back. As if she had more definite knowledge that some sort of tragedy *would* befall her, making Albert's ascent to the throne inevitable.

"We understand that Nyro has pulled back to Spanbrook with her army," Albert said, "and that she's spending most of her time in Drengrvollr, but making nightly visits to Spanbrook. Do we know what she's planning to do next? Or have any idea what she's waiting for?"

Jezebel and Allison spent a few minutes updating them on everything they'd learned in recent days. "We believe Nyro will trigger my sister's metamorphosis into a sorcerer and use her to bind a new crop of demons. And although we're not sure why she delays, we can surmise that she may be having trouble deciding *which* demons to bind. Those from her Sacred Circle were special. They retained their identities and personalities much more than most. And any she can find now would be more like animals."

"Unlikely to be leading armies for her, then," Salerna observed.

"We don't believe so," Jezebel confirmed. "But again, all of this is speculation at this point. One way or another, we believe Nyro will want to rally the various forces at her disposal before attacking again to ensure a decisive victory. She likely would have defeated us in Stoutwall had it not been for Syllith. Our combined armies suffered great losses, and while the dragons did give us an advantage, standing against the combined might of the Sacred Circle threatened to overwhelm us.

"Nyro still has sixty thousand soldiers. And despite the loss of her demons, she remains as strong as ever thaumaturgically. We can count on her binding new demons. She may bring other spectral forces to bear as well, such as ghouls or even wraiths. And it's possible she's waiting for more troops to arrive. They'd have to make the journey from the elven lands by ship, which will take weeks.

"With the combined armies of Blacksand, Keepstone, Spanbrook, and Stoutwall and all of the mages concentrated in Stoutwall, it's a good bet that's where she'll attack again. It would be best for us to marshal all available forces to resist her there. We have examined the possibility of a sneak attack in Spanbrook, but do not believe it would be successful."

"Only twenty thousand soldiers remain in Stoutwall, and despite our complement of sorcerers, Nyro remains stronger than all of us combined," Allison said. "We're hoping to change that dynamic soon, but it will take time."

"Change it how?" Salerna asked.

Allison caught Jezebel's gaze, and she nodded. She spent the next several minutes telling them about Shadow and her plans to bind the demon and become a necromancer. The information seemed to shock Albert, but Salerna didn't seem surprised.

"A necromancer?" the prince said, stroking his beard. "Except for Myrddin, we have not seen a necromancer in Anoria since Nyro's downfall. This is grave news indeed. You believe taking this step would make you Nyro's equal in power?"

"Perhaps not at first, but in time," Allison said. "Unlike a sorcerer, a necromancer's potential is limitless."

"They can increase their power by binding more demons?" Albert asked.

"Yes," Allison confirmed. "Princess Salerna, did you foresee my transformation into a necromancer?"

Salerna took a deep breath, collecting her thoughts for a moment. "The looking glass has not given me any glimpse of the future in many years. But yes. Long ago, it showed me your arrival here with Princess Jezebel ahead of a great battle."

"When the crystal tower falls?" Jezebel asked.

"Yes," Salerna said with a sigh. "And in that vision, you were a necromancer," she added to Allison. "Your irises were white. I believe that battle may be upon us now."

Allison wondered if perhaps they should consider abandoning Stoutwall and bringing their forces here. With Nyro's greater numbers, she could afford to divide her troops like she did last time, sending enough here to lock down Highgate's army and prevent them from joining the battle. Gathering everyone here would allow them to bring their combined strength to bear against the enemy.

"Where does Bayfast stand?" Allison asked. "Will Princess Miranda come to our aid? The last we heard, she had a standing army in excess of twenty thousand. Her force combined with the army in Stoutwall and the troops here in Highgate may well tip the scales in our favor."

Salerna exchanged a glance with Azure.

"Unfortunately, we have been unable to reach Princess Miranda," the sorcerer said. "I have been in communication with her chief mage, Beast, and while he has assured me Bayfast's army stands ready to fight, he's been rather, ah, evasive when I've asked about coming to our aid here or in Stoutwall."

"We could stop in Bayfast and ask Her Highness directly," Jezebel said. "We can leave as soon as we're done here."

"I believe that does conclude our business," Salerna said, "however I'd hate to see you leave so soon. Won't you join us for dinner this evening? You're welcome to stay overnight, and you could depart at first light."

"That would be lovely, thank you," Jezebel said with a smile.

"Your Highness, I wanted to inquire about the tome Khaldun and Mira brought here to be translated," said Allison.

"Ah, yes," Azure said. "I have the original and a bound copy of the translation for you."

"Perfect," said Allison.

The meeting adjourned, and Allison and Jezebel followed Azure down to the undercroft. The space was massive. It seemed like it extended far beyond the castle and beneath the city. The place seemed familiar somehow, though Allison couldn't place it. She didn't think she'd ever been down here before.

Azure led them into his workshop and retrieved the two volumes from his bookshelves, handing them to Jezebel. They were thicker than Allison thought they would be.

"It occurred to us that Saliman or one of his descendants might have recorded Nyro's true name somewhere," Allison said. "Do you know if the text contains any reference to that?"

"The scholars who worked on this didn't mention anything," Azure said.

"We'll have to give this a read and see what we can find," Jezebel said, thumbing through the pages.

"I've read some of it," Azure said. "It's dense and dry, I'm afraid. Why don't I check with our people and see if they recall anything?"

"That would be fantastic, thank you," said Jezebel.

Azure led them back up to the main level, where they met Salerna's steward, who showed them up to their quarters for the night. Their chambers included a washroom with running water, so Allison and Jezebel filled the tub with hot water, stripped out of their clothes, and slipped into the bath together.

"I needed this," Jezebel said with a sigh.

"Agreed," she said with a grin.

After relaxing for a few minutes, they took turns cleaning each other and rinsing off the soap, then lay together in the water. Allison held her in her arms as Jezebel reclined against her.

"I was thinking," Allison said, harkening back to their conference with Salerna. "In the last battle, Nyro divided her forces, leaving part of her army here. Which kept Salerna's troops from joining the fight."

"Yes, and Nyro outnumbers us, so such is sure to be the case again the next time she attacks."

"Precisely. Perhaps we can convince Augustine to abandon Stoutwall. We could fall back here and present a united front against the elves. If we can convince Miranda to send aid, we could erase Nyro's advantage in numbers."

"Assuming she hasn't sent reinforcements from the elven continent by then."

"True. But even still, this would give us the largest possible force when the battle is joined."

"Yes," Jezebel said with a sigh. "We should reach out to Okset again, too. If Prince Kamari would send troops, that could make all the difference."

"He's been pretty reluctant to get involved thus far," said Allison. "But things have changed since our last communication with him. Perhaps he'll reconsider."

They sat in silence for a minute.

"I wanted to ask you who that other dragon rider was," Jezebel said. "When Alanna followed us on our way here."

"Ah," Allison said. "I've been meaning to talk to you about this. I'm not certain, but I believe it was a boy named Soren." She spent a few minutes telling Jezebel about her newfound abilities, and what she'd learned about Alanna's relationship. "She tells me she has no intention of taking him to bed, but promised to talk to me first if she changes her mind. I've got Shatter preparing the potion to prevent pregnancy."

"She's still so young," Jezebel said. "I knew this day would come, of course, but I thought we'd have more time."

"She made sure to point out that she's the same age we were when we first made love," Allison said.

Jezebel chuckled. "Yes, I'm not surprised she'd bring that up. If we forbid her from seeing this boy, it will only prompt her to defy us."

"My thought exactly. I think we've done everything we can."

"I agree. Tell me more about your sympathetic magic, though. Have you tried it on anyone else yet?"

"When Salerna told us about including Albert in our planning sessions, she was keeping something from us," Allison told her. "She seems to know for certain that her end is near. I wonder if she's ill."

"She does look much older than the last time we saw her," Jezebel said. "But when I came here with Khaldun, she told me the looking glass had never shown her anything beyond the battle where the crystal tower falls. Though she never said so explicitly, I had the impression that she did not believe she would survive that battle."

"That could be," Allison said. "Perhaps she's convinced herself of that over the years."

"Can you read me?" Jezebel asked.

Allison focused for a moment. "You're thinking back to our wedding," she said with a smile.

"That's incredible," Jezebel said. "How about now?"

"The girls being born," Allison replied.

"Can you see any memory of mine that you want?"

Allison concentrated, trying to see other events from their past in Jezebel's mind. "I don't think so. I can see what you're thinking about, but it doesn't seem to go any further than that."

"I wonder if that's how it works for Nyro, too," she said. "When she infiltrated the castle, Augustine told her Syllith wasn't there, and she was able to see where you'd brought her. But maybe she couldn't have seen that if he hadn't been thinking about it."

"That could be," Allison said with a shrug. "I'll have to ask Shadow about this next time I see her. Allure's going to work with me on blocking sympathetic magic, too, so hopefully I'll be able to prevent Nyro from reading my thoughts."

"What's your range?" Jezebel asked. "Can you read people across long distances?"

"I don't think so," Allison said. Closing her eyes, she concentrated for a moment. "There's a woman in the next room—a member of the staff—cleaning up after the guests who stayed there. They left this morning, and she's disgusted with the mess they left."

Jezebel chuckled.

"I can't sense anyone else, so it would seem they have to be pretty close. I believe Allure requires physical touch to do her readings. Augustine was in the courtyard with Nyro when she read him; I don't know if she can do it from farther away."

"Another question for Shadow," Jezebel said.

That evening, they joined Salerna and her wife, Jennifer, as well as Albert, his wife, and Azure for dinner in the private dining room. Allison hadn't brought any clothing other than her armor, and Jezebel had only her traveling clothes, so Salerna's master of wardrobe supplied them with evening gowns.

Azure told them that the book they'd translated for them contained no reference to Nyro's true name. However, it did chronicle Saliman's descendants all the way to the time of Nyro's downfall. Azure told them their people would see if they could trace the family line to the present time.

"It's possible some information could have been handed down within the family," he said, "from one generation to the next. If we can find any living descendants, they might know something."

"It's certainly worth a shot," Jezebel said. "Thank you for doing that for us."

"There was an interesting anecdote concerning one of Saliman's last descendants before Nyro's downfall," Azure said. "She became enraged over something and invoked his true name. It destroyed him the same way it would a sorcerer, though he wasn't even a mage."

"We were discussing this recently," said Allison. "The idea that *everyone* has a true name."

"That's the common belief," Azure said. "There's no way to test the theory, of course, but this incident does at least prove that it holds the same power over a non-mage that it does over a sorcerer."

"It seems like everyone *must* have a true name," said Jezebel. "How could Saliman and his descendants have one, but not the rest of us?"

"It's possible that the situation was created when Nyro reversed her bond," Azure said. "No one understands how she accomplished that. So perhaps the magic she used endowed Saliman with a true name, and he hadn't had one before that."

"Which means inheriting her bond must have endowed each of his descendants with one, too," said Allison.

"Indeed," Azure agreed. "I don't think we'll ever know for sure. But I'm inclined to believe everyone has a true name, though for the vast majority, it's never revealed, even to them."

They stayed up late, drinking wine and sharing stories with Salerna and Jennifer. Allison was tired by the time they retired to their chambers, but Jezebel wanted to make love. She tore Allison's dress off, devouring her as if they hadn't seen each other in weeks.

"Allure must be right," she told her at one point. "Whatever Shadow did has unleashed your magnetism. I can't get enough of you!"

Jezebel drifted off to sleep, and Allison pulled Allure's scroll out of the void. Calling a small flame to provide some light, she spent some time memorizing the spells. They weren't too long, so this wasn't difficult. Focusing on the words, she sensed the power in them. The rite used only the magical force, which was her forte. She formed the magic in her mind, careful not to execute it. Using this to bind Shadow shouldn't pose any problem. It was far simpler than the rite used to bind a sorcerer to a conjurnor. Allison terminated the spells and went to sleep.

The two of them woke at dawn. Once they'd dressed, and Allison tucked the history books into the void, they went down to the great hall for breakfast. Azure met them there and escorted them to the keep roof when they were done.

"Princess Salerna asked me to bid you farewell, and wish you a safe journey," he said. "We look forward to learning how you fare in Bayfast."

"Thank you again for everything," Jezebel said.

Allison removed her carpet from the void. They took their seats and launched off the roof. Bayfast was much farther away than Stoutwall.

They flew for half the day, then landed in the foothills of the Green Mountains to rest and eat. Salerna's steward had supplied them with enough food for their journey to Bayfast and back to Stoutwall.

They continued on their way after that, flying until sunset. They landed again in a clearing in a forest. Not having planned on an overnight voyage, they didn't bring a tent, so they took turns sleeping under the stars. Jezebel slept for the first half of the night while Allison kept watch, and then they switched.

The next morning they resumed their course, reaching Bayfast a little after noon. Allison landed on the keep roof, where they found one of Miranda's wizards standing guard. He explained that the princess was away, but escorted them inside to meet Beast, the princess's sorcerer.

Beast was a large man with straw-colored hair and a long beard. He was a shapeshifter but could change only into a tiger. Allison's understanding was that all shifters were different. Semblant had been able to take any form he wished, and could also change objects as long as he was touching them. They'd change back as soon as he broke contact. Beast could shift only himself.

They found the sorcerer in the princess's council chambers, meeting with the household staff. The wizard announced them, and he got to his feet to greet them.

"We're sorry to disturb you," Jezebel said, "but we were hoping to speak to Princess Miranda."

"Mm, yes, well, I'm afraid she's not here," he said with a shrug.

"Your wizard mentioned that," Jezebel said. "Do you know where we might find her?"

"I know where she is," he said. "It's unlikely she'll want to see you, though."

"Could you find out?" Jezebel asked. "I'm assuming you must be able to reach her by mirror."

Allison could tell he was uncomfortable. A vision came to her. She saw the princess—a woman with long, blond hair, whom she'd never met, but she was sure it had to be Miranda—sitting outside a small castle overlooking a lake.

Beast took a deep breath, letting it out in a long sigh. Pulling a mirror out of the void, he said, "If Your Highnesses would excuse me for a moment?"

"Of course," Jezebel said.

The two of them waited outside the council chambers, and he closed the door behind them. Allison could sense that he'd cast the spell to prevent anyone from listening in on him. They couldn't hear a thing, but only a few minutes later, he emerged again.

"Your Highnesses," he said, looking back and forth between them. "Have you eaten? Perhaps we could discuss the situation over a meal?"

"I'm famished," Jezebel said.

"I could eat," Allison agreed.

"Perfect," Beast said, sounding relieved.

He led them out of the castle and through the city. They reached a tavern overlooking the bay, sitting at a table on the rear patio. The staff here seemed to know the sorcerer well, and Allison had the impression he was a regular.

"I'm afraid the princess has refused to meet with you," Beast said, once they'd been served ale and he'd taken a swig. "Between you and me, she hasn't been herself lately. She knows about the invasion, of course. And, ah, let's just say she's not taking it very well."

"How do you mean?" Jezebel asked.

Beast hemmed and hawed for a moment, and Allison said, "She's shirking her responsibilities. You haven't seen her since the first reports arrived about the elvish armies landing in Anoria."

"How do you know that?" he said with a frown.

"That's not important," said Jezebel. "Why is she reacting this way?"

"I'm afraid I don't know for sure," he said. "I've tried discussing it with her, but she refuses. It's cowardly if you ask me. Shameful. Bayfast has never abandoned its allies. If her father were here… well, it's not for me to say, now, is it?" He drank more of his ale.

"Is there anything we can do to help?" said Jezebel. "Nyro will attack again, and we could use Bayfast's help. Together with Highgate and Stoutwall, we may yet have a chance to prevail."

A man served their food. "Give me a minute," Beast said. "I don't think so well on an empty stomach."

Allison and Jezebel dug into their meal, too. It was a fish stew, the best Allison had ever tasted. She washed it down with her ale, then sat back in her chair waiting for Beast to say something.

"Her Highness told me she does not wish to speak with you," he said finally. "Didn't give me any orders beyond that. She owns an estate out in the forest overlooking a lake. Her father, the prince, built the place when he was young, and Princess Miranda loves it there. Finds the quiet and solitude comforting, I guess.

"If I happened to describe its location in great detail, and the two of you decided to take a look, I wouldn't be violating my nonexistent orders... right?"

Allison chuckled, and Jezebel said, "You would know the answer to that better than we could. But we would be eternally grateful."

Beast explained how to find the estate. "I can tell you this much. The princess never wanted to rule. But she was an only child, and her father passed away when she was barely an adult. And she's a wise and just ruler. Warfare, though, is beyond her ken. One of the smartest people I've ever met, but she doesn't have a mind for combat."

"She must have military advisers on staff," said Allison.

"Yes, of course," Beast said. "Ultimately, she's still the one who has to make the decisions, though. And I'm not sure she knows what to do with the situation at hand. Maybe that's behind her decision to withdraw. I don't know. But I'm hoping the two of you might be able to talk some sense into her."

"That is very helpful," Jezebel said. "We will certainly do our best."

They thanked him, and after another ale, left the tavern with him. Bidding the sorcerer farewell, they mounted Allison's carpet and took off.

Allison took them north into the forest. Miranda's private estate was only twenty miles or so from the city. Beast's directions had been simple and clear, and she had no trouble finding the place. She spotted the lake first, and sure enough, as Beast had told them, the castle was nestled in the woods by the northeast shore.

Flying in closer, Allison spotted the princess sitting on an upper-level terrace. As she took them in closer, Miranda must have seen them. She got to her feet, retreating inside the castle. They landed, getting to their feet, and Allison tucked the carpet into the void. A pitcher of wine sat on the little table next to where the princess had been sitting, her glass half-finished.

A woman came rushing out to meet them, wringing her hands. "I'm terribly sorry, but Her Highness is not accepting visitors."

"We must speak with her," said Jezebel. "I am Princess—"

"Princesses Jezebel and Allison from Spanbrook, yes, our sorcerer did tell us you turned up at the castle looking for Her Highness. But I'm afraid she's not well and cannot speak with you now."

"We have urgent matters to discuss with her," Jezebel said, "and we're not leaving until she hears what we have to say."

"Oh, I am so very sorry, but—"

"It's all right," a voice said. Allison turned to see Miranda emerging from a side entrance. Her long blond hair was disheveled and her eyes were red, as if she'd been crying. She was wearing a robe, as if she'd just risen from bed. "I'll speak to them. Please, leave us."

"Are you sure, Your Highness?" the woman said. "You need your rest—"

"Yes, Alice. I'll be fine."

The woman hurried inside. Princess Miranda retook her seat, finishing her glass of wine and pouring another. "What do you want?"

"Your Highness," said Jezebel. "As you know, Nyro has invaded Anoria. Her armies have defeated us in Rockport, Blacksand, Spanbrook, and Keepstone. We have retreated to Stoutwall, where we faced her once again in battle, and managed to—"

"Eliminate her Sacred Circle," Miranda said. "I know. I've received Beast's reports."

"Nyro is regrouping and she will attack again," Jezebel continued. "As it stands now, we are badly outnumbered. But if you come to our aid, together with Highgate, we could—"

"When I was a girl, my father told me stories about Nyro," Miranda said, drinking some of her wine. "In hindsight, I believe they were meant to be instructive. To serve as a warning against despotism. Yet he succeeded only in terrifying me. I grew up having nightmares about her, dreading that someone like her might rise again. And now the nightmare has become reality. I cannot face this. I hoped the northern princedoms would defeat the invaders before—"

Allison heard a groaning sound coming from inside the castle. Miranda stopped talking, her eyes going wide with fear. "What was that?"

"What was what?" Jezebel asked her, looking confused.

"You heard it?" Miranda said, meeting her gaze.

The noise repeated, louder this time, and Miranda whimpered. Gazing through a window, Allison could swear she saw an enormous shadow moving about. The door burst open, startling Jezebel, and a cloud of dark smoke oozed onto the terrace, taking human shape.

"A demon?" Allison said.

"Where?" Jezebel said, backing away from the door and clinging to Allison. For some reason, she couldn't see it.

"You see it, too?" Miranda said to Allison, on her feet now. "Thank the stars—no one else ever has. I thought I was losing my mind!"

Allison banished the demon, and it turned to smoke again, blowing away on the breeze. "How long has it been harassing you, Your Highness?"

"For years now," she said. "It used to be that I could come here to escape it. But now it follows me no matter where I go."

"A haunting?" Jezebel asked.

"I'm afraid so," Allison said.

"I told Beast that a spirit was appearing to me when it first started," Miranda said. "He couldn't see it, and found no evidence of spectral activity."

"Hauntings are rare," Allison told her. "And it's not uncommon for a demon to hide itself from anyone but the object of its desire."

"When the invasion started, it got worse," Miranda said. "It told me that Nyro would destroy our princedom and murder every last one of us. The reports confirmed that Nyro was behind the invasion, so I didn't know what to believe.

"The demon said Bayfast might be spared if I refused to get involved. Part of me thought I was seeing things—that this demon was only a figment of my imagination. That I was going insane. But it knew things. It would tell me how your battles had gone, and then the reports from Beast would confirm what it told me. I didn't understand why no one else could see it, but I thought by retreating here, I might save our people."

"Could Nyro be controlling this demon somehow?" Jezebel asked Allison.

"I don't think so," Allison said. "She certainly couldn't have used Syllith to bind it. If she had, it would be gone now. I suspect that it was drawn to Nyro like a moth to a flame. If it learned of her plans, it could have used that information to terrorize the princess for its own purposes."

"Is it gone now?" Miranda asked.

"I banished it, but it could still come back. How often does it appear to you?"

"Every night since the invasion started," Miranda said. "Can you make it stop?"

"I believe so, yes," Allison said. "We'll have to wait until it returns."

Princess Miranda invited them inside. They sat down at her dining room table, and she told them more about what she'd experienced. Allison's heart went out to the woman; it reminded her of her own haunting all those years ago. Luckily for the princess, the demon hadn't been able to possess anyone, so there had been no rape. But it had been driving her toward madness.

After dinner, Alice showed Jezebel and Allison to the guest quarters. Allison kissed her wife goodnight and told her to stay in her chambers no matter what. The battle with the demon would most likely grow violent, but she assured her she could handle it. After that, Alice escorted Allison to the princess's chambers. Miranda had already gone to bed, lying under the covers with her eyes open. An oil lamp on her bedside table provided the only light.

"Is there a certain time of night the demon typically shows up?" Allison asked her.

"It always seems to wait till I've fallen asleep," she said. "But other than that, it could happen at any time."

"Very well. Then try to get some sleep, and I will stay here until it makes an appearance."

"You're sure about this?" the princess asked. "I wouldn't want any harm to come to you on my behalf."

"Don't worry, Your Highness," Allison told her. "I can handle this."

Allison sat down in the chair in the corner of the room, and the princess blew out the lamp. Turning her ring around her finger, Allison waited.

Within minutes, the princess was snoring softly. Faint moonlight streaming through the window provided limited illumination, but Allison could make out no more than the shape of the bed in the middle of the room.

Allison remembered her own haunting only too well. To this day, she had nightmares about it. What a difference her magic had made. Back then, her power had never manifested itself—she had no idea she'd ever become a mage, much less a sorcerer. If only she'd possessed the abilities then that she did now, things might have been very different.

A couple of hours passed, and Allison started to wonder if the demon would return. But then she saw it. An oily blob moving among the shadows. Getting to her feet, Allison cast a spell that would prevent the demon from retreating to the spirit realm. With a thought she lit the oil lamp, and sensing her presence, the demon roared.

Miranda woke with a start, sitting up in her bed and screaming. The demon turned to smoke, trying to engulf her, but Allison summoned it, forcing it to leave the princess alone. The monster turned its attention to Allison, trying to possess her. Allison called the magic that would prevent the demon from entering her body.

The demon surrounded her, trying to find a way through her protections. Allison called a dozen smaller spirits, and they started consuming the demon's spectral substance. The monster howled in pain, desperately trying to flee to the spirit realm, but unable to escape.

Flames erupted around the room, and the bed started bouncing violently up and down. Miranda screamed again, cowering against the headboard.

The demon tried to fight off the little spirits, but they continued gnawing away at its essence. Allison called spectral fire, and the demon's remaining substance began to smolder. It howled once more, and then it was over. The bed went still, and the flames disappeared. Allison banished her spectral minions, and Miranda's sobs were the only sound that remained.

CHAPTER EIGHT
ESCAPE ATTEMPT

mma woke with a start. It took her a moment to remember where she was and what was happening and when she did, she wanted to scream. For all the good it would do. She was lying naked in the enormous bed she'd been forced to share with Nyro. What her obsession with nudity might be, she'd never understand. The covers were bunched up by her feet, and she vaguely recalled waking in the middle of the night covered in sweat after a nightmare.

"You're finally awake," the voice from her nightmares said. Nyro was standing in the doorway, her sleek elvish body naked as always. Emma had tried to think of her as "Estrid," believing that perhaps an elven mage and senator would terrify her less than the most powerful necromancer Anoria had ever seen. She was wrong. Not once had she stopped being completely terrified since arriving here. "You should get up and have some breakfast. We have a busy day today."

"Why? What are we doing?" Emma asked, but Nyro walked away without answering.

Emma slipped out of bed, wishing she could cover herself, but it was no use. Nyro had incinerated her clothes. When she'd tried covering herself with a bed sheet before going downstairs one morning, she'd burned that away, too. She'd reduced her staff to ash, ensuring she could perform no magic. At least until she triggered her transformation into a sorcerer. Which Emma knew had to be coming. She didn't understand the delay but had no doubt Nyro had her reasons.

Padding through the house and down the stairs, she found a feast waiting for her at the dining room table. In the beginning, she'd considered refusing food as a way to protest. But Nyro could use magic to force her to eat. She wanted Emma alive, that much was sure. She sat down to eat, and Nyro watched her for a minute before digging in herself.

"You'll be accompanying me to the senate today," Nyro said. "The others are growing impatient. I told them our campaign in Anoria would be nearing completion by now, but of course, that bitch, Syllith, dealt us a grievous blow. Now, instead of delivering the promised victory, I'll be requesting more troops.

"I already know they're going to vote against it. But this will expose some of the obstructionists who've been trying to work only in the shadows. They won't openly argue against me, but they'll vote with the vocal ones when the time comes. And then we'll eliminate them. It will take time, but my people in the other provinces will ensure that only loyalists run in the elections to replace them."

Emma didn't understand why she bothered sharing her plans with her. And she didn't always. Sometimes she'd go an entire day in silence. Other times, she muttered unintelligibly. More often than not, though, she'd talk to herself, almost as if she'd forgotten that Emma was there. This was only the third or fourth time she'd addressed her directly.

"Why do you need more troops?" Emma asked. "Your army already outnumbers ours. And your elves are far stronger than our soldiers."

"I'm done taking chances. I will attack again only when I'm certain I can crush the enemy. Which I would have done with my Sacred Circle. Losing them has cost me more than any number of deaths on the battlefield would have. Added to that, your side has those cursed dragons now. Our soldiers might outnumber yours, but those beasts tip the scales in your favor. I'll neutralize your sorcerers and decimate your army by sheer force of numbers, but I'll need something special to counteract those dragons."

"How can you neutralize the sorcerers?" Emma asked. "With your new demons?" Nyro said nothing, eating her breakfast in silence now. "I don't see how you can combat the dragons. They're almost impossible to kill and their fire makes them more powerful than any weapon you possess."

Nyro was done talking.

Once they'd finished eating, Nyro cast an illusion of clothing over herself. A royal blue gown fit for an empress, with a tight bodice and long, flowing skirts. And a bejeweled crown on her head. After making her appear as an elf, she cast a similar spell for Emma but gave her the simple brown dress of a servant.

Nyro summoned the elf mage, Gorm, and spoke to him in the elven tongue for a minute. Emma didn't understand the language but assumed she was leaving him instructions to carry out during their absence. Next, she cast the spell of compliance on Emma. Her head felt foggy, but she tried to concentrate, determined to remember what happened to her this time.

Pulling the pyramid out of the void, Nyro created a portal, and they walked through it. Emma took in their new surroundings as she returned the artifact to oblivion. They were in the entry hall of what looked like an enormous mansion. Emma had learned that both the island castle and the senate building were in Drengrvollr's capital city of Krokr, so they couldn't have gone very far.

A servant hurried over, opening the front door for them. Emma followed Nyro outside and found a horse and carriage waiting for them. Another servant opened the carriage door, giving Nyro a hand climbing inside. He helped Emma, too, and she sat next to the empress.

"You will appear to others as my deaf and dumb cousin from Mestrland, as Syllith did before you," Nyro told her. "This will ensure there is no need for you to speak to anyone. When we arrive, you will proceed upstairs to the balcony. I will have local mages in the audience to keep an eye on you. Not that you'll be able to get away, but the resistance has figured out that all is not as it seems with their great leader. So one of them may make an attempt to take you. My mages will prevent that. I thought about leaving you on the island, but I don't want to let you out of my sight."

A crowd gathered around their carriage when they reached their destination. Several guards approached, one of them opening the door for them and helping them out while the others held the crowd at bay.

The senate building was a humongous marble structure with a golden dome. Nyro led the way inside, proceeding across the atrium and through a set of giant double doors. One of the guards took Emma by one arm, leading her up the stairs to the balcony level. She took an aisle seat near the front, gazing down at the chamber below.

Tables and chairs filled the space, arranged in a semi-circle facing the dais at the front. Dozens of elves packed the floor, most of them cheering for Nyro as she made her way to the front, stopping to chat with various senators.

Finally, she reached the dais, and another elf called the chamber to order. Emma couldn't understand a word he said, but the room grew quiet and the elves took their seats when he called out to them. He must have introduced Nyro—or Estrid, as they knew her—because she stepped up to the lectern to raucous cheering and applause.

As Nyro addressed the chamber in elvish, Emma's concentration waned. It was hard to keep paying attention when she could comprehend nothing. The senators cheered most of what she said, but now and then, one group would remain silent. Emma was sure they represented the opposition, but not even they dared to boo or jeer their empress.

Emma must have dozed off because she started awake when someone poked her in the back. She assumed it had been an accident until a voice whispered in her ear.

"I know you are not who you appear to be," the person said—in Anoria's common tongue. "Nyro has cast an illusion spell over you. I'm a mage and a member of the resistance movement. Do not speak! I will ask you questions and you can answer by nodding or shaking your head. Keep your movements subtle—we do not want Nyro to realize I'm communicating with you. Do you understand?"

Emma nodded slightly. Small movements like this were the most she could manage under the enchantment.

"Good. We would like to remove you from the building. Rescuing you from her island would have been impossible, but here, we have a better opportunity. Will you cooperate with our efforts?"

Emma nodded, her heart pounding in her chest now. She'd been holding onto a glimmer of hope that Allison and the other sorcerers might find a way to save her. But this was better than nothing.

"Now, listen carefully. I'll be casting two separate spells simultaneously. One to make you invisible, and the other to create an illusion of you still sitting here. There will be a momentary glimmer as the two spells take effect, so I'll have to execute the magic when Nyro is facing away from us, otherwise, she's sure to notice. Once that's done, we'll need to leave. Are you ready?"

Emma shook her head. Nyro had taken away her ability to function autonomously. She couldn't get up and walk away. But she didn't know how to explain that without being able to speak.

"Is there some sort of problem with the plan?"

Emma nodded.

The stranger said nothing for a few moments. "I understand. There's another spell in place that prevents you from leaving. I'll cancel that first. Make sure not to start moving until I tell you. Do you understand?"

Emma nodded.

She felt his first spell wash over her, and she nearly slumped out of her seat. She could move of her own volition now.

"You're free now," the elf told her. "Next I'm going to cast the other two spells. Be ready to move."

He hadn't asked a question, but Emma nodded anyway. She was very much ready to leave this place.

Nyro continued her speech, slowly gazing back and forth around the chamber. Her gaze seemed to linger in Emma's direction, though, and she worried she'd realized something was amiss. But finally, she swept her gaze to the opposite side of the room.

Emma felt the mage's spells washing over her.

"Now, let's go," he hissed in her ear.

She got to her feet, stepping into the aisle, and felt someone grip her arm. It was an elf, taller than most, with a thin, wiry build.

He had to be invisible, too—no one around them looked in their direction as they moved.

Leaving the chamber, they hurried to the stairway and down to the main level. Emma could see that she was still wearing the simple brown dress, meaning Nyro's illusion spell was still in place. Better that than moving through the city as a naked human. The elf led her out of the building and up the street.

"We should find somewhere to hide," the mage told her. "Remove our invisibility and change our appearances before we go any farther." He led her up an alley, moving behind one of the buildings. "This should do."

Before Emma could say anything, he lifted all the spells. Gaping at her, he said, "Why aren't you wearing anything?"

"You'd have to ask Nyro," she said, trying to cover herself. "Can you please cast a new illusion?"

"Yes, yes," he muttered.

Emma felt him cast his spell. Now, she appeared as an elf wearing a bright blue dress. His appearance changed, too, both his facial features and his attire. "Thank you. Now, who the hell are you?"

"We need to keep moving," he said. "The resistance maintains a hideout nearby. Once we get you there, I promise to answer all of your questions."

Emma nodded.

They hurried along, the elf leading the way, up one street and down the next. Their course stuck fairly close to the shoreline, in a more-or-less westerly direction. Over the next half hour or so, they moved from the city center to the less crowded outskirts, finally slackening their pace a bit.

"How much farther is it?" Emma asked when there were no other elves in earshot, but the mage shushed her anyway.

Only a few minutes later, the elf stopped, and Emma stood next to him. He looked around for a minute, then produced a key and unlocked the door to a small house. Ushering Emma into the building, he stepped inside, closing and locking the door behind him.

"This way," he said before she could start asking questions.

He led her through the house, which looked like it had been vacant for quite some time, and down to the cellar. There were no windows, so he called a flame to light their way. Canceling an illusion spell, the elf revealed a doorway in the back wall. They moved into a tunnel, and he closed the door behind them, replacing the illusion spell.

"We're almost there," he told her, leading the way up the passage.

Five minutes later, they emerged into a large cavern. Emma could smell the sea and thought she heard crashing waves in the distance.

"This is it," the elf said, removing his illusion and sitting down on a rocky shelf.

"Leave my illusion in place, please," she said.

"Yes, of course," he agreed.

"Now tell me who you are."

"My name is Arvid. I'm a member of the resistance," he said, taking a deep breath. "We grew suspicious a while back that Estrid was not what she seemed, and a compatriot of mine uncovered the truth. That she is Nyro. And that she was holding a human sorcerer in her island castle. He freed her and helped her board a ship for Anoria. She wanted to warn your people of the coming invasion."

"Yes, Syllith," Emma said. "She reached us, but it was too late." Emma told him briefly about the battle in Stoutwall.

"That explains why she's demanding more troops," he said. "I need to get word to Asmund."

"He was the one who freed Syllith, wasn't he?" Emma asked, recalling the name from Syllith's account of her long ordeal.

"Yes, that's correct. He's one of the leaders of our movement."

Arvid pulled a mirror out of the void, stared into it for a few moments, and then began speaking in Elvish. Emma could hear someone's replies but didn't understand what they were saying.

"We must wait here," the elf said, tucking the mirror back into the void. "He's going to send some people for you."

"Will they take me home?" Emma asked, her eyes welling up with tears.

"They'll negotiate passage for you aboard a ship heading for Anoria," he said. "But they'll need to take you out of Krokr first. Nyro will come looking for you when she realizes you're missing—which she may have done by now. Her people are sure to be watching any outgoing ships from the port here."

"How did you know Nyro had me in her castle?" Emma asked.

"Ever since Asmund discovered the first sorcerer there, we've kept a watch on that island," he explained. "We saw it when she first took you there through her portal."

Emma was excited and hopeful for this opportunity to return home, but an ocean voyage would take weeks. And she had no way to let Jezebel or Allison know she'd escaped. In the meantime, if Nyro failed to recapture her, she was sure to take someone else from Anoria she could use the same way Emma was sure she'd been planning on using her.

"Can you use your mirror to communicate with my people back home?" she asked. Not being a sorcerer, she'd never been entirely clear on how the magic worked. "Several of them have mirrors, too."

"Unfortunately not," he said. "Mirrors must first be linked before they can be used this way."

"Do you have any other means to send a message to Anoria?"

"No, I'm sorry."

They sat in silence after that, the crashing of the waves the only sound. Emma lost track of time, unsure if minutes or hours had passed. She thought she heard something at one point—rocks falling, perhaps. Arvid scanned the area but didn't seem alarmed.

Suddenly, Emma's dress disappeared. Her illusion spell was gone.

"What happened?" she asked, trying to cover herself.

Arvid stared at her for a moment before getting to his feet, frantically searching the cave. A bolt of lightning hit him, hurling him into the cavern wall. Arvid fell face-first on the ground, blood oozing from his skull. Emma screamed, standing up and trying to run back to the passage they'd used to get here.

Two elves appeared directly in front of her, grabbing her before she could move around them. One of them hit her with a spell, and everything went black.

Emma's eyes fluttered open, and she sat up with a start. She was lying in bed, back in Nyro's island castle. Tears streamed down her cheeks and she stifled a scream. For a brief time, she thought she might actually have been saved.

"Don't worry," Nyro said, walking into the room and smiling at her. She was nude, and Emma realized she still was, too. "You were never in any danger. I had a feeling they might make a move while I was busy with the senators. They got you farther than I wanted, but it worked out in the end.

"Now, I'll need you to come with me. We have some business to handle."

Emma slipped out of bed, and by the time her feet hit the floor, she was wearing her elven guise but still no clothes. Nyro led her downstairs. It was light out, but she wasn't sure if it was still the same day or not.

They reached the dining room and Emma gasped. A dozen elves were suspended in midair, without any sign of what might be holding them there, all of them naked, with wounds all over their bodies dripping blood on the floor. Emma thought she recognized a few of them from the senate chamber. One of them opened her mouth and seemed to be speaking to her, but no sound came out.

Nyro sat down at the table, pouring herself a glass of wine from a pitcher. She drank some of it, then sat back in her chair. "The opposition," she said, smiling at Emma. "With them out of the way, I'll have no trouble getting my extra troops."

Nyro pointed at the first elf, and he opened his mouth in a silent scream. Fire consumed him from the inside out, moving slowly from his feet up his legs. Emma was familiar with this spell, but Nyro was dragging it out much longer than usual. Several minutes went by, and the elf writhed in agony as the fire moved up his body. She was pretty sure he'd already died before it reached his head.

Emma watched as Nyro drank her wine, taking her time killing her prisoners. She seemed to be enjoying herself. Emma felt sick, and it was everything she could do to stop herself from vomiting. She tried running upstairs—she did not want to witness this. But Nyro cast the spell to limit her mobility.

Finally, Nyro finished the grisly work, and nothing remained of the senators but so many piles of ash.

"That was invigorating, don't you think?" Nyro said, getting to her feet. She'd finished most of the pitcher. "Nothing like a little torture to get the blood flowing."

Emma tried to scream, but couldn't escape her enchantment.

"I'm getting hungry, but we have some more work to do," Nyro said, pulling her pyramid out of the void. She created a portal, and Emma could see and smell the ocean cavern on the other side. "After you," she said, and Emma felt herself walking through the portal, though she was not making herself move. Once Nyro was through, she collapsed the gateway behind her, tucking the pyramid back into the void.

Emma spotted Arvid's body lying nearby, exactly where it had landed before. But now, there were four more elves, suspended in midair like the senators had been. They were naked and bloody, too, with wounds all over their bodies. One was missing an arm, another a leg, only bloody stumps remaining where the limbs used to be.

Another elf was standing nearby, and he bowed as Nyro approached. He alone was clothed, wearing what looked like mage's robes. He handed Nyro something, and they spoke for a minute. Although she couldn't understand the words, Emma knew that Nyro was not pleased.

"Useless," Nyro said, returning to Emma's side. Her mage held out one hand, and one of the captives started burning from the feet up, like the senators had back in the castle, his mouth open in a silent scream.

Nyro held up the mirror Arvid had used. "These were the other members of the local resistance cell. Their mage used this mirror to communicate with one of the leaders, but the others didn't even know his name. Yes, Asmund, that's right," she said, flashing Emma a smile. A shiver ran up her spine, knowing Nyro had read that thought in her mind.

"My fool of a mage was too eager," Nyro continued. "He tried using the mirror himself, tipping our hand. Asmund wisely severed the link." She threw the now-useless mirror across the cavern. "Had this one not been so impatient, there's a good chance I could have used the link to locate my foe."

Emma almost thought she could sense waves of rage rolling off of Nyro.

Her mage finished with the resistance members and turned to face Nyro with a bow. Nyro held out one hand, lifting the elf off the ground. His eyes went wide with fear as he tried to escape her spell. Nyro called fire, setting one of his little toes on fire. The mage screamed and screamed, writhing in agony. Nyro didn't silence him.

"He's still useful to me, so I'll let him live," she told Emma. "Hopefully this will teach him not to act so impulsively in the future."

Emma covered her ears, trying to drown out his screaming.

CHAPTER NINE
SHAPESHIFTING

llison and Jezebel woke at dawn. Allison had returned to her chambers after destroying the demon and helping Princess Miranda calm down. She seemed skeptical that the specter was truly gone at first, but Allison stayed with her until she drifted off to sleep. Alice served them breakfast, and as the morning wore on, remarked that it was extremely unusual for Miranda to sleep in so late. The princess finally wandered downstairs, sleepy-eyed and tousle-haired.

"I have to thank you, Princess Allison," she said with a yawn. "That's the first time I've had a good night's sleep in many months. I feel like a new woman!"

"You're quite welcome, Your Highness," Allison said with a smile, thinking she *looked* like a new woman, too.

Allison volunteered to fly Miranda and Alice back to Castle Bayfast, but they declined. They were both terrified of heights, so it never would have worked. They'd traveled to the lake on horseback and that was how they intended to return. Miranda did assure them she would resume her duties and that Bayfast would be ready to come to their aid when the time came and asked them to keep Beast apprised of their plans.

"I do have one last request," Miranda said as Allison and Jezebel took their seats on their carpet and prepared to depart. "Could you keep my, ah, ordeal to yourselves? I'd hate to have Augustine or Salerna thinking me weak."

"Your secret is safe with us, Your Highness," Jezebel said.

Miranda thanked them, and they took off.

It was a day and a half back to Stoutwall, so they landed in the foothills of the Green Mountains that night. Once they'd eaten, they contacted Azure and Shatter by mirror to let them know Bayfast was back in play, and the two of them said they'd inform Salerna and Augustine. Shatter also let Allison know her potion was ready. After that, they chatted with Khaldun, who assured them Alanna and Leda were on their best behavior.

Allison and Jezebel slept under the stars that night, resuming their flight at dawn the next morning. They made it to Castle Stoutwall late that afternoon. Allison set them down outside the castle walls by the lake, and the two of them got up and stretched. She rolled up the carpet and tucked it into the void, removing the two books from Highgate.

Inside the castle, they went to see Khaldun and Mira. Allison gave them the books.

"Oh, thank you," Mira said. "I was planning on adding them to our library in Castle Barclay..."

"Hold onto them for now," Jezebel said. "The day will come when you can add them to our collection. I promise you that."

"We should tell them about Leda," Mira said.

"Leda?" Jezebel said. "What did she do? I would have expected something from Alanna."

"Oh, no," said Khaldun, "it's nothing bad. We picked up their magic lessons while you were gone. Leda came to me after our lesson yesterday—Alanna was off riding her dragon—and asked if I could teach her void magic."

"Void magic?" Allison said. "That's pretty advanced. Not many non-sorcerer mages ever pick that up."

"True, but I think she might get it," he said with a shrug. "She's been able to cancel illusion spells for a while now. And we'd been working on casting one before the invasion, and she can do it now. Only a small one—she made a cat appear. But she does seem to have an affinity for the magical force."

"I think she must want something to compete with Alanna's dragon," Jezebel said.

"That was my thought as well," said Mira. "I know she's feeling a little left out."

"Well, Alanna's shown no special aptitude for the magical force, so this could be Leda's thing," Jezebel said.

"I hope so," said Allison. "They've always been each other's equal until now."

"Also, Allure came to see us at breakfast this morning," Khaldun said. "I'll be going with her to see Shadow at the university tonight. She's going to unlock my latent shapeshifting abilities."

"That's great news!" Jezebel said.

"I think I'd like to accompany you if you don't mind," Allison said.

"Not at all," he replied with a grin. "The more the merrier."

"I'll be remaining here to keep the null intact," Mira said. "And I wouldn't be able to enter Shadow's tower anyway."

Allison hadn't considered that. But if she was right that it was akin to void magic, she was correct. Nothing like that could work on Mira.

Allison went to see Shatter after that, collecting her potion and thanking him for taking care of it for her. The girls weren't in their chambers, but as expected, they found them with Sigrid, frolicking in a meadow by the lake. One of Augustine's castle guards stood nearby, a young raven-haired woman, possibly Kongese. Soren was there with his dragon, too, so Alanna grudgingly introduced him to Jezebel and her. Allison found it hard to believe he was three years older than Alanna—they looked to be the same age. But he told them he'd flown his dragon in the battle along with the rest of the crash.

Soren did seem quite smitten with Alanna. Allison knew that look in his eyes as he watched her play with Sigrid. Alanna was much more interested in the dragons, though, and didn't seem to pay Soren much attention at all. Allison breathed a sigh of relief. Though she knew it was inevitable, she wasn't yet ready for the girls to become romantically involved with anyone.

Allison met Allure and Khaldun outside the castle that night, not long after dark. They took Allure's carpet, and with the three of them calling air, they made it to the university in no time. As before, they found Shadow inside her tower. She appeared as a spark of light before taking the glowing outline of her human form.

"Welcome, Khaldun," she said. "Allure tells me you've got some latent shapeshifting abilities you'd like to bring out."

"Yes," he said, "if it's not too much trouble. I've been working on it for years, without much progress to show for the effort."

"Let me see what I can do," Shadow said, placing her hand on the side of his head. "Yes, I do believe Allure is correct. Shapeshifting is so tough to pin down—it's different for everyone. I cannot tell exactly how your talent will manifest, but it is there. I will call it forward. This could be a little unsettling—are you ready?"

"Yes, I am," he said, taking a deep breath.

Shadow did something; Allison could feel a blast of magic. Khaldun stood there and blinked for a moment before he swooned. Allure and Allison managed to catch him before he hit the stone floor, laying him down gently.

Allure took a knee next to him, taking his head in her hands and closing her eyes. "He's all right," she said after a few moments, standing upright. "Give him a minute and he'll come around."

"I wanted to ask you about Nyro's sympathetic magic," Allison said to Shadow. "Do you know how much she can read from someone's mind? I've found I can sense what a person is thinking about, but cannot penetrate their memories. Is it the same for Nyro?"

"It was always like that for her, too," Shadow said. "Although things may have changed over the centuries. In the beginning, she required physical touch to read a person, but over time, gained the ability to do her readings from a distance."

"Do you know what her range might be?"

"Again, my information could be outdated," Shadow said, "but the last I knew, she needed physical proximity. Perhaps fifty or sixty yards? I never knew exactly."

"What about you?" Allure asked. "Do you have a sense of your range yet?"

"I was able to read someone in the next room in Castle Highgate," Allison said, "but not any farther than that. I'll have to experiment more and see if I can build on that."

Sure enough, Khaldun came around very quickly. Allison helped him to his feet, but he had no trouble standing on his own. He tried shifting his shape, but nothing happened.

"Give it time," Shadow said, and Allison heard the sound of tinkling bells. "Your body will probably need a few days to adjust."

"Thank you," Khaldun said, bowing his head.

Shadow disappeared, and the three of them left the tower. They flew back to Stoutwall, and Khaldun spent a few more minutes trying to change once they'd landed. It was fruitless, though, so they went inside and said goodnight.

Allison rose at dawn, heading down to the great hall to meet Shatter, Battleaxe, and Imani before their training session. Imani had yet to arrive, but much to her surprise, she found Khaldun sitting next to Battleaxe.

"What brings you here so early?" she asked, sitting down and pouring herself a cup of coffee.

"I had a dream," he said, grinning from ear to ear and practically jumping with excitement. "I turned into a bear and I was running through the forest. It felt *so real*—I think I would have transformed in my sleep had it not been for Mira's null."

"Have you tried it in real life yet?" Allison asked, taking a sip of coffee.

"No, I've been waiting for you to arrive."

"I'm ready," she said, getting to her feet. She took a few more sips of coffee and added, "Let's go!"

"I want to see this, too," said Battleaxe, getting up from her chair.

Shatter was only halfway through his breakfast, so he stayed behind, but Allison and Battleaxe headed out to the grounds with Khaldun.

"Oh, yeah," he said with a nod as they left Mira's null. "I can feel it. I know exactly what I need to do." They moved a little farther from the castle, and then he added, "All right. I can do this."

Khaldun closed his eyes, focusing for a moment. It happened all of a sudden. His body seemed to turn to liquid, growing and changing shape. Sure enough, he shifted into an enormous brown bear. Still standing on his hind legs, he roared, then ran off on all fours.

"I'll be damned," Battleaxe said, following his progress toward the lake.

He returned and retook his usual shape. "I knew it! Hah! This feels great!"

"Can you turn into a dragon?" Allison asked.

"I think so," he said. He focused, and his body turned protean. Allison and Battleaxe backed away as he grew to massive size and his arms turned into wings. After only a few seconds, his transformation into a dragon was complete. He was a smaller one, maybe Sigrid's size, but a dragon nonetheless.

Khaldun took off at a trot, wings extended, building up speed as he headed toward the lake. The air caught his wings, and he soared over the water, circling once before going into a dive. He started flapping his wings, desperately trying to gain altitude, but it was no good. He crashed into the lake.

Battleaxe bent over laughing as Khaldun retook his usual form and swam to shore. Her laugh was infectious and Allison couldn't help but giggle.

"That's going to take a little practice," Khaldun said when he reached them, but he couldn't stop grinning.

"Yes, I think that attempt was a little off," Battleaxe said, trying to catch her breath.

Khaldun called air to dry himself off.

"Your robes transform with you," Allison observed. "Can you change other objects?"

"That's a good question," he said. He pulled his sword out of the void. Holding it by the hilt, he concentrated for a moment and turned it into a bullwhip. "I guess I can."

"What happens if you put it down?" Allison asked.

He dropped it, and it turned back into a sword.

"Interesting," he said. He picked it up again, turning it into a spear this time, but it changed back the moment he let go of it. "Let me try something else," he said. This time, he kept its shape the same but made it half again as large. And when he put it down, it retained its greater size. "This seems to be similar to what I was able to do before," he said. "I can alter its features, but not its inherent nature."

"Can you change anything else about it?" Battleaxe asked.

Khaldun tried changing the shape of its cross guard, making it more curved, and added an engraving of a serpent to the blade. Those changes stuck. He curved the blade, making it more of a saber, and this time, it reverted to its previous shape when he put it down.

"I'll have to experiment with this more," he said, tucking the weapon back into the void.

Shatter and Imani had emerged from the castle while Khaldun was testing out his new ability. "What about me?" Allison said. "Can you make me larger?"

"I think so," he said with a shrug. "I'm not sure if this would hurt you, though. Would your internal organs change with you?"

"Yours must have," Allison said. "Let's try it. Go slow, and if anything goes wrong, you can always change me back, right?"

Khaldun nodded. He focused, and at first, Allison felt nothing. But then she noticed her armor growing tighter. "Stop there," she said.

"I don't see any difference," Battleaxe said, looking her up and down.

"I can feel it," she said. "You three start without me. I want to work on this with Khaldun." Battleaxe shrugged, and the three of them headed over to where Imani and Shatter's squires were waiting with their plate armor. The usual crowd had gathered, and they were all watching Allison and Khaldun. "I'm going to make us invisible," Allison said. She cast the spell around them, and added, "Come with me," taking off toward the lake. They moved along the shore a ways, finally stopping when they were out of view. Allison kept the invisibility spell in place just in case, and said, "Can you change my armor, too? It's too tight now."

"Yes," he said, and Allison felt it loosening.

"I want you to make me as tall as Shatter and Imani. But you'll have to keep adjusting the armor, too. Can you do it?"

Khaldun nodded and got to work. He went slowly, taking turns increasing her body size and enlarging her armor. Before long, Allison towered over him.

"How do you feel?" he asked.

"Huge," she said with a grin. "But otherwise, no different than before. My internal organs seem to be functioning as well as ever."

"Good," he said, sounding relieved. "Jezebel would have killed me if I hurt you."

"No, no, this was my idea," she said. "I'm the one she would kill. Can you make my muscles larger, too?"

"One way to find out," he said with a shrug. He focused on her right arm, but nothing happened. "Uh… I think I need to be able to see what I'm working on."

Allison stripped out of her armor and Khaldun turned a deeper shade of gold. "Try now." Within seconds, the muscles of her right arm bulged, much larger than before. "Maybe not that much," she said. He reduced some of the bulk, and she said, "Perfect. Do my other arm."

Khaldun matched her left arm to her right and then spent the next twenty minutes bulking up her legs and torso. "That should do it," he said when he was done. "Not as grossly muscular as Shatter, but bigger than Imani."

"You'll have to adjust my armor, too," she said. Khaldun expanded it, and Allison tried it on, but it was much too loose. They spent a few more minutes adjusting it until it was form-fitting again. "I hope all this tinkering didn't affect the spells," she said. Allison had spent years weaving protective magic into the material that repelled the four basic forces. "Can you hit me with a fire spell?"

Khaldun threw multiple spells at her, but the armor didn't seem to have lost any of its power. Only its size and shape were different.

Allison removed her new sword from the void, swinging it around for a minute. She stopped, grinning at Khaldun. "Shatter's not going to know what hit him."

"You do look like you could slice him in half now," he said. "The added size and bulk haven't affected your balance or coordination?"

Allison spent a few more minutes moving around with her sword, going through some of her training exercises. She didn't feel like she'd lost any of her physical abilities. The blade no longer felt too large for her, either.

She canceled the invisibility spell, and the two of them walked over to the practice session. The crowd had Shatter, Imani, and Battleaxe completely surrounded, so they had to jostle their way through them. Imani and Shatter were in the middle of a match. Battleaxe spotted Allison, and said, "Holy shit!", her eyes nearly bulging out of her head.

Shatter and Imani stopped their fight to see what had prompted Battleaxe's reaction. "Heaven above," Imani said, looking her up and down with a big grin. "You're a fucking monster!"

Shatter chuckled. "Now, this is going to be fun."

"I forfeit," Imani said. "She's all yours."

"Let's go," Shatter said, beckoning to her.

Allison squared off with him. Holding her blade in one hand, she pulled the short sword out of the void with the other—it felt more like a dagger now. They circled each other a couple of times, then she attacked. She couldn't believe how fast she could move now; the transformation had increased her speed as well as her strength. Shatter seemed slow by comparison, and she had no trouble getting through his defense and landing a killing blow, stopping her blade before it decapitated him.

Shatter went on offense next, coming at her with an intensity she hadn't seen from him before. But Allison parried and evaded his every attack, finally disarming him and sweeping his legs out from underneath him. Shatter hit the ground hard, and she pressed the tip of her longsword against his throat.

They went a few more rounds, but each one ended with Allison the victor. The next time they faced off, Shatter went after her like a wild man, slashing and stabbing with his longsword with total abandon. Allison lost her footing as she retreated, nearly falling over, and Shatter took advantage of her misstep, grabbing her by the throat with one hand. He tried lifting her off her feet, the blood vessels popping out of his head and neck as he strained with the effort, but he couldn't do it.

Allison smiled at him. Tucking her weapons into the void, she grabbed him with both hands, lifting him off the ground. Shatter flailed his arms, struggling to free himself from her hold, but it was no use. She tossed him through the air, and the crowd scrambled to get out of the way.

Shatter slammed into the turf, creating a ditch as he skidded across the ground, and tried to regain his feet. Allison was on top of him, grabbing him in a chokehold. The giant man fought to free himself, but Allison was too strong. Finally, he yielded.

The crowd roared its approval as Allison got to her feet, and she couldn't stop grinning. For the first time, she felt like she could face Nyro in single combat and emerge victorious.

"I want a turn," someone said.

Turning away from Shatter, Allison saw that it was Khaldun. She was surprised, to say the least—he could hold his own in a fight, but he wasn't in the same league as Shatter, Imani, and Battleaxe. "Are you sure?"

"Yes," he said with a mischievous grin before turning into a giant bear.

"Oh shit," Allison muttered as he charged.

Khaldun tackled her, knocking her around with his paws as she tried to regain her feet. Allison might be big now, but as a bear, Khaldun was much larger. Turning onto her back, she managed to kick him off of her with both legs, giving her a chance to get to her feet.

The crowd had scattered, giving them plenty of space. Allison tried over and over again to defend herself against Khaldun's onslaught, but it was no use. He knocked her down every time, and it took her several attempts to stand up again. If he'd been using his claws, he would have torn her to shreds.

Finally, after sending her sprawling yet again, he sat on her. Allison struggled and fought to push him off of her, but he was too massive. It was hard to breathe, and though she said "I yield!" several times, she doubted he could hear her. She clapped him on the backside several times, and he got off of her.

Changing back to his human form, Khaldun grinned at her and said, "Good fight."

"You're an ass," she said, chuckling as she gave him a shove. "But that was well done."

CHAPTER TEN
MAGES GALORE

yro sat at the head of her table, the girl in the adjacent seat, and the usual feast laid out before them. She wasn't hungry, but she drank some wine. Maybe she should forgo the alcohol, given the tasks at hand, but she was enjoying it too much. The girl ate but didn't seem enthusiastic about it.

"You should drink some wine with that," Nyro told her.

She didn't reply. Nyro had finally felt her sexual desire returning for the first time since losing her Sacred Circle, and this one sitting here with her slim figure and perky breasts was only adding to it. She could force her into bed, of course, but for some reason, she didn't want to go that route this time. With Syllith, it had been different. She'd been denied the pleasures of the flesh for centuries, and it didn't matter how she sated her desire. Now, she wanted to be wanted. And that wasn't going to happen with this one.

"It's time to find ourselves a mage," Nyro said, finishing her glass of wine and pouring another. "Once we have one, I'll trigger your transformation and they can bind you to me."

The girl blanched but said nothing.

"We'll start binding some demons after that. But I think I have another project for us to work on first."

There were mages all over Anoria, but it would be easiest to go somewhere known to have a concentration of them. Arthos, for example. Or the university. Nyro wanted to start in Stoutwall, though. Remind them that she was still out here, biding her time before engaging them again. Once the pieces were all in place.

Yes. She wanted to go to Stoutwall. "Let's go," she said, getting to her feet.

The girl started to ask where they were going, but Nyro didn't feel like having a conversation just then. She cast the spell to make her compliant and limit her mobility. She didn't bother disguising or clothing her. Let the puling children see her and wonder why Nyro hadn't transformed her yet. Pulling the pyramid out of the void, she tried to open a portal into the courtyard of Castle Stoutwall, but the magic failed.

It had to be the null. She must be keeping that odd magic of hers in place to prevent exactly what Nyro was trying to do now. Once more she attempted it, putting every ounce of her power into the spell, but it was no use. No amount of force could overcome that null. Gods, what she could do with that one if only she could be subverted somehow.

Those fools from Fosland had managed it once, but the logistics were completely different now. The null hadn't been protected back then, sitting in the middle of the university. Once they'd gotten through the barrier, it had almost been easy. Now, they had her in one of the most fortified locations in all of Anoria.

And being a null, it was impossible for her to move through a portal. Nyro would have to take her to Spanbrook by carpet. But to get close to her, she'd have to relinquish her power. Which would mean taking her by force of arms.

The null cared for this girl, so she could use her as leverage, as they had the princess the last time. But with the null's magic in effect, they'd have to breach the castle by force. She'd done that once already, and they'd blocked off the secret entrances after that. At least the ones Nyro knew about.

No, acquiring the null wouldn't be feasible at this time. Even if she could, that one was older and wiser now. There was a good chance she'd refuse to cooperate no matter what Nyro did or threatened to do to this girl. The null had had many years to contemplate what the fools had done to her, and by now, had probably steeled herself against such manipulation.

Oh, well. She was hardly necessary to Nyro's plan.

Nyro created a portal to the grounds outside the castle walls instead, a little way into the forest, walking through it with the girl right behind her. She closed the portal behind them, taking in their new surroundings. The army camp was nearby. The other mage with the dual inheritance was inside the castle, still asleep. Protected by the null—which thankfully didn't affect sympathetic magic. No getting to that one, then.

Nyro noticed something this time, though, that she hadn't before. This one possessed a latent ability. One which she would sacrifice much to obtain. It was subtle—the absence of a thing more than the presence of one. No wonder she'd missed it until now. And while Nyro could bring the talent forward, she doubted it would ever manifest on its own. She would have to devise a way to acquire this one.

Noises drifted over to her from the lake. What was going on there? Dozens of people swimming in the nude? Was this some sort of orgy? Nyro didn't think these people had it in them.

Moving toward the water, she realized it wasn't sexual at all. Purely innocent, all of them playing like children. Nyro would have enjoyed this in her younger days. So many centuries ago. Several of the sorcerers were there—the giant, the boy, and the warrior woman among them. As well as one Nyro didn't recognize. A female version of the giant. Who the hell was this?

Nyro moved closer and failed to stifle a gasp. It was the princess. Only she was as big as the giant and nearly as muscular. And gods, the sexual energy emanating from her now. How on earth had she done this? If she'd possessed untapped magic, Nyro could have brought it out of her. Someone else must have done so—that might account for the magnetism.

Could she be a shapeshifter? That could explain it—this was no illusion. If someone had brought out her untapped abilities, shifting could have been one of them.

The princess froze for a moment, turning toward Nyro and snapping her gaze to hers. Nyro tucked the girl into the void—she wanted to learn more, but wouldn't risk losing this one. Marching out of the woods and toward the lake, she focused on the princess.

It was the boy. *He* was the shapeshifter. But he'd changed the princess. Permanently, it would seem. How interesting.

The princess left the water, pulling a massive two-handed sword out of the void. Nyro had no weapon—nothing tucked into the void could come through the portal—and she hadn't expected to need one. She sensed nothing but confidence from this foe.

"You've grown stronger," Nyro called out, smiling as she took in her body. "And someone's unlocked your full potential."

"Shut up and fight," the princess said, glaring at her.

Fucking hell. She'd made contact with the forsaken one. She was hiding out in that tower at the university. This explained a lot. And in addition to her sympathetic magic, she'd unleashed her full power over the spirit realm. The princess was no necromancer, though. Nyro didn't think her ancient mentor would allow anyone to bind *her*. She was too proud for that.

The princess charged, and it was all Nyro could do to evade her onslaught. She would make an interesting opponent, but not today. Summoning her full power, Nyro caused an earthquake, creating a massive chasm in the earth between her and the princess. Withdrawing both the girl and the pyramid from the void, she opened a portal to the university, walking through it right behind the girl. As she closed the gateway behind her, she realized the princess had read her thoughts.

Well, shit. They knew where she'd gone. And they were sure to warn the governors. No matter. She still had another target. Opening another portal, Nyro walked into a field just outside of Arthos, the girl right behind her. She closed the rift and tucked the pyramid into the void. She would have to work on closing her mind before facing the princess again. This was an ability she'd discovered long ago but hadn't had much use for, so she hadn't bothered practicing. She was confident it would only take a little work.

Nyro hadn't thought to bring her carpet, but that was all right. The day was warm and sunny, and she felt like walking. She had much to ponder after that encounter.

They'd need disguises for this visit. Nyro cast an illusion to make the girl look like another she'd known in her youth. A blue-eyed blond she'd taken to bed a few times. For herself, she chose her human appearance from that same time period. Raven black hair and dark eyes. It wouldn't do to walk through the free city naked, either, so she added simple but attractive dresses to the illusions.

Setting off toward their destination, Nyro contemplated the meaning of the forsaken one's involvement with her enemies. She shouldn't be surprised. Of course she would take their side. That tower possessed magic that would ensure Nyro could never find her. Her demons had sensed it when they took Syllith there, and it had made her wonder. She'd always been clever, Nyro had to give her that.

The princess was sure to bind a demon before their next battle. At least one. Which didn't matter too much—Nyro could still overpower her. But she'd have to accelerate her plans a bit and make sure she bound the demons she wanted before the princess could get to them. She wondered if any of the others might attempt the transformation, too. The tiny one was the only other with any affinity for the spirit realm. She might try it. Nyro doubted anyone else would.

Perhaps she'd be facing two necromancers in addition to the rest. So be it. Forewarned was forearmed. This changed nothing.

The forsaken one's direct involvement concerned her more. After Nyro, she was the most powerful entity left in the world. Formidable to say the least. But Nyro could use the girl to bind her if she came close. Of course, she'd refuse if she tried to summon her. Her power paled in comparison to Nyro's, but she was certainly strong enough to resist a summoning. The spells they'd put in place to preserve themselves ensured that would be the case.

If she came close during the battle, Nyro could take her. She very much doubted she'd risk that. Maybe she only planned to assist her foes from behind the scenes. She'd unlocked the princess's and the boy's latent talents, and perhaps that was all she would do.

The princess had grown more powerful than any of the others, but she was still no match for Nyro. Not even close. Single combat was another matter. It had been centuries since Nyro had faced her equal in battle. The princess just might be up to it. This could be interesting indeed.

They reached the city, but it was early, and they'd have to wait till evening to carry out what Nyro had in mind. They spent a little time walking around so Nyro could refamiliarize herself. She hadn't been here in centuries, after all. It was surprising how little had changed. Arthos was old, even from her perspective, and it had always been free of any princedom. Nyro had allowed the tradition to continue during her reign. The place had been a favorite getaway when she attended the university, and to this day, she harbored a certain nostalgia for those carefree holidays.

They took their lunch at a tavern early in the afternoon. Nyro kept an eye on the other customers, but there were no mages here. Not to worry; her plan was a good one. She cast an illusion spell, using the non-existent coins to pay for their meal. They'd disappear from the till eventually, but Nyro would be long gone by then.

Evening finally came and Nyro chose a large inn with a busy common area. Walking inside, she scanned the room and found almost a dozen mages among the patrons. This would be perfect. Moving out to the reception area, she spoke to the woman at the front desk and reserved a room for the night, casting a spell to make her believe Nyro had paid. Taking the keys, she returned to the common area.

She sat at the bar, the girl right next to her, letting her natural magnetism do its work. Sure enough, only minutes later, a couple of young wizards sat down next to them. Nyro used no magic but had them eating out of the palm of her hand. She invited them to her room, and they followed her upstairs.

Once inside, she closed the door, had the girl sit down on the chair in the corner, and lay on the bed, removing the illusion of clothing. "I'm all yours, boys, do whatever you want with me." They chuckled, removing their robes. One lay next to her, kissing her and caressing her breasts. The other moved toward the girl. "Not her. Only me."

The two of them turned out to be quite creative, and Nyro enjoyed their attention to the fullest. Once they were done, she incinerated their robes and their wands.

"What the hell?" one of them demanded, getting out of the bed and standing there, looking irate. Nyro tucked the two of them into the void. She removed the spells on the girl, returning her to her true appearance, without any clothes, and restoring her free will.

"I do *not* want to watch this!" she said, getting to her feet and trying to leave the room. Nyro called earth to keep the door closed. "LET ME GO!"

"You know I can't do that," Nyro said. "But I won't make you watch anymore." She tucked the girl into the void. No doubt, she'd tell the other two who she was, and what was likely to happen to them. Which was fine. Let them contemplate their fate for a little while.

Nyro restored the illusion of her dress and returned to the common room. She sat at the bar and drank a few ales, letting her sympathetic magic do its thing. This time, she returned to her room with a witch. She enjoyed women so much, but couldn't decide if she preferred them to men. Depended on the individual, she supposed. This one wasn't as creative as the last two. When they were done, she burned her clothes and staff and moved her into the void with the others.

A young married couple made their move on Nyro next. She brought them back to her room, and let them have their way with her. Then she added them to her collection.

The common room grew busier as the night wore on, and Arthos being a haven for mages, she had no shortage of new candidates. It took most of the night, but she assembled twelve mages total, equally split between men and women. Perfect. She needed one more, though, and this time it would be best to find one with the dual inheritance. None of the ones she'd captured so far had it. Which was a little surprising, but random chance was what it was.

Nyro sat at the bar for another hour, turning down several men and women, and even another couple. She started thinking she'd have to return the following night when in walked a sorcerer. Nyro had no idea who she was, but this would save her the trouble of having to transform her. She was attractive, too. Kongese, by the look of her.

The sorcerer walked past Nyro, giving her an odd look, but not initiating conversation. She went to the back of the common room and sat down with her two companions, a witch and a wizard. Nyro wasn't in the mood to waste any time. Getting up from the bar, she walked over to the table and sat down with them.

"Hello," the wizard said, chuckling. "Who might you be?"

"You're from Kong?" Nyro said to the sorcerer, ignoring the boy.

"No, Shifar," she said, her voice deadpan.

"Funny. What brings you to Arthos?"

"Just a little holiday with my friends, here," she said.

"You're from the university," Nyro said. "Still in training—no assignment yet?"

"How could you possibly know that?" the sorcerer said with a frown.

"Fang, that's an unusual name. I love it."

"What the hell is going on here?" the wizard demanded, gripping his staff. Nyro incinerated it with a thought. "Hey!" he said, getting to his feet and hovering over her angrily.

"Sit down, Jonas," the sorcerer said, and Nyro didn't need to read her thoughts to sense her fear. She, at least, had an inkling that Nyro wasn't what she appeared to be. "Who are you?" she added in a whisper, giving Nyro a puzzled look.

"Why don't you come with me?" Nyro said, hitting the other two with sleep spells.

"I'm not sure if I want to do that," she said.

"Oh, you definitely do," Nyro said, getting to her feet and casting a spell of compliance.

The sorcerer stood up and followed her up to her room. Nyro's body was sore after all of the evening's activity, and as attractive as she found this one, it would have to wait until another time. She tucked her into the void.

Now she needed to take this rabble back to Drengrvollr with her, and she couldn't do that with them all in the void. She left the inn, walking through the city and humming to herself. It was late—only a few more hours till dawn, she believed. All the alcohol had gone to her head, and she felt good. Her plans were unfolding nicely. No longer did she have any worries about the princess or the forsaken one. Nyro now had all the mages she'd need.

Reaching a field east of the city, she removed her acquisitions from the void one at a time, casting the spell to make them compliant before they could flee. Once they were all out, she withdrew the pyramid and opened a portal back to her private island. It was daytime there, so a blinding light filled the field, but that didn't matter. She'd be long gone by the time anyone came to investigate.

Nyro herded her sheep through the portal as quickly as possible—she couldn't keep it open very long. She walked through, and it collapsed right behind her of its own accord. Gorm was waiting for her, and he eyed their guests with a curious look. Let him wonder.

He opened a gateway for them in the protective barrier, and Nyro led them through it and into the castle. She took them to the dining room and ordered the staff to prepare a feast. All that sex took a lot of energy, and she was famished.

Nyro sat at the head of the table, drinking her wine, and appreciating the beauty of these mages she'd collected. She'd have to work with the girl and the sorcerer first. There was no way around that.

Once she'd eaten and downed a few more glasses of wine, she got to work. Releasing the sorcerer from her spell, she invited her to sit with her at the table. She hesitated, terror in her eyes, but then she sat down.

"Fang, I truly do love that name," Nyro said with a smile.

"The girl, Emma, told me in the void that you're... you're *Nyro*? Is that true?"

Getting to her feet, Nyro removed the illusions she'd cast over herself, revealing her elvish body and retaking her seat. "She told you the truth. This body belonged to an elf mage and senator named Estrid. But it's mine, now."

"Where are we?" she asked.

"My private island castle in Drengrvollr," Nyro said. "We're on the elven continent," she added in answer to the sorcerer's blank stare. "I'm going to trigger the girl's transformation into a sorcerer, and I'll need you to bind her to me."

"W-what? That's impossible—you can't *make* someone transform—"

"Oh, but I can."

"I don't know the spells of binding, though. I'm no governor!"

"No matter, I know them. I've had to modify them a bit to make them work on an elvish body but I'll, ah, guide you through that when the time comes." She'd worried about losing Syllith when she'd done this the first time. It had taken quite a bit of experimentation to get it right. The girl should have a much easier time of it.

"W-what are you going to do with me after that?" Fang asked.

"My first instinct would be to kill you," Nyro said with a sigh. Fang whimpered, her eyes filling with tears. "But unlike last time, I don't have my Sacred Circle anymore. I could use a good sorcerer. We'd have to bind you to me, of course. Would you be willing to enter my service?" If not, she'd kill her. It would be enough work constantly forcing the new demons to obey her. She didn't have the patience to do it with a sorcerer, too.

"I want to live," she said, her bottom lip trembling. "I'll do whatever you want me to do."

"Good. That's a wise choice. Very well, then. Let's proceed, shall we?"

Nyro released the girl from her spells. She gazed around at the other mages, all of them standing there naked and slack-jawed, and started sobbing. "W-what are you going to do with them? What the fuck is this?"

"You'll see," Nyro said with a grin. Pointing a finger, she triggered her transformation. The girl dropped, howling in pain and writhing around on the floor. She started foaming at the mouth as her skin turned golden.

"I don't believe it," Fang said, watching the metamorphosis with her eyes wide, her voice barely more than a whisper.

"It is something to witness, isn't it?" Nyro said.

The girl's transformation finished and she got to her feet, staring down at her body in disbelief.

"Now for the fun part," Nyro said. "Go ahead and lie down, flat on your back."

The girl stared, her expression defiant. Nyro put her under her spell, forcing her to comply. Once the bonds had grown out of the floor, securing the girl by the wrists and ankles, she cast her enchantment over the sorcerer, too. Sure enough, she was able to complete the rite of binding in a single shot this time.

Once that was done, she made the girl perform the rite for the Kongese one. This time was the easiest of all. Nyro had the two of them stand before her, walking around them with a glass of wine in one hand. She was pleased. They were beautiful specimens, their chiseled, golden bodies perfect in form. Their vacant red eyes stared straight ahead, and she knew their true names. If the Kongese one gave her any trouble, she wouldn't hesitate to eliminate her. She'd need to keep the girl at all costs, though.

Although, perhaps it would be better to use the Kongese for that. She seemed more compliant. More accepting of her fate. Nyro could eliminate the girl—she wanted nothing to do with her role here. Then again, she was her doom's sister. It still seemed fitting to let her keep her place of honor in Nyro's grand designs. Yes, that would be best. She'd stick to her original plan. The Kongese one would have her uses, she was sure.

Nyro sat down and drank her wine. What next? She recalled the princess's newly unleashed spectral powers and decided she'd have to make the girl bind the demons next. The other mages could wait.

CHAPTER ELEVEN
FALLOUT

espite Khaldun smacking her around, Allison felt great. Finally big and strong enough to defeat Shatter, she felt like she could take on anyone in single combat. Now she needed to bind Shadow and take her thaumaturgic prowess to the next level, too. Splashing around in the lake with Khaldun, Shatter, Battleaxe, and Imani, she worked on her sympathetic magic. Shatter was in the middle of a friendly wrestling match with Battleaxe, each trying to dunk the other under the water. Allison couldn't read him at all. Battleaxe's only thought was to get the big sorcerer into bed. She had to stifle a giggle.

Many of the soldiers around Imani were drawn to her sexual magnetism, both men and women. Those closest to her felt it the strongest. Imani herself seemed oblivious to all the attention, thinking instead about ways to beef up her training regimen. She felt the others surpassing her in their practice sessions and wanted to reverse that trend. Allison tried expanding her reach, but at this distance, she couldn't read anyone in the castle or the army camp.

At that moment, she felt powerful magic wash over her. Gazing around the lake and the grounds, she tried locating its source, but came up empty. That was strange. What could have generated so much power?

Allison spent several more seconds searching for the source, and then she froze. Someone was reading her. Turning, she spotted two people out in the trees. She gasped—it was Nyro and Emma. She strode out of the water, pulling her sword out of the void. Emma vanished—she was pretty sure Nyro had tucked her into the void—and then, Nyro marched out of the trees to meet her.

"You've grown stronger," Nyro called out, looking her up and down. "And someone's unlocked your full potential."

"Shut up and fight," Allison said, but couldn't help her thoughts flickering to Shadow.

Nyro bore no weapon, but she wouldn't let herself underestimate this foe. Allison charged, slicing at Nyro over and over again, but she moved like water, always just out of reach. The earth started shaking, and Allison had to back off and concentrate on keeping her balance. A chasm opened in the ground between Nyro and her, and Allison retreated lest she be swallowed up by it.

Powerful magic washed over her again, and Allison realized that Nyro had produced her pyramid from the void—along with Emma—and opened a portal. Allison didn't recognize the meadow beyond but could see in Nyro's mind where they were going. The two of them stepped through the gateway and it disappeared.

Tucking her sword back into the void, Allison retrieved her armor, pulled her mirror out of its pocket, and reached out to Governor Amelia at the university.

"Princess Allison," the governor said as her face appeared in the glass.

"Nyro just moved through a portal to the university," Allison told her. "She's got Emma with her, and she hasn't transformed yet. She must be planning to acquire a mage there who can bind her."

"Oh, no," Amelia said, going pale. "Thank you, Your Highness. I will alert the others and do everything in our power to stop her."

"Keep me apprised," said Allison.

Amelia nodded before disappearing from the mirror.

Allison called air to dry off her armor before putting it on. Running toward the castle, she felt her magic die in the null before reaching the gates. Hurrying inside, she found Mira in the entry hall.

"What happened?" she asked. "I felt something powerful crashing into my null."

Allison told her what had taken place.

"Nyro here," Mira muttered, fear in her eyes.

"We need to gather the council," Allison said. "Can you alert the steward and have him get the word out? I'll recall the others from the lake."

Mira nodded and hurried off. Allison left the castle but found Shatter, Khaldun, Battleaxe, and Imani hurrying over to her.

"That was Nyro?" Khaldun asked.

"I'm afraid so," she confirmed.

Jezebel came running through the gate, stopping short when she saw Allison. She stared at her with a blank expression for a moment before screaming. "What *happened* to you?" she said, looking her up and down.

"I'll tell you everything, I promise," she said with a grin, "but we've got to get inside for a council meeting."

Ten minutes later, they were sitting in Augustine's private dining room with all the usual rulers, mages, and military commanders. Allison spent a few minutes explaining what had happened with her transformation and Nyro's brief visit.

"Nyro still hasn't triggered Emma's transformation?" Augustine asked once she'd finished.

"No, but I'm sure she only came here to try and acquire a sorcerer who could perform the rite of binding for her," Allison said. "Which means she must be getting ready to proceed with her plans."

"There are plenty of young mages at the university she could take," Allure said with a sigh. "Have you heard anything back from Governor Amelia since your warning?"

"No, but I can check now," Allison said. "I'll be right back." Hurrying out of the castle and retrieving her mirror, she reached out to the governor again.

"Your Highness," Amelia said. "I've gathered the other governors and faculty, and we've made our stand around the dormitory buildings. We've instructed the students to stay inside, but so far, we've seen no sign of Nyro here."

"Thank you," Allison said. Tucking the mirror back into its pocket, she returned to the council and told the others about her conversation.

"Nyro might have sensed you reading her," Sage said. "In which case, she could have gone elsewhere to find her mage."

"And that means she could be anywhere by now," Mist said.

"If I were Nyro," Khaldun said, giving them a pensive look, "I'd want to go somewhere I knew for sure I would find a high concentration of mages."

"Arthos," Mira said.

"We should get word to the city council," Allison said. "Does anyone have a mirror linked to one of them?"

"I do," Battleaxe said, getting to her feet. "I'll warn them now. The trouble is that the city is enormous. It's unlikely they'll find Nyro before it's too late." She hurried out of the room. A couple of minutes later, she returned, letting them know she'd delivered the warning.

"We've done what we can," Augustine said. "With Princess Allison and Lord Khaldun's new abilities, we should be better equipped for Nyro's next attack."

"It's not enough," Allison said. "I need to bind Shadow and become a necromancer. Only then will I have any chance of matching Nyro's power."

"I'll speak to Shadow when we're done here and find out if she's ready yet," Allure said.

"Once I do this, I should use the pyramid to go to Drengrvollr and rescue Emma," Allison said.

"It would be ideal if we could get you there *before* Nyro binds any new demons," Jezebel said.

"For Emma's sake, I agree," said Khaldun. "But that will only slow Nyro down. She'll abduct another mage and use them to bind her demons instead."

"And I'm afraid it may already be too late for Emma," Allison said with a sigh. "Nyro read me when she was here. She knows Shadow unlocked my full potential. It wouldn't be such a leap for her to realize I'll be binding the demon soon."

"Which may prompt her to accelerate her own plans," said Khaldun.

"Exactly," Allison replied.

"It would still behoove us to rescue Emma," said Sage, "regardless of how far along Nyro might be. We know from Syllith's account that Nyro shared her plans with her. There's a good chance Emma can provide insight into what Nyro's got in store for us."

"Not only that," said Allison, "but as much as I wish we could spare Emma any further suffering, rescuing her *after* Nyro binds her demons would actually *help* our war effort. She must be taking her time in part to find the strongest candidates for binding, knowing that there are no demons as well-suited as her Sacred Circle. Once we have Emma, we can reassign her bond, and Nyro will lose her command of those specters. Unlike the Circle, they'll have no interest in continuing to do her bidding."

"The only trouble is that without Nyro, Emma will lack the power to control them on her own," Khaldun said. "It would be like what happened to Myrddin, only worse."

"There's no way around that," Allison muttered. "We'll have to keep her inside Mira's null. As long as Emma's isolated from the specters, they should pose no threat to any of us."

"That's true," said Allure. "I'll ask Shadow about this, though. Perhaps there's some way to fortify Emma's command over them. As far as Emma providing us with information about Nyro's plans, that should be possible without physically rescuing her."

"How?" said Khaldun.

"Shadow can move through the spectral plane to Drengrvollr," Allison said. "Doing so now would put her at risk—Nyro could bind her if she comes too close. But once I've bound her, that threat will be removed."

"So, she could communicate with Emma and find out what she knows?" Khaldun said. Allison nodded. "In that case, it might also be helpful to have Shadow locate the elf mage who helped Syllith escape. Asmund was his name, I believe. He was a leader in the resistance movement over there. Perhaps they could send some aid."

"That could be," Sage said. "It sounds like Nyro has already taken command of the entirety of the elven continent's military resources, but it would be worth investigating. If the resistance has amassed any kind of army, we could certainly use their help."

"Even if they can send mages, it could make a difference," Shatter said.

"I still want to go to Drengrvollr in person," Allison said. "We can send Shadow to do some reconnaissance for us, but rescuing Emma must be a top priority."

"It will be dangerous, Your Highness," said Augustine. "After losing Syllith, she's sure to have fortified her island against such incursions. And correct me if I'm wrong, but it's likely that she knows the university has another pyramid in its possession. She may be expecting a rescue attempt."

"I appreciate your concern," Allison said. "And I have no intention of being reckless. But once we've assessed her defenses, if there's any possibility of getting Emma out of there, I plan on making the attempt."

Augustine nodded. "Very well. Where do we stand with Bayfast and Highgate? They will send troops when Nyro attacks again?"

"We can count on Salerna and Miranda," Jezebel confirmed. "Your Highness, the problem is that if Nyro divides her forces again, sending troops to Highgate like she did last time, she could effectively tie up any aid we might otherwise have expected from those princedoms."

"There may not be any way to prevent that," Prince Carlo said. "We would have to choose one fortress from which to make a last stand, abandoning the others. Gather all available troops around the same castle. I cannot imagine Salerna or Miranda would be willing to make such a sacrifice."

"Prince Carlo is right," Allison said. "And of the three, Highgate is the most heavily fortified. I hate to ask this of you, Prince Augustine, but abandoning Stoutwall and Bayfast, and uniting all of our forces in Highgate would provide the best chance of success."

Augustine sat back in his chair, taking a deep breath and heaving a long sigh. "Abandon Stoutwall," he repeated, shaking his head.

"Never did I think I would see the day. But I fear you may be right. Would Princess Miranda agree to such a plan?"

"I'll have to consult with her," said Allison. "I have a feeling she might. We should reach out to Prince Kamari from Okset as well. His army is larger than all of ours combined."

Khaldun shook his head. "Kamari will never agree to abandon his city. He refused to believe Nyro survived the war with the elves, much less that she was any threat to us now."

"That was before the invasion," Mira pointed out. "He'd be hard-pressed to deny the reality of our current situation."

"It's worth a shot, I suppose," Khaldun said with a shrug. "I'll reach out to his sorcerer, Siren, once we've finished here."

"If we're going to abandon Stoutwall anyway, we should consider laying a trap for Nyro," Shatter said. "It might be possible to draw her into the castle again. Once she's inside, with all of our mages acting in concert, we may be able to destroy her."

"What would we use as bait?" Augustine asked. "Last time, she entered the castle to abduct Emma. If she's gone to Arthos to acquire the other mages she needs, I'm not sure what else might draw her in."

"Me," Allison said. "I could sense that she saw me as a challenge. She had no weapon this morning. If we presented her with an opportunity to face me in single combat, she might just take it."

"Or me," said Mira. "Dredmort told me Nyro never had a null during her reign. I'm sure the prospect of acquiring me would be attractive to her."

"We'll have to think on this," Augustine said with a nod.

"What about the old gods?" said Khaldun. "When we were taking the first artifact to the university, we stopped at an ancient temple. The monks there tried to use the pyramid to release their gods from some other plane of existence. I guess Nyro banished them there in ancient times? I doubt they're true gods, but they did seem like powerful mages. Could they help us against Nyro?"

"We could use the pyramid to bring them here," Sage said. "But there's no telling what they might do. Perhaps they would help us in the fight against Nyro, using our resources to defeat her. But what then? They may try taking Anoria for their own. If the stories are true, they would be loyal only to themselves."

"I agree," said Allure. "Unleashing those beings could prove disastrous. We cannot trust them."

"Very well," said Augustine. "We will consider sacrificing our castle for the sake of consolidating our forces in Highgate and perhaps setting a trap for Nyro. Princess Allison will reach out to Bayfast to see if Miranda would be agreeable to such a plan. And Governor Allure will find out if Shadow is ready for her rite of binding. I believe that should conclude our business this morning."

The meeting adjourned, and Allison headed up to her chambers with Jezebel. Leda and Alanna were awake but still in bed. They spotted Allison and both screamed the way Jezebel had.

"You're a giant!" Alanna said. "Who did this to you?"

"You remind me of Shatter," Leda said with a frown.

"Khaldun did this if you must know," Allison told them, "because I asked him to."

"Why?" Leda said.

"Don't worry about it," Jezebel told her. "It's none of your business anyway. Why don't you both go down to the great hall for breakfast?"

"I was going to go visit Sigrid first," Alanna said.

"Not today," Jezebel said. "I think the two of you had better stay inside the castle for now."

"What? Why?" Alanna said. "I *have* to see Sigrid! She'll be so sad without me!"

"She can come to the castle and see you in the courtyard," Jezebel said. "Nyro showed up on the grounds this morning so I do not want you two wandering about."

"*What?*" said Leda. "Nyro was *here?*"

"Yes," said Allison, "and we believe she was looking for another mage to abduct. So, please, promise us you will stay in the castle!"

"I swear on my sister's life I won't go anywhere," Leda said.

"Hey!" Alanna said, pushing her and nearly knocking her out of the bed. "I agree. You should have told us that from the start!"

Jezebel coaxed them out of bed, and they headed down to breakfast. "Now let me get a proper look at you," she said, sitting on their bed and flashing Allison a sultry smile. "Take off that armor."

Allison chuckled. She stripped out of the leather, turning slowly in place to give her a full view. "If we don't like it, I can always have Khaldun change me back once the war is over."

"I think I like you this way," Jezebel said. "It'll take a little getting used to, however. Why don't you come to bed and let me get a little more familiar with this new body."

"I don't know how you can think about lovemaking at a time like this," she said, sliding into bed next to her.

"It's all I can think about since your last visit with Shadow," she said, kissing her hungrily.

They made love, but Allison was distracted. Nyro showing up here had rattled her, and all she could think about was the rite of binding. She didn't understand what was taking Shadow so long. Everything depended on her becoming a necromancer. She didn't know precisely how things would unfold yet, but felt certain this was the only path to victory—and to saving Anoria.

Later that morning, Allison and Khaldun tried to help Shatter and Battleaxe close the chasm Nyro had opened. The four of them called earth, but couldn't generate enough power to do it.

"I don't understand," Khaldun said after they'd tried a few times. "I've opened chasms like this before, so why can't the four of us together close this one?"

"This is different," Shatter said. "Nyro opened this rift deep into the bedrock. None of us possess that kind of power."

"Hopefully people watch where they're going out here," Battleaxe said, peering into the abyss. "It's a *long* way down!"

Later that morning, Allison contacted Beast by mirror. She explained their proposal to gather all of their armies in Highgate, abandoning Stoutwall and Bayfast, and using Castle Stoutwall to lay a trap for Nyro. He said he would relay the message to Miranda.

Only an hour later, Miranda used Beast's mirror to respond. She told her she supported the proposal wholeheartedly. When the time came, she could evacuate her city, and personally lead her armies to Highgate.

"I understand the threat Nyro represents," she said. "We must not allow her to destroy Anoria. If joining forces in Highgate is the best way to stop her, then Bayfast will be there."

"Thank you, Your Highness," Allison said. She promised to keep her informed.

Allure came to find her after that. She explained that she'd been unable to reach Shadow, but suggested that they experiment with their sympathetic magic to see if Allison could keep her out of her mind. Allison was happy for the distraction.

The two of them left the castle, walking up to the top of the waterfall. Sitting on the bench there, they turned to face each other. Allure placed one hand against Allison's cheek and closed her eyes.

Allure told her she was reading her, but Allison felt nothing at first. Until suddenly she did. It was subtle, but she could sense her presence inside her mind. Allison focused on pushing her out, and after a few seconds, it worked. They repeated the experiment several times, and Allison found it easier to sense her every time, and took less and less time to force her out.

"We know this works now," said Allison. "But I'll need to learn how to stop Nyro from initiating a reading in the first place, rather than only kicking her out once she's begun."

"This is better than nothing," Allure said with a smile. "And besides, if it comes to combat, this should be good enough."

"That's probably true," Allison conceded.

"I want to try this, too," said Allure. "Try reading me and I'll see if I can stop you."

Allison nodded. Staring into her eyes, Allison opened her senses. Allure was thinking about how attracted she was to her, and wished she could take her to bed. Allison giggled nervously.

"I'm sorry—I'll try to think about something else. It's hard, though. I'm not used to being on the receiving end of someone else's magnetism."

Allure didn't think about anything else, but did manage to close her mind to her. They repeated the exercise several times, and like Allison, she improved every time but was unable to stop her from *initiating* a reading.

"We should both work on this," Allure said. "Mira's able to control her null even when she's asleep, so I feel like this should be similar. If we can learn to *keep* our minds closed, we could make it a habit the way she has."

That evening, Allison headed to the great hall for dinner with Jezebel and the girls. But Augustine's steward caught up to them in the entry hall to let them know that the prince had invited them to dine with him and his family. So the four of them went to his private dining room instead.

Once they'd sat down, Augustine told them that he'd decided abandoning Stoutwall and uniting their combined forces in Highgate was their best way forward. And he supported the idea of using his castle to set a trap for Nyro.

"I'm not sure how best to execute that plan, however," he concluded. "You and the other sorcerers should probably be the ones to figure this out and orchestrate it when the time comes. I think those of you with her kind of power best understand how her mind works."

"We'll put our heads together and come up with something good," Allison assured him. Though she didn't know yet what that might be.

CHAPTER TWELVE
MISSING

Nyro needed to get on with it. The demons she'd chosen were the very same ones the princess was certain to select as well. Forcing the girl to bind them now would ensure the princess could not. She only had to hope it wasn't already too late.

Sitting in her dining room and leaving the girl under her enchantment, she forced her to summon the one known as Cyclone in life. She resisted, and Nyro had to channel her full power through the girl to call her forward. Finally, the demon rose through the floor as smoke, coalescing into a human shape.

"I knew it had to be you," she said, engulfing Nyro and trying to possess her.

Nyro laughed, and the specter withdrew. "This body is elvish. There's nothing you can do to it."

"What do you want?"

"Your existence," Nyro said with a smile. "The girl is going to bind you, and through her, I shall control you."

Cyclone seemed to notice the two sorcerers for the first time. "You can't do this."

"I think you'll find that I can."

"I won't do your bidding. I'll refuse your every command."

"You are welcome to try," Nyro said. She forced the girl to perform the rite of binding, and the demon screamed. It took a few moments for the spells to take hold, and then she said, "Now you are mine."

Nyro summoned the next demon, the one known as Legion in life. This one offered less resistance than the first. They seemed almost resigned to their fate as if they'd seen this coming. Nyro had wondered if this one would manifest as multiple demons, but it was not to be. It remained to be seen if they'd retained their special talent in death. Nyro so hoped that they had. Once she was done forcing the girl to bind them, she sent them back to the spectral plane.

She completed the rite with the last five, wishing there were more. In hindsight, she realized she might have been a little hasty in forcing Syllith to invoke the oaf's true name. He'd been the most powerful of the bunch and would have been quite useful to her now. If only she'd foreseen the demise of her Sacred Circle... Oh, well. What was done was done, and there was no use dwelling on it.

It was a little surprising that the princess hadn't bound any of the demons from this group already. Nyro wondered why that would be. Could the forsaken one be allowing her to bind her, after all? The woman she'd known never would have allowed that. Yet that was a very long time ago. Circumstances had certainly changed. And death could change a person quite radically, as Nyro knew only too well.

Facing the combined power of the princess and the forsaken one might change things. Nyro felt a twinge of doubt. She gazed at her two sorcerers, standing there like statues. The girl had now merged her soul with the seven most powerful demons after the forsaken one. But if the princess really was going to bind *her*, it wouldn't be enough. Nyro reconsidered her previous plan.

There was no reason the Kongese couldn't bind demons, too. Only the wild ones remained, so there was no other choice. Yes, this was the right course of action.

Nyro summoned the strongest one she'd been able to find during her research, and it roared as it rose through the floor, rattling the chandelier. It tried possessing her, and Nyro had to force the Kongese to get it under control. This demon was far too strong for the necromancer, and were it not for Nyro channeling her power into her, it would certainly take her over if she tried binding it. This would be a dangerous undertaking, but she had no choice. She forced the Kongese to bind it, then sent it away.

Nyro made her bind only three more demons. She'd have to test this out with those first and make sure her control would hold. As far as she knew, no other mage had ever attempted anything like this. So it remained to be seen how successful it would be. No great loss if it failed; at this point, the Kongese was disposable.

Next, Nyro used the girl to summon Cyclone again. She was hoping the spell she'd used on her Sacred Circle might help preserve her new demons' identities. As an elf, she could not wield this magic herself, of course, so she tried to make the girl do it. This proved challenging, as the girl's natural talent wasn't very strong. She was sure it would have been much easier using Syllith. But in the end, she got the job done. Cyclone should now retain her sense of self as much as her Sacred Circle had. Nyro repeated the process with each of the other six.

Night had fallen by the time Nyro was done. This had been a lot of work, but the critical steps were now completed. When she first contemplated binding these demons, she'd debated whether she wanted to leave them in spectral form and decided that she did. Now, though, with the Kongese commanding the second group, perhaps she could have the best of both worlds. Yes. This would be the best way forward. And it would have certain fringe benefits as well.

Once she'd cast illusions to make the girl and the Kongese appear as elves, Nyro pulled the pyramid out of the void, opening a portal to Krokr's port and walking through it, her two necromancers in tow. Closing the portal, she turned to survey the situation. Already more than two dozen ships had docked and taken on fresh soldiers, proceeding to anchor out in the bay. Half a dozen more ships were loading their passengers now. Right on schedule. Nyro walked along the pier until she found the commander in charge of this operation.

"Your Majesty," he said, taking a knee. "My apologies, we weren't expecting you today."

"Rise," she told him with a smile. "You are doing well; I am pleased."

"Thank you, Your Majesty."

"I require seven of your mages for a special assignment. Six males and one female. You may select them yourself."

He bowed and hurried off. Ten minutes later, he returned with seven other elves, all of them with an air of smug pride for having been chosen. Poor fools. Nyro led the group back to land, then produced her pyramid and created a portal back to her castle.

Back in her dining room, she cast sleep spells to knock out the new arrivals. They dropped, lying peacefully on the floor. Nyro used the girl to summon Cyclone again. This time, she forced her to possess the girl. Using that body, Cyclone kneeled next to the female elf. Nyro cast the spell to stop her heart, then called fire to burn away her clothes. Cyclone placed a hand on her chest, and the area began to glow.

Free of the demon, the girl gasped before regaining her feet and taking her place by the other necromancer's side. It worked—Cyclone had reanimated the elf. She stood up and approached Nyro, a look of horror on her face.

"What the hell have you done to me?" she demanded, gazing down at her body.

"Don't you like it?" Nyro asked with a smile. She cast an illusion to make Cyclone appear as she had in life. "Perhaps this is better?"

Cyclone met her gaze. "Why are you doing this? What are you going to do with me?"

"You shall see in good time. Now, please, have a seat. We have to take care of the others."

Cyclone sat down at the table, glaring at her. She wasn't happy, but happiness wasn't required. Only obedience. And so far, she seemed to possess that quality in abundance.

Nyro summoned Legion next. Once they'd reanimated an elf body and Nyro had cast an illusion to give them their human appearance, she tried forcing them to make copies of themselves. Much to her chagrin, this didn't work. Apparently it was not a talent that carried over into death. Too bad. But they would still be quite useful. They sat down next to Cyclone.

She completed this same process with the other five demons, ordering each of them to take a seat at the table when it was done. It was getting late, and she was growing tired, but there was one more thing she wanted to test. Using the Kongese, she summoned the strongest demon. It roared and thrashed, trying to escape her control, but it could not. Good. Nyro sent it through the spirit realm to Stoutwall.

It was daytime there, and Nyro could see the castle and the surrounding area through the demon's eyes. Just like old times, she reminisced. The demon could not move into the null, but that was hardly surprising. It could still see into the courtyard. She sent it swooping around the army camp, and then out into the forest by the lake where the dragons were hunting. Its passing caused quite the ruckus among the beasts, who could sense its presence far better than any human.

That was enough for now. She released the demon and brought her focus back within herself. Sitting down at the table, she gazed around the room. She'd accomplished a lot in one day. Seven elven bodies reanimated by the strongest demons available. Two necromancers. Plus the twelve human mages, still standing where she'd left them earlier, under their compliance spells. One project left to complete, but that would have to wait until another time.

Allison rose at dawn the next morning and went to train with Shatter, Battleaxe, and Imani. She had no trouble winning every bout. Shatter took the most effort, but her increased size and strength gave her the advantage—he'd never encountered his equal in physical power before.

After their usual swim in the lake, they went into the great hall for breakfast, where Jezebel and the girls joined them, along with Khaldun and Mira. After the meal, Allison went to speak with Allure in her chambers, but she still hadn't heard from Shadow. Allison's impatience was only growing.

She checked in with Governor Amelia again, but she assured her all was well at the university. There had been no sign of Nyro, and none of the students or faculty were missing. Allison figured she must have gone on to Arthos or some other city with a lot of mages, but they'd had no word from anyone else, either.

That night, she went into the city with Mist, Battleaxe, Imani, and Khaldun, and they visited their usual tavern. The minstrel, Thomas Broadpaunch, was there again, entertaining the sparse crowd with his songs. They chatted over ales for several minutes, then the conversation turned to recent developments. Allison told them that Miranda and Augustine had both agreed to gather their forces for a last stand in Highgate.

"I spoke to Prince Kamari," Khaldun said, taking a swig of his ale.

"You mean his sorcerer, Siren," Battleaxe said with a knowing grin. "From what I hear, Kamari won't speak to anyone by mirror."

"Oh, no, I spoke to the man himself," Khaldun said. "I started with Siren, of course. Explained what we were planning, and how much we could use some aid from Okset. She told me she would see what she could do, but not to expect any miracles."

"She said not to expect *miracles*?" Mist said with a chuckle.

"Her exact words," Khaldun confirmed. "And no surprise, she got back to me several hours later to apologize, but the prince was unwilling to part with any of his soldiers. So I told Siren it would be on the prince's head when Nyro burned down the rest of Anoria, exterminating every man, woman, and child, and leaving no one to stop her from marching into Shifar."

"You did not say that," Imani said.

"Yes, I did, and apparently she relayed that exact message to Kamari. Because only *minutes* later, he reached out to me himself, using her mirror. And once we got through the insults and chest pounding, I think he was actually afraid."

"As well he should be," said Allison. "So did he agree to send aid?"

"No," Khaldun said with a sigh.

"How can he possibly refuse us?" said Allison.

"He says what happens outside of his princedom is none of his concern. Nyro hasn't landed any ships or sent any armies anywhere in Shifar, so why should he waste his resources? He's got a standing army seventy-thousand strong, so he'll let Nyro 'blunt her blade' on us first, and then he figures his forces should have no trouble taking care of the rest."

"Blunt her blade?" Battleaxe said, her tone angry and exasperated. "That's what he said," Khaldun confirmed.

"Does he understand that Nyro is most likely waiting for reinforcements to arrive from Drengrvollr?" Allison said. "She could attack with a hundred thousand or more."

"He's aware," said Khaldun. "And he'll more than match that once he calls in his levies. With all of our sorcerers here, plus the dragons, he figures we can reduce their numbers pretty significantly before they march on Okset. *If* they ever do—he still believes they'll stop with Maeda and Dorshire."

"He's a fool," said Battleaxe.

"No, he's not," said Imani. "But he *is* an isolationist. His family always has been."

"Well, we're not getting any aid from Okset, that much we know for sure," Khaldun said, finishing his ale and ordering another.

Allison was furious. What arrogance! How could a ruling prince with such resources at his command refuse to come to their aid in the face of the gravest threat to Anoria in centuries? How she'd love to give him a piece of her mind. Though she doubted it would do any good, it sure would feel satisfying.

The next morning, Governor Amelia contacted Allison again. She was outside for their training session, watching Imani's fight with Shatter, so she pulled her mirror out of its pocket to talk to her.

"It turns out one of our students *has* gone missing," Amelia said. "A sorcerer named Fang. She went on holiday to Arthos with a couple of friends, a witch and a wizard. The other two returned, but they don't know where Fang went. According to their report, a woman approached them in a tavern, sitting down at their table. She carried no instrument and didn't appear to be a sorcerer, but she incinerated the wizard's staff and knocked them both out with a sleep spell. When they came around, Fang was gone."

"Did they get a description of this woman?"

"Long, black hair and dark eyes. Several inches over five feet tall. Exuding a strong sexual attraction."

"Nyro," Allison said. "It had to be. Do you know the name of the inn?"

Amelia told her the name and where to find it in the city. Allison thanked her and bade her farewell. She told the others she had some business to take care of and returned to her chambers. Jezebel was there with the girls, so she gave her the news and told her she was going to Arthos to investigate.

"It seems pretty obvious Nyro must have taken her," Jezebel said. "What else is there to find out?"

"I'll figure that out when I get there," Allison told her. "It's Nyro, so who knows what other mischief she made."

"All right," Jezebel said with a sigh. "Don't go alone, though. Take Khaldun with you."

"I'll see if he's free," she said. Kissing her, she strode out of the chambers.

Khaldun was free and just as intrigued as she was. Once he'd let Mira know what was going on, he left the castle with Allison, flying off on her carpet. They reached Arthos, and Allison set them down in the general area where Amelia had told her the inn was located. She tucked her carpet into the void, and the two of them set out on foot.

They hadn't found the place after a couple of minutes, so Allison asked a passerby for directions. It was only a couple of blocks away. They went inside, finding the common room almost empty. There was a barkeep on duty, though, so they went to talk to him. Allison told them they were looking for a sorcerer from the university who'd gone missing.

"She wasn't the only one," he said, giving her a dark look. "We've had reports of several other customers disappearing that night, too. I've worked here almost twenty years and we never had a problem like this before. A lot of mages frequent the place, so it tends to be pretty safe."

She caught Khaldun's eye and gave him a meaningful look. "Do you know what table the sorcerer was sitting at?" she asked the barkeep.

"Not exactly, but I was told it was one of the ones in the back over there," he said, nodding toward the rear of the common room.

"Thank you," Allison said.

"Frequented by mages," Khaldun said as they made their way across the room. "Exactly the kind of place Nyro would target."

"Yes," Allison agreed. Holding out one hand, she opened her mind, and immediately the echoes of powerful magic accosted her. "Someone cast a spell here," she told Khaldun. Focusing for a moment, she created a vision of what had happened.

The light in the room dimmed, and suddenly it was crowded. Sure enough, a Kongese sorcerer was sitting at a nearby table with a witch and a wizard. A woman with black hair and dark eyes sat down with them. They had a brief conversation, and then the wizard gripped his staff, looking angry with the woman. She incinerated his staff, and he got to his feet, standing over her menacingly.

The woman hit the witch and wizard with a sleep spell, then got up and walked away with the sorcerer. Allison kept her spell going, and she and Khaldun followed the pair upstairs. They went into one of the rooms, lit only by an oil lamp on the nightstand, and the sorcerer disappeared.

"She tucked her into the void," Allison told him.

The woman left the room and Allison's spell faded. Daylight streamed in through the window.

"More magic was performed here," Khaldun said. He focused for a moment, and the daylight disappeared, replaced by the light of the oil lamp. The door opened, and the dark-haired woman led a young wizard into the room. She lay on the bed and her clothes disappeared. The wizard took off his robes and had sex with her. When they were done, the woman tucked him into the void.

"What the fuck?" Allison said.

Khaldun shrugged. But he revealed several more scenes, all essentially the same. The mystery woman led people into the room—men, women, and even two couples—had sex with them and then tucked them into the void.

The first such encounter involved two men. But that time, there was another girl present, sitting in the corner. Once the woman had tucked the men into the void, she released the girl from a spell, and she screamed at her. The woman told her she wouldn't make her watch anymore before tucking her into the void as well.

"This must be Nyro," Allison said. "And I'm willing to bet the girl in the corner was Emma."

"She took twelve mages in addition to the sorcerer," Khaldun said, his expression grim. "I can think of only one reason she'd need so many non-sorcerer mages."

"Wraiths," said Allison. "She needed the sorcerer to bind Emma to her. And the mages so she could create wraiths."

"We'd better get back to Stoutwall," Khaldun said.

Back at the castle, they told Jezebel and Mira what they'd seen, and then Allison went to notify Shatter. He would let Augustine and the others know.

Allison remembered Henry's wraiths only too well. She supposed it made sense that Nyro would create more of them here. Without the Sacred Circle, she had to replenish her thaumaturgic forces any way she could. No doubt she'd use Emma to bind a new crop of demons, but they wouldn't be as powerful as her last group. The wraiths could help fill that gap.

That night, she returned to the tavern with the same group from the previous night. No sooner had they sat down, though, than Allure reached out to her by mirror. It was too loud in the tavern, so Allison went outside to talk to her.

"I'm sorry, it was too noisy in there," she said. "What were you saying?"

"Shadow is ready for you. It's time for the rite of binding."

Chapter Thirteen
The Rite of Binding

 llison asked Allure to notify Jezebel, who would want to accompany them to the university for this. Going back inside the tavern, she let the others know she needed to go.

"Where are you off to, Princess?" Battleaxe asked, earning a glare from Allison.

"Shadow's ready for me," she said. "We're doing the rite of binding."

They wished her luck, and Allison headed out. She flew back to the castle, meeting Allure and Jezebel out in front of the gates. Once the three of them had positioned themselves on the carpet, they took off. Reaching the university, Allison opened a gateway through the protective barrier, closing it again behind them, and landed outside the seven-sided tower.

Allure cast the spell to allow them entry, and they walked inside. Allison gazed around the blackness and spotted the little spark of fire almost immediately. Shadow took the shape of a woman, glowing around the edges.

"Welcome," she said, and Allison sensed none of her usual amusement. "The time has finally come. Though I have long anticipated this moment, now that it is upon us, I find that I am terrified."

"You're not the only one," Allison said with a nervous grin. "I know there's no undoing this. Once we complete the rite, you and I will be eternally inseparable."

"Yes," Shadow said. "I am glad you're here as her conjurnor," she added to Jezebel. "This will be a big change that affects you as well as us."

"I wouldn't have missed this for anything," Jezebel said.

"Well, then, let us proceed. Allure, can you please confirm for Her Highness that I have taken the necessary steps to ensure she retains full control?"

Allure closed her eyes, holding out one hand toward Shadow for a few moments. "It is done," she told Allison. "Shadow has initiated the rite, so there will be no chance of her overpowering you."

Allison nodded. She'd memorized the spells, but just to be sure, she pulled the scroll out of the void, unrolling it and casting a small flame to better illuminate it. She read the words, forming the magic in her mind and focusing it on Shadow. Holding out one hand, she executed the spells.

Shadow arched her back and gasped, the glow around her flaring for a moment. And that was it. Allison sensed her bond with the demon immediately. She could see the three of them from her perspective and felt Shadow's power joined to her own.

"This space no longer serves any purpose," Shadow said, and it took Allison a second to realize she'd heard the words only in her mind. *"With your permission, I'll collapse it before we leave."*

"Can you recreate it should it ever become necessary?" she replied without speaking out loud.

"Yes, even more easily than before now that we've joined."

Allison told her to do it, and her entire body tingled for a moment as the expansive blackness dissolved. They were left standing in a dusty chamber as a wooden door formed in one wall.

"Whoa," Jezebel said, taking in their new surroundings by the light of Allison's flame. "What happened?"

"Shadow created the void that was here to hide her from Nyro," Allison said. "Now that she's bound, that's no longer necessary."

"Your eyes have changed," Jezebel said, meeting her gaze. "The irises are white now." She stroked her cheek with one hand, adding, "And your skin—it's like Myrddin's was. Translucent."

Allison held out her hands and she could see the difference. Between this and the adjustments to her physique Khaldun had made, she looked nothing like she had only days earlier.

They left the tower. Allison put out her flame, tucked the scroll back into the void, and withdrew her carpet. They took off, and with her power increased more than twofold, she propelled them faster than ever.

"I want to thank you for everything you've done for me," Allison told Allure once they'd landed in Stoutwall. "Tonight wouldn't have been possible were it not for you."

"It was my pleasure, Your Highness," she said. Allison embraced her, and Allure headed into the castle.

"I'm much too excited to sleep," Allison said to Jezebel, "and I'd like to explore my new abilities a bit before coming to bed."

"I'm not sleepy either," Jezebel said. "Let's see what you can do!"

"I feel like I could move the world," Allison said. "The well of power within me is so much deeper now." Gazing across the grounds, awash in moonlight, she focused on the chasm Nyro had created. Calling earth, she focused deep beneath the ground, concentrating on closing the rift. The ground shook beneath them and the chasm closed.

"Holy shit," Jezebel muttered. "Literally moving the world."

Closing her eyes, Allison summoned Shadow, viewing the area from her perspective when she arrived. She sent her to Spanbrook. Shadow moved through the spirit realm—which Allison saw as a black void with blobs of color shooting in all directions—emerging high above Castle Barclay. The enemy camp stretched across the fields to the east, campfires dotting the landscape.

Allison directed her to the castle, and they found Camilla on the ramparts, keeping an eye on the elves. Shadow made the witch invisible and cast the spells to contain sound and prevent magical observation, then appeared to her, taking her glowing human form. Camilla gasped, backing away from her and pointing her wand.

"Camilla, it's me, Allison," she told her, speaking through Shadow. "I've bound a demon and I just wanted to see what I can do now."

"You-you're a necromancer now?" she asked.

"Yes. The entity in the seven-sided tower at the university was Blaze from Nyro's Sacred Circle. She was the one who betrayed her to the elves."

"This will take a little getting used to, Your Highness," Camilla said.

Allison chuckled. "Yes, for me as well."

Camilla told her that Nyro hadn't appeared in Spanbrook for a couple of nights. Allison wasn't surprised—Nyro had been busy.

She returned her focus to her own body and told Jezebel what she'd done.

"That's incredible," she said. "You can communicate with anyone this way without the need for a mirror."

"Yes, that's true," Allison said. "It should be possible to reach Emma this way."

"That could be dangerous if it alerts Nyro to your presence."

"Hmm." Allison summoned Shadow, and she appeared before them, taking her human shape. Allison explained what she wanted her to do. "Will Nyro sense you if we do this?" she asked out loud.

"That's tough to say. She cannot perform necromancy in her elvish body. So I do not believe she would normally be able to sense the presence of a demon. However, moving from the spirit realm to the human world makes use of the magical force, and there's a good chance she would sense *that*. And of course, she would see me if I took this form and hear my spoken words."

"Could she read your thoughts?" Jezebel asked.

"She could read demons when she was still human," Shadow said. "Now, I don't know. But I too possess sympathetic magic, and I learned long ago to close my mind to her. That was the only way I was able to betray her to the elves without her knowledge. She will not be able to read me."

"It's worth a shot," Jezebel said. "Emma may be able to tell us what Nyro's been up to since her incursion into Arthos. You should say nothing about a rescue attempt, though. We don't want to tip our hand—Nyro's sure to interrogate her if she realizes you were there."

Allison nodded. "Let's do it."

Shifting to Shadow's perspective, she sent her through the spirit realm to Drengrvollr. The demon appeared high above Nyro's island. It was morning here, a rainy, dreary day. Allison could sense the barrier Nyro had put in place, identical to the one protecting the university. She spotted four elf mages patrolling the perimeter of the castle.

Shadow moved through the spirit realm again, emerging inside the barrier. She flitted around the castle for a minute, looking through various windows. Finally she found the main bedroom, and two figures were lying in the bed, apparently asleep.

Shadow moved inside. Getting closer, Allison recognized Emma and Fang, both of them sound asleep. Through Shadow, she cast the spell to wake Emma, and the demon took her human shape, standing next to the bed.

Emma sat up, rubbing the sleep from her eyes. She spotted Shadow, gasping and scurrying across the bed to get away from her. Her skin was golden and translucent and her irises were white.

"Emma, it's me—Allison," she said through Shadow.

"What? How can that be?"

"I'm a necromancer now. I've bound the entity from the seven-sided tower at the university. Can you tell us what Nyro's been doing?"

"Y-yes—Allison, she made me a sorcerer! And she forced me to bind demons to become a necromancer!"

"We figured as much," Allison said. She'd worried about Nyro using so many compliance spells on her. Those types of spells could cause madness, but her metamorphosis would protect her from such effects.

"It gets worse, though. She made me bind the sorcerers we lost fighting Henry and her. Cyclone and Semblant, Intuit, Vision. Legion, Warhammer, and Spring. She cast the spells to prevent them from deteriorating like she did with the Sacred Circle. And she made them reanimate the bodies of elf mages like she did with the others."

Allison sighed. They should have realized this would be the case. These were the most recently deceased sorcerers, and as such, would retain the most of themselves from life. "Do they still have their special talents?"

"All of them but Legion. Semblant is still a shapeshifter, Vision can still see events from afar, and Spring can run and jump. I don't know about Intuit—Nyro had him try reading her, but she didn't say whether it worked or not."

"Damn," Allison said.

"She made Fang bind some demons, too," Emma continued. "More animalistic ones—she's keeping those in spectral form. They're not reanimating elves."

"Has she used the other mages to create wraiths?"

"Wraiths?" Emma said with a gasp. "No—is that what she's planning to do with them? Those mages are here in the castle, but she hasn't revealed their purpose yet."

"I'm not sure what else she might have in mind," Allison said. "If she does go with wraiths, she'll force you to perform the rite of binding on them, making her their conjurnor."

"M-meaning I'll have to kill them and bring them back to life?" Emma said, her eyes welling up with tears.

"I'm afraid so."

"My life is a living hell here," Emma said, taking a deep breath as the tears ran down her cheeks. "I have no control of my actions—neither does Fang. She uses magic to force us to do what she wants. It's worse than my darkest nightmare—I'd rather be dead! Can you use your demon to get us out of here somehow?"

Allison couldn't see any way that would work. Shadow might be able to call the basic forces against Nyro and her elf mages, but couldn't possess them. And operating alone, it would be impossible for her to overcome Nyro's defenses.

"Can her elf mages create an opening in the barrier surrounding the island?" Allison asked.

"Only the main one," Emma said. "Gorm. He's the strongest of the four. And the biggest."

Shadow could use the magical force to make him comply with her commands. She could make him open a barrier for them, giving

Emma and Fang a way off the island. But if Nyro were around, it wouldn't matter. She could stop them.

"Hold on," Allison said. "I'll be right back."

She sent Shadow through the castle. They found Nyro in the dining room, sitting at the table and muttering to herself. Allison gasped when she got a look at the people occupying the other chairs. Cyclone, Vision, Warhammer—all of their lost sorcerers. She knew it was only illusion, and they'd all taken elf bodies beneath the spells. But seeing them again in the flesh still took her breath away. A dozen men and women, all naked, were standing along one wall. Allison recognized them as the mages Nyro had abducted from Arthos.

Nyro gave no indication that she'd sensed Shadow's presence. Allison sent her back to Emma's room. "Nyro's here right now, so there's nothing we can do."

"She never leaves the castle without me," Emma told her. "After losing Syllith, she's taking far more precautions. And the city is crawling with her mages and soldiers. Even if we could find a way off the island, I don't know how we'd escape Krokr.

"She took me to the senate with her one day. One of the mages in the resistance movement made contact and smuggled me out of the building. He took me to a hideout and they were going to try to get me out of the city and onto a ship back to Anoria. But Nyro found me first."

"*I cannot neutralize Nyro on my own*," Shadow said to Allison in her mind. "*With you here in person, it may be possible.*"

"Can't I bring my full power to bear through you?" Allison asked. She'd always believed that was how this would work.

"*Yes, but we are not yet her equal in thaumaturgy. She would overpower us. Adding your physical prowess, who knows?*"

"We'd like to make contact with the elvish resistance movement," Allison told Emma. "Do you know how we might do that?"

"I don't know where to find them," Emma said. "But the one who tried to rescue me did say that they've had someone watching Nyro's island ever since they found Syllith here."

"That could prove very helpful," Allison said. "Do you know anything more about what Nyro's planning?"

"She's sending more troops," Emma told her. "They've loaded at least a few dozen ships with soldiers headed for Anoria, but I don't know when they're leaving or where they'll land. I think she's waiting till they get there before launching her next attack, though. She wants to bring enough force to bear to wipe us out this time."

"That's not unexpected," Allison said with a sigh. "Do not despair. These powers are still new to me. Let me consult with the others and we'll discuss the possibilities. One way or another, I promise you we will prevail. But this may take some time. Stay strong, Emma."

"I'll try," she said, her lip quivering.

Allison hated to leave her, but there was nothing more she could do from afar. She had Shadow withdraw to the spirit realm and returned her focus to her own surroundings. For the next few minutes, she told Jezebel everything she'd seen and discussed with Emma.

"You could get there using the pyramid now, right?" Jezebel said when she was done.

"Yes, I believe that's the case," Allison said. "And now would be the perfect time—Nyro's in a different room and didn't seem to sense Shadow's presence."

"Let's see if Allure's still up," Jezebel said with a grin.

They hurried into the castle, running up to Allure's room. She was still awake, so they explained what they wanted to do.

"Let's give it a try," she said.

The three of them left the castle together, and Allure retrieved the pyramid from the void, handing it to Allison. She was surprised by its weight—it was heavier than she'd expected.

"I've never used portal magic, of course—I'm not powerful enough," Allure said. "So I won't be able to help you with this."

Allison held the pyramid in her palm and swept her other hand over it. She could sense its power and had no trouble comprehending how it must work. "It's literally a portal. It's closed now, but if I focus on a destination, all I'd have to do is open it."

"Wait," said Jezebel. "Didn't Nyro lock the other one on her? Isn't that how she was able to communicate with Khaldun and Syllith?"

"Yes, but she never did so with this one," Allure said. "Shadow examined it when Enigma brought it to her. There were no extra spells placed on it."

"You should try using it to go somewhere other than Drengrvollr first," said Jezebel. "To make sure you can do this properly."

"Good idea," Allison said. She thought of Shadow's tower at the university, then channeled her magic into the pyramid. It was difficult—like lifting a massive weight—and she had to pour every ounce of her power into it, but finally, a portal opened before them, and she could see the structure beyond, illuminated by the twin moons. "After you," Allison said with a grin.

Jezebel and Allure walked through the portal, Allison right behind them. She closed the portal again behind her. It took so much power, she didn't feel like she could have kept it open much longer anyway.

"This is incredible," Jezebel said, gazing around the campus.

"Now, can you take us back?" Allure said.

Allison took a deep breath. Thinking of Castle Stoutwall, she concentrated on the pyramid and tried opening a portal. It didn't work—she felt like she'd been repelled somehow. Of course—Mira's null. She'd been visualizing the courtyard. Trying again, picturing the grounds out in front of the castle this time, it still took tremendous effort, but she had no trouble opening a portal. The three of them walked through it.

"I'd say you've got it," said Allure. "Ready to try Drengrvollr?"

"Yes, I think I am," she said. "I'll open the portal in the bedroom. Grab Emma and Fang and bring them back with me before I close it."

"Let's hope Nyro's still downstairs," Jezebel said.

"I should send Shadow again, just to be sure," Allison said. Summoning the demon, she sent her to Nyro's castle. Sure enough, Nyro was still sitting at her dining room table, and the other two were in the bedroom. She released Shadow again. "All right. This is the best chance we'll get." Focusing on the bedroom, she opened a portal.

The magic didn't work as expected. She felt something repelling it. Channeling more power into the pyramid, she finally opened a portal. But it wasn't the bedroom on the other side.

"That's not right," Jezebel said, gazing through the gateway.

"That's Nyro's island," said Allison, "but it's outside her barrier." She closed the portal. "Something blocked the magic. It was similar to how it felt when I tried going inside Mira's null. That made it impossible for the portal to form, though, while this seems to have redirected it."

"Could Nyro have woven extra magic into her barrier to prevent the portal magic from penetrating it?" Jezebel asked.

"That must be the case," Allure said. "I never knew that was possible, but this is Nyro we're talking about. She's taken her magic further than any other mage in history, so it wouldn't surprise me if she found a way to do this."

"Let me try again," Allison said.

"Be careful," Allure told her. "If Nyro did modify her barrier to prevent this, there's a good chance she'll know it when your spell hits her magic."

"Just like Mira could tell when Nyro tried getting through her null," Allison said. "You're probably right." Taking a deep breath, she focused on Emma's bedroom and tried again. She poured all her power into the pyramid, but it made no difference. The portal opened outside the castle again. This time, they spotted two of Nyro's mages on the other side, hurrying toward them. Allison closed the portal. It was getting progressively more difficult to open them—as if the weight she was trying to lift kept getting heavier. She doubted she'd be able to open another one without giving herself time to recover first.

"Nyro might have modified the magic to allow *her* through using a portal, but no one else," Allure said. "That's how the barrier magic works when you pass through it the normal way."

"Damn," Jezebel said. "We should have known it wouldn't be this easy."

"Nothing ever is," Allison replied. "I want to look inside that castle one more time." She summoned Shadow again and sent her to Drengrvollr. Looking through the demon's eyes, she saw Emma cowering in the bed, Fang still sleeping next to her. Turning, she saw Nyro in Estrid's body standing by the foot of the bed.

Nyro seemed to look right at her, and Allison gasped.

"You," Nyro said, and Allison felt her trying to use Emma to bind her demon. "I was right, then. You *did* allow the princess to bind you. So be it. I'll enjoy destroying you all the more."

A shiver ran down Allison's spine. Unreasonable though it may be—she knew Nyro couldn't touch her—she was terrified. She pulled Shadow out of there, sending her back to the spirit realm.

"She knew I was there," Allison told the other two. "And she knows Shadow is bound to me now."

"Let's get some sleep," Jezebel said, gripping her arm. "Tomorrow, we'll sit down with everyone else and come up with a new plan."

CHAPTER FOURTEEN
RESCUE

ack in their chambers, Allison tried reaching out to Shadow. She wasn't sure if this would work from inside Mira's null. It didn't. Which wasn't too surprising. The dragons and their riders communicated using sympathetic magic, but there was no reason to believe her connection to the demon would work the same way. It was still necromancy, after all, which was a branch of thaumaturgic magic.

The next morning, Allison and Jezebel joined Prince Augustine and all the others in his private dining room for a council meeting. Allison felt like a good night's sleep had replenished her magic after opening so many portals. She told them about the previous night's events and her desire to rescue Emma.

"Your transformation represents a dramatic shift in our capabilities," Augustine said. "Both the ability to send your demon anywhere in the world and your command over the pyramid artifact to travel wherever you wish in physical form."

"Agreed," said Sage. "Rescuing Emma will still be difficult and dangerous, however. With the spells Nyro has added to her protective barrier to guard against portal magic, using a compliance spell on her mage may be the only way to get inside."

Compliance spells used the magical force, not sympathetic magic, to work on a person's mind, much like sleep spells and memory modifications. They could cause madness in non-sorcerers, and thus the university had strictly banned them. Hearing one of the governors recommend such a spell gave Allison pause.

"Could Lady Mira accompany you?" Prince Carlo asked Allison. "Surely her null would take down the barrier."

"Would it, though?" asked Princess Yolanda. "You attended the university without collapsing the barrier there, didn't you?" she asked Mira.

"When it comes to things like the barrier, shield spells, invisibility spells, and the like," said Mira, taking a deep breath, "my null eliminates them only if it encompasses the majority of the magic. And the one protecting the university is much too large for that. Otherwise, my passage merely pokes a hole in the spell as I move through it."

"Either way, you could breach the barrier surrounding Nyro's island," said Carlo.

"The real problem would be getting you to Drengrvollr," Allison said. "Your null makes it impossible for you to travel through a portal, and taking you there by ship would take weeks. No, Sage is right. Spelling Nyro's mage is my only way in. But how do I do that without attracting her notice?"

"Well, even Nyro has to sleep eventually, right?" said Khaldun. "You could have Shadow stay inside her castle and monitor the situation. Alert you once Nyro is asleep, and then you could make your move."

"That is the best opportunity I'm likely to get," Allison said. "But I sensed it when she formed her portal here, so I'm sure mine would alert her as well. It may be enough to wake her."

"You could create the portal on the mainland," Allure said. "Use your carpet to fly to her island from there."

"Yes," Allison said. "I don't think she'd sense it from that far away. Nothing in the void can travel through the portal, so I'll need to carry the carpet and my sword on the way through. But that's not an issue."

"What about her passage through the protective barrier?" said Jezebel. "Would Nyro sense that as well?"

"Assuming her barrier is like ours at the university, then yes," said Sage. "And Nyro can most likely control who *can* and *cannot* open a gateway through the barrier even if they know the spell. That's how ours works. But in her case, her mage is probably the only one with access."

"But forcing Gorm to open one shouldn't prevent *me* from passing through it," Allison said.

"That's correct," Sage confirmed. "And he must open gateways to pass through the barrier himself now and then. So it's possible his doing so for you won't rouse Nyro from sleep."

"I wouldn't count on it, though," said Allure. "From what Emma reported, she's become much more vigilant since losing Syllith."

"My thought exactly," said Allison. "For efficiency's sake, once inside the barrier, I should use the pyramid to create a portal to Emma's bedroom. I'm guessing that would work?"

"I don't see why not," Sage said with a frown. "Nyro added magic to prevent you from creating one *through* the barrier, but that shouldn't stop you from creating a portal from one point inside the barrier to another."

"You should take Gorm with you when you go inside," said Jezebel. "Tuck him into the void, maybe. Chances are you'll need to make a quick escape, and you're going to need him to open a gateway through the barrier on the way out, too."

"You could just leave the gateway open," Khaldun said. "That would eliminate the need to open one again on your way out. But if it works anything like the barrier at the university, then Nyro will certainly be alerted if the gateway stays open that long."

"Yes, that's a good point," Allison said with a sigh. "This is not going to be easy," she added with a chuckle.

"We are taking an enormous risk here," said Augustine. "We may lose you in this endeavor. And I'm not sure there's much in the way of potential gain. Taking Emma away from her would mean one of you could reassign her bond to someone here. Nyro would lose her demons again. But there's nothing stopping her from abducting someone else and binding more."

"That still gives us one advantage, Your Highness," said Allison. "She's bound the demons of *our* deceased sorcerers. Their deaths occurred recently enough that they won't have deteriorated much compared to any of the other demons she could bind. And they'll surely be more cooperative for us than they would be for her. Nyro's already bound some of the more animalistic ones using her second necromancer, Fang. But this move would be a blow.

"And on top of that, Emma's family. We have an opportunity here, and I refuse to squander it, no matter the risk if it means we have a chance of bringing her home."

"I agree," Jezebel said, her eyes welling up with tears.

"Very well," Augustine said with a nod. "If you could find a way to destroy some of their troop ships while you're there, that would be helpful as well. The fewer of those vessels that make it to Anoria, the better."

"I'll do what I can," Allison agreed. "If I can rescue Emma, I'll want to bring her here first. Then I can go back and try taking out those ships."

"You should not do this alone," said Shatter. "Your Highness, allow me to accompany the princess."

"Yes, it might be best to send a small team," said Prince Leto from Keepstone. "Despite Princess Allison's recent transformations, Nyro remains formidable."

"With all due respect, Your Highness, I must disagree," said Allison. "Putting anyone else in such close quarters with Nyro could prove disastrous. Were she to capture one of our sorcerers, she could reassign their bond and make them hers."

"I agree," said Allure. "Princess Allison alone among us possesses sufficient power to go toe-to-toe with Nyro. It will still be dangerous, but it could prove catastrophic to send anyone else with her."

Prince Augustine sat back in his chair and sighed. "I do believe Princess Allison should go alone. However, I still harbor grave misgivings, for the exact reasons you point out. What if Nyro captures the princess, and reassigns *her* bond?"

"Her transformation into a necromancer makes that much less likely than it might seem," Sage said, taking a deep breath. "We are talking about Nyro, so anything is possible. But bear in mind that Princess Allison has essentially become two separate beings sharing a single soul.

Even if Nyro did manage to incapacitate her somehow, as an elf, she cannot affect Allison's *demon*, but the demon *can* liberate the princess."

"That's a good point," Allure said. "If Nyro were to overpower me and force one of her necromancers to perform the rite of binding, I'd have no way to stop her. It's completely different for the princess. Shadow is vastly stronger than any of the demons Nyro has bound. Neither Emma nor Fang can overpower her. The best Nyro could hope for would be a stalemate. She abducts Allison, but cannot bind her, and meanwhile, the princess cannot escape."

"Nyro could still kill her," Khaldun pointed out.

"And that's a risk I'm willing to take," said Allison.

"If the princess does succeed, Emma could make the perfect bait for our trap," Shatter said. "Nyro would undoubtedly want to recapture her."

"That is true," Allison said. "I hadn't thought of that. Nyro would lose Emma's demons the moment we reassign her bond. But she could get them back the same way. Nyro would be sure to come for her herself, too, rather than sending one of her minions."

"We can't put Emma's life in danger like that again," Jezebel said. "We'll have to think of another way."

"In any event, with Nyro waiting for her reinforcements to arrive in Anoria, I daresay we have a few more weeks to find a solution," Augustine said. "I would like to raise another point. My understanding is that Lord Khaldun is responsible for Princess Allison's remarkable *physical* transformation?"

"Yes, Your Highness," Allison said.

"Lord Khaldun, might you be able to do something similar for some of our troops?" asked Augustine. "The elvish soldiers are far bigger and stronger than ours. Any advantage we can gain would be helpful at this point."

"I should be able to do that," said Khaldun. "The only issue will be time. This is not a quick process by any means. And I'll need to transform their armor as well, making it take even longer."

"We should leave the Eagle Company out of this, Your Highness," said Imani. "At least those of us from Shifar. We are already much closer to the elves in size and strength to begin with, and if you make us any larger, we will have trouble moving about inside your castles and dwellings."

The others chuckled.

"I agree," said Jezebel. "We should provide this help where it's needed most."

"Very well," Augustine said. "Princess Jezebel, Prince Carlo, and Prince Leto, perhaps we can have our commanders take some time today to decide which regiments to choose, and Lord Khaldun can get started tomorrow."

The meeting adjourned, and Allison went up to her chambers with Jezebel. Leda and Alanna were awake but still in bed. Allison explained to them what she was going to do, and implored them to be on their best behavior while she was gone. She gave them each a hug farewell, and they headed down to the great hall for breakfast.

"Please, be careful," Jezebel said, embracing her. "I want Emma back as much as you do, but I need *you* to come back to me, too."

"Don't worry," Allison said, holding her tight. "I'm not planning on sacrificing myself, I promise. I think I'm going to go to Drengrvollr now. I'll send Shadow into the castle to keep watch, but observing Nyro's island from the outside could provide valuable insight into her activities, too."

"Come and have breakfast with us before you depart," Jezebel said. "Who knows when you'll get the opportunity to eat again?"

"That is an excellent point," she said with a smile.

The two of them went to the great hall to eat with the girls. They'd sat down at a table with Khaldun and Mira, Battleaxe, and Imani, so Allison and Jezebel joined them. When they were done, they all wished Allison luck. She embraced the girls once more, then headed out of the castle with Jezebel.

Once they'd moved outside of Mira's null, Allison removed all of her weapons, the carpet, and the pyramid from the void. Nothing could move through the portal in the void, so she needed to physically carry whatever she needed. Her mirror, helmet, and facemask were tucked into the pockets in her armor. She rolled up her two-handed sword in the carpet, hoisted that over one shoulder, and held the pyramid in her other hand. Jezebel promised to look after the rest of her weapons while she was gone.

It was daylight in Stoutwall, which meant it might be dark in Drengrvollr—Allison wasn't sure what the exact time difference might be. But she didn't want to risk shooting a blinding light across the city, potentially alerting Nyro to her presence. She didn't know the geography around the city, either, so she summoned Shadow and sent her ahead to choose an uninhabited location somewhere nearby.

Moving through the spirit realm, it took Shadow very little time to find the perfect spot, a clearing in a wooded area. Seeing the place from Shadow's perspective in her mind's eye, Allison opened a portal. She kissed Jezebel and walked through it, closing it from the other side.

It was dusk in Drengrvollr, so it was a good thing she hadn't tried opening a portal in Krokr. Allison unfurled her carpet on the ground, tucked the sword and pyramid back into the void, took off on the carpet, and made herself invisible. Shadow helped her find the city, and she circled high above, finding a rooftop with a good view of Nyro's island. Landing there, she tucked her carpet into the void and took in the scene for a minute.

The island sat in the bay, not far from shore. Allison could see flickering lights inside several of the castle windows, but there were no other signs of activity. She sent Shadow into the castle and took a seat on the roof.

Moving through the spirit realm, Shadow had no trouble getting into the building. She found Nyro sitting at the head of her dining room table, Emma and Fang to her right, and the reanimated elves to her left. The human mages were still lined up by the wall. Nyro gave no sign that she'd detected Shadow's presence.

Servants hurried about, removing the remains of an enormous feast from the table. Fang and Emma sat there with blank expressions, undoubtedly under Nyro's compliance spell. The reanimated elves looked so much like they had in life, Allison had to hold back her tears. Little things caught her notice, like Semblant's scowl, and the way Cyclone held her head in one hand, her elbow propped up on the table. She imagined Allure having to face Semblant in battle and wished there were some way they could spare her that pain.

Nyro hooked one leg over the arm of her chair and drank her wine. She was muttering to herself, but Allison couldn't understand what she was saying. Why were they all just sitting there? Was Nyro waiting for something?

Allison paid attention to the elf mages patrolling the island outside the protective barrier. She could see only the front and right side of the castle from her vantage point, and only two of the four mages. Mostly they stood guard, but periodically walked along their side of their property, from one end to the other.

Full night fell, and finally, Nyro got to her feet. She extinguished all the torches on the wall but one, then called air, moving one of the human mages to the floor. She lay him down, flat on his back, and roots grew out of the floor, binding his wrists and ankles.

Nyro was going to create her first wraith. Cold dread crept up Allison's spine; they hadn't faced wraiths since Henry's attack on Highgate. A part of her wanted to do something to save these people from their doom. But if she did that, she'd lose the element of surprise, most likely making it impossible to rescue Emma. This was a terrible choice, but any attempt to save these mages with Nyro right there in the same room was sure to fail.

Allison stayed on her rooftop as Nyro forced Emma to get to her feet and stand over the wizard, behind his head. Allison knew the rite of binding well. Several years earlier, she'd spent some time at the university, and this was one of the things they'd taught her.

Allison had never witnessed the rite used to create a wraith, however. It was mostly the same with some adaptations made to account for the subject being a normal mage, not a sorcerer. The initial flames that consumed the wizard charred him, burning away sections of skin altogether—they didn't affect a sorcerer that way. It would still tether the mage's soul to a conjurnor, though, and she had no doubt Nyro would fill that role for all of the ones here.

There was a spell they used to transfer the power from a mage's wand or staff into their body when they became a sorcerer, and Allison had learned that it was normally incorporated into the modified rite to create a wraith. She'd seen no sign of these mage's instruments, however, and suspected that Nyro had destroyed them. Nyro had modified the rite, however, using Emma to call forth the mage's full power instead of transferring it from an instrument.

Emma produced a dagger, dropping to her knees and plunging it into the wizard's heart. From Shadow's perspective, floating by the ceiling, it was impossible to tell for sure, but she believed that the man died. Emma spoke the words that would tether the man's soul to Nyro in Estrid's body.

The rite concluded, the roots disappeared into the floor, and the wraith got to its feet, standing before Nyro. She caressed its face with one hand and sent it to stand behind the reanimated elves.

Emma repeated the rite over and over again until all twelve mages had been transformed. It had taken hours, and Allison had to believe it was exhausting for Emma. The wraiths had lined up along the wall behind the reanimated elves. And now Nyro stood in front of the first. Holding out one hand, she cast some sort of spell. Shadow could sense magic as well as Allison, and whatever this was, she was using the magical force.

When Nyro was done, the wraith's features seemed darkened, as if it were standing in shadow. Allison recalled the shield spell they'd used on the wraiths during and leading up to Fosland's attack on Highgate. Wraiths were extremely sensitive to sunlight, and the spell had protected them from it. Whatever this was, it seemed to do the same thing, but the spell imbued their bodies with the light-repelling magic, instead of using a shield to do it.

Nyro performed the same spell on all twelve wraiths. Meaning these would have no trouble functioning during the day.

"I've never seen anything like this," Shadow told her in her mind. "Though she did have centuries to think up new magic when she was incarcerated in Pytha."

"*I have a feeling this is a more recent invention,*" Allison replied. "*It's similar to the shield spells they used last time. She could have adapted that magic to do this.*"

Nyro retook her seat at the head of the table, pouring herself a glass of wine and drinking half of it in one gulp. Then she ordered Emma and Fang to bed. The two necromancers moved to the stairway and disappeared from view as they made their way up to the second floor. Nyro sat there, drinking her wine.

Allison wondered where Nyro slept. She sent Shadow up to the second floor to have a look at the other bedrooms. None of them showed any evidence of being used. She had a terrible thought—was Nyro sharing a bed with Emma and Fang? This shouldn't surprise her, but she hadn't considered the possibility. After reading Syllith's account, Khaldun had told her that Syllith mentioned Nyro sharing a bed with her. She hadn't understood that it was *every night*.

Allison sent Shadow back to the dining room. This was probably the best chance she was going to get. Trying to rescue Emma with Nyro lying next to her in bed would be impossible. Nyro finished her wine, then sat there, lost in thought. Not asleep, certainly, but not fully alert, either. Part of her wanted to make the attempt *now*. If Nyro were to get up and go to bed with the other two, then she would lose her chance. Yet opening a gateway through the barrier with Nyro awake was almost certain to get her attention.

Allison decided to take the cautious approach. If she couldn't execute the plan this time, she could always come back and try again. She waited twenty more minutes, and fortune smiled on her. Nyro started nodding off, and before long, her eyes closed and her chin came to rest on her chest.

"*Stay here and let me know if Nyro shows any signs of moving,*" Allison said to Shadow. "*I'm going in.*"

"*Good luck.*"

Allison mounted her carpet and took off toward the island. Swooping around the castle once, she had no trouble picking out the largest of the four elf mages. This had to be Gorm. Flying in closer and staying invisible, she cast her spell, forcing the elf mage to obey her. She made him open a gateway through the barrier.

This was it. She had to move *fast*. Flying through the opening, she forced Gorm to move inside the barrier and then close the gateway behind him. She landed, tucking Gorm and her carpet into the void and tethering them to that spot, and withdrawing her sword and the pyramid. Focusing on Emma's bedroom, she opened a portal. It worked, and she heaved a sigh of relief.

Walking through the portal, Allison closed it behind her, tucking her sword into the void. Calling a flame to provide some light, she roused Emma, removing the sleep and compliance enchantments. Emma sat up with a start, and Allison cupped one hand over her mouth, as her eyes went wide with surprise.

"We're getting you out of here," Allison whispered. "Come on!"

"Take Fang, too," Emma said as she slipped out of bed.

Allison was about to wake her when Shadow said, *"Nyro's coming!"*

"Shit," Allison muttered. Opening a portal back to the castle exterior, she told Emma to go through it, but it disappeared.

"I knew you would try something like this," a voice said. Nyro had entered the room, moving around the foot of the bed.

Allison tucked her pyramid into the void and retrieved her sword. "Take Fang and wait in the hall," Allison told Emma, hitting the Kongese necromancer with a spell to wake her. Emma grabbed her, pulling her out of the bed, and the two hurried out of the room. Allison held up her weapon.

"How I've been looking forward to this," Nyro said, flashing her a smile as she withdrew her own sword from the void.

CHAPTER FIFTEEN
BAIT

After breakfast, Khaldun and Mira went up to Jezebel's chambers with her and the girls. They knew she'd be nervous about Allison and wanted to support her as much as they could. The girls retired to their room, and Jezebel closed the door behind them before sitting down at the small work table with Khaldun and Mira.

"I hope Allison will be all right," she said, tears welling up in her eyes. "I swear if I lose her now, I'll never forgive myself."

"You didn't force her to do this," Khaldun said. "Hell, I doubt you could have stopped her. You know better than any of us how stubborn she can get once she's set on a plan of action."

Jezebel giggled. "Yes, I suppose you're right."

Khaldun couldn't blame her, though. He'd feel terrible if they lost Allison like this, too.

"I'm not worried," Mira declared. "I think back to the first time I met the princess, and it's remarkable how much she's grown since then. And I don't just mean her recent transformations, either—she's gained so much confidence over the years. If anyone can pull this off, she can. And if she can't, I know she'll find a way to return to us safely."

"Thank you," Jezebel said, holding her hand. "I hope you're right."

"If her rescue attempt does succeed," said Khaldun, "Shatter has a valid point. Emma would be the perfect bait for our trap."

"No," Jezebel said, shaking her head. "We can't ask that of her. It would be far too dangerous. And after the ordeal she's endured… There has to be some other way."

"I would have to agree," said Mira. "I still have nightmares about my time in captivity with Henry and Dredmort. This is too much to ask."

"I know it's a lot," Khaldun said, "but think of the stakes. If we succeed here, *we win*. There are two huge problems with this idea, though, and one is choosing bait that's sure to lure Nyro here *in person*. Emma would definitely do that.

"We've seen that Nyro prefers to send her underlings to lead her operations. She launched the invasion without making an appearance herself. Not until Mira arrived with the dragons did she enter the battle—that's what it took to bring her into the fray.

"But according to Syllith, Nyro collected the elf mages she needed for her Sacred Circle to reanimate. Even once she'd helped the first few with their new bodies, she still took care of all the rest herself. She could have had the first ones take care of the others, but she didn't. And this time, she went to Arthos to collect the witches and wizards she needed herself."

"She had no choice," said Mira. "After what happened with Syllith, there was no way she would risk sending Emma on her own to do something like that. And her Sacred Circle is gone, so she had no one else to do the work for her."

"True," Khaldun conceded. "But if she saw an opportunity to retake Emma, I cannot imagine her sending anyone else to take care of that. And who or what else do we have that Nyro would want that badly?"

"Allison or me," Mira said with a shrug.

"Yes, but from her perspective, I doubt either of you seems attainable," he said. "Allison's too powerful now. Even if Nyro could manage to overpower her—which may no longer be possible—you heard Sage and Allure. Now that Allison has bound Shadow, Nyro would be hard-pressed to bind her.

"You would make a more tempting target, I think," he added to Mira. "The trouble, though, is that Nyro knows your null makes it almost impossible for her to capture you. And you're keeping it in place night and day to protect the castle. So your suddenly appearing here alone and without your null would appear highly suspicious. Nyro's not stupid—she's sure to see through such a ploy."

"Not only that, she *can't* use magic to force you into compliance," Jezebel added. "She must know that. Though I suppose she could use Emma as leverage the way they used Allison last time."

"Forgive me for saying this, but I would not obey her regardless of what she did to Emma," Mira said, taking a deep breath. "I've had years to think about this. And it's *Nyro* we're talking about here. She's planning to exterminate the entire continent—I could never help her. Your sister is family to me, but I'm sorry, not under any circumstances would I ever help Nyro."

Khaldun knew better than to question her resolve, yet he wondered how long *he* would be able to hold out in such a scenario if Nyro tortured Emma in front of him day after day. He'd like to believe he could hold out, but faced with that reality? He'd known Emma since she was a little girl. Something like that was sure to wear down the best of them over time. He kept these thoughts to himself, though.

"Nyro may believe she could persuade you," he said, "but my point stands. Any situation where you were easily attainable would be sure to alert Nyro to our ruse."

"What's the second problem?" Jezebel asked.

"Oh, right," Khaldun said. "Well, supposing we do come up with suitable bait—whether that ends up being Emma or not—and Nyro takes it. What then? For this to be worthwhile, we'd have to *destroy* her. Not just kill her body—that would be an inconvenience for sure, but she could always kill another elf mage and reanimate their body."

"Yes, well that is the problem, isn't it?" Jezebel said. "No matter what we do—whether setting a trap for her here succeeds or not—at some point, we'll have to find a way to destroy her. The elves couldn't do it all those centuries ago, so I don't see how we can. Yet short of that, whatever else we do, she won't stop until she's killed us all."

"We have to find her true name. That's the only way to destroy her, isn't it?"

"We'd have to ask Allison or Allure," said Khaldun. "This isn't exactly my area of expertise. We used that spike against Myrddin's demon, but Enigma told us Nyro and her Sacred Circle were far too powerful for that."

"Well, that's sobering," Mira said with a sigh. "Here I was thinking we could open a chasm in the ground, toss her in, and be done with it. But that would only kill her body."

The door to the girls' room opened, and Leda burst through it, crying hysterically. Jezebel got to her feet and hugged her, patting her back and saying, "Leda, honey, what's the matter?"

Alanna walked in behind her, looking glum, but not crying. "She's afraid Mother Allison's going to die," she said, plopping down on Jezebel's bed. "I'm kind of worried about that, too."

"You listen to me," Jezebel said. "Mother Allison is tougher than you know. Everyone dies eventually, but today is not going to be that day for her. She'll come back to us, alive and well. I'm certain of it."

Leda couldn't stop sobbing. Alanna said, "How can you know that? What if Nyro catches her?"

"I know this is hard to believe, but now that she's bound Shadow, Mother Allison is nearly as powerful as she is. Nyro might stop her from rescuing Emma, I won't deny that. But she will come back to us no matter what."

Leda calmed down a bit, taking a few deep breaths and hiccupping a couple of times. "I hope you're right."

"You two need to do something to get your mind off of this for a while," Jezebel said. "For that matter, so do I. There's no way to tell how long it's going to take, and sitting around fretting about it isn't helping anyone."

"I know the perfect thing," Mira said with a grin. "We haven't conducted any lessons since leaving Spanbrook."

"And if Mira gives me a good report, we could spend some time on your magic later, too," Khaldun added.

Leda choked back a sob and flashed him a smile. He'd told her that he'd help her learn void magic and knew how much she was looking forward to it.

"Oh, great, lessons," Alanna said, rolling her eyes. "I guess that is better than sitting around staring at the ceiling."

"I suppose I can take that as a compliment?" Mira said.

The girls headed to the library with Mira. Jezebel told Khaldun she needed to confer with Amari to decide which of their regiments to send to Khaldun for physical augmentations. With nothing else requiring his immediate attention, he left the castle, heading over to the lake.

Tapping into his power, Khaldun changed his shape into that of a dragon. He hadn't had much time to work on shapeshifting since first acquiring the skill, and with his new duties commencing the following morning, might not have another chance for a while. Spreading his wings and taking off at a run, he soared into the sky.

He'd been flying on a carpet for years, but this was completely different. The former relied solely on his magic, whereas the latter was an entirely physical undertaking. Catching an updraft, he climbed higher and higher before circling the lake.

Last time, he'd struggled to get any lift from beating his wings, and he wanted to improve with that. He went into a dive, but this time, pulled up sooner, gliding for a moment before powering his flight with his wing strokes.

This worked better than it had last time—he avoided a water landing, at least. But it still felt much more difficult than it should. Flying high, he spent some time bulking up the musculature that controlled his wings. And this did the trick. After his next dive, he had no trouble powering through an ascent.

Khaldun had always loved flying on his carpet, but as with anything experienced enough times, it had become routine over the years. Flying as a dragon reminded him of those early days with the carpet, rekindling his love of soaring through the air. He circled the castle and the lake a few times for the sheer joy of flight. Before long, a dragon joined him in the sky, and he recognized Sigrid. The beast seemed like she wanted to play, moving in close a few times before surging away.

Khaldun gave chase. Sigrid was much faster than he was. She would slow down and allow him to catch up, only to speed off again. He had the feeling that she recognized him. Perhaps there was some sympathetic magic operating here; he couldn't tell for sure. But her behavior toward him had an air of familiarity. The other dragons stayed away.

Sigrid returned to her kin after a while, and Khaldun landed by the top of the waterfall. He wanted to try breathing fire. After a few minutes adjusting his breathing, trying both deeper and shallower breaths, fast and slow exhalations, he realized he had no idea how this worked. Was there some internal organ responsible for this ability that his shapeshifting had failed to reproduce?

Finally he remembered that dragon fire was magical. He tried exhaling and calling fire at the same time and startled himself when he belched a jet of flame. Now that he understood how it worked, it turned out to be easy. He could breathe fire at will.

With the entire crash here, he doubted he'd be taking this form in battle, however. They were far better at being dragons than he would ever be, so it made sense to leave them to it. He spent the next several minutes trying out various other animal forms, including a bear, an octopus, and a giant wolf. It occurred to him that he shouldn't be limited to real-life animals, so he tried mixing elements from various creatures. He tried a winged horse, a bear with dragon-hide, and a lion with horns.

The bear with dragon hide appealed to him the most. But he wondered if the dragon hide would repel magic the way a real dragon's would. Taking the form of an eagle, he flew back to the castle. He required no magic to sustain different shapes once he'd assumed them, so he tried flying into Mira's null. Sure enough, it didn't affect him at all. He landed out in front of the castle, retook his true shape, and then went inside to find Battleaxe.

She joined him out on the grounds, and he transformed into the dragon-bear. Battleaxe tried hitting him with a variety of spells, including fire, air, and earth, but none of them could penetrate his hide. He decided this was the shape he'd most want to use in battle. It would give him the ability to cause maximum destruction to the enemy lines while protecting him from their mages.

That afternoon, Leda and Alanna came to find him after they'd finished with Mira. They couldn't practice magic inside the null, so they went out on the grounds. Jezebel, Mist, and Battleaxe came to watch. After Nyro's recent incursion, the princess was nervous about letting the girls outside of Mira's null. So she asked the two sorcerers if they wouldn't mind joining them just to provide a little extra protection.

Khaldun spent several minutes reviewing their spells. Both Alanna and Leda could call all four basic forces. Alanna was a little stronger with fire spells than her sister. Khaldun suspected she must have inherited that from Jezebel. Leda was a little stronger with earth. They'd both become proficient with canceling each other's magic, too.

After that, Khaldun had them work on illusion spells. Leda had no trouble creating the cat she'd produced last time. She could make it prance around and rub up against their legs and even climb a tree, so he had her start working on a tiger.

Alanna hadn't been able to cast any illusions last time, so he spent some time with her on that. For most mages, the magical force was much tougher than the four basic ones. Khaldun had been unusual in that he'd made himself invisible at a young age before he'd received any training. Alanna's progress was more typical. After a half hour, she still couldn't cast even a simple illusion and was growing frustrated.

Khaldun told her to take a break and reviewed Leda's progress. She'd managed to produce a realistic-looking tiger but had more trouble making it move around than she had with the smaller cat. This was a common difficulty and one Khaldun had had himself as a young man.

Sigrid swooped out of the sky to visit them, and that coupled with Alanna's ongoing frustration with illusion spells meant he'd totally lost her attention. She ran around the grounds, frolicking with her dragon. Battleaxe and Mist stayed close to her, while Jezebel remained behind.

Khaldun took advantage of the opportunity to work with Leda on void magic. Pulling one of his daggers out of oblivion, he held it in one hand. He was going to review the spell with Leda, but she remembered it from their previous lesson. Leda tried tucking the weapon into the void several times, but couldn't do it.

"I've never been able to do this," Jezebel said. "Not for lack of trying, either. So don't feel bad if you can't get it at first."

"Few non-sorcerer mages ever acquire this skill," Khaldun added. "I have a feeling you might be one of the special cases, though."

"Based on what evidence?" Leda asked sardonically.

"Nothing I can pinpoint," he told her. "Try it again."

Leda waved her wand and cast the spell, but nothing happened. Khaldun offered her a few tips—putting the stress on different syllables, and adding a bit more force to her wand-waving. She tried it again, and the dagger vanished with a little pop.

Leda squealed. "Was that it? Did I do it?"

"You did," Khaldun said with a chuckle. "Much sooner than I thought you would."

They spent another twenty minutes working on the skill, but Leda was unable to reproduce her initial success. That was often the way, however, and Khaldun remained confident she'd get it consistently before too much longer.

Allison faced Nyro, sword in hand, her heart pounding. She felt her enemy trying to read her and closed her mind. Nyro charged, cutting and slicing with otherworldly speed and efficiency. Allison evaded and parried every attack. Nyro backed off and she advanced. Over and over she swung her sword, driving her opponent toward the window, but Nyro moved with a fluidity she'd never encountered before.

Back and forth they vied, neither able to gain any advantage. Finally, Allison summoned a ghoul. The monster erupted out of the floor, grabbing Nyro by the throat and pinning her against the wall. Unfortunately, it was blocking Allison's access to her opponent. She moved around the monster, trying to stab Nyro in the neck, but she called fire, hitting the ghoul with lightning bolts. The force of the spell knocked both the ghoul and Allison off their feet. The ghoul faded to smoke as Allison lost her concentration.

Nyro launched herself at her, chopping with her sword, barely missing as Allison rolled out of the way, sending sparks flying with every impact on the stone floor. Calling air, Allison hurled the bed at her, giving herself a chance to regain her feet. The bed slammed into the wall, missing Nyro by inches and breaking into several pieces as it fell to the floor.

Allison squared off with her opponent again. As Nyro advanced, Allison shot lightning at her as she evaded her onslaught. Nyro canceled her spell, hurling air and earth spells at her as Allison pressed her counterattack.

Nyro dodged and parried, and though Allison came close to landing several killing strokes, they were never close enough. Finally, as Nyro came at her again, Allison summoned Shadow. She had the demon hit her opponent with fire and lightning as Allison defended herself.

Allison went on the attack again, and four demons appeared in the room, attacking Shadow. These must be the specters Fang had bound. They kept Shadow busy as Allison continued her fight with Nyro.

Nyro gasped at one point, and Allison had no idea what had prompted that reaction. The demons' battle raged, and neither she nor Nyro could get the upper hand against the other. Nyro started edging along one wall as they fought, and it took a minute for Allison to realize she was trying to get to the doorway. She tried driving her back, but Nyro called air in an attempt to throw her into the wreckage of the bed, and in the moment it took Allison to cancel the spell, Nyro darted out the door.

Allison charged after her, reaching the hallway in time to see Nyro, Emma, and Fang flying through a portal on a carpet right before the gateway closed. "Shit!" she shouted, kicking the bedroom door in frustration.

The demons fighting Shadow withdrew to the spirit realm, leaving Allison to contemplate her next move. She'd seen only sky and forest on the other side of the portal, and it looked like it was nearing sunset—or perhaps only a little after sunrise—wherever they'd gone. It was high above the ground, too, explaining why Nyro had taken her carpet.

Where the hell had she gone? And why so abruptly? Allison had no answers. She considered waiting in the castle for Nyro to return, but there wasn't much point. Nyro would be ready for another rescue attempt. Allison had tipped her hand and would not get the element of surprise again.

Pulling the pyramid out of the void, she opened a portal to the castle exterior and walked through it. Closing the portal behind her, she liberated Gorm and her carpet from the void, restored her compliance spell, and tucked her sword and pyramid into oblivion. Mounting her carpet, she forced Gorm to open a gateway in the barrier, then flew through it, shooting high into the sky.

Allison circled the port once, but the ships were gone. She flew over the bay and out to sea. Dawn was cracking the eastern horizon, providing a bit of light, but she couldn't find the vessels anywhere.

Returning to the city, she made herself invisible and landed on the same rooftop she'd used earlier. She figured she'd wait here for a while to see if Nyro returned. Perhaps she could glean some clue as to what had prompted her sudden departure. Summoning Shadow, she sent her into the castle. If Nyro were to return, there was a good chance she'd open a portal to the interior of the building.

Allison sat there as the sun rose, climbing higher in the sky. There was no sign of Nyro. She got to her feet, thinking she'd return to Stoutwall, when a voice said, "Hello there. I can't see you, but I know you're up here."

Turning, Allison spotted an elf approaching. His hair and beard were both long and white, contrasting with his ebony skin. She could feel the power emanating from him and knew he was a mage. Preparing a shield spell and making herself visible, she said, "Who are you?"

"My name is Asmund. I believe we have a common enemy."

CHAPTER SIXTEEN
CLOSE CALL

lanna enjoyed playing with Sigrid but wanted to ride her. What was the point of being a dragon rider if she couldn't *ride*? Sigrid wanted it, too. She kept showing her visions of the two of them soaring over the lake.

But her mother had forbidden her from leaving the castle grounds, and with Battleaxe and Mist hovering the way they were, there was no way she could get away.

She went to the great hall for dinner with Leda and Mother Jezebel. But she spent the whole time trying to figure out a way to escape the castle unnoticed for a little while. They had guards at the gates around the clock, and Alanna was sure they'd have strict orders not to let Leda or her leave on their own. And with the moat around this place, it wasn't like she could slip out a window. Normally, she would use an invisibility spell to sneak out, but Mira's null made that impossible.

She could summon Sigrid and meet her in the courtyard. But someone was sure to see her flying away on her back and report it to her mother. Assuming Mother didn't see it with her own eyes—she rarely let her out of her sight these days.

The one secret tunnel she'd known about didn't exist anymore. She knew there had to be others but had no way of finding them. And there was no chance any of the people who did know about them would tell her.

Leda wouldn't be any help, either. Not this time. Nyro's visit had scared her shitless and there was no way she was going to risk breaking Mother's rules. Alanna had been afraid, too, but Nyro hadn't made another appearance. No one had. And she'd be riding Sigrid, and the enemy mages didn't seem to have any interest in the dragons since the battle.

If she could find a way out of the castle, she'd have to decide where to meet Sigrid. The dragon riders' camp would be perfect. Far enough from the castle to avoid attention. And she'd get to see Soren, too. She did miss him, if not as much as she missed riding Sigrid. He was fairly attractive, and she knew he was smitten with her. Which made flirting with him a lot of fun.

After dinner, Alanna returned to her chambers with Leda. Mother had gone to visit Khaldun and Mira, so the two of them had their rooms to themselves.

"Why are you so sulky?" Leda asked as Alanna plopped onto the bed. "You got to play with Sigrid. I figured you'd be happy now."

"I want to *ride* her," Alanna said with a sigh.

"It's too dangerous," Leda said, sitting down at the table by the window. "What if Nyro comes back?"

"Why would she, though? She only came here to find more mages, but she ended up abducting a bunch of them from Arthos instead. There's no reason for her to return here."

"I guess that's true," Leda said with a shrug.

"Doesn't matter. I don't know how I'd sneak out of the castle anyway."

"You could ride Sigrid out of the courtyard."

"I said *sneak*. Mother would see me if I tried that. Or someone else would and they'd report it to her."

Leda seemed lost in thought for a few moments.

"What's wrong?" Alanna asked.

"There might be a way," she said. "Come with me," she added, getting to her feet.

"Where are we going?" Alanna asked without moving.

"Do you want to ride Sigrid or not?"

Alanna stared at her a moment longer before getting out of bed. They left their chambers, and Leda took her down to the courtyard and over to the stables. One of the prince's guards was there—a young Kongese woman. Alanna had seen her around quite a bit recently; she'd even accompanied them the last time they went to the lake to see Sigrid.

"Your Highnesses," the guard said with a smile.

Leda kissed her, and Alanna's jaw dropped. Leda was romantically involved with her? And she'd kept it from Alanna? She closed her mouth and tried to act naturally before either of them noticed her reaction.

"This is Scarlett," Leda told her. "She's a member of the castle guard and recently started working for the master of horse."

"It's a pleasure to meet you," Alanna said.

"We've been confined to the castle," Leda told the woman. "But Alanna's desperate to ride her dragon. You told me you know one of the secret passages, right?"

"That I might," she said with a grin.

"Could you take us out of the castle?" Alanna asked, smiling ear to ear.

"When would you like to go, Your Highness?"

"Right now," Alanna said.

"Come with me," she said.

Scarlett led them to the last stall by the outer castle wall. She pulled down one of the wooden wall braces, and Alanna realized it was a lever. "This frees the mechanism holding the stall in place," she told them. They helped her slide the structure away from the stone wall, revealing a small opening behind it. Crawling through that, they found a stairway leading below ground.

Alanna and Leda followed the woman down the steps. At the bottom, she took a flint and steel set from a ledge on the wall and used that to light the torch sitting in the lone sconce. Illuminating their way with the torch, she led them through a short stone passage and down a much longer stairway.

At the bottom, they reached a dank tunnel. They followed that, and unless Alanna's sense of direction had failed her, it was taking them toward the waterfall. It sloped upward, and after a while, Alanna was sure she could hear the roar of the falls ahead. Finally, they reached a set of steps. There was some light here coming from above. Scarlett left the torch in a sconce on the wall, and they climbed the steps. It grew steadily brighter as they moved higher. Sure enough, they reached a small cavern behind the waterfall.

"You'll get a little wet on the way out, but there's no avoiding that," Scarlett said with a grin.

"Thank you so much," Leda said, kissing her again.

Alanna and Leda dashed through the falling water, emerging on a ledge overlooking the lake. They were right at the edge of the falls, and after a short trek through the woods, the castle came into view.

"I had no idea you were involved with someone," Alanna said as they strolled along the lakeshore, taking their time to avoid attracting attention. "How did you hide this from me?"

"I've been sneaking out in the middle of the night," Leda said, failing to stifle a giggle.

"She's beautiful," Alanna said. "How old is she?"

"Seventeen," Leda told her. "Her mother is in the household guard but she used to provide security for an antique dealer hauling artifacts out of Pytha. She met her father in a brothel in Hido."

"Her father was a prostitute?" Alanna said, her eyes wide.

Leda giggled. "Yes. She's never met him."

Alanna was shocked. This was the first time her sister had ever done anything so mischievous. At least, as far as she knew.

They found the trail to the dragon riders' camp, and Alanna led them into the forest. A few minutes later, they reached the camp in a clearing in the woods.

The dragons were hunting, and she could see several of them flying over the lake. Reaching out with her mind, she called Sigrid. There was a roar in the distance, and the dragon appeared over the trees moments later, swooping over them once before landing. Sigrid lowered his head, and Alanna stroked his snout.

"Alanna!" a voice said. She turned to see Soren hurrying over to them. "I thought you weren't allowed out of the castle!"

"I'm *not*," she said with a grin. "But I missed riding Sigrid, so we sneaked out."

"I think you missed me, too," he said, embracing her. "It'll be dark soon—you're welcome to stay the night with us."

"That won't work," she said with a frown. "We need to get back before they notice we're gone." She kissed him, plunging her tongue into his mouth. He kissed her back, and she felt the familiar tingling between her legs. "Next time, perhaps. Our mother should return from Drengrvollr soon, and she might allow it."

"Mm," Soren said, kissing her again. "You're ready to share my bedroll, then?"

"I didn't say *that*," she said. "One day. Maybe." She shot him a mischievous smile as she backed away. Sigrid nuzzled her with her snout, nearly knocking her over. "Hey! Watch it!" she said, rounding on her as Soren chuckled.

"She wants you to take her for a ride," he said.

"Yes, let's go," Alanna said to the dragon, showing her a memory of the two of them flying over the lake. "Wait here for me—I'll need your help getting back in the castle!" she added to Leda. Sigrid lowered her head and one wing, and Alanna climbed onto her back.

Moments later, they were soaring high into the air. She spotted another rider approaching as they circled the lake and knew it had to be Soren. His mount and Sigrid loved playing together, and Alanna screamed for joy as Sigrid banked first one way and then the other, trying to get behind Soren. Maneuvers like this had terrified her at first, but she'd gotten over her fear very quickly and now she loved this more than anything.

Sigrid roared, giving up the chase and pulling up short, beating his mighty wings to hold them in place above the lake. Out in front of them, Alanna spotted a dark patch in the sky. It wasn't a cloud, she was sure of that, and as she stared at it, trying to decide what it was, a carpet flew through it, headed straight for them.

Suddenly, Sigrid dropped like a stone, plummeting toward the lake. As they fell, Alanna spotted three riders on the carpet. One was an elf with a scar running down one cheek. This had to be

Nyro, which meant the other two must be Emma and Fang. Alanna screamed as Sigrid went into a dive, pinning his wings to his sides. He spread them again, pulling up hard, and managed to regain his flight right before they plunged into the water.

Gazing around her, Alanna spotted the carpet approaching fast from behind. Beyond it, she saw Soren's dragon gaining on the carpet. The beast blasted the carpet with a jet of fire, and Alanna screamed again—he'd kill Emma along with Nyro! But there was a shield spell in place that repelled the dragon fire. Soren's mount roared, bellowing his fury to the sky.

Sigrid climbed, flying fast and erratically to avoid any more spells from the carpet. Alanna knew a mage could cancel the air beneath a dragon to rob it of its lift. She couldn't stop screaming, and terror verging on panic threatened to overcome her.

Suddenly, two more dragons swooped in from above, flying in the opposite direction. Alanna turned in time to see them breathe fire on the carpet, but they couldn't get through the shield spell, either. Within moments, a dozen more dragons converged on their position, all of them attacking the carpet. Word must have spread among them, because they stopped using fire, instead trying to rend it apart with their teeth and claws.

Nyro managed to cancel the air beneath a couple of them, and they plunged into the lake. Before long, it seemed like the entire crash had come to their aid, though, and their attacks overwhelmed her. Another black patch formed above them, and Nyro flew through it, disappearing as the portal closed behind her.

Khaldun had gone up to his chambers with Mira after dinner, and Jezebel had joined them. They were worried about Allison, but Jezebel didn't want to contact her by mirror for fear of interrupting if she was in the middle of infiltrating Nyro's castle. They knew this could take a while. The whole day had gone by without any word, though, and Khaldun was starting to think it might be worth risking the mirror. Jezebel wanted to hold out, though.

They talked for a while, rehashing what they'd discussed before about setting a trap for Nyro. Khaldun found his mind wandering, and gazing out the window, spotted a couple of dragons chasing each other back and forth above the lake. He wondered if any of the others would warm up to him in dragon form as Sigrid had.

Suddenly, a dark patch of sky appeared over the water. It was too far away to be sure, but he thought he saw something shoot out of it. What the hell was going on? The lead dragon started falling from the sky. He managed to catch some air before hitting the water, climbing higher as the second one gave chase.

As they picked up speed, the rear one shot fire toward the leader—that's when Khaldun spotted the spherical void in the dragon fire. A shield spell. Someone had flown a carpet through a portal. And other than Allison, only one person possessed the ability to do that.

"Nyro's here," he said, getting to his feet.

"*What?*" Jezebel said as she and Mira both rose from their seats, nearly knocking them over. "Where? And how do you know?"

He told them what he'd seen, and the two of them stared out the window. Several more dragons were rushing to assist. "I've got to get out there. One of you should alert Shatter, Battleaxe, and the others."

"I'll do it," Mira said, as Jezebel gasped.

"What's wrong?" Khaldun said. She ran out of their room, and he followed her.

Reaching her own chambers, Jezebel threw the door open, calling for Alanna and Leda. They were gone. "I've got a bad feeling that's Alanna and Sigrid out there," she said, tears welling up in her eyes as she met his gaze.

Khaldun nodded before hurrying off. He ran down to the entry hall and out onto the grounds. The moment he was outside Mira's null, he pulled his carpet out of the void and took off. Flying over the lake, he raced toward the dragons. By the time he reached them, the carpet was gone. His heart jumped into his throat—had Nyro taken Alanna?

No. He spotted her riding Sigrid. Flying in closer, he waved at her, getting her attention. There would be too much wind noise for her to hear him, so he pointed toward the shore. Alanna nodded. Sigrid turned around, heading for land, and Khaldun followed them back.

They landed, and Khaldun spotted Jezebel running over to them with Allure, Battleaxe, Mist, Sage, and Shatter in tow. Alanna climbed down from Sigrid's back, and Jezebel hugged her tight, crying and sobbing.

Once she'd calmed down, Jezebel held her daughter by the shoulders. *"Don't you EVER do that again, do you hear me?!"*

"I'm sorry, Mother," Alanna said through her tears. "I missed Sigrid so badly and—"

"That was *NYRO*! She could have taken you like she did Emma! Is that what you want? Is it?" Before Alanna could respond, Jezebel's eyes went wide. "Where's Leda?!"

"She was in the dragon riders' camp—she should be safe," Alanna said, the fear in her eyes belying her words.

Khaldun was about to go looking for Leda when he spotted her running toward them from the woods. Jezebel took off, meeting her halfway.

"We should all fly patrol for a while," Allure said to the rest of the sorcerers. "This incident could be a prelude to a larger attack."

"I'll alert the prince," Shatter said, hurrying off.

The rest of them took off on their carpets, flying above the castle and the grounds. Khaldun had a lot of questions. It made no sense, but the way this had unfolded sure made it seem like Nyro had targeted Alanna specifically. What would she want with the girl? She was a novice mage, without any special abilities. He knew she'd inherited magic from both parents, so it was possible she had the metamorphosis in her.

He had to remind himself that it didn't matter if she had it within her or not—Nyro could trigger the transformation in anyone with the dual inheritance. Could she have sensed some other latent ability in the girl?

But if that were her reason for attempting this, why hadn't she taken Alanna when she abducted Emma? They'd both been there at the time. And on top of that, how could she have known Alanna had left the castle? As long as she stayed within Mira's null, she was safe. Somehow Nyro had known the moment she ventured out on her own? He couldn't understand it.

After an hour or so, there had been no further incursions, so Khaldun landed out in front of the castle gates. Allure and Battleaxe were already there, and Mist, Sage, and Shatter joined them over the next few minutes.

"We have a problem," Allure told them. "Nyro's got one of her demons watching Stoutwall. I had a suspicion that might be the case, and sure enough, I found him hovering high above the grounds. I banished him, but he returned almost immediately."

"It must be one of the ones she used Fang to bind, then," Sage said. "The others have reanimated elvish bodies."

"I believe Nyro must have targeted Alanna specifically," Khaldun said. "And this would explain how she knew Alanna left the castle without any of us. The demon was keeping watch for her." He explained the questions he had about Nyro's motives.

"I should give Alanna a reading," Allure said. "The last one I did was years ago, and she was too young."

Khaldun went into the castle with the others and led Allure up to Jezebel's chambers. Unsurprisingly, Jezebel was still furious and was scolding her daughters as they sat in their bed, cowering against the headboard. Jezebel didn't typically inspire fear in them, but she was in a towering rage. Mira was there, too, giving Khaldun a concerned look. He gently interrupted Jezebel and explained what Allure wanted to do and why. Jezebel agreed.

Allure sat down on the bed next to Alanna, holding her face in her hands and closing her eyes. "Yes, you do have the transformation in you," she said.

"Y-you mean I'll become a sorcerer one day?" she asked.

"It's not certain, but it is within you. Nyro could have triggered it regardless… but there's something more."

"A latent talent?" Khaldun asked. "What is it?"

Allure shook her head, squeezing her eyes tighter. "It's… strange. I don't think I'm reading a talent, but rather a lack of something. A void that I can't penetrate."

"I don't understand," Jezebel said, her tone impatient.

"I'm not sure I understand it, either," Allure said, opening her eyes. "But I believe she has the potential to become a null."

"A *null*?" Alanna repeated. "That can't be! I can *do* magic!"

"I could too in the beginning," Mira said. "But that changed as I got older."

"I'm reasonably sure you would never become a null on your own," Allure said. "The void I sensed was small and not very strong. But I'm willing to bet it's something Nyro could bring out in you."

"That's why she wanted her," Khaldun said. "Nyro would probably give anything to get her hands on a null. But acquiring Mira would be nearly impossible at this point."

"That could well be," Allure said.

"Why didn't Nyro take her when she abducted Emma?" he asked.

Allure frowned for a moment. "The void I sensed is subtle—I nearly missed it. My guess is that Nyro didn't notice it when she took Emma. She was focused only on finding a mage she could turn into a sorcerer. But she could have sensed the same thing I did at a later time. Perhaps when she came here and fought Allison."

"So at that point, she stationed the demon here," Khaldun said. "Alanna was inside Mira's null then, so Nyro couldn't get to her. The demon spotted her riding Sigrid tonight and alerted Nyro."

"That would certainly explain it," Allure said. "Once Allison returns, we should see if she can destroy this demon."

Khaldun had an idea, but didn't want to discuss it in front of Jezebel—she and the girls had endured enough for one evening. They said goodnight to Jezebel and her daughters, and then Allure left with Khaldun and Mira.

"Could we speak to you in private?" Khaldun asked Allure once they'd closed the door behind them.

"Of course," she said.

Allure followed them to their chambers.

"We've been exploring this idea of setting a trap for Nyro," Khaldun said as the three of them sat at their table. "And in the interest of doing that, it might be better to let Nyro's demon remain."

"Because once we plant our bait, we'd *want* it to alert Nyro," Mira said.

"Yes, exactly," said Khaldun. "Would you or Allison be able to station a demon to keep watch on *Nyro's* demon?"

"The trouble would be getting it to remain here longer than a few hours," Allure said. "Allison could do it if she binds another demon, though."

"Perfect," Khaldun said. "I'll ask her about it when she returns. When the time comes, we now know that Alanna would make the ideal bait."

"Jezebel is *not* going to like this," Mira said.

"I know. And that's why I didn't want to discuss it in her presence. But think about this. Nyro came here for Alanna herself—she didn't send one of her minions. And knowing now that she has the potential to become a null, it's not remotely surprising that Nyro would want to acquire her."

"She would be perfect," Allure agreed.

"We have another problem, though," Khaldun said. "There's no point setting a trap if we don't have the means to destroy her. Killing her body isn't enough—she'd just reanimate another one. Maybe we can find her true name by then. Maybe not. Jezebel and I used a spike to capture Myrddin's demon, but Enigma told us Nyro's far too strong for that. So do you know of any other way?"

"Nyro would have been too strong for the spikes Syllith used," Allure said. "She acquired those from the Darkhold, and they hadn't been designed for a demon that powerful. But I know the spells required to create those spikes. Working with Augustine's blacksmith, I could make one strong enough to hold Nyro. Especially if we use Stoutwall steel. There's no guarantee, of course. It *is* Nyro we're talking about after all, so she may be ready for this tactic. I don't see how, though."

"Why did Enigma say Nyro was too powerful for this?" Khaldun asked.

"I wasn't there, obviously, but I'm sure he must have been talking about the process, not the spike itself," Allure replied. "Keep in mind, he didn't know exactly how Syllith was doing it at the time. She had to keep it from him to ensure the demon didn't find out."

"Oh, that's right," Khaldun said.

"And Nyro—or any of the Sacred Circle for that matter—*would* have been too powerful for that. Enigma was allowing them to possess him so Syllith could seduce them. Which is not difficult with the lesser demons."

"But Nyro's demons retained enough of themselves to spot the trap," Khaldun said with a nod. "They wouldn't have been consumed with their carnal desires like the lesser ones. And once one of them had possessed Enigma, there would have been no stopping them."

"Precisely," said Allure. "Syllith never would have had the opportunity to trap them in the spike."

"That's it, then," said Mira. "We have the ideal bait and a means of destroying Nyro."

Khaldun felt hope blossoming in his chest in a way it hadn't done in a long time. "We'll need to discuss this with the full council."

CHAPTER SEVENTEEN
FOREIGN EMISSARY

smund?" Allison repeated. "The mage who found Syllith in Nyro's castle?"

"One and the same," he said with a slight bow. "And who might you be?"

Allison sensed no active magic in place around him. No illusion or compliance spells—he was what he appeared to be. She could also sense his desire to defeat Nyro and wrest control of his homeland from her regime. "My name is Allison. I'm from Spanbrook in Dorshire."

"*Princess* Allison, the great sorcerer, unless I'm much mistaken," he said. "Only, you are a necromancer now?"

"Yes, I am. How did you know I was here?"

"We often use this rooftop to keep our watch on Nyro's island," he said. "It does provide the ideal vantage point, does it not? I heard you rustling over there and sensed an invisibility spell."

That explained it. She hadn't expected anyone else to be using the roof or she would have been more careful. "I'm glad you found me. We wanted to talk to you about joining forces against Nyro." Allison spent a few minutes explaining the military situation in Stoutwall.

"I may be able to assist," he said when she was done. "I helped establish our resistance movement. We have organizations in every kingdom and most cities. I operate independently now, but I do know the leader here in Krokr."

"Do your people command any military resources? Or mages? Nyro's forces outnumber ours as it is, and she is sending additional troops. We could use some reinforcements of our own."

"We have no fighting force, I'm afraid. There are a handful of mages operating here in Krokr, though."

"A handful?" she repeated, her heart sinking.

"There are more throughout Drengrvollr and the other kingdoms. But we have to be extremely careful. Nyro's mages infiltrated our organization in the early days and we lost many of our people. Now, no one knows any resistance members outside their own local group. The leaders know some of the others nearby, but only the overall director in a given kingdom knows all of them. None of them know any of the local leaders from the other kingdoms."

"So pulling from the entire movement, there could be... dozens? Hundreds of mages?"

"Hundreds, I would guess. But I have no way to know for sure. To send significant numbers to your aid, the orders would have to come from the directors. And to reach them, we'd have to start with the local leader here in Krokr and work our way up the chain of command."

"You helped create the movement, though," she said. "Don't you know any of the directors yourself?"

"Not anymore. The people who started with me have all been killed or captured. Like I said, we have to be extremely careful."

Allison nodded. She was about to ask where they could find the leader when she sensed someone reaching out to her through her mirror. "Excuse me," she said to Asmund. Pulling her mirror out of its pocket, she found Jezebel staring back at her.

"Are you all right?" Jezebel asked. Her eyes were red as if from crying.

"Yes, I couldn't rescue Emma, but I'm fine. What's wrong?"

Jezebel told her briefly what had happened with Nyro and Alanna. "With Nyro and Emma showing up here, and no word from you, I couldn't help but worry."

"I'm sorry—I should have contacted you. I didn't know where Nyro had gone, but this certainly explains her sudden departure.

Thank the stars Alanna's safe." She told her about Asmund and the situation with the resistance movement.

"Could you return here for the night before you set out with him?" Jezebel asked. "Leda and Alanna were terrified something might happen to you, and we all miss you terribly."

Allison smiled. "Of course. Let me talk to Asmund and I'll return immediately."

"If he's willing, it might be good for him to come with you. We're holding council in the morning, so he could meet Augustine and the others. Discuss our strategy against Nyro."

"That's a good idea. I'll ask him."

Allison stowed her mirror and explained her situation to Asmund. She invited him to go to Stoutwall with her, and he agreed. Allison rolled up her carpet, hoisting it over one shoulder, and freed Shadow to return to the spirit realm. Then she removed the pyramid and her sword from the void and opened a portal back to Stoutwall, the grounds and castle visible on the other side.

"After you," she said to Asmund.

The elf's eyes had gone wide, and he reached through the rift with one hand, pulling it back as if he'd touched something hot.

"It's perfectly safe, I assure you," she said with a grin.

"Perhaps you could go first?" he said.

Allison stepped through the portal, and Asmund followed slowly. It took all of her strength to keep it open for so long. Once he was through, she let the portal collapse, tucking the pyramid, sword, and carpet back into the void.

"We are standing on the human continent now?" he asked, taking in his surroundings.

"That is Castle Stoutwall in the old kingdom of Maeda," she said.

"Incredible," he muttered.

Allison led him across the moat and into the castle. Asmund gasped when their magic died. "What is this? My power is gone? I have never experienced anything like this…"

Allison told him about Mira's null. "She keeps it in place at all times in case Nyro attacks. She's shown up here twice since the battle, so it's proven to be a wise choice."

Allison found Augustine's steward and asked him to introduce Asmund to the prince and take care of his accommodations for the night. She said goodnight to the elf, and he walked off with the steward. Running up to her chambers, she found Jezebel and the girls waiting for her. She embraced the three of them, grateful that Alanna was safe and uninjured.

"How do you feel about Allure's reading?" Allison asked Alanna after the four of them had spent some time together. "You've always wanted to be a sorcerer one day, right?"

Alanna frowned. "*Someday*."

"Not now?" Allison asked. "Shadow could probably trigger your transformation."

"I don't think so," Alanna said. "In a few years, perhaps. And I definitely don't want to become a null. I love doing magic."

"Fair enough," Allison said, hugging her again.

"You should let Khaldun and Mira know you've returned," Jezebel told her. "They were as worried as I was, I think."

Allison walked over to their chambers, and Mira let her inside, embracing her and saying, "I'm so relieved you're all right."

"I never had any doubts," Khaldun said with a grin.

"He was as nervous as I was," Mira said to Allison. "Don't let him fool you."

Khaldun chuckled, hugging Allison and saying, "We're glad you're safe. While you're here, would you have a few minutes?"

"Yes, of course," she said.

The three of them sat down at the table and Khaldun told her about the demon Allure had found watching the castle and their ideas about the trap for Nyro. Jezebel had told her about Alanna's ordeal in great detail but had only touched on the demon.

"Using Alanna as bait," Allison said with a sigh when he was done. "I don't like it. The poor girl has already been through so much. But I believe you are correct that we could lure Nyro here that way."

"Jezebel would never approve this plan, though," Mira said.

"She might," Allison said pensively. "I'll bring it up with her. I'm sure Alanna would be agreeable. We'd have to do everything we can to ensure her safety, of course."

"What do you think about the demon?" Khaldun asked. "Could you summon one to keep watch over it?"

"I believe so," she said. "As Allure noted, I'd have to bind one first. I have some ideas about that—I'll discuss them with Allure before I retire for the night. Who else knows about the possibility of using Alanna as bait?"

"Only the three of us and Allure," he said.

"Good. Let's keep it that way for now. It would be best for Jezebel to hear it from me first, and I'm not sure when I'll get an opportunity to discuss it with her."

Allison bade them goodnight and went to see Allure. The sorcerer was still up. They discussed the incident with Alanna and Khaldun's ideas for a minute. Allure confirmed Allison would need to bind a demon to set it on a perpetual watch over the castle.

"It would be best to do this right away," Allison said. "I've got something in mind—would you be willing to assist me? Despite binding Shadow, I still feel a little unsure of this."

"It would be my pleasure," she said with a smile.

The two of them left the castle. Allison gazed up at the sky, and sure enough, she could sense the demon up there. "We should do this somewhere else to make sure our friend doesn't catch on." Retrieving the pyramid from the void, she opened a portal to the university, and the two of them walked through it.

Once she'd closed the gateway and tucked the pyramid back into the void, she called a flame to provide some illumination and said, "I've got these little specters I'm fond of using for most tasks. Unlike normal demons, they're not the spirits of ancient sorcerers."

"I thought that's where all demons came from," Allure said.

"So did I, but not these. I believe they're native to the spirit realm, but I'm not sure. I'll have to ask Shadow about it sometime. They should be perfect for our current situation."

"Are you sure they can be bound?"

"One way to find out," she said. "I'll try the spell on one of them and see what happens."

"What do you need me to do?"

"Hopefully nothing. I draw confidence from you, that's all. And if something does go wrong, I'm hoping you can save me."

"I'm sure you'll be fine," Allure said, flashing that sultry smile of hers.

Allison summoned one of her minions. Taking a deep breath, she formed the spells for the rite of binding and released the magic. She felt the spirit's power joining with hers. "I've got the first one," she told Allure. "That was even easier than it was with Shadow. Can a demon stop us from binding it?"

"They can't stop the rite, no," Allure said. "It cannot be canceled. As long as you can summon the demon and prevent it from returning to the spirit realm, you can bind it."

"And a demon more powerful than me could resist the summoning," Allison said. "Or escape again even if I did manage to force the summoning."

"Yes, exactly," Allure said. "And of course, binding a demon stronger than you would be extremely dangerous to begin with. Although at this point, Nyro is the only one *you* couldn't overpower."

For the next several minutes, Allison summoned and bound the rest of the spirits. There were an even dozen all together. They returned to Stoutwall, and she set three of them to keep watch on Nyro's demon. She instructed them to stay hidden and to alert her if the monster did anything but watch or if it departed.

"That's it," she told Allure. "Now we'll know if anything changes."

"I'm planning on working with a blacksmith after tomorrow morning's council meeting to see if we can create a spike for Nyro," she said. "I can teach you the spells if you'd like to join me."

"Yes, I would like that," Allison said. "Haven't you done this before?"

"I made a few at the university after we found the spells in Fosland," she said, "just to make sure I could do it. Those were simple, but we'll need something much stronger to contain Nyro. The mage who recorded the spells did specifically recommend using Stoutwall steel for more powerful demons."

"Augustine's smithy isn't in the castle, is it?" Allison asked. It would be impossible for Allure to weave her spells into the steel inside of Mira's null.

"No, it's in the city," she said. "I've already discussed this with Shatter, and he was going to let their blacksmith know he has permission to forge our spike with their special steel. I guess its formulation is a closely guarded secret."

They returned to the castle and said goodnight as they went their separate ways. Jezebel was still awake when Allison reached her chambers. She stripped out of her armor and slid into bed next to her. They discussed what she'd done with her new demons, but kept it brief.

Allison wanted to make love to her wife, and Jezebel was more than responsive. This would be their last opportunity for who knew how long, so they took full advantage of it. They were always passionate but became particularly so on this night.

Jezebel lay in her arms when they were done, and they probably would have drifted off to sleep at that point. But Allison wanted to bring up the idea she'd discussed with Khaldun, and wouldn't have another chance before leaving for Drengrvollr. So, she took a deep breath and told Jezebel what they were thinking, keeping her voice as low as she could. The girls were sleeping in the next room, and she didn't want them overhearing.

"I hate this idea," Jezebel said when she was done. "How can we ask our own daughter to put herself in harm's way like that? I know she'd probably jump at the chance, but that's beside the point."

"I'm not sure it is," Allison said. "If things turn out how we want, she could stand to inherit an entire kingdom one day. And she's not a child anymore. Putting her life at risk to defend that kingdom wouldn't exactly be a bad lesson."

Jezebel heaved a sigh. "You're right, of course. It's hard to accept how quickly they've grown up, but she is at an age where she could handle this. And I have to concede she *would* be the perfect bait. Nyro wants her and she'll come for her herself."

"Yes, exactly," Allison said. "And she is known for wandering off on her own, so creating a situation where she appears to be accidentally left behind would seem authentic. Not a setup that would be believable for Mira at all."

"Hardly," Jezebel said, taking a deep breath and sighing again. "Let me think about it. Maybe I'll discuss it with Alanna while you're gone."

Allison knew that was the best she could hope for, so she let it lie.

"Did you know Leda has been seeing someone romantically?" Jezebel asked.

"I had no idea!" she said. "Who's the lucky boy?"

"The lucky *young woman* is named Scarlett," Jezebel told her. "She's a member of Augustine's household guard. She's the one who showed Leda and Alanna how to get out of the castle. Apparently, Leda's been sneaking out of our chambers to meet her in the middle of the night."

Allison chuckled. "This is not something I would have expected from Leda."

"Which part? The interest in women or the sneaking out?"

"Both, I suppose."

"Agreed," Jezebel said with a sigh. "I wish they could have stayed little girls just a little longer."

"Does Augustine know Scarlett was involved with the girls' transgression?"

"No, and I don't plan on telling him," Jezebel said with a sigh. "I've spoken with Scarlett myself, and now that she's aware of the gravity of the situation, she feels terrible. Punishment enough, I think."

"Fair enough," she agreed.

Allison rose at dawn and trained with Battleaxe, Imani, and Shatter before the council meeting. She and Jezebel reached the prince's private dining room before any of the others. Once everyone had arrived and taken their seats, Allison introduced Asmund to the group.

Sage said something to him in elvish, and his eyes went wide with surprise. They conversed in his language for a few moments, and then, in the common tongue, he said, "I did not expect to find anyone in this land who could speak elvish."

"Sage is our preeminent scholar," said Allure. "She's probably the only person in Anoria who knows your language."

The elf told them the story of Nyro's rise to power as Estrid in Drengrvollr, her conquest of their continent, and the organization of the resistance movement. Allison knew they'd all heard pieces of this story before, but was sure none of them had heard all of it in so much detail.

"As I explained to Princess Allison, we have no military resources under our command," he told them. "But I do believe we have many mages who would be willing to come to Anoria's aid. Once Princess Allison and I return to Krokr, we will meet with the local leader and go from there."

"Thank you, Asmund, for coming here to meet with us," Augustine said. "I wonder, do any of your mages know the enchantments the ancient elves used to incarcerate Nyro and her demons in Pytha?"

"I do not believe so," Asmund said. "Only a few of the mages who came here then were still alive as Nyro rose to power. She slaughtered them. Those who had already passed handed down their secrets to their protégés, but Nyro sought them out and killed them, as well. I believe she considered this revenge upon those who had imprisoned her."

"Your Highness," said Khaldun, "even if we could recover those spells, we must not settle for incarcerating Nyro this time. Doing so would only pass on this problem to another generation of Anorians.

"I've been consulting with some of the others, and we believe we have discovered a way to lure Nyro here once we've evacuated *and* to destroy her for good."

"That is welcome news," Augustine said. "Would you care to elaborate?"

Khaldun met Allison's gaze for a moment, and said, "Not at this time. We are only in the early stages of working out the details. I would prefer to wait until we have a complete solution."

"Very well," Augustine said. "Have we been able to destroy the demon observing the castle?"

"There has been a change in plans," Allison told him and explained what she'd done. "We'll want Nyro's demon in place when it comes time to spring our trap, so this is our best way forward."

"Understood," Augustine said. "Do you know how long your journey to elvendom will take?"

Allison turned to Asmund.

"It's hard to say," the elf replied. "Only a day to make contact with the local leader in Krokr. Beyond that, it will depend on how receptive the territorial directors are. And the disposition of the available mages across the continent. It will all go much faster using the princess's portal, of course. I would say anywhere from a few days to a couple of weeks."

"You won't have much longer than that," Prince Leto said. "The ships carrying Nyro's reinforcements will arrive in Anoria in three weeks, maybe less."

"We will bear that in mind," Asmund said.

"Princess Allison," said Augustine, "will you require anyone else to accompany you on this journey?"

"I don't think so, Your Highness," she said. "Asmund will be my guide, and I should be able to handle any trouble we encounter myself."

"It would be best for the two of us to handle this on our own," Asmund said. "Forgive me, but our people are distrustful of humans. And I'm afraid the prejudice has only worsened among those who know Estrid's true identity. The princess's fair complexion, blond hair, and light eyes will make this difficult enough as it is. Taking any more of you with us would only complicate matters."

"We could change her appearance if that would help," Khaldun said.

"Like your sorcerers, our mages can sense the magical force," said Asmund. "An illusion spell would only rouse their suspicion."

"Understood," Khaldun said with a grin. "But I can create a physical transformation in Her Highness."

"That's impossible," Asmund said.

"It's not," Allison told him. "I used to be the same size as Princess Jezebel."

Asmund looked back and forth between the two of them with an expression of disbelief. "Even if what you say is true, turning you into an elf might cause more harm than good. They'll know you cannot be one of them."

"A Shifari, then," Imani said with a grin. "She's already got the height. Khaldun can make it so she'd pass as my sister."

"That could work," Asmund said with a nod. "Our history books do tell us that your people were descended from ours. And the prejudice against humans doesn't run as deep against the Shifari as it does the rest of your kind."

"Perfect," Allison said. "I need to attend to a matter with Allure first, but then we can depart for Drengrvollr as soon as Khaldun has taken care of my appearance."

The meeting adjourned, and Allison left the castle with Allure. Once outside of Mira's null, she pulled her carpet out of the void and they flew to the city. Allure told her where to find Augustine's smithy.

Sure enough, the blacksmith was expecting them. Allure described the spike they would need, and he got to work.

"As big as my forearm?" Allison said to her as they watched his progress. "I could close my fist around the one we used on Myrddin's demon."

"Nyro is vastly more powerful," Allure said. "Even using the special steel, we simply need more mass."

Allison paid attention as Allure formed the spells the first time, weaving them into the steel. Allure repeated them several times as the blacksmith worked, and once she was sure she had it, Allison took over the spell work. Allure explained that the more layers of magic they could work into the metal, the better it would contain Nyro's essence.

The process was taking longer than she'd anticipated, so Allison asked if Allure wouldn't mind taking over again.

"No problem," Allure said. She embraced her, kissing her on the cheek. "Good luck, Allison. Return to us safely."

"I will," she promised.

Leaving the smithy, she flew back to the castle. She found Khaldun by the army camp, consulting with Amari and Shatter. He excused himself and came over to meet her.

"I'm starting the troop transformations this morning," he said with a sigh. "This is going to become quite tedious, I'm afraid."

"The price you pay for your unique talent," she told him with a grin.

"I suppose so," he said. "Are you ready?"

"You're sure you can change me back to my original appearance once we've defeated Nyro?" she said. "Taking this next step won't make it impossible to undo my previous transformation?"

"I don't see why it would," he said, shaking his head.

"All right, let's do it. Let's find somewhere a little more discrete before I strip, shall we?"

"You can keep your armor on this time," he said with a grin. "Skin color is one thing I've been able to change for years, so I have a lot more practice."

"You don't need to see what you're working on?"

"I did in the beginning, but not anymore."

Allison nodded. Gazing up at the sky, she felt Nyro's demon and said, "Actually, it might be best to do this elsewhere anyway." She didn't know if changing her skin color would tip off Nyro to their plans or not, but it couldn't hurt to play it safe.

Allison used the pyramid to create a portal to the university again, and once the two of them had moved through it, Khaldun got to work. Allison held out her hands, and he darkened them to a deep mahogany.

"How's that?" he asked.

"Perfect."

He worked his magic over her entire body. Allison pulled back her armor near her waist, confirming the transformation had included her unexposed skin. Khaldun made her eyes dark and turned her hair jet black.

"That should do it," he said, looking her up and down. "Not much family resemblance to Imani, I'm afraid, but you could pass for a distant cousin, I'm sure."

Allison chuckled. "Thank you for this. Let's hope it helps."

"Anytime, Your Highness."

"Listen, I broached the topic of using Alanna for our trap with Jezebel last night," she told him. "And she was more receptive than I would have thought. I don't think she's convinced yet—for that matter, I'm not sure *I* am. But we'll both think about it more while I'm away. She might discuss the idea with Alanna, too, but I have no doubt she'll be eager to play her part."

"That's excellent," he said. "I worried what Jezebel's reaction might be."

Allison cast an illusion to return herself to her previous appearance. She could remove it once she reached Drengrvollr with Asmund. They returned to the castle, and Allison ran inside. Mira's null removed her illusion spell, but she would recreate it when she left the null again. She hurried up to her chambers to bid her family farewell.

Jezebel was in the front room with Mira. They both embraced her and wished her luck, and Jezebel kissed her. "You have your mirror, right?"

Allison nodded. "I'll keep you apprised of our progress, I promise."

Alanna and Leda were awake, but still in bed. Allison sat on the edge of the mattress and told them that she was leaving for Drengrvollr.

"You'll be gone a lot longer this time?" Leda asked.

"Yes, but there's no way to know *how* long. No more than two weeks or so, and possibly much less." She took a deep breath. "I want you two to *promise* me that you'll stay inside the castle this time. It worked out in the end last time, but Nyro is the cleverest, most persistent mage who's ever lived. She's sure to try again, and there's no telling what tactics she might attempt. Mira's null provides the best possible protection."

"I promise," said Leda. "I only helped last time because she was so sad and pathetic I couldn't bear it."

"Hey," Alanna said, smacking her arm. "I was never *pathetic*. Desperate, perhaps. But I promise I'll behave. I have no desire to encounter Nyro again. Sigrid will have to do with visits in the courtyard."

"Good," Allison said with a smile. "I'll return as soon as I can."

She hugged them both tight, said farewell once more to Mira and Jezebel, and then headed out. Asmund was waiting for her in the great hall, so she collected him, and the two left the castle together. She cast her illusion spell again as they left Mira's null.

Allison removed her sword, carpet, and the pyramid from the void. It would be dark in Drengrvollr now, so she opened a portal to the same location in the countryside she'd used last time. She felt herself becoming more fluent with portal magic, but it still took an immense amount of power. Once they'd stepped through it, she closed the gateway behind them, tucked the sword and pyramid back into the void, removed her illusion spell, and unfurled her carpet on the ground.

Once they'd taken their seats, she cast her spells and launched them high into the sky. Asmund screamed his head off, and Allison couldn't help but giggle.

CHAPTER EIGHTEEN
ANGUISH

nce he'd finished making Allison appear Shifari, Khaldun got to work transforming the first regiment of soldiers. It was a group from Stoutwall and included the princedom's elite units. Most of them were already large and muscular, both the men and the women. Khaldun's job was to augment those physical attributes.

He still couldn't do this kind of work sight unseen, but these soldiers didn't seem troubled by public nudity. On the contrary, he was pretty sure he'd seen many of them joining in on the morning swims in the lake with Allison and her training partners.

When the first male soldier asked him to increase the size of his manhood as part of the transformation, Khaldun had to laugh. He knew he should have seen this coming. At first, he refused, saying this sort of thing wasn't part of his assignment. Some of the nearby troops had overheard the request, though, and egged him on. Khaldun granted the soldier's wish, and the others whistled and cheered.

One of the women asked him to make her breasts bigger, so he complied with that request as well. Before long, though, things were getting out of hand with soldiers requesting different eye, hair, and skin colors, in addition to enhanced genitalia. This was going to take forever, so he finally put his foot down, giving the remaining troops only the increased size and strength delineated by his initial orders.

It was still slow-going. In addition to changing their physique, he had to adjust their armor to match. He worked until sunset and had only transformed a few dozen soldiers. It was exhausting work, and yet at the rate he was going, he'd be hard-pressed to get through a single regiment by the time Nyro's reinforcements arrived.

Khaldun called it quits for the day and met Mira in the great hall for dinner. Jezebel and the girls were sitting at the head table with Augustine and his family, so they sat with Allure, Battleaxe, Mist, and Sage, and he told them about his day. The others chuckled at some of the requests he'd received.

"Two cocks, huh?" Battleaxe said. "While that might be, ah, interesting in bed, I fail to see how it would help in battle."

"Yes, well, I did refuse that particular request," he said, shaking his head.

"I wonder if there are other things you could do with your shapeshifting we haven't thought of yet," Allure said, giving him a pensive look.

"Like what?" said Battleaxe. "Three tits?"

The others guffawed, but Allure said, "No… I was thinking along the lines of granting mages new powers."

"You could turn all these ruffians into shapeshifters to lighten your workload," Mira said with a grin.

"This ruffian is *not* changing anyone's genitals for them," Battleaxe said.

"You really are obsessed with genitals, aren't you?" Sage said, giving her an appraising look.

"Can't help it," she said with a shrug. "I told you I haven't been laid in a while."

"No luck with Shatter, then?" Mist said with a knowing grin.

"Ah, no. I've all but raped him in the lake after our training sessions, and he hardly notices. I think it's a lost cause."

"To answer your question," Khaldun said to Allure, talking over the others, "everything I've done so far is purely physical. I'm not sure if I can effect changes in someone's magic. I'll have to give it a try."

"That's a good idea," Battleaxe said. "And if you can give someone more magic, then why not more intelligence? Or musical abilities? Maybe the sky's the limit!"

"Could be," Khaldun said with a shrug. "I'll have to test this out at some point."

"I'm free now," Battleaxe said, getting to her feet.

Khaldun chuckled, heading out of the castle with her. Out on the grounds, he tried giving Battleaxe his shapeshifting ability or increasing her intelligence but had no sense of how to do any of it. Changing people physically was becoming easy, but anything beyond that seemed to be beyond reach.

They returned to the great hall, and after dinner, Allure asked Khaldun and Mira to come to her chambers with her. She showed them the spike she'd had forged that morning.

"This thing is massive," Khaldun said, taking it from her. "And even heavier than I expected. We'll have to have Shatter be the one to do the honors when the time comes."

"Or Allison, for that matter," Mira said, taking it from him and testing its weight before she handed it back to Allure.

"You should get a feel for it outside of the null," Allure said to Khaldun as she placed it on her table. "I wove a ton of magic into it as it was forged, and the thing was pulsating with power when we were done."

"It would have to be to contain Nyro," Khaldun said.

"A thought occurred to me while we were making this," Allure said. "Nyro will be able to read anyone who's present when we set this trap for her."

"Oh, shit," Khaldun said. "I hadn't considered that, but you're right."

"We might have to avoid telling Alanna too much," Allure said. "If she ends up being involved, of course."

"Yes, and limit the participants as much as possible," Khaldun said. "We'll need someone there as bait. And I cannot imagine making this work without Mira. Without her null, Nyro would have her full power available to her, and we wouldn't stand a chance."

"We should think this through a bit more," Allure said. "Mira would have to extinguish her null at first to have any hope of drawing Nyro in. It would have to appear that Alanna is alone. Only once Nyro takes the bait should Mira expand her null."

"And then what?" Mira asked.

"That's a good question," Khaldun said. "Normally, the spike must penetrate the person's flesh *while* the demon is possessing them. But this is a very different situation."

"It is," Allure said, taking a deep breath. "Nyro isn't merely possessing Estrid's body—she has essentially become its life force. Her spirit can only leave when that body dies."

"Meaning we'd need to impale her with the spike while she's alive," Khaldun said.

"Yes," Allure replied. "And then kill the body to release her spirit into the spike. But that cannot happen inside the null."

"But the moment I extinguish my null, Nyro regains her magic," Mira pointed out. "And then we lose."

"Maybe not," said Allure. "Normally, the spike prevents someone from doing magic while it pierces their flesh."

"All right," Khaldun said, his brow furrowed in concentration. "So we draw Nyro into the castle, expand Mira's null to take away her magic, impale Nyro with the spike, extinguish the null, and then kill the body. Right?"

"I'll want to run this all by Shadow beforehand, but yes, I believe that's how this will have to work. And we must make sure *not* to kill the body while the null is in effect. That would release Nyro's spirit without trapping it in the spike."

"Meaning she'd be free to start over with a new elvish body," said Khaldun.

"We're overlooking one important detail here," Mira said. "Magic or no, Nyro won't just stand there and let us impale her. My null won't diminish her fighting skills in the slightest."

"Yes, that is a problem," Khaldun said with a nod.

"Luckily, we have time to work out the kinks," Allure said. "In the meantime, we'll have to train anyone who's going to be involved to close their minds. And that may be impossible for Alanna at this point."

"Why is that?" asked Mira.

"Her magic isn't very strong yet," Allure said. "On the other hand, communicating with her dragon does make use of sympathetic magic. I'll have to work with her and see what I can do."

"Failing that, we can keep Alanna in the dark," Khaldun said. "I'm not sure how that would work, but we'll figure it out."

"What about me?" Mira asked Allure. "Do you think I can learn to close my mind?

"Yes, I believe so. Allison and I have been working on it, and we can both do it at will. And like Alanna, you're using sympathetic magic every time you communicate with your dragon."

"I should probably learn to do this as well," Khaldun said. "However this works out, the three of us and Allison are likely to be the ones executing this mad plan of ours. And Shatter, perhaps, but he's already immune to sympathetic magic."

"Yes, so you two will be needing the lessons," Allure said. "This may be the most difficult for you, Khaldun. You have no experience with sympathetic magic. We should start working on this as soon as possible."

"Let's start now," Mira said. "If you're free, of course," she added to Allure.

"As it happens, I am," she said.

"Why don't you two get started?" Khaldun said. "I want to go speak with Jezebel for a moment."

He went over to her chambers, but no one answered when he knocked. Going back to the great hall, he checked for them there, but they'd left. He heard a roar coming from the courtyard and figured he knew exactly where they'd be.

Sure enough, he found Alanna and Leda playing with Sigrid, and Jezebel sitting on a nearby bench. Khaldun sat down next to her.

"Do you have a moment?" he asked.

"Of course," she said. "Is something wrong?"

"No, no, it's not that," he said. He explained what they'd discussed about Alanna's potential role in their plans for Nyro. "If it's all right with you, Allure will work with her on closing her mind to sympathetic magic. But in the meantime, it might be best not to discuss our plans with her."

"Yes, that makes sense," she said. "I want to think about this more before bringing it up with her anyway. And Allure is welcome to work with her. It would be good for Alanna to learn this regardless of our decision."

"Perfect, thank you," Khaldun said, getting to his feet. "I'll let Allure know."

He returned to his chambers, and Mira told him she could already close her mind.

"That fast?" he said. "I'm impressed. I was only gone a few minutes."

"No, she could *already* do it," Allure said. "She didn't need my help."

"I had no idea, but it must be from working with Magna, or my null, or the combination of the two," Mira said.

"That's great!" Khaldun said. "I have a feeling this isn't going to come to me nearly as readily."

"One way to find out," Allure said. "Have a seat." He sat down facing her. Allure closed her eyes, holding his head in her hands. "I'm reading you now. Can you feel it?"

"No," he said with a frown. "Wait—yes, I think I can."

"Good, now try to stop it. Push me out of your mind."

Khaldun tried, but couldn't do it. They spent a half hour on this, but it was no use. He had no feeling for how it was supposed to work. Mira and Allure both tried explaining how it felt when they did it, but it was no help. They decided to call it a night. Allure wished them a good night and returned to her chambers.

Khaldun rose early the next morning. He and Mira had breakfast together in the great hall, then he went out to the army camp to continue transforming the soldiers. This time, he made it clear from the outset that he would not be taking requests. And he found he was hitting his stride, getting through each transformation much quicker than he had the day before. He'd completed nearly a hundred by sunset.

He was heading back into the castle, intending to sit down for dinner in the great hall, when he sensed someone trying to contact him. Pulling out his mirror, it took him a moment to recognize the face staring out at him.

"Princess Jelena!" he said. He hadn't heard from her since before the battle. Her children, Susan and James, had come to Stoutwall with Jezebel's parents and taken refuge out in the countryside. "How are things in Rockport?" Part of the elvish fleet had landed there before proceeding to Spanbrook.

"It's been fairly quiet since the enemy departed for your princedom," she said. "They left a small occupying force here, large enough that we didn't dare risk an attack. Something's going on, though. We've noticed them bringing groups of our people—humans, that is—into their camp. None of my people have gone missing, and we haven't recognized any of the prisoners. If they were coming from Rockport, I'd expect that one of us would have known at least some of them. But not a single one looked familiar."

"So they must be bringing people there from elsewhere," Khaldun said. "Did they look like soldiers?"

"Not that we could tell," she replied. "We've tried to determine where they're taking them, but they always disappear inside the camp, and then we lose track of them."

"Disappear as if with an invisibility spell?"

"That's what we believe," she said. "My wizard, Roman, has tried locating any hidden structures and he had no luck until today. He's no sorcerer, so of course, he can detect spells only as they're being cast. But he heard noises coming from one of the fields just outside the city. He tried canceling invisibility and exposed part of a pen with dozens of people inside. The spell was much larger, but he lacked the power to cancel the entire thing. The part he did cancel reformed almost immediately."

Khaldun thought back to Camilla's report of human-sized armor being fabricated in Spanbrook and thought he finally understood. "Did he get a sense of how large the pen might be?"

"He says it was impossible to tell from the little section he saw. But there's more. He felt an overwhelming sense of dread as he moved through that area—more than this discovery warranted. That's a sign of wraiths in the area, isn't it?"

"Yes, it is," he said with a sigh. "Let me discuss this with Princess Jezebel. I'll get back to you as soon as I can."

"Thank you," Jelena said before disappearing from the glass.

Khaldun found Jezebel in the great hall, having dinner with the girls. He pulled her aside to tell her about his conversation with Jelena.

"Wraiths in Rockport," she said, shaking her head. "Well, it was only a matter of time before Nyro put them in play. She must be planning on using our own people against us."

"That was my thought, too," Khaldun said. "It would explain the armor in Spanbrook. What I don't understand is how she can get them to fight against us."

"Compliance spells?" she said.

"That would make the most sense. But she could have thousands of such people for all we know. Casting that sort of spell on so many would take time. And the spells would wear off after a while. It doesn't seem too practical."

"We should send someone to investigate further," Jezebel said.

"I could leave immediately," he said.

"No, no," she said. "Depending on what you found there, this could take an extended period of time. We need you transforming the troops."

"We do have several more sorcerers here. Augustine will want Shatter to remain, I'm sure, but we do have four from the university."

"Yes, but I wouldn't want to deplete our defenses too much," Jezebel said. "Talk to Allure. See if she and Battleaxe would be willing to go. That would leave Sage, Mist, and Shatter here."

Allure had returned to her chambers after dinner, sitting on her bed in the dark, hugging her knees to her chest. Though she'd been doing her best to hide it from everyone else, since Semblant's death in the battle, she was barely hanging on. Her will to live was nearly depleted, and the only thing driving her now was an intense desire to see Nyro destroyed. She had nothing else to live for anymore.

Semblant was the love of her life. True, he'd never been the same since his resurrection fifteen years earlier. But their love for each other hadn't changed. She knew facing Cyclone, Vision, or Intuit in battle would be tough. But fighting Semblant might rip her heart out.

A knock at the door startled her. Slipping out of the bed and igniting the oil lamp with a thought, she opened the door to find Khaldun standing there.

"Come in, please," she said, flashing a smile she didn't feel.

They sat down at her work table, and he told her about human prisoners in Rockport.

"I would prefer to investigate this further myself," he said with a sigh, "but I must remain here to continue transforming the troops. Princess Jezebel wanted me to ask if you and Battleaxe could look into this for us."

"It would be my pleasure," Allure said. "I've been feeling rather useless since the battle."

"You're hardly useless," he said. "Were it not for you, neither Allison nor I would have unleashed our latent talents."

She was going to point out that Shadow was responsible for that, not she, but decided to let it go. Allure bade him goodnight and went to Battleaxe's chambers. There was no answer, and she wasn't in the great hall, so Allure was pretty sure she knew where to find her.

Leaving the castle, she took off on her carpet, flying to the tavern in the city. Sure enough, Battleaxe was there with Imani and Mist. It was loud—it seemed like more and more of the city's residents were returning to the city, many of them frequenting the tavern. Allure asked Battleaxe to step outside with her, and explained Princess Jezebel's request.

"Sounds like fun," she said with that irrepressible enthusiasm of hers. "When do we leave?"

"I could leave now," she said with a shrug.

"That works."

Battleaxe went inside to let the other two know she was departing, then took off with Allure on her carpet. As they flew, Allure steeled herself against a possible encounter with Semblant. Nyro had deployed her wraiths, so there was no reason not to believe their lost sorcerers would be in Anoria now, too. Even with the two of them calling air, it still took half the night to reach Rockport.

Allure made them invisible as she took them in low over the elvish army camp. It was dark with scattered campfires providing the only light, so it was hard to tell for sure, but Allure estimated they had around a thousand soldiers here.

Flying east of the city, she sensed a powerful invisibility spell covering one of the fields. At the same time, a feeling of dread came over her, and she knew there were wraiths down there. Summoning her power, she canceled the invisibility spell and, at the same time, called a giant fireball high above them to illuminate the area.

Allure gasped. The spell had been hiding a massive pen holding *thousands* of people. They had a wraith at each corner to maintain the invisibility spell.

The wraiths started firing off indiscriminate spells, trying to find them, so Allure had to get them out of the way before she was able to get a full estimate of the headcount in the pen. Once she'd moved them to a safe range, she asked Battleaxe what she thought.

"I would guess roughly five thousand," she said. "Nyro's got twelve wraiths, though, right? So there could be additional pens."

Allure circled the surrounding fields, and sure enough, they found two more pens, with wraiths stationed at each corner to maintain a giant invisibility spell.

"Fifteen thousand prisoners," Battleaxe said with a tone of disbelief. "Using compliance spells on so many seems a little unrealistic."

"That can't be their plan," Allure said. "Maintaining that many spells for any length of time would be impossible."

"If we get Mist and Sage here, we could do the same thing we did on the way to Stoutwall," Battleaxe said. "Drawing power from each other, we could tuck all three groups into the void and get them out of here." They had taught Mist and Sage how to do this after the battle in Stoutwall.

"It'll be tough with those wraiths working against us," Allure said. "And I'm sure they've got mages in the camp, too. But we've got to make the attempt. I'll contact Sage."

Before she could produce her mirror, a blinding light appeared in the sky. Shielding her eyes, Allure could see it was a portal. Four carpets shot through the rift, and it closed behind them.

"Oh, shit," said Battleaxe. "I bet I know who that was."

Allure's stomach clenched with dread. Witch fires sprung up all around the three pens and the wraiths canceled their invisibility spells. The four carpet riders touched down by the four corners of one of the pens. They were too high to see much in the way of details, but one of them was huge. It could only be Semblant. Allure's throat burned and she had to wipe tears from her eyes.

As they watched, all the people in the pen disappeared, and Allure felt a wave of power wash over her. One of the newcomers had tucked the entire group into the void. They moved to the next pen and one of the others did the same with that group. Once they'd completed the spell with the third group, all four riders took off on their carpets, heading south before going invisible.

"Well, shit," Battleaxe said. "How much do you want to bet they're taking them to Spanbrook?"

"It would only make sense," Allure said. "That's where their army is camped. We'd better take a look."

"I'll update Jezebel on our progress," Battleaxe said. "Should we ask her to send Sage and Mist?"

"Not yet," Allure said. "It won't take long to get to Spanbrook from here. Let's appraise the situation when we arrive before we make a decision."

With both of them calling air, they reached Spanbrook in very little time. The army camp and the surrounding area were illuminated by countless little fires. Nyro's sorcerers had already arrived and released their captives from the void in three separate groups. Dozens of soldiers were standing guard around each while work crews constructed new pens for them.

"No need to bring Mist and Sage here," Allure said. "It would be the four of us against all of their sorcerers and mages, plus the entire army."

"Yeah," Battleaxe said with a sigh. "Trying to tuck so many people into the void with such an overwhelming force bearing down on us isn't my idea of a good time."

The trouble was that they didn't have enough sorcerers to tuck all of the prisoners into the void at once. It took one of them drawing power from three others to handle five thousand people that way. They'd have to repeat the process three times, like the enemy mages had. And the enemy wasn't about to stand there and let them do it.

"Nyro tucked her entire army into the void on her own when they left Stoutwall," Allure said. "Which means Allison may be able to do so with all the prisoners on her own."

"Might be able to pull that off in a sneak attack," Battleaxe said. "With the rest of us covering her."

"We'll have to discuss this with her when she returns," Allure said.

Battleaxe checked in with Jezebel again, and the princess told her she'd spoken to Camilla. The witch reported that they'd moved the human armor from the forges in the city out to the army camp. They'd had their mages working spells on the entire lot around the clock for the last day and a half, but she couldn't tell what kind of magic it was. She asked if Allure and Battleaxe could look into it.

Allure circled the camp, and they had no trouble spotting the ongoing project. There were several massive piles of armor, and even now more than a dozen mages were imbuing the equipment with magic.

Making sure they were invisible, Allure flew them directly over one of the piles of completed armor. She took them in lower, hovering directly over the top of the heap, and Battleaxe grabbed a breastplate.

Allure took them higher, and Battleaxe said, "Oh, damn." Her heart sank when the sorcerer told her what the magic was.

Something hit them—a spell of some sort—and their carpet dropped like a stone. Someone had canceled all of her air spells. Allure restored them before they lost too much altitude, and she spotted another carpet swooping toward them in the light of the fires below. Her heart nearly stopped when she spotted the massive rider, and she froze up, unable to hit him with any spells.

Luckily, Battleaxe had spotted Semblant, too, and fired off a barrage of spells to unravel the magic keeping his carpet aloft. Allure launched them toward Stoutwall with all the power she possessed. She'd known it was only a matter of time before she'd encounter him, and she'd steeled herself against it, but she was still overcome with sorrow. The love of her life a slave to their mortal enemy… This was more than she could bear.

It was light out by the time they'd reached Stoutwall, and Allure went into the castle to find Jezebel. She wasn't in the great hall, so she went upstairs and found her in her chambers.

"This is from Spanbrook?" Jezebel asked when Allure handed her the breastplate Battleaxe had swiped.

"Yes, Your Highness," Allure said. "They're imbuing the metal with compliance spells. It will force anyone wearing it to obey whatever orders Nyro's commanders give them."

"So the armor is casting a spell over its wearer?" she asked incredulously. "I've never heard of such a thing."

"Neither have we," Allure said. "You can't see it inside Mira's null, but the magic gives the metal an iridescent sheen, much like the armor our troops wear to repel magic. It must have taken Nyro ages to come up with this. But using it, she'll add fifteen thousand of our own people to her numbers. Undoubtedly she'll put them on the front lines, sacrificing them and fatiguing our troops before they face her main force."

"It doesn't seem like these prisoners are even soldiers," Jezebel said. "Common citizens from the conquered princedoms, most likely. They don't stand a chance against trained soldiers."

"Having to kill their own people is sure to demoralize the troops, too," Allure said with a sigh. She also told her about the possibility of Allison rescuing those people.

"That gives me hope," Jezebel said with a smile. "I don't want to interrupt her with this now, but I'll discuss it with her as soon as she returns. Thank you," she added, squeezing Allure's hand.

CHAPTER NINETEEN
RESISTANCE LEADERS

aking them invisible, Allison flew to Krokr, hovering high above the city. Thankfully, Asmund had stopped screaming.

"Where will we find the local leader?" she asked.

"I'll have to contact him," Asmund said. "Not even I know where he resides, and we never meet in the same place twice. Could we land somewhere?"

Allison flew to the same rooftop where they'd met. Asmund got to his feet, moving away from the carpet, doubled over, and vomited. Allison grimaced.

"My apologies," he said. "At my age, my stomach can barely tolerate a boat ride on a calm lake, never mind a magic carpet ride."

He pulled out his mirror, and after a few moments, started speaking to someone in elvish. Allison summoned Shadow, instructing her to remain invisible. *"Do you understand elvish?"*

"I do. Would you like me to translate?"

"Not yet. Just listen, and once he tells me what's being said, let me know if he's telling the truth."

Asmund's conversation stopped, but he continued staring into the mirror. A minute later, Allison heard a different voice, and Asmund and the newcomer spoke briefly. Finally, he put the mirror away and said, "The local leader, Erling, will meet us now. We'll need to fly to a farm east of the city."

"All right," Allison said.

"He spoke to someone else first. A lackey, by the sounds of it. And he didn't tell Erling that he was bringing anyone else to the meeting. So your presence is sure to be a surprise. Otherwise, he told the truth."

"Perhaps we could go a little slower this time," Asmund said as they took their seats on the carpet. "Erling will be traveling over land, so there's no hurry."

Allison chuckled. "I'll make it as smooth as I can."

They lifted off and she headed east. The landscape was awash in moonlight, so Asmund had no trouble navigating. Fifteen minutes later, they landed on a farm. The place seemed deserted, and Allison sensed no magic nearby.

"That flight was much more agreeable," Asmund said as they got to their feet. "Thank you."

Allison rolled up her carpet and tucked it into the void, and he said, "This way."

He led her into an old, stone granary with a couple of sections of its wall missing. Allison asked Shadow to keep a lookout outside and warn her if anyone approached. She called a small flame to provide some light.

"Erling is younger than me, but still quite advanced in age," Asmund told her. "He does not speak your tongue, but I will translate for you."

After several minutes, Shadow told Allison that a lone elf was approaching on horseback. Powerfully magical. There was a dirt road leading to the farm, and he was leaving that, making his way across the field toward them.

"I think he's here," Allison said to Asmund.

"How can you tell?" he asked, narrowing his eyes.

"I have my ways."

Allison heard noises outside, and Shadow let her know that Erling had arrived and was dismounting his horse. The elf walked into the granary moments later. He stopped short when he spotted them, and he and Asmund exchanged heated words for a moment.

"Erling demanded that Asmund identify you. He's upset that Asmund didn't warn him to expect a third party and says he wouldn't

have come if he knew there would be a human present. Asmund told him that's why he didn't warn him."

"Erling welcomes you to Drengrvollr," Asmund said to Allison.

"He said nothing of the sort," Shadow told her. Allison smiled and nodded to Erling anyway.

The two elves spoke for a few more minutes. Finally, Asmund said, "Erling agrees that we should send as many mages as we can to aid Anoria in your fight against Nyro. She has a stranglehold on our people here, and we have no way to break free. Joining forces with your army, however, we can help defeat her, and that may be the only way to retake our own kingdoms.

"The trouble is that he doesn't know how many mages we have left. Only a handful remain in Krokr. He will speak to the director of the movement's Drengrvollr territory and see if they would be willing to meet with us. It may take him a day or two to receive a response, but he will notify me once he does."

"Everything he said is true. But Erling also cursed him for bringing you here. He said the territorial director may not agree to his bringing a human along. So, you may need to wait elsewhere while Asmund speaks to them. Asmund told him he would only agree to that if there was no other way."

"Excellent, please thank him for me," Allison said.

Erling left the granary and rode away on his horse. Allison and Asmund took to the air on her carpet, and she said, "Where do we go from here?"

"Are you hungry?" he asked.

"I could eat."

"Take us back to the city."

Allison took her time, and he directed her to a small home in Krokr's northwestern outskirts. They were invisible, and Asmund had agreed it would be best for no one in the city to see her. A couple was strolling up the road in front of the house, so Allison waited until they were out of sight before landing.

"Welcome to my humble abode," Asmund said. "My domestic assistant will cook for us. I trust her, but it might be best for her to believe you are an elf." Allison cast an illusion to make herself look like a native and removed their invisibility spell. "That should do nicely."

"How do we get around my inability to speak the language?"

"I'll tell her you're a mute," he said. "Come on."

Allison tucked her carpet into the void and followed him inside. It was a two-story brick structure, small but cozy. Asmund led her into the kitchen, speaking to the elvish woman they found there. Shadow told her that he'd introduced her, so Allison smiled and nodded. She sat down at the table with Asmund and the woman got to work cooking them a meal.

Delicious aromas filled the small space, and Allison's stomach started rumbling. The woman served the food, and Allison believed it was some sort of fish. She tried a bite and thought the sauce might burn a hole in her mouth. It was delicious, though. She had to eat slowly and drink a lot of water, but she finished her plate.

Asmund's assistant departed once she'd cleaned up after them, so they were able to speak freely, and Allison dropped her illusion spell. They chatted for a while about the local cuisine, and then Asmund suggested they retire for the night. It was the middle of the day as far as her body was concerned, and Allison wasn't tired, but neither did she know when she'd get the opportunity to sleep again. Asmund led her upstairs to the guest bedroom, and she lay in the bed to rest. She sent Shadow to keep an eye on the surrounding area and alert her if anyone suspicious approached the house.

Pulling out her mirror, Allison contacted Jezebel and spent a few minutes updating her on her progress so far. It didn't sound like anything new was going on back in Stoutwall.

Allison dozed off eventually and had slept a few hours by sunrise the next morning. She headed down to the kitchen to find Asmund sitting at the table, and his assistant cooking for them again.

She would have enjoyed a tour of this ancient city, but Asmund advised against it. The place was crawling with Nyro's mages and soldiers, and it was too great a risk that one of them would realize Allison wasn't what she appeared to be.

So they waited in the house. Asmund had a small library, and Allison perused some of the books for a while, but they were all in elvish. Sitting around like this felt so strange—there was always something that needed doing back in Stoutwall. But there was nothing they could do until Asmund heard from Erling.

The elf finally made contact that afternoon. He told Asmund that the territorial director would meet them in the mountains at the northern end of Drengrvollr, near the border with Askaheimr. They lived in that region and would be using the home of an adviser for their meeting.

Asmund unrolled a map of the continent on the kitchen table and pointed out the approximate location of their destination. Allison sent Shadow to have a look. She wanted to traverse most of the distance by portal, then fly the rest of the way on her carpet. Their contact was sure to wonder how they'd managed to get there from Krokr so quickly, which could be problematic, but Asmund assured her it would be good to let the director wonder. He wouldn't reveal her secret, and they would let the director believe Allison possessed unknown powers.

Between the map and Shadow's scouting efforts, Allison was able to use the pyramid to open a portal to a location in the foothills. She walked through it with Asmund, closing it behind her, and then they took off on her carpet. Allison sent Shadow ahead to help her navigate. For the next couple of hours, they drew closer and closer to the mountains.

Before long, Allison spotted a large, wooden structure nestled on a saddle point between two peaks, just above the tree line. As they moved closer, she could sense a shield spell protecting the place. She landed outside the boundary, on the trail leading up to the house.

They got to their feet and she tucked the carpet into the void. She sent Shadow into the building to give her a better idea of who or what was waiting for them. Shadow reported the presence of three elf mages—two males and a female—a half dozen guards, and several others who appeared to be household staff.

Allison walked up to the edge of the protective spell with Asmund, and they waited. A few minutes later, two enormous elvish guards approached and spoke to Asmund. One of them spoke to someone by mirror, and the protective spell disappeared. They followed the guards up the trail, and the shield magic reformed.

Wooden terraces and porches surrounded the house, and the guards led them up one of the porches to the entrance. Inside, they found the two mages waiting for them. Asmund spoke to them for a moment, and they invited them to sit down in a room with an enormous fireplace and a beautiful view of the surrounding mountains.

Asmund spoke with the mages further, and Allison waited patiently. Finally, he said, "The female is the territorial director, and the male is her second in command. They tell me that they support a temporary alliance with your people for the purpose of defeating Nyro. The resistance movement in Drengrvollr currently includes roughly thirty mages. They believe Mestrland has a similar number, perhaps a few more. Ellrivollr's mages were the first to suspect Nyro was not who she appeared to be, provided more resistance, and saw their people culled in greater numbers, so they probably have somewhat fewer mages. Askaheimr and Snaerverold have much smaller populations to begin with, so the resistance in those kingdoms might have a handful of mages each.

"However, they have heard that Nyro has imprisoned many mages in a fortress in Snaerverold. How many, they cannot say. Perhaps hundreds. Nor do they know the location of this fortress. They'll need to contact the other directors to ascertain their willingness to send aid."

"He's telling the truth," Shadow told Allison. "But the director, whose name is Gyda, did ask how you were able to travel here so quickly. Asmund hinted that you were responsible for that, but didn't explain how you did it."

"How soon can they contact the other directors?" Allison asked.

"I will reach out to them by mirror as soon as we are done here," Gyda said.

"You speak the common tongue?" Allison said.

"Not so common for my people, but yes," she said. "One of my advisers lives here. His people are preparing a feast for us now. You and Asmund are welcome to wait for us in the dining room, and we will join you once we have reached the others."

As if on cue, one of the household staff appeared by the doorway. Allison and Asmund followed her to a spacious dining room with cathedral ceilings.

"That went better than I could have hoped," Asmund said as they took their seats.

"If we can find and liberate the mages Nyro captured, this could make a big difference in the war," Allison said.

The staff poured wine for them, and Allison and Asmund drank and talked while they waited for the others. Dinner was served, and moments later, Gyda and her lieutenant joined them.

"My counterpart in Mestrland refuses to take part in your war," Gyda told them. "She does not trust the humans and believes if we can liberate the mages being held in Snaerverold, we should have enough aid without her.

"The director in Ellrivollr does not believe we will succeed and is not willing to sacrifice his few remaining mages to our cause," she continued with a sigh. "Askaheimr is not willing to part with the few mages they have, and I have not been able to reach anyone in Snaerverold."

"Should that concern us?" Asmund asked.

"I don't think so," Gyda said. "The director there tends to be reclusive. I'm sure we'll make contact eventually, but it typically takes a couple of days."

Allison enjoyed the food and the wine. Thankfully, the fare wasn't as spicy as what Asmund had served. The wine was strong, and she felt it going to her head.

Once they'd finished eating, Gyda asked Allison how she and Asmund had reached them so quickly. She didn't see how it could hurt, so she pulled the pyramid out of the void, holding it in her palm to show them.

"I've heard of these, but I've never seen one," Gyda said. "My understanding is that when our mages came to your people's aid against Nyro in ancient times, she used an artifact like this to evade them at first. They found a way to prevent the portal magic from working. It was the only reason they were able to keep her from escaping the final battle."

"That must be where Nyro got the idea," Allison said pensively. She explained how she'd woven spells into the protective barrier around her island that prevented anyone else's portal magic from penetrating it.

"Do you know where the pyramids came from?" Gyda asked. "I do not believe Nyro created them, but neither have I ever learned of their origins."

"I've always assumed she took them from the elves," Allison said.

"I don't believe so," Gyda replied. "The only time I've ever heard of them being used was in the battle with Nyro." Allison had never given this much thought. She'd have to ask Sage about it when she returned to Stoutwall—if anyone knew their history, she would. "My mentor told me Nyro used a pyramid to bring monsters from other realms to fight against our people in the war."

Allison knew the pyramid could be used to access the spirit realm. And Khaldun had encountered a group of monks who tried to use it to release one of their "gods" from some other place. So it didn't come as much of a surprise that Nyro would have used it that way. They'd have to remain vigilant—she could do it again in the coming battle. "Your mentor participated in the ancient war with Nyro?" she asked.

"Yes. He helped cast the spells that incarcerated Nyro and her Sacred Circle in the land of Pytha. And he was one of the last surviving mages from that era before Nyro assassinated him during her recent rise to power."

"I'm sorry to hear that," Allison said. "Did he teach you the magic they used to imprison her?"

"No, I'm afraid not," she said with a sigh. "I believe he intended to eventually, but never had the chance. The mages who contained Nyro in Pytha were the most powerful among us. Much knowledge was lost when she assassinated them and their protégés. None of our surviving mages have matched their prowess."

"That's a shame," Allison said. She'd wondered about this—it was clear none of the elvish mages they'd faced in battle possessed that kind of power. "Given the other directors' unwillingness to send aid, I'm surprised you were so agreeable."

"The Drengrvollri have always been the most warlike of our people," Gyda said. "In old times, we were the ones who conquered the rest of the continent. Masquerading as Estrid, Nyro tapped into that tradition to launch her own conquest of the other kingdoms. And now, those of us who remain free want revenge, no matter the cost."

"I'll drink to that," Allison said, raising her glass. The others clinked their glasses with hers, and she finished her wine.

She sat up late with Asmund and Gyda, and the two elves shared stories about Drengrvollr's glory days. Allison liked these two. She could read them and knew Gyda was being honest with her. If they ever managed to defeat Nyro and restore peace in Anoria, she'd love to return here with Jezebel one day and learn more about their history and culture.

Gyda tried reaching someone in Snaerverold again the next day with no luck. Allison had checked in with Jezebel the previous night to let her know how it was going. And she spoke with her and the girls a couple of times that day. Two more days went by before Gyda finally reached someone. It was one of the director's advisers, not the director himself, but he spoke on his behalf and arranged a time and place for them to meet. He started out trying to arrange for something in a few weeks' time, but Gyda told him they could be there as soon as that same day. They settled on the following morning.

Gyda told them it would be best for her to travel with Allison and Asmund on her own. For one thing, she didn't want to expose her lieutenant to any of the other directors. If anything were to happen to her, he would take over in Drengrvollr. But moreover, Snaerverold was cold, snowy, and inhospitable. She saw no reason to subject her guards to such conditions.

Before bed, Allison spoke with Jezebel by mirror and let her know the plan. Early the next morning, she sat down at the table with Gyda, and one of the staff brought them a map. She needed some sense of where they were going, so Gyda pointed out their approximate destination. Like last time, Allison sent Shadow to get a look at the area.

The household staff provided the two elves with heavy furs. Allison wouldn't need any. Once they were ready, the three of them went out on the terrace, and Allison opened a portal to Snaerverold.

The moment the gateway opened, a blast of icy wind nearly knocked them off their feet. Allison called fire to heat up her armor and pushed her way through the portal, Asmund and Gyda right behind her. Closing the gateway, Allison retrieved her helmet and facemask from their pockets, donned those, and heated them as well.

The wind was far too strong to allow for a carpet flight, so they trudged across the snowy landscape on foot. Allison had chosen a location very close to the meeting point. It was unlikely that anyone would see their arrival through the blowing snow.

They spent a minute struggling against the gale before Allison finally cast a spell to repel wind—the same one used for carpet flights. Despite their proximity, it still took them twenty minutes to reach their destination, toiling through the snow the entire time.

The structure they were seeking didn't become visible until they were almost on top of it. It was squat and semi-spherical and appeared to be constructed from blocks of snow or ice. The whole thing was glowing as if there were a fire inside. There was a hatchway leading to the interior, and Allison followed Gyda and Asmund inside.

They found a lone figure sitting across from them, with a roaring fire in the middle. He spoke to the other two in elvish for a moment.

"This is Einar," Asmund told Allison. "He is the director of the resistance movement in Snaerverold. We've explained the situation, and he says he doesn't have any mages he could send to Anoria. However, he is willing to tell us where to find Nyro's ice fortress. He says the last he knew, she was keeping over three hundred mages there."

"*That was an accurate and complete translation,*" Shadow told her.

"*Three hundred?*" Allison repeated out loud. "I won't be able to get that many through the portal." She could keep one open for only a few seconds. Maybe eight to ten people could pass through at once? She could open additional ones, but portal magic took an enormous amount of power. After opening a few in a row, she'd need time to replenish herself before she could open any more.

"There may not be that many left," Asmund said. "His information is at least a year old. And Nyro's had her people torturing the captives."

"We'll have to go there and see for ourselves," Gyda said. "He's provided the location, so we can proceed there immediately."

Once Gyda had explained where to find the ice fortress, the three of them bade their host farewell and went outside. After the calm and quiet inside the dome, the conditions outside were an assault on Allison's senses. She cast her air spell to shield them from the wind again, and sent Shadow to stake out their next destination.

The demon had no trouble finding the fortress, standing like daggers of ice on a bluff high above the sea. She wanted to get a look at the place with her own eyes, so they'd have to travel to a nearby plateau first, then figure out a way inside.

Summoning her power, Allison opened a portal to the plateau. They walked through, and she closed it behind them, tucking the pyramid into the void. The wind here was fiercer and colder than it had been outside Einar's dwelling, and Allison had to reinforce her protective spell.

It was daytime, but the blowing snow and cloud cover were so thick, it seemed like dusk. The ice fortress loomed out of the darkness like a giant's icy crown. Allison didn't see any obvious way inside. She sent Shadow ahead to scout the structure and its surroundings, and they waited for her report.

CHAPTER TWENTY
ICE FORTRESS

he fortress itself is heavily fortified. Walls of stone covered with several feet of ice. Two sets of gates that appear to be frozen shut under many layers of ice. There is a postern gate but it is buried under a dozen feet of solid ice. The windows have thick steel bars embedded in the stone. If Nyro ever comes here, she must use her pyramid to open a portal, because there is no physical way inside."

Allison told Gyda and Asmund what Shadow had reported.

"This fortress looks like something the ancient Drengrvollri would have built," Gyda said. "My guess is that it sat here abandoned for centuries. Nyro has probably only *ever* accessed it using her pyramid."

"There is a holding cell in the undercroft and that's where they're keeping the mages," Shadow continued. "Only thirty-six remain alive, many of those on death's doorstep."

"Thirty-six out of three hundred?"

"That estimate may have been exaggerated. There are many dead mages in there, too, but no more than a hundred or so."

"What about guards?"

"This is where it gets interesting. There are beasts that I would have to describe as snow trolls."

"Snow trolls?" Allison repeated.

"Giant, human-shaped creatures, taller even than the elves, but much bulkier. Like Shatter, but with lots of flab and fur."

"Wonderful. How many?"

"A dozen total."

"So we'll have to open a portal in the undercroft, kill or incapacitate the guards, then free the mages and take them back to Stoutwall."

"It may not be that simple. The holding cell is inside a protective barrier, like the one at the university and Nyro's island castle."

"Ah. So if she's used the spells to stop portal magic, we'll have to hope one of the guards knows the spell to get inside."

"I can't tell if she's added preventative spells to the barrier. You'll have to try using the pyramid and see what happens."

"She might not have—I can't imagine she expected us to come here. This may be much simpler if that's the case. It would save us from having to fight the snow trolls."

"I'm afraid not. Four of them are inside the barrier. And it looks like they've been feeding on the dead mages. There are many piles of bones."

"How lovely." Allison gave Gyda and Asmund the news. "Could Nyro have brought the snow trolls here from one of the other realms using the pyramid?"

"No, they're native to Snaerverold," she said with a grin. "I've never encountered one before, though."

"I wonder why Nyro hasn't taken them into battle," Allison said.

"She might have tried, but they can't survive anywhere warmer," Gyda told her.

Allison sent Shadow back inside the fortress to the holding cell. Viewing the area from her perspective, she could open a portal directly into the chamber, they could take out the four guards, and hope the others didn't know the spell to get inside.

Allison thought of letting Jezebel know what they were about to do—it would be good to give those in Stoutwall at least some warning that a bunch of elf mages were about to appear on the grounds. But there was no way she'd be able to hear her over the roaring of the wind, so she didn't bother.

Withdrawing the pyramid and her sword from the void, Allison summoned her full power and opened the portal. She had no trouble getting through the protective barrier. The three of them hurried through it and she closed it behind her, tucking the pyramid into the void. Their sudden appearance seemed to startle mages and guards alike, but in the case of the guards, it lasted only a moment. They roared in unison and converged on their position.

Allison stepped into the first one's advance, using her sword to remove his head. Blood sprayed everywhere as the corpse hit the stone floor. Another rushed her and she called fire, incinerating it from within. The monster screamed until the flames abruptly cut off the sound. She turned to see that Asmund and Gyda had taken out the other two guards.

The rest of the guards stood outside the barrier, roaring at them, but unable to get inside. It didn't seem like these beasts possessed *any* magic, much less the spell to get through the barrier. Asmund and Gyda spoke to the captive mages. Shadow told Allison that they were letting them know what was happening, and that they'd be taking them to the human continent. And that fighting alongside the humans against Nyro was the one condition being placed upon their liberation. None of them objected.

By the look of them, they were all close to death. Mostly, it didn't appear they'd eaten in a long time, or at least not enough to sustain them. Hopefully they could rectify that in short order once they got to Stoutwall.

Gyda told her they were ready. Asmund volunteered to go through the portal with the first group to let anyone on the other side know what was happening. None of these mages spoke the common tongue, so without Asmund, it was possible the castle guards would think this was an invasion.

Summoning her power, Allison created a portal back to Stoutwall. Asmund made it through with eight of the mages before she had to close it again. They repeated the process thrice more, and Allison had to close the portal a little sooner each time.

"This is taking more out of me than I thought," she said after getting only four mages through her last portal. "I don't know if I can open another one." Twelve mages remained, plus Gyda and her.

"Rest for a minute," Gyda said. "The guards don't seem able to penetrate the barrier, so we have time."

Allison nodded, taking a few deep breaths. Finally, she tried opening another portal, but it was no use. She needed more recovery time.

"*Can you draw power from these other mages the way you've done to tuck armies into the void?*" Shadow asked.

"*That's a good idea.*" Allison told Gyda what she was planning, and she relayed the message to the others. Calling on their collective power, Allison opened another portal, and they managed to get eight of the twelve mages through before she had to close it. Allison collapsed, exhausted from the effort. "I don't think I can do that again. We're going to have to wait."

Gyda helped her sit up against the wall. She should let Jezebel know what was happening, so she pulled her mirror out of its pocket. But at that moment, she felt a massive wave of power wash over her. A portal opened outside the barrier and Nyro walked through it.

"Oh, shit," Allison muttered, struggling to her feet. One of the guards must have alerted her.

"So you've found my hidden fortress," Nyro said with a mocking smile. "And transported most of the remaining mages to Stoutwall. Clever girl." Allison hadn't thought to close her mind, so she did it then. "Opening portals is grueling work, isn't it? Well, no matter. These fools refused to serve me, and I've long since extracted any useful information out of them. I left them here to die, with the understanding that I'd liberate any of them who agreed to enter my service. Shocking that not a single one of them took me up on my offer."

Allison tried summoning her power, expecting it to be futile, but discovering that she could wield the basic forces without any trouble—only the magical force was depleted. She tried hitting Nyro with a fire spell, but only portal magic could get through the barrier.

Nyro chuckled. "No, that won't work. This unexpected visit has been pleasant, but I have other matters demanding my attention. Farewell, Princess." She held out both arms, and Allison felt the stone floor starting to shake. Nyro had triggered an earthquake.

Allison sent Shadow after her, and the demon hit Nyro with fire and lightning spells. It was a wasted effort, though. Opening another portal, Nyro rushed through it, closing it behind her.

The snow trolls fled, disappearing up the stairs. Allison tried opening a portal again as the quaking grew stronger, but even drawing power from the others, she couldn't manage it yet. A section of the opposite wall by the stairway collapsed, opening the undercroft to the elements. One of the elf mages screamed, but the sound of the roaring wind drowned him out almost immediately. The barrier spell kept the weather out, but not the sound.

Allison tried again and again to open a portal, summoning every ounce of her power, but it wasn't enough. Her ability to harness the magical force was completely spent. The tremors continued, and the floor outside the barrier disappeared, exposing the abyss below. And a moment later, their chamber broke free and plummeted into the chasm.

Khaldun and Mira joined Jezebel and the girls for breakfast in the great hall, and the princess told them about Allure and Battleaxe's trip to Spanbrook.

"That's incredible," Khaldun said when she was done. "Nyro found a way to imbue armor with magic that subjects its wearer to a compliance spell?"

"So it seems," she said with a shrug.

"That does explain a lot," Mira said. "Nyro could force those people to fight for her. How awful!"

"I'd like to get a look at that armor if you don't mind," Khaldun said.

"Of course," Jezebel said. "I have it in my chambers—come up with me after we're done here."

Khaldun nodded. "I do hope Allison can rescue those people." He had to agree with Allure that the logistics of that situation would not work out otherwise. With anyone but Allison, it would simply take too much time.

Khaldun went up to Jezebel's chambers with her after breakfast, and she gave him the breastplate Allure had brought back from

Spanbrook. He left the castle with it, and the moment he left Mira's null, he felt its magic spring to life. Spending a few minutes examining the spells, he was sure Allure was right. He had to give Nyro credit—she might be evil, but this was some highly complex and clever magic. Khaldun was sure it never would have occurred to him to even attempt such a thing. Not that he could pull it off if it had.

Once he'd returned the armor to Jezebel, Khaldun headed out to the army camp to begin the day's transformations. This was the most tedious and exhausting task he'd ever undertaken. And he seemed to have reached a plateau after that first day. Despite working as fast as he could, he only managed to complete the magic with just over one hundred soldiers.

Khaldun and Mira sat with Imani, Battleaxe, and Mist at dinner that night, and Allure joined them halfway through their meal. Battleaxe told him they were heading into the city to hit the tavern after dinner, and invited Khaldun and Allure to join them. Khaldun felt bad that Mira could never go due to the need for her null. But he was also feeling wiped out from all the work, so he declined. Allure agreed to go, though, which was unusual. He hoped that meant she was starting to feel better.

Mira and Khaldun retired to their chambers, deciding to go to bed early. They made love for a while first, and then Khaldun drifted off to sleep. After what felt like only a few minutes, he started awake. He didn't know what had woken him until he realized someone was knocking. Answering the door, he found Battleaxe standing there. He was about to move into the corridor to talk to her when Mira sat up and invited the sorcerer inside.

"Sorry to disturb you," Battleaxe said once Khaldun had closed the door behind her. "I was wondering if the two of you might be willing to talk to Allure."

"Why, what's wrong?" Khaldun asked.

"She, ah, had quite a lot to drink. And she's pretty small and doesn't drink often, so, you know how that goes."

"Oh, no, is she ill?" Mira asked.

"She was, but that's not our real concern. I think she's still extremely upset about Semblant. And it, ah, might be my fault, but she kind of lost it at the tavern. Started lighting things on fire, saying that Nyro's going to burn down the whole continent anyway, so she might as well get it started for her…"

"Wait, how is this your fault?" Khaldun asked.

"I'm the one who's been harassing her to go to the tavern with us, and after the other night, I should have known better," Battleaxe said, and he realized she was tearing up. He'd never seen her cry before. "She had to fight Semblant, for fuck's sake. I should have known better than to let her drink. Nobody would be in their right mind after something like that."

"It's not your fault," Mira said, sliding out of bed and gripping Battleaxe's arm. "Allure's been through a lot—we all have. You were only trying to help her get through it."

"Where is Allure now?" Khaldun asked.

"In her chambers," she said. "Mist is sitting with her. She's stopped trying to burn things down, at least. But Mist and I are out of our depth, and let's just say all the alcohol isn't helping matters."

"We'd be happy to help," Mira said.

Khaldun and Mira went over to Allure's chambers with Battleaxe. Mist's relief was palpable. Khaldun suggested that the other two sorcerers go sleep it off, and he and Mira sat down with Allure at her table.

"I'm sorry they woke you up," she said with a belch. "Honestly, I'll be all right. I feel so foolish."

"Facing Semblant could not have been easy," Mira said. "You can't blame yourself—anyone would be struggling after that."

Allure burst into tears, and Mira slid her chair closer and hugged her.

"I still c-can't believe he's gone," she said with a hiccup. "In my mind, I always imagined we'd grow old together. Never did I think I'd have to live without him." She sobbed, and Mira rubbed her back. "I thought about summoning him after he died. But I decided against it. He deserves his peace, and I have to learn to let him go. Bringing him back as a demon would never be the same."

"Losing someone like that is never easy," Khaldun said. "I still remember how much it hurt when I lost Nomad. It was devastating. He was like a father to me, and I never thought he'd die so young. It took me a few years to accept that. I still miss him to this day, but the grief has diminished over the years. You *will* feel better in time."

Allure cried quietly for a few moments before saying, "I miss him *so* much. Gods, I hate Nyro for doing this to me." She broke down sobbing again, and Mira held her tight.

Allure calmed down after a few minutes, and sitting up in her chair, met Khaldun's gaze with an odd expression on her face. She started to say something but then shook her head.

"What is it?" he asked.

"It's… nothing. Too much to ask. I couldn't."

"We'll do whatever we can to help," Mira said. "Please. What do you need?"

Allure giggled nervously, then started crying again. "I just… Khaldun's a shapeshifter now. After the other night, I would give anything to be with Semblant one last time…"

Khaldun's eyes went wide, and he shot Mira a pleading look. "I don't think I could—"

"I'm not asking you to sleep with me," Allure said. "Just hold me."

Khaldun was about to refuse, but Mira said, "Yes, of course he can do that."

He didn't want to be unfaithful to Mira, despite what she said. "I'm not sure I'm comfortable—"

"It's all right," Allure said. "It was selfish of me to ask."

"Give us a moment," Mira said, getting to her feet. She took Khaldun by the hand and led him out of the room, closing the door behind her. "The first few nights after I returned to Blacksand when my father and brother died, were some of the darkest of my entire life. I would have given *anything* to hold you once more. You can do this for her."

"I don't want to violate your trust," he said, caressing her cheek with one hand. "I've never been disloyal and I'm not about to start now."

"I appreciate that, but you won't be. She'll be holding Semblant, not you. And I trust you. Please, she's one of our dearest friends and she needs this."

Khaldun nodded. "All right. I'll need to go outside to transform."

Mira went back into Allure's room, and Khaldun headed out to the grounds. He'd known Semblant well and had no trouble taking on his appearance. Going back inside the castle, he checked his reflection in one of the windows and was satisfied with what he saw.

Running back up to Allure's chambers, he found Mira lying with her in the bed, leaning against the headboard. Lifting her gaze, Allure got a look at him and sobbed, holding out both arms. Khaldun slid into the bed next to her and held her tight. Mira left them alone, and Allure sobbed into his chest for several minutes, squeezing his arms with both hands. Khaldun said nothing, just lying there and rubbing her back.

Allure calmed down eventually, and after crying softly for several more minutes, seemed to have drifted off to sleep. Khaldun slid her over to the other side of the bed as gently as he could, lying her head on her pillow, before slipping out of bed. Allure was snoring quietly. He left the castle to retake his normal appearance before returning to his own chambers. Mira was lying in bed, still awake, with the oil lamp providing some light.

"How is she?" Mira asked as he slid into bed next to her and extinguished the lamp.

"Asleep," he told her, as she cuddled against him.

They lay quietly for a few minutes, and he thought Mira had drifted off, until she said, "You're a good man. That's what I love most about you."

Khaldun kissed her, and they went to sleep.

Allure sat with them at breakfast the next morning, thanking them and apologizing profusely for her behavior the previous night. Mira and Khaldun both assured her there was nothing to apologize for, and that they were glad to help. She told them she'd be staying away from the tavern for a while.

Khaldun spent every waking hour working on the troop transformations. He didn't get any faster, but it seemed to take a little less energy as time went on. Jezebel kept them updated on Allison's progress with the elves, but there wasn't much to report at first. After a few days, she told them Allison would be going to Snaerverold with Asmund and the leader of the Drengrvollri resistance movement. They were hoping the director there could tell them how to find Nyro's prison fortress, which might hold hundreds of elf mages.

That night, Khaldun and Mira went up to Jezebel's chambers with her and the girls. Jezebel hadn't heard from Allison again but knew she'd probably have left for Snaerverold by then—early morning for Allison, but after dark in Stoutwall.

The mood in the princess's chambers was tense but giddily hopeful. As the night wore on, though, with no further word from Allison, it grew steadily more anxious. Khaldun suggested contacting Allison by mirror, but Jezebel didn't want to interrupt her in case they were in the middle of something important.

After a couple more hours, Khaldun started to fear the worst. Alanna and Leda had grown extremely worried, and while Jezebel tried to express hope, Khaldun could tell it was only for her daughters' sake.

There was a knock at the door, and Jezebel answered it. It was one of the steward's messengers. "I'm sorry to disturb you, Your Highness, but the elf mage, Asmund, has appeared on the grounds with several other elves—"

Jezebel was out the door before he could finish. She turned around, though, reminding the girls they were not to leave the castle under any circumstances, before hurrying out again. Mira stayed behind as Khaldun hurried off after Jezebel. They found Asmund with eight sickly-looking elves in the entry hall, along with two of Augustine's house guards.

"Where's Allison?" Jezebel asked, gripping Asmund by the arm.

"She should be here soon," he said. "We found Nyro's fortress. There were too many mages for Allison to send through all at once. So I came here with this first group. More should be on their way."

Jezebel hurried out to the grounds, Asmund and Khaldun right behind her. Several more guards followed them out. They ran into others escorting seven additional mages toward the castle, but no sign of Allison. A minute later, Khaldun felt a powerful spell somewhere nearby and spotted a portal forming. Five more elves emerged through it, and Khaldun caught a glimpse of a stone chamber beyond before the portal disappeared.

Only a minute later, yet another portal formed, but this time, only four elves came through. "I see her!" Jezebel yelled. Khaldun knew she was referring to Allison and he spotted her, too, right before the portal closed, recognizing her at first only because she was holding the pyramid in one hand. He'd forgotten for a moment that he'd transformed her to appear Shifari.

Several more minutes passed without any more portals forming. Jezebel started fretting. "What the hell is going on? Where is she?"

"Don't forget, portal magic takes a lot of power," Khaldun told her. "Opening so many in a row must have drained her."

"Yes, that's it exactly," Asmund said. "She told us this would happen. Give it some time."

Finally, another portal formed, and eight more elves stepped through before it disappeared. Asmund spoke to them in elvish for a moment before a couple of the guards escorted them toward the castle.

"They said Princess Allison needed to draw power from them to open that portal," he told Khaldun and Jezebel. "Only four more mages remain in the holding cell, plus Gyda, the leader from Drengrvollr, and Her Highness. She may need a little more time before attempting one final transport."

Several more minutes turned into a half hour, and still, there was no sign of Allison or the others. Jezebel tried contacting her by mirror, but couldn't reach her. Khaldun tried to talk Jezebel into returning to her chambers, but she refused.

Suddenly, he noticed a spark of light bobbing around by the castle. It moved toward them, finally becoming the glowing outline of a female form.

"Shadow," Khaldun said.

"There's been an accident," the demon told them.

"What kind of *accident*?" Jezebel demanded, a note of panic in her voice.

Shadow explained that Nyro had shown up before Allison could open the final portal. She'd caused an earthquake, destroying the fortress. The holding cell had plummeted to the rocky shore far below, with Allison, Gyda, and the other four mages still inside. The barrier spell had held, providing them some protection from the fall. But it had included some of the fortress's rocky foundation, and that had broken loose, hitting those inside the cell. One of the elf mages had died from a shattered skull. Allison and Gyda had managed to call air, protecting them from the worst of it.

"They're alive and they're safe," Shadow concluded. "Allison's mirror shattered on impact, so she won't be able to contact you that way. She needs to sleep for a while—that may be the best way for her to replenish her power before attempting to open the final portal. Try not to worry. I'll watch over them until they're ready to return."

Chapter Twenty-One
Laying Plans

llison watched from Shadow's perspective as she updated Khaldun and Jezebel, then the demon returned to Snaerverold. It was frustrating being trapped like this, but there was nothing more she could do. Other than creating a portal, there was no way to breach the barrier enclosing them without knowing the spell. The chamber had landed mostly intact, with the loose section of stone wall now forming a debris pile. They were wedged between boulders on the rocky shoreline, and sea spray kept hitting the barrier. The magic allowed air and fine particles to pass through, so Allison felt a cold mist hit her face every time a wave crashed on the shore.

The three surviving elf mages had sustained minor injuries during the fall. Gyda was tending to their needs the best she could. They'd moved the bodies of the snow trolls and the dead elf as far away as they could. Allison was lying on an unbroken section of the stone floor, now pitched at an uncomfortable angle, hoping to get some sleep. This was the best way to replenish the magic she needed to create a portal.

"*How are you?*" Shadow asked her.

"As well as can be expected," Allison replied. "*I miss my girls. Did you ever have children?*"

"*No. We talked about it, but Nyro and I were both necromancers, so neither of us could conceive a child. Yours are lovely, though. Spitfires, the both of them. I'm sure they have a bright future ahead of them.*"

"If they have any future at all," Allison said with a sigh. "*I fear for them, Shadow. I fear for everyone in Anoria if Nyro prevails.*"

"We'll make sure she doesn't. I believe the universe conspired to bring the two of us together for this very purpose."

Allison was glad Shadow was here; her presence comforted her. It almost felt like having her mother back again.

"*I need to sleep, but I can't quiet my mind. I should have Gyda spell me under.*" She hardly knew the woman, and the thought of allowing her to cast any magic on her was distressing. Yet if she fell asleep on her own, she'd be defenseless against Gyda anyway. And Shadow would be vigilant.

"*I can take care of that for you, if you'll allow me,*" Shadow said. "*Don't worry, I will watch over you while you sleep.*"

Shadow cast her spell and Allison drifted off immediately.

Allison awoke to find nothing had changed. With the intense weather outside their chamber, it wasn't any darker or lighter than it had been before. "How long was I out?" she asked Gyda.

"It's hard to say. Several hours, I believe."

"*It is dusk,*" Shadow told her in her mind.

"I feel better," Allison said, getting to her feet. "We should try going to Stoutwall."

"I'm ready," Gyda agreed.

Removing the pyramid from the void, Allison held it before her and summoned her full power. It was still difficult, like lifting a massive weight, but she created a portal. She followed Gyda and the three other mages through it, letting it close behind her. Gazing around the grounds outside Castle Stoutwall, she breathed a sigh of relief. It was just after dawn here.

Augustine had posted extra guards outside the castle, and a few of them came rushing over to them. They escorted the new arrivals inside. The steward met them in the entry hall, assuring Allison he would see to the elvish mages' needs. Allison hurried upstairs to her chambers.

Jezebel woke up when Allison opened the door. "Oh, thank the stars you're back!"

Allison sat next to her in bed and held her tight, crying tears of joy as relief filled her very soul. "I'm sorry for putting you through this ordeal. Opening so many portals drained me even more than I had imagined."

Allison went to say good morning to the girls, waking them from their slumber. They welcomed her back as she embraced them. She spent a few minutes with them, then they lay down to go back to sleep.

"We have much to discuss," Jezebel said as Allison returned to their room. "Are you hungry?"

"Famished," she said with a grin. "Let's talk over breakfast."

Heading down to the great hall, they sat down at a table with Khaldun, Mira, and Allure. She told them more about her trip to Drengrvollr and Snaerverold, and they updated her on everything that had happened during her absence.

"I would very much like to rescue the prisoners from Spanbrook," Allison said. "And I believe you're correct that tucking them into the void in one shot is probably the only way to get them all. Yet I remain unsure if I possess sufficient power."

"Nyro moved more than that when she retreated after the battle here," Allure said. "And you're nearly her equal now. I believe you can do this."

"It's worth an attempt, at least," Khaldun said.

Allison took a deep breath. "I'll want a couple of you with me for backup. Once they realize what we've done, they're sure to come after us. And I won't be able to use a portal to return here." Nothing in the void would go with her if she did that.

"Battleaxe and I can accompany you," Allure said. "We'll want the others to remain behind to maintain our defenses here."

"The extra thirty-five mages from Snaerverold should make a difference, I would think," said Mira. "They're as powerful as a typical sorcerer, aren't they?"

"Yes, that's true," said Jezebel. "They'll probably need a couple of days to build up their strength, but once they're ready, we should be able to send Mist and Sage to Spanbrook, too."

"We could send some of the dragons, too," Mira suggested. "It'll take them a couple of days to get there. So if they head out today, and the rest of you use a portal, you could all arrive at the same time."

"That would be terrific," Allison said. "Even if they send all seven reanimated elves after us on carpets, the dragons would give us the advantage."

"They could have some of the regular elf mages equipped with carpets by now, too," Khaldun pointed out.

"Yes, I've been wondering about that," said Jezebel. "Camilla hasn't reported any increase in carpet activity, though. And any new riders would need some time to practice."

"She could be taking them elsewhere for that," Allure said. "She must suspect that we're watching Spanbrook."

"Yes, that could be," Allison said. "We should recall Camilla and the band of survivors she encountered. I can station a few of my minor spirits there to keep an eye on things for us going forward."

"I'll let Camilla know," Jezebel said.

"We should take care of them first, before the prisoners," Allure suggested. "Nyro's people aren't likely to notice *their* absence."

"Agreed," said Allison. "You were able to finish the spike to contain Nyro?"

"It's ready to go," said Allure. "We'll need to come up with an alternative plan soon if Alanna won't be participating."

Jezebel caught Allison's gaze. "We still need to discuss this further."

They finished breakfast, and Allison asked if Khaldun could make a new mirror for her. She knew the spells well enough, but his mirror was already connected with all the others, so it would be easier for him to take care of this for her. Khaldun offered to change her back to her original appearance. But Allison told him she liked this new look and wanted to stick with it a while longer. After that, she went to speak with Gyda. She and Asmund were sitting at the head table with Augustine and his family.

"We'll need to return to Drengrvollr to transport the rest of your mages here," she said to the elf mage.

"I will contact the local leaders and see how many they're willing to send," Gyda said. "It may not be many. Most of the groups have only one and won't want to go completely defenseless. But I will see what I can do."

Allison and Jezebel returned to their chambers and roused the girls. Once those two had gone down to the great hall for breakfast, they sat down at their table.

"So, what do you think about allowing Alanna to take part in our trap for Nyro?" Allison asked.

"I still don't like it," Jezebel said with a sigh. "But she would give us our greatest chance of success, there's no denying that. Nyro craves power, and adding a null to her arsenal would give her capabilities she's never had before. That's sure to be tempting. And given Alanna's penchant for wandering off on her own, she would be more credible than Mira."

"Not only that but if she did take her, she'd be sure to bind her once she triggers her transformation," Allison said. "And if she doesn't bring out her null until after that, she would end up with a *bound* null, which is impossible with Mira. I'm not sure if that's feasible or not, but it would only make Alanna an even more attractive target."

"I hadn't thought of that," Jezebel said. "You think we should do this, then?"

Allison took a deep breath. "I believe we should let Alanna decide. She's old enough to have some say in this. We weren't much older when you traveled the continent in search of Enigma. And that was only to save *me*. Now, we're talking about the lives of every man, woman, and child in Anoria."

"I feel the same," Jezebel said, "and I was hoping you would talk me out of it."

"My apologies," Allison said with a grin.

"We should discuss this with her as soon as possible. And we must take every precaution to ensure her safety."

"We will," said Allison. "But it won't be without risk. Nyro remains the strongest mage the world has ever seen. She's clever and persistent. If there's a way out of our trap, she'll find it."

"Then we'll have to make sure there isn't one," Jezebel said.

"Yes," Allison agreed. "Now, the only trouble with leaving this to Alanna is that she can't very well make an informed decision if she doesn't know the facts. And unless she can close her mind, we can't risk her knowing the plan lest Nyro read it in her thoughts."

"Let's take Alanna to Allure first," Jezebel said. "If Alanna *can* close her mind, this becomes a moot point."

Alanna and Leda returned after breakfast. Allison told Alanna that she was taking her to see Allure.

"For what?" she asked suspiciously.

"Some, ah, extra work on your magic," Allison told her.

"Why doesn't Leda have to go?"

"Because I can already do void magic, and you can't even cast an illusion," Leda said.

"Brat!" Alanna said.

Allison dragged her out of the room, taking her to see Allure. They found the sorcerer in her chambers, and she invited them inside.

"We were wondering if you could try teaching Alanna to close her mind," Allison said. "In case she were to encounter Nyro again."

"Are you expecting her to attack again?" Alanna said, giving her a suspicious look.

"It's Nyro, so you never know what she might be planning," Allison told her.

"I'd be happy to help," Allure said.

The three of them sat down at her table, and Allure moved her chair so she was facing Alanna. Placing one hand on either side of her head, she said, "I'm reading you now. Can you feel it?"

"Yes," Alanna said. "Just like I could last time."

"You sensed me reading you when I found the potential null inside of you?"

"Sure, I did. It's the same thing I feel when I talk to Sigrid."

"That's intriguing," said Allure. "Can you stop me from reading you?"

"I think so," Alanna said, furrowing her brow in concentration. "Like that?"

Allure gasped. "Yes, exactly like that," she said, opening her eyes. "She did this as easily as Mira," she said to Allison. "It must have something to do with their connection to the dragons."

Allure had Alanna repeat the skill a few more times to be sure, and Alanna could do it on command. She could even stop her from reading her in the first place.

"That settles it," Allure said. "There's no reason to keep her in the dark."

"In the dark about what?" Alanna demanded.

Taking a deep breath, Allison told her about their plan, emphasizing how dangerous it would be. "Mother Jezebel and I want to leave this decision to you. If you're willing to—"

"Did you truly think I would refuse an opportunity like this?" Alanna said.

Allison had to laugh. "I would have been shocked if you had. But you must understand the risks involved. This is *Nyro*—"

"Yes, yes, I am well aware. I have never been so frightened in my life as I was when she chased me on her carpet. But I also understand what's at stake and I want to help."

"I'm proud of you," Allison said, getting to her feet and embracing her, trying hard to fight back the tears. "You must understand how important it is to keep all of this to yourself. Outside of the three of us, only Khaldun, Mira, and Mother Jezebel know everything, and we need to keep it that way."

"I can't tell Leda?"

"Definitely not," Allison said. "And you can't taunt her about knowing something she doesn't either. Act like nothing is afoot whatsoever."

"This is going to be difficult," she said with a grin. Allison gave her a stern look, and she added, "Don't worry, I promise I'll be on my best behavior."

Alanna and Allison returned to their chambers and found Mira there chatting with Jezebel. Alanna went into the other room with Leda, and Allison sat at the table with the other two.

"I've spoken to Kashi from the dragon riders," Mira told her. "Of course, I can't leave the castle, so I had to send a messenger to invite him here," she added with a sigh.

"It must be frustrating being stuck in the castle," Allison said.

"It is, but it's for the best," she said. "The worst part is not being able to ride Magna. He visits me in the courtyard, but I can tell he misses flying with me almost as much as I do. Anyway, Kashi will assemble a team of five dragons to leave for Spanbrook as soon as I send word. Are we ready for them to depart?"

"Yes, I don't see why not," Allison said, turning to Jezebel.

"I agree. The sooner we can rescue those people, the better."

"I'll let Kashi know right away," Mira said, getting to her feet.

"Have them meet us at Rockhedge," Allison said. "That should be far enough from the castle for them to avoid the elves' notice."

Mira nodded and headed out to find another messenger.

That evening, after dinner, Allison joined Mira and Khaldun in Allure's chambers to discuss laying the trap for Nyro. Khaldun had prepared Allison's new mirror, too. Allison took it from him, tucking it into the pocket in her armor.

"As we discussed last time," said Khaldun, "we must draw Nyro into the castle, expand Mira's null to eliminate her magic, embed the spike in her flesh, extinguish the null, and only then kill the elvish body."

"And the key to this whole plan is to make Alanna's presence believable," said Allison, "so that Nyro doesn't anticipate the trap. We should wait until the elvish reinforcements arrive. If we remain here, her next move will be to attack Stoutwall again. Once her forces arrive, we can evacuate everyone—the army, all the castle occupants, everyone. Tuck them into the void and take them to Highgate."

"Only you can take so many at once," Khaldun pointed out.

"True, but Sage, Mist, Allure, and Battleaxe can each take five thousand. So let them take care of the army, and Shatter can handle everyone from the castle. We won't have nearly the same time pressure as we will in Spanbrook."

"Fair enough," Khaldun said with a nod.

"Once everyone else has left, we can have Alanna run into the courtyard and appear to panic as if she's been left behind accidentally. As long as Nyro's demon is still watching the castle, it should alert her immediately. She may or may not accompany her armies for the attack, but she's sure to investigate when she receives the demon's report."

"And we can have Mira waiting inside the keep with her null extinguished," Khaldun said. "The moment Nyro arrives, she'll expand it to take away her magic."

"And now comes the hard part," Allison said. "How do we impale Nyro with this spike? I might be her match in single combat now, but this will be no training session. Even if I manage to best her, it's not like she's going to yield. I'd have to kill her, and then we lose our opportunity to use the spike."

"Unless you can pin her long enough for one of us to impale her with it," said Allure.

"Unlikely," said Allison. "Even if I could pin her, she'd struggle mightily when she sees that spike coming."

"As long as she's inside the null, I can hold her down long enough for someone to embed it in her flesh," said Khaldun. "I've practiced shifting into a giant octopus. With that many limbs, I should have no trouble pinning her arms and legs."

"The only trouble with that is Nyro could read you," said Allison. "But you and I can wait somewhere nearby. Not close enough for her demon to sense us, but perhaps in the city, and I'll have Shadow keep watch. The moment Mira expands her null, we can use a portal to return here. It'll have to be outside the castle, but we can enter through the gates."

"I'll pin her, you embed the spike, Mira extinguishes her null, and then I tear her limbs off and let her bleed out," Khaldun said.

"Or I can decapitate her with my blade," Allison said. "That would be faster."

"We'll need to make sure Sigrid understands what we're doing," said Khaldun. "If she realizes that we've left Alanna behind, she might come here to rescue her. That could complicate things."

"That's a good point," Mira said. "It might be best to send her to Highgate ahead of time with some of the others."

"This sounds like a plan," Allison said. "We'll keep Alanna and Mira in the castle, and Khaldun and I will wait in the city until Nyro takes the bait. No one else needs to be involved."

"Yes, I think we've got it," Khaldun said with a nod. "Is there anything we haven't considered?"

"The timing is going to be critical," Allison said. "Nyro's sure to come here using her pyramid. She could open a portal very close to Alanna, take her to the other side, and close it again very quickly. Mira, your reaction time will need to be as short as possible."

"I'll be ready," Mira said. "My null will collapse her portal instantly."

"Could Nyro open the portal so close to Alanna that she could grab her without even stepping through it herself?" Allure asked.

"I can't," Allison said. "When I tried rescuing Emma, I couldn't get it that close to her. The spell doesn't have that much precision. I was able to open it inside Emma's bedchamber and choose which side of the bed it appeared on, but that was the best I could do."

"Nyro has had much more experience with portal magic," Khaldun pointed out. "Could she have greater accuracy?"

"It's possible," Allison said. "I'll ask Shadow. She must have seen Nyro use the pyramid many times in the old days." She couldn't summon the demon inside the null, so it would have to wait until later.

"We should run the entire plan by Shadow and make sure there's nothing else we're missing," Allure said. "And the rest of us should try to think of any additional pitfalls. The more contingencies we can plan for, the more likely it becomes that we'll succeed."

Allure gave Allison the spike, and she left the castle with it to examine its magic outside Mira's null, taking care to make herself invisible to avoid the watching demon's notice.

The spike pulsated with power, vastly stronger than the one they'd used against Myrddin's demon so long ago. Allison summoned Shadow, and she agreed it should be more than strong enough to contain Nyro. Allison tucked it into the void.

She discussed their entire plan with Shadow, and she saw no reason it shouldn't work. She told her Nyro's precision with the portals wasn't any greater than Allison's. In fact, she'd complained about that very issue on a few occasions.

"And consider this. No matter how convincing you make this ruse of yours, Nyro will still be extremely suspicious. I'm sure she'll want to investigate herself, but I doubt she'd risk opening the portal so close to Alanna. She's aware of Khaldun's new abilities, and for all she'll know, it could be him waiting for her. Her demons can't read people, so she'd have no way to tell for sure without coming here herself."

"And if it were Khaldun, he could turn into some sort of beast and rip her apart."

"Yes, exactly. Nyro could reanimate a new body at that point, but it would still be an inconvenience. One she could avoid by simply opening her portal halfway across the courtyard."

Allison thought for a moment that baiting the trap with Khaldun disguised as Alanna might not be a bad idea. Of course, the moment Nyro arrived, she *could* read Khaldun, and then the game was up. Her inability to read Alanna was sure to deepen her suspicion, but it didn't give anything away.

"What if Nyro sends her demon into the keep?" Allison asked. "It could find Mira waiting there as easily as you could."

"I can handle her demons," Shadow said. "I'll scatter and confuse any she sends while remaining hidden myself."

Allison ran into Gyda on her way up to her chambers. The elf told her that she'd finally reached her people in Drengrvollr.

"We can bring eight more mages here," she told her. "All from Krokr and the neighboring provinces. There are three more who could join us from the outlying territories, but that would mean three more portals. Or waiting two to three weeks for them to travel to the city. The rest could be there tomorrow."

"Three more won't make that much difference," Allison said. "Let me know where I can meet the ones from Krokr, and I'll fetch them tomorrow. It should take only two trips through a portal."

Allison returned to her chambers. Jezebel had an oil lamp lit, but she'd dozed off in bed. She started awake when Allison came in. Removing her armor, she lay next to her and told her about their plan for trapping Nyro. The girls were asleep, so she kept her voice down to avoid waking them.

"This all sounds pretty thorough," Jezebel said when she was done. "Replacing Alanna with Khaldun *does* sound tempting. But you're right—Nyro could read the entire plan in his mind. I do worry about Alanna being so unprotected. It'll take a little time for you and Khaldun to get there, even using the portal. Perhaps we should have Imani and several of her soldiers waiting in the keep with Mira. We can keep them in the dark—there's no reason for them to know the plan. Tell them only that they're to wait inside unless and until a threat to Alanna presents itself."

"Yes, I like that. A cornered animal is a dangerous one, and once Nyro realizes it's a trap, there's no telling what she might do to Alanna."

Jezebel fell asleep after that, but Allison couldn't stop thinking about possible flaws in their plan. She lay awake worrying about it for several more hours.

CHAPTER TWENTY-TWO
LURING THE ENEMY

he next morning at breakfast, Gyda told Allison that the elf mages were ready to come to Stoutwall. "It would be best if I accompany you to Krokr. I can guide you to the meeting place, and then speak to them before we bring them here. They do not know about your portal magic yet."

"Why don't they?"

"I did not tell the group leaders *how* we'd be transporting the mages. It's best to share only information that's absolutely necessary."

Allison could see no good reason for keeping this from them. Nyro already knew she possessed a pyramid. She figured secrecy was just her way.

"You could take five of the mages back with you on the first trip," Gyda continued, "and I'll stay behind with the others. Then I can return with them on your second trip."

"That should work," Allison agreed.

She went to find Augustine's steward, and let him know they'd be bringing eight more elf mages to Stoutwall, then left the castle with Gyda. Allison removed her sword, carpet, and pyramid from the void, hoisting the carpet over one shoulder and handing Gyda the sword. It would be dark in Drengrvollr, so she opened a portal to the same location she'd used last time to avoid attracting attention with the sunlight streaming through. Once on the other side, she tucked her sword and the pyramid back into oblivion.

Allison and Gyda sat down on the carpet and took off. Unlike Asmund, she didn't seem fazed by this mode of travel. Allison made them invisible, and once they'd reached Krokr, the elf guided her to an old building by the sea. The rear of the property was enclosed behind high stone walls, so Allison landed there, making them visible.

Gyda led her inside the building. They found the eight mages waiting for them on the lower level. Gyda spoke to them in elvish for a minute, then told Allison the first five were ready to go to Stoutwall.

Allison withdrew the pyramid from the void and opened a portal to Stoutwall. She led the first group through the rift, closing it behind her. Asmund was waiting outside with a couple of the guards, so Allison led the group to them. Asmund spoke to them briefly before taking them into the castle with one of the guards.

Opening a portal to the building where she'd left Gyda, Allison went back to Drengrvollr for the second group. They returned to Stoutwall, and Gyda escorted them to the castle with the remaining guard.

Allison went to see Allure and found Mira sitting with her, discussing the trap for Nyro. She told them about Jezebel's idea of having Imani stationed in the keep with some of her soldiers. They agreed that would be for the best, as long as they kept them in the dark.

That night, Mira told Allison that Kashi and his team had reached Rockhedge with the dragons. Allison met Allure, Sage, Mist, and Battleaxe out on the grounds. They pulled their belongings out of the void—Allure and Allison were the only two taking carpets—and Allison opened a portal to Rockhedge.

The dragons and their riders were waiting for them. Allison told Kashi they'd go to the castle to collect their people there first. She'd signal him when it was time for the dragons.

"What kind of signal, exactly?" he asked. As with the rest of the riders, the spirits here in Rockhedge were making him nervous. The dragons were unfazed.

"You'll see," she said with a grin.

Allison mounted her carpet, and the other four sorcerers took their positions on Allure's. The two of them took off, making themselves invisible and heading into Spanbrook. They'd cast the spells that let them track each other's progress before leaving Stoutwall, so they had no problem staying together. Allison circled the enemy camp once. There was a heavy guard surrounding the pens with all the prisoners, and they had a couple of their mages flying patrol on their carpets. This time, the pens abutted each other in such a way that the three of them shared a common vertex.

Allison landed on the roof of Castle Barclay's keep, Allure and the others right next to her. Jezebel had alerted Camilla that they'd be coming, so she was there with one of the soldiers. She greeted them and sent the soldier to bring the rest of the group to the roof. Once they'd arrived, Sage tucked them into the void.

Summoning Shadow, Allison sent her to notify Kashi it was time for the dragons. She watched as the demon took her glowing human shape in Rockhedge, and Kashi nearly jumped out of his skin. Perhaps she should have warned him, but his reaction made her chuckle. Shadow delivered the message, and the dragons took off.

Allison summoned three of her minor spirits and set them to keep a watch on the enemy camp. Allure and the other three sorcerers took off on her carpet, going invisible as they soared over the ramparts. Sitting on her carpet, Allison flew after them, casting her own invisibility spell.

She circled the pens for a minute and smiled when she heard the dragons roar as if announcing themselves. They swooped around the pens, shooting jets of fire at the guards. The elves must have had some mages in the area because, after the initial attack, someone canceled the dragons' flames. Not to be deterred, the dragons dove, grabbing soldiers in their jaws and flinging them into the air.

Under the cover of chaos, Allison made her move. Landing by the vertex of the three pens, she summoned her power. Concentrating on all three groups of prisoners, she cast her spell to tuck them into the void. The air around her seemed to vibrate as if someone had struck a giant gong as the magic did its work. She almost whooped for joy when she realized it had worked. The pens were empty.

Taking to the sky, she sent Shadow to let Kashi know it was time to go. The dragons were sending the elves scrambling as they flew back and forth, tossing random soldiers high into the air. Their mages had done a good job neutralizing their fire but hadn't managed to bring any of the beasts down. Allison realized they were focusing on the riders, but the dragons were turning and twisting to keep their bodies between the mages and the riders.

As if guided by a single will, the dragons soared into the sky, heading toward Stoutwall. Allison followed, and she spotted Allure's carpet flying a parallel course. Three of the enemy carpets gave chase, their riders trying to cancel the air beneath the dragons. The sorcerers canceled their spells, and Allison hit one of them with a fire spell, igniting the carpet. That one fell away, and the other two had put shield spells in place by the time Allison hit them with fire.

Two of the sorcerers on Allure's carpet—Allison couldn't tell which—canceled the air beneath their pursuers' carpets. They gave up the chase after that. Allison was a little surprised they'd given up so easily. On the other hand, though, these prisoners weren't even soldiers. They were never going to make a huge difference in the outcome, only tire and demoralize their troops.

After a few hours, they landed by a small river to give the dragons a rest and let them drink some water. Allison conferred with Allure and the others. They agreed that the enemy's lack of effort to recapture the humans seemed suspicious.

"They could have people waiting along our return route to ambush us," Battleaxe said. "Hell, Nyro herself could be waiting for us."

"And although we're keeping ourselves invisible, they could find the dragons easily enough," Sage pointed out. "It would be difficult for us to contain them inside an invisibility spell. They're too spread out."

"We should change our flight path," said Battleaxe. "Head east from here, then follow the Torsa to Stoutwall. If they are planning an ambush, there's no reason for us to fly right into it."

"One of us should fly with Princess Allison," said Allure. "It's the prisoners Nyro will want. With two people calling air, she can get back to Stoutwall faster while the rest of us stay with the dragons."

"I'll go with the Princess," Battleaxe said.

They took off again, and Battleaxe flew with Allison. The two of them called air, leaving the others far behind. It still took a little longer to reach Stoutwall along their new course, but Allison felt this was the right choice.

The sun had risen by the time they reached the castle. Allison landed on the grounds, and Battleaxe went inside to fetch the steward's assistant, who was expecting them. He left the castle on horseback as Battleaxe emerged through the gates.

Allison and Battleaxe took off again, this time landing in the fields outside the city. Taking a few deep breaths, Allison prepared to release the prisoners from the void—this would take as much power as sending them there had. She cast her spell, and once again, the air around them vibrated as the people filled the surrounding fields as far as the eye could see.

"Damn," Battleaxe said, scanning the area. "Sometimes I envy you."

The steward's assistant had gone into the city, where he'd be gathering a group of citizens who'd volunteered to help resettle these people. Stoutwall's population had evacuated to the countryside and they had established camps all across the princedom, hoping to ride out the war by staying in hiding. The volunteers would help get these people to the camps.

Using the magical force, Allison amplified her voice and explained to the crowd what was happening. By the time she was done, the steward's assistant had arrived with the volunteer group. Allison remained a few minutes longer to make sure they had the situation under control before flying back to the castle with Battleaxe.

Allison checked in with Allure a few times that day, and the sorcerer reported that all was well. They had encountered no pursuit from Spanbrook and no ambushes. She made it back to Stoutwall with their comrades and the dragons that evening.

Augustine called a council meeting the next morning. All of the usual rulers, mages, and commanders were present, along with Asmund and Gyda.

"Good morning, everyone," he said, "and thank you for coming. The time has come to decide our next moves. Nyro's reinforcements will arrive in Anoria within a matter of days, and if we remain here, she is sure to attack Stoutwall again. Are we prepared to lay our trap for her?"

"We are, Your Highness," said Allison. "Lord Khaldun, Lady Mira, and I will be springing the trap. Along with Commander Imani and a contingent of soldiers."

"And who do you plan on using as bait?" the prince asked.

"Our daughter, Alanna," Allison said. "She possesses a latent ability that Nyro greatly desires. We would prefer not to share any further details, however. With Nyro's ability to read people's thoughts, it would be best to contain the finer points of our plan as much as possible."

"She'll be able to read my people and me," Imani said, "and we know it's a trap."

"By the time she's close enough to read you, Mira will have extended her null," Allison said. "As long as you don't know anything more specific, this changes nothing."

"We will need to discuss the broader plan, however," said Augustine.

"Of course," Allison agreed. "We should maintain our presence in Stoutwall, giving every outward sign that we plan on engaging the enemy here. But once they arrive and prepare their attack, we will evacuate.

"Working together, Sage, Allure, Battleaxe, and Mist can tuck the combined armies into the void and fly them to Highgate. And if we gather the castle's remaining occupants in the courtyard, Shatter can do the same with them. The dragons should take off for Highgate at that time as well.

"Mira will remain inside the castle, her null extinguished, along with Imani and her soldiers. And once everyone else has departed,

Alanna will emerge into the courtyard, appearing to have been left behind. As long as Nyro's demon is maintaining its watch, it should alert her to Alanna's presence immediately. And once Nyro comes for her, we'll spring our trap."

The others sat in silence for a minute, absorbing everything she'd told them.

"You are taking a great risk putting your daughter in harm's way like this," Augustine said finally. "Are you sure this is the best path forward?"

"Yes, Your Highness," said Jezebel. "We are. Alanna wants to help. And she's old enough to make this kind of decision for herself. We will be taking every possible precaution to keep her safe."

"Very well," Augustine said with a nod. "Then we shall proceed as if we plan on engaging the enemy here in Stoutwall. And when the time comes, we will fall back to Highgate. If our trap succeeds, victory shall be ours. And if not, our forces will gather in Highgate for one final battle."

Over the next several days, the tension inside the castle became palpable. With Shatter's help, the steward spread the word about the coming evacuation. They quietly started releasing anyone not essential to the war effort or the running of the household, and those people left for the countryside a few at a time.

Alanna summoned Sigrid to the courtyard. She did her best to explain to the dragon that she would need to fly ahead to Highgate with some of her companions. Sigrid was resistant at first, but Alanna managed to convince her. Kashi arranged for two of the other riders to escort Sigrid with five other dragons. The next morning, Alanna bade Sigrid a tearful farewell in the courtyard, and the dragon took off with the others.

Allison continued her early morning training sessions with Battleaxe, Imani, and Shatter. Khaldun kept up his work transforming soldiers, adding a little over a hundred physically augmented specimens every day. He also found time every night to practice his own shapeshifting, focusing especially on his giant octopus and dragon-bear shapes.

Allison, Mira, and Alanna worked on keeping their minds closed to sympathetic magic, and after the first few days, were able to do it perpetually without conscious effort—much the same way Mira could control her null. Allure worked with Khaldun several more times, but he simply wasn't able to acquire this skill. It did seem that having some pre-existing talent for sympathetic magic made all the difference.

Using her specters, Allison kept a constant watch on Spanbrook, but nothing seemed to change there. The army camp betrayed no signs of moving out, and the reanimated elf mages kept up their air patrols using their carpets. One night, her spirits alerted her to some unusual activity in the camp. Allison sent Shadow, and through her eyes, saw that the wraiths had arrived outside the camp, along with another thousand troops.

Allison contacted Princess Jelena, and sure enough, she reported that all the enemy forces in Rockport had disappeared. Nyro or one of her mages must have tucked them into the void and flown them to Spanbrook.

Neither Jelena nor their contact in Northcoast reported any incoming ships. Allison's specters confirmed Nyro's demon continued to watch over Castle Stoutwall. But there was no sign of Nyro anywhere. Allison sent Shadow to Nyro's island castle in Drengrvollr, and she found the place abandoned. The barrier was gone, as well as the household staff and guards.

Gyda checked with her people, and they told her that the mages guarding the castle exterior had gone inside a couple of days earlier, and they'd seen no further activity on the island. Their lookout points on the mainland were too far away to detect Nyro's barrier spell in the first place, so they couldn't confirm when it had gone away.

A few more days went by without any changes to the situation. Until finally, one morning, their contact in Northcoast reported seeing dozens upon dozens of ships approaching from the east. They didn't know yet if they'd be landing in Northcoast or Rockport, but either way, Jezebel and Augustine agreed they should send their sorcerers to do whatever damage they could.

So, after breakfast, Allison went out to the grounds with Khaldun, Sage, Allure, Mist, and Battleaxe. They took off on their carpets, and Allison opened a portal to Northcoast. Once they'd all flown through it, she let it close and tucked the pyramid into the void.

Making themselves invisible, they flew over the sea, and Allison spotted the ships almost immediately. There were at least a couple of hundred of them—far more than the number that had left from Drengrvollr. The other kingdoms must have supplied additional troops, too. Moving in closer, she called fire, trying to ignite the closest vessel's sails. Nothing happened—they must have used the spells to make them impervious to fire. The same was true of the hull. Allison tried hitting a few different ships with much the same result.

One of the others called air, trying to blow some of the vessels into each other. But someone canceled their spell almost immediately. Allison tried hitting a ship with an earth spell that should have knocked a massive hole in its hull, but it died before reaching the target. She tried several other spells, but it was no use. Someone canceled her magic every time.

Before long, it became clear the ships were making for Northcoast. Most of them dropped anchor off-shore, while others moved toward the docks. Allison and the others kept trying to hit them with magic, but someone had cast a shield spell over the group heading toward land. The demon mages in their reanimated elf bodies had to be nearby, probably flying invisible on their carpets just like they were.

The first ships docked and started unloading their passengers. Allison and the others kept up a constant barrage, throwing fireballs, tornadoes, and fire orbs at the soldiers. Their invisible opponents managed to cancel most of their magic, but not all of it, and their unrelenting attacks started taking a toll.

A few times, Allison or one of the others managed to use their opponents' spells to locate and make them visible. They found Cyclone, Vision, Intuit, and Semblant that way. But every time, they cast a new invisibility spell, and they lost them again. The enemy exposed Battleaxe, Mist, and Sage that way, too, before the sorcerers could go invisible again.

More and more ships unloaded their troops, and the ones who made it through the bombardment started forming lines in the fields south of the city. Allison refocused her attacks there, but someone had erected a massive shield spell, too strong for her spells to penetrate. She had a feeling Nyro had to be here—none of the others could pull off something with so much power. Allison sent Shadow inside the shield, and she kept up a constant barrage of fire and earth spells. The elf mages canceled most of them, but she managed to take out some additional soldiers.

Allison returned to the lines moving away from the ships and hit them with everything she had. It took many hours for the enemy to get all the new arrivals unloaded, and Allison and the others inflicted as much damage as they could. In the end, she estimated Nyro had brought forty thousand fresh troops, and she and the others had managed to reduce that by five thousand or so.

Not long after the last soldiers moved inside the shield spell, they began disappearing, several thousand at a time. Someone was tucking them into the void; it took seven spells to remove them all. It had to be the demon mages. Allison flew around and around the area, sending Shadow to do the same, but she couldn't find them. They had to be out there somewhere, most likely on carpets, but they were probably long gone.

Allison regrouped with the others and they decided to return to Stoutwall. She opened a portal and they flew through it, removing their invisibility spells as they landed out in front of the castle.

"I'll be damned," Battleaxe said as she tucked her carpet into the void. "That shield spell they used was impregnable. That *had* to be Nyro."

"Not even Nyro's shield spell could withstand an assault like that without degrading," Sage said. "She must have found a way to draw power from her demon mages when she cast it."

"Like we've done with our void magic," Battleaxe said. "That makes sense."

"You must be right," Allison said. "I did the same thing creating portals from Drengrvollr."

They met Shatter in the entry hall, and Allison told him how it had gone in Northcoast. He went off to inform Augustine, and Allison went up to her chambers.

"Any reduction in their numbers is helpful," Jezebel said once Allison had recounted their efforts.

Allison sent Shadow to search the area between Stoutwall and Northcoast, hoping she might sense the demon mages. Her specters in Spanbrook reported no change in the army's disposition there. She knew their attack was imminent, and it was only a matter of time now. They'd done everything they could to prepare, and all they could do was wait.

Jezebel and the girls went to bed that night, and Allison stayed with them for a little while, but she knew there was no way she could sleep. Not only that, her demons couldn't reach her in the null. So she left the castle, flying her carpet high above the grounds to give her the best possible view of the area, awash in the light of the twin moons.

A couple of hours later, her specters in Spanbrook told her that the army there had disappeared—all sixty thousand troops in one shot. That had to be Nyro's doing. Shadow continued her search for the demon mages. They easily could have reached Stoutwall by then, so Allison felt certain they'd be somewhere nearby, ready to release the new army from the void. Most likely, they were only awaiting for Nyro's arrival with the army from Spanbrook before putting things into motion. Not even Nyro could use a portal to move anything in the void, so she had to be traveling via carpet.

Sure enough, as the first light of dawn cracked the eastern horizon, Allison felt the air around her vibrate. The spell was fainter than the one in Northcoast, and she didn't see anyone nearby. Flying beyond their own army camp, she found the source of the magic. Sixty thousand elvish troops had appeared in the fields north of Castle Stoutwall. As she circled the new arrivals, seven more groups of soldiers joined them, totaling thirty-five thousand additional troops. The armies from Spanbrook and Northcoast had arrived.

Now was the time to set their trap.

CHAPTER TWENTY-THREE
SPRINGING THE TRAP

Flying back to the castle, Allison used her mirror to contact Imani and Amari and warn them that the elvish armies had arrived. Only moments later, she heard the horns rousing their troops. Landing on the grounds, she tucked her carpet into the void and ran inside, nearly crashing into Shatter in the entry hall. He'd spotted the armies arriving, too, and was on his way to alert the prince.

Allison ran up to her chambers, waking Jezebel and the girls. "It's time. Nyro's armies are here."

The three of them got out of bed and quickly got dressed. Once they were ready, Allison escorted them down to the courtyard. She hugged Jezebel and Leda, wishing them well—they'd be departing with Shatter.

Khaldun and Mira emerged from the keep, and Allison hurried over to see them, Alanna in tow. "Are you ready?" she asked them.

"I'm leaving now," Khaldun said. "I'll meet you in the city, outside the tavern."

He kissed Mira, then rushed off, leaving the castle. Mira was going to leave her null in place until the last minute, so he couldn't take off from the courtyard.

"You stay with Mira," Allison told Alanna. "I'm going to make sure the others depart without incident, and I'll be right back."

"Yes, Mother."

"I've sent word to the dragon riders," Mira told her. "They should be leaving any moment now."

Allison nodded before hurrying out of the castle. She ran into Imani and her soldiers on the way out and told her where to meet Alanna and Mira. Out on the grounds, she found Allure, Mist, Sage, and Battleaxe gathered by the army camp.

"We're ready to go," Allure told her.

"Be safe," Allison said.

She embraced them each in turn, and they ran off to take their positions surrounding the camp. Once the others were ready, Allure focused for a moment, drawing power from the others, and tucking five thousand troops into the void. One by one, the other three executed their spells, and the rest of the army disappeared. After that, the four sorcerers mounted their carpets, taking off and going invisible as they soared into the sky. Allison watched the dragons rising above the trees, beating their mighty wings as they headed east. Magna was in the lead, dwarfing all the others.

Inside the courtyard, Allison spoke to Shatter. The castle's occupants were all there, ready to go. Allison went into the keep and let Mira know it was time to extinguish her null. She did so, and Shatter tucked the entire group into the void before flying off on his carpet, going invisible before he cleared the castle wall.

Allison turned to face Mira, Imani and her soldiers, and Alanna. "This is it. I'm leaving for the city now, and then it's Nyro's move."

"We're ready, Your Highness," Imani told her, without her usual grin.

"Wait till I'm gone," Allison said to Alanna, "then wander into the courtyard. Play your part the best you can—you've just discovered that everyone's left without you, and you're distraught. And make sure you close your mind!"

"I already have," she said. Allison tried reading her, and sure enough, couldn't access her thoughts.

"Good girl," she said, hugging her tight. Pulling away, she held her by the shoulders and said, "I'm proud of you."

Alanna rolled her eyes. "Can we just do this already?"

Allison chuckled. "Good hunting, all of you," she said to Mira, Imani, and the soldiers. Making herself invisible, she pulled her carpet out of the void, walked into the courtyard, and took off.

As she soared over the castle, Allison reached out to her specters keeping watch over Nyro's demon. They reported that it was still there. She summoned Shadow and told her it was time to spring their trap.

"Don't worry. Victory will be ours."

Allison hoped she was right.

She flew to the city, landing by the tavern, where she found Khaldun waiting for her. "Everyone's in place," she told him.

Khaldun nodded. His body turned protean and he changed, taking the form of a giant octopus.

Allison watched the castle from Shadow's point of view, floating above the courtyard. Alanna wandered out of the keep, yelling, "Hello? Where is everyone?" She ran over to the stables, and then the armory, her body language increasingly frantic.

"Mother! Leda! *Where are you?!*" Her voice cracked, and sending Shadow closer, Allison realized she was crying. She had to give her credit—she looked and sounded genuinely hysterical.

"Nyro's demon is moving in closer," Shadow told her in her mind. "It's just above the courtyard now—I'm casting the spell to confuse it. That worked. It's drifting around the grounds."

"You're sure Nyro won't realize what happened?"

"She might suspect it, but I've hidden myself from her. She'll have no way to know for sure."

Alanna ran up the stairs to the ramparts, moving along the castle walls, and frantically searching the grounds. She was playing her part well. It was making Allison nervous, though—she was pretty far from Imani now. If Nyro were to open a portal near her, this could be disastrous.

Alanna returned to the courtyard, and Allison breathed a sigh of relief. She moved to the keep, sitting down, hugging her knees to her chest, and sobbing.

There was no sign of Nyro. Allison sent Shadow higher to get a look at the enemy army. They were making camp, with no indication that anything odd was happening in the castle. Shadow moved back to the courtyard.

Nyro's demon returned, taking position above the castle, and making no attempt to move in closer this time. Minutes passed, and nothing changed. Still no sign of Nyro anywhere.

What was going on here? Clearly she knew Alanna was alone. Had she detected their ruse somehow? Allison didn't see how. Mira had kept her null extinguished. Shadow had kept the demon from searching the castle but otherwise hadn't exposed her presence to Nyro. Had that been enough to tip her off?

A few more minutes went by, and Allison was getting ready to call the whole thing off. And that's when Shadow said, "*She's here. On the ramparts. I sensed no portal magic, so she must have taken her carpet.*"

"I don't see anyone," Allison said.

"*There's an invisibility spell. I suppose it could be one of her demon mages.*"

Could they have been wrong? Had Nyro sent one of her underlings for Alanna after all? It was time to find out.

Producing her mirror, Allison reached out to Mira. Her face appeared in the glass, and Allison said, "It's time. Expand your null."

Mira nodded, and her face vanished from the mirror.

"*It's her,*" Shadow said. "*She's running down the steps to the courtyard. Come quickly.*"

"Let's go!" Allison said to Khaldun, stowing her mirror. She pulled her pyramid out of the void, opening a portal to the castle grounds outside the null.

Khaldun slithered through the rift, surprising her with his speed. She had no idea he could move so fast in this form. Allison followed him through, closing the portal behind her. She pulled the spike out of the void and they hurried across the moat. Rushing into the courtyard, they found Imani and her soldiers battling Nyro. They had her surrounded. Wielding her sword, Nyro was trying to fight her way out of the circle, but they kept her contained. Alanna was cowering against the wall, and Allison was sure her sobs were real now.

"Khaldun, now!" Allison said.

He hurried across the courtyard with remarkable speed, and the soldiers moved so he could pass.

"*NO!*" Nyro screamed as he approached. She tried escaping through the other side of the circle, frantically cutting and slashing, and felling one of Imani's soldiers in the process.

But Khaldun had her. He wrapped his tentacles around her arms and legs and one around her neck. Nyro tried cutting him with her sword, but with only her wrist able to move, couldn't generate enough power to do any damage. Khaldun used an extra tentacle to rip the blade out of her hand and toss it across the courtyard.

Nyro writhed and screamed, struggling mightily against Khaldun's hold. Allison rushed in, impaling her with the spike, right through the gut. Nyro went silent, fixing Allison with her stare, and it felt like she'd bore right through her skull with the force of her gaze.

"Mira, now!" Allison yelled.

Terror bubbled up in her belly as she felt her magic return. If they were wrong about this step, the result could be catastrophic. But they weren't wrong. Nyro had no magic.

Allison pulled her sword out of the void. "Release her neck," she said to Khaldun. He removed the tentacle, and Allison raised her weapon.

"You will pay for this, you bitch," Nyro said, staring into her eyes.

Allison said nothing, decapitating her in one stroke. The head rolled across the ground as the body twitched. Khaldun released it, and the corpse slid to the flagstones.

Returning to his normal shape, Khaldun said, "I've never been so terrified in my entire life."

Mira ran over to them, embracing Khaldun. "We did it? This mad plan actually succeeded?"

Allison was watching the spike. It was so hot, it was glowing, and the corpse was sizzling where it made contact with the metal. "Something's wrong," she said. Sections of the spike started pulsating, growing lighter and darker as if something were moving around inside of it. Which was impossible—it was solid metal. "We'd better get out of here."

"Wait—there's something tucked into the void," Khaldun said. He cast the spell to remove whatever it was, and a carpet appeared on the ground.

"What about her pyramid?" Allison asked. If she'd survived somehow, taking that from her would at least give them some advantage.

"It's not here," Khaldun said, shaking his head. "Only the carpet."

An extra carpet could always come in handy, but Allison didn't trust this one. Nyro could have woven extra spells into it that would harm anyone else riding it. She incinerated it with a thought. "All right. Let's move."

Khaldun removed his carpet from the void, and Mira took her seat, strapping herself in. Imani took the rear spot as Khaldun tucked the other soldiers into the void. One of them had sustained injuries, but they'd have to tend to her once they reached Highgate.

Allison ran over to Alanna, helping her to her feet and holding her tight. "You did great," she told her, patting her on the back.

Alanna couldn't stop sobbing, and Allison knew she wasn't faking it anymore. She pulled her carpet out of the void, and once they'd taken their seats, she launched them high above the castle, Khaldun right next to them.

The spike was now emanating a jet of sparks that was climbing higher every second. Allison couldn't understand what was happening here. Had Allure been wrong about the amount of power needed to contain Nyro? Shadow had agreed the spike should be more than enough.

Gathering every ounce of power she possessed, Allison called earth, channeling her spell deep into the bedrock beneath the castle. The entire structure started shaking, and with an earsplitting crack, the ground broke, a chasm opening and splitting the castle in two. Allison could see tongues of fire flickering in the deep as the spike and Nyro's corpse fell into the opening. Allison kept adding power to the spell. The chasm opened wider, and the entire castle slid into its depths.

Taking a deep breath, Allison called earth again, causing a second earthquake, this time closing the rift. "It's done. Let's get out of here."

They headed east, leaving the elvish armies behind. Allison wanted to believe Nyro was gone. She was the most powerful mage in the history of Anoria—maybe the spike was supposed to react this way. Perhaps her spirit was still trapped in the metal.

"Mother, look!" Alanna yelled, terror in her voice.

Glancing over her shoulder, she saw that Alanna was looking behind them. She turned them around and gasped. In the distance, roughly where Castle Stoutwall had stood, a plume of fire was shooting high into the sky.

Allison knew in her bones that Nyro had survived. She couldn't comprehend how she'd done it, but there was no doubt in her mind.

Agony. Nothing else existed. She didn't know who she was, never mind where, or how she'd gotten there. Searing pain rending her mind asunder, leaving her incapable of thinking of anything else.

Focus. Surrender to the agony. Let it persist as something separate, not part of her. She was Nyro. And she'd prepared for this centuries ago.

Never had she expected the pain.

She'd seen this possible future in prophecy. Not the events that had led to it, only being trapped in this infernal instrument. And she'd discovered a way to save herself. Taken the steps to inoculate her soul against the magic. It had required her to consume the spectral energy of numerous lesser demons. A process that had nearly destroyed her, yet it had worked. And this was the proof. Her essence resisted the enchantments in this metal. Kept itself separate.

This was far from ideal. She'd seen the bitch princess coming at her with that spike and knew she'd fallen for their trap. Understood the difficulties she was about to endure.

But not the pain. She'd never seen this agony coming. And now it took every particle of her will and focus just to form a thought.

Fire. To free herself, she had to melt the metal. That's all it would take. Nyro became the essence of flame, channeling all the power she possessed into this one force. On the fringes of her mind, she could sense those other beings, still tethered to her. And she drew their power into her spell, too, adding it to her own.

Like the very sun brought to earth she became, concentrating the power of fire into this substance that held her. And suddenly she was free. The agony subsided and slowly, she returned to herself, able to think and remember.

She had no body. As she'd been for centuries, Nyro was once again no more than spirit. And that spirit was weak. Nearly destroyed this time, but not quite. She needed to heal. Gather her strength. In her present condition, she doubted she could produce the magic to reanimate a new body.

There was time. The enemy would gather their forces in Highgate in case their plan had failed. Nyro was still tethered to those other souls—the two girls. And through them, she retained her connection to all those others. She would regroup and then they would know hell on earth.

She would take Gorm's body. He was male, but that hardly mattered. Among all the elf mages under her sway, he was the most powerful. She'd moved the two necromancers to a new castle on a different island, along with the guards and household staff. This campaign wouldn't be like the last. Without her Sacred Circle, she'd need to oversee the operations herself. Those demon sorcerers could not be trusted to carry out the spirit of her orders, much less make important command decisions on their own.

Nyro could not risk taking the two necromancers into battle with her. Yet she'd learned the hard way the risks involved in leaving them behind. She had no choice. But she'd take every possible precaution. She'd purchased the new island using an assumed name. No one could trace it to Estrid—or her—this time. And she'd put the same barrier in place she'd had on the first island. And doubled the guard. She'd have to replace Gorm, but there was no way around that.

It would take a day or two to recover, then she'd need to possess a human and retrieve the pyramid artifact. She'd suspected a trap in Stoutwall and couldn't risk losing it to the enemy. So she'd tucked it into the void, tethering it to a tree deep in the forest north of the castle, and setting one of her demons to stand guard over it.

Using the human, she could retrieve the artifact and open a portal back to Drengrvollr. Then she could dispose of the human and take Gorm's body.

This was a setback, nothing more. And despite the inconvenience, it had been worth the risk. Acquiring the null could have changed everything. She never thought those righteous fools would use their own daughter as bait. Now she knew better. And she had to admire the ruthlessness of it—she didn't think they had it in them.

Time. She only needed a little time to heal. Then, as she always did, she would begin again.

CHAPTER TWENTY-FOUR
FALLING BACK

llison sent her specters to keep an eye on whatever was going on in Stoutwall. Halfway to Highgate, she spotted the dragons gamboling by a river far below. One of them flew up to meet them, and she recognized Magna. She had no doubt he was communicating with Mira using that special bond they shared. After a minute, he returned to his crash.

Reaching Highgate, Allison circled the city once. The army from Stoutwall was still making camp on the plain below the city walls, not far from Highgate's forces. She landed on the keep roof, Khaldun, Mira, and Imani touching down right next to her. They got to their feet and Khaldun released the other soldiers from the void.

One of Salerna's mages hurried over to meet them. Khaldun told him that one of their soldiers required a healer. He led them all inside, where they met the steward, who hurried off with the injured soldier. Alisson and Alanna followed Khaldun, Mira, and the others as the mage led them to the great hall. The rest of the group from Castle Stoutwall was here, waiting for Salerna's staff to escort them to their chambers.

Allison and Alanna found Jezebel and Leda, and she gave Jezebel the bad news.

"Oh, no," Jezebel said. "You're sure of this? I don't understand how Nyro could have survived."

"Neither do I," she said. "But we need to hold a council meeting with Salerna and the others immediately."

Fifteen minutes later, she and Jezebel joined Princess Salerna, her son, Albert, Azure, and Highgate's military commanders in her council chamber, along with Princes Augustine, Leto, and Carlo, Princess Yolanda, and all the various mages and military commanders from their princedoms. Azure put the spells in place to prevent magical observation of their meeting.

"I like your new look, Princess Allison," Salerna said with a contemplative expression. "This is not how you appeared in the looking glass all those years ago."

"We believed it was best for my visit to the elven lands, Your Highness," she replied, "and I decided I like the change."

Salerna nodded. "We are writing our own futures, it seems. This gives me hope. Please, proceed."

Allison gave them her report about the events in Stoutwall and what she thought it meant.

"I left some of my specters behind to monitor the situation," she told them. "The jet of fire shooting out of the ground has ended, leaving only a blackened pit, wide enough to engulf a small house. There is no sign of Nyro anywhere in the area. Her troops remain camped where they were when we left them, and her demon mages are flying patrol on their carpets."

"This is dire news indeed," Salerna said. "But we always knew this possibility existed, did we not?"

"Your Highness, the fear was that we wouldn't be able to trap Nyro in the spike," Allure said. "Allison did that. So, I'm afraid I have no explanation for how this might be possible."

"We're certain Nyro has escaped?" Azure asked.

"Yes, we are," Allure said. "Had this worked, we would have finished the job by destroying the spike, using ancient spells designed for this purpose. But it is clear that the spike failed to contain Nyro. It makes no sense—we wove more than enough magic into the metal for this to work. But somehow, it didn't."

"Shadow agrees," Allison said. "She believes Nyro must have foreseen this potential outcome ages ago and made preparations against it. None of us understand what that might have entailed, but it wouldn't be the first time Nyro invented new magic to prevent her own demise."

"What do we do now?" Prince Carlo asked.

"We must proceed with our original plan," Augustine said. "Gather our forces here in Highgate, prepare for Nyro's next attack, and do everything we can to defeat her."

"Yes, I agree," Salerna said. "We'll need to bring Princess Miranda here from Bayfast along with her mages and her army. And it wouldn't hurt to reach out to Prince Kamari in Okset once more. With twenty thousand troops from Bayfast, the twenty thousand new arrivals from Stoutwall, and Highgate's standing army of twenty-five thousand, we have a force sixty-five thousand strong. But with her reinforcements, Nyro's army now numbers somewhere above ninety-five thousand. My understanding is that Okset has a standing army of seventy thousand, plus as many as thirty thousand more once he calls in his levies?"

"That is our understanding, as well," Jezebel said.

"Working together, Allure, Sage, Mist, and Battleaxe can transport Miranda and her people here," Allison said. "I'll contact Beast to arrange that. Traveling by portal, I can take our sorcerers to Bayfast, then proceed on my own to Okset and see if I can persuade Kamari to come to our aid."

"In that case, you might as well make contact with Princess Zuri in Horn, too," said Salerna. "Their standing army may be smaller than Okset's, but it would still improve our situation, especially if Kamari remains stubborn."

"Yes, Your Highness," Allison said with a nod.

"We don't know Nyro's present location?" Prince Leto asked. "Or how long it might be before her next attack?"

"Unfortunately not," Allison said. "She'll need to acquire a new body. But she could do that immediately. We have to assume her attack here is imminent and prepare accordingly. I'll keep my specters in Stoutwall, so we should have plenty of warning before her army moves here. And I'd like to return to her castle in Drengrvollr. She's abandoned it, which means she must have moved her two necromancers elsewhere. I may be able to find some clues as to where they went."

"Would you try rescuing Emma and Fang again if you do?" Allure asked.

"Perhaps," Allison said with a shrug. "It will depend on what her defenses look like. Assuming it's the same as her previous stronghold, it may be possible. Especially if she keeps them there and comes here herself to lead her forces."

"That's a good point," Khaldun said. "That would provide an opportunity you didn't have last time."

"Yes, exactly," Allison said. "I have to find them first. And she may not leave them behind after what happened with Syllith."

"Surely she wouldn't bring them here with her," Battleaxe said.

"I doubt it," Allison agreed. "But she may elect to stay behind to guard them herself."

"You are welcome to try finding them in the looking glass," Salerna said. "My joints are too stiff to make the trip up to the top of the crystal tower anymore, but Azure could take you when we're done here."

"I would appreciate that, Your Highness," Allison said. She'd forgotten that the looking glass could locate people. After Jezebel's journey all those years ago, she'd thought only of its ability to show visions of the future. An ability that had been greatly diminished since Mira's transformation into a sorcerer.

"Azure, have you had any luck tracking down Saliman's heirs?" Khaldun asked.

"We haven't found a living descendant yet, but I believe we're coming close," the sorcerer said. "Our people have been scouring the Hall of Records and managed to trace the family line through several generations here in the city. They've changed their surnames a few times, so it's made it a little difficult. It seems like they haven't wanted to be found."

"That's hardly surprising," Battleaxe said. "If I had a family history like theirs, I wouldn't want to be found, either."

A few of the others chuckled.

"We should redouble our efforts," Salerna said. "If Saliman's living heir has information regarding Nyro's true name, we could end this war without any further bloodshed."

"Yes, Your Highness," Azure said.

"Princess Salerna, we should consider having Lady Mira put her null in place around the castle," Augustine said. "That will eliminate Nyro's ability to come here using a portal."

"Yes, I agree," she said. "Please proceed, Lady Mira, if it's not too much trouble."

"No trouble at all, Your Highness," Mira said. She concentrated for a moment, and Allison felt her null snuff out her magic.

"Your Highness, this will prevent me from communing with my spirits," Allison said. "As well as making communication by mirror impossible. Might you have somewhere in the city I could stay, outside of the null, to keep those channels open? Preferably not too far from the castle."

"We do have a townhouse on the city's fourth level, right outside the castle wall, that we normally use for visiting dignitaries here on extended visits," Salerna said. "You're welcome to reside there as long as necessary. I don't believe it's occupied at the moment."

"It is not, Your Highness," Azure confirmed. "I'll have our steward show you to the property once we're finished with the rest of our business," he added to Allison.

They spent the next hour discussing their plans for defending the city against Nyro's attack. Once the meeting had adjourned, Allison and Jezebel headed out with Azure. The sorcerer led them up to the keep roof and over to the crystal tower. He opened the great iron door, and the three of them went inside, climbing the spiral staircase.

Partway up, Allison felt her magic return and knew they'd moved out of Mira's null. Her thighs were burning by the time they reached the top. Azure opened another iron door and they moved into the chamber. It was eight-sided and made entirely of crystal. Openings at the bottom of each wall allowed air to pass, making it quite windy inside. The view was amazing—more expansive than anything she'd seen without riding her carpet.

In the center of the chamber was a circular basin of water sitting on a crystal base. This had to be the looking glass. Azure invited Allison to have a look.

She moved to the basin and staring into the water, saw only her own reflection. "How does this work?"

"Her Highness typically used verbal commands," Azure said. "But as long as you focus on the person you want to see, it should show them to you."

"Show me Emma Barclay," Allison said. The reflection on the water's surface changed. It went black, except for two glowing figures lying on their backs. Emma and Fang. They seemed to be unconscious.

"I don't understand," Jezebel said. "Why is it so dark?"

"They must be in the void," Allison said. "Nyro must have moved them there to add an extra layer of security. If someone were to infiltrate her new base of operations, they'd never know these two were there. Unless they were a sorcerer."

"That's assuming Nyro tethered them in place," Azure pointed out. "She could be taking them with her, wherever she goes."

"Perhaps," Allison said. "She'd have to remove them from the void before moving them through a portal. And if she participates in the battle, keeping them with her that way could prove dangerous."

"Can you see where this void is located?" Jezebel asked.

Allison focused on the vision in the basin, and said, "Show me where this is." The image vanished, showing her only her reflection again. Allison and Azure both tried various approaches to get a look at what they wanted, but the looking glass wouldn't—or couldn't—cooperate.

"Show me Nyro," Allison said finally. Her reflection faded, and the looking glass showed a blur of color, moving fast. "What is this?"

"I'm not sure," Azure said. "I've never seen it do this before. Nyro could be using the spells that prevent magical observation."

"I've always wondered if those would work against the looking glass," Jezebel said.

Allison wondered if Nyro was moving through the spirit realm. This vision was similar to what she'd seen from Shadow's perspective when they went there. They spent a few more minutes with the looking glass, but couldn't glean anything further. Finally, they made the long trek back to the keep.

The steward told them his people would need a little time to prepare the townhouse for Allison, so she went up to Jezebel's chambers with her. She had a bedroom and a washroom that connected with the girls' chambers.

Allure came to find Allison and told her that she and the others were ready to go to Bayfast whenever she was. The townhouse was ready, so she went to see that, and Allure, Mist, Battleaxe, and Sage went with her.

"This place is beautiful," Battleaxe said, going out on the second-floor terrace from the main bedroom. Allison would enjoy the gorgeous view of the city and surrounding plain. "And there's a tavern next door. Can't beat that!"

The other three joined them on the terrace, and all five sorcerers removed their carpets from the void. Allison produced her pyramid and created a portal to the keep roof of Princess Miranda's castle. They walked through, and she let it close behind her.

Their sudden appearance startled Beast, who had been dozing in the far corner as a tiger. He whined before shifting into his human form, completely naked. Allison and the others tucked their carpets into the void.

"Well, hello there," Battleaxe said with a grin as Beast approached, looking him up and down.

"Princess Allison," the sorcerer said with a bow. "To what do we owe this unexpected pleasure?"

She gave him a brief update on the recent events in the war with Nyro. "I'm afraid she could attack at any moment, so the time has come to marshal all of our resources in the defense of Highgate."

"Yes, of course," he said. "I can take you to see Her Highness immediately. Without any notice, it will take us a while to prepare. It's a long march to Highgate."

"No march will be necessary," Allison told him with a grin. "This is Allure, Battleaxe, Sage, and Mist, from the university. They can transport your entire army and any support staff you require by carpet."

"That must be an awfully large carpet," he said with a confused grin.

"I'll allow Allure to explain," she said. "I must continue to Okset."

"Has Prince Kamari reconsidered sending aid, then?" Beast asked.

"Not yet," Allison told him. She bade the other sorcerers farewell, then took off on her carpet. Her next stop would be whatever room in his palace Kamari was currently occupying, and she didn't want him to recognize her whereabouts. This would be a bold move, and she didn't want to implicate Bayfast or any of the other princedoms in her actions.

Flying across the river and well south of the city, she found an empty field and landed there. She sent Shadow ahead to the prince's palace. It took her only moments to locate the prince in his council chambers with several of his advisers. Rolling up her carpet and hoisting it over one shoulder, Allison opened a portal, walking right into the chamber and startling Kamari and his people. She let the portal close, tucking her carpet and pyramid into the void.

"Who are you?" the prince demanded, getting to his feet. The two guards standing by the door rushed into position to protect their prince from her. "What is the meaning of this?"

"I am Princess Consort Allison Barclay from Spanbrook," she told them. "I had business in Drengrvollr and Snaerverold, so we altered my appearance to appear Shifari."

"Why?" the prince's sorcerer asked. She was the only non-Shifari in the room. This had to be Siren.

"The elves are prejudiced against humans," Allison said. "Less so when it comes to Shifari, apparently—but that's not important right now. I am here to demand that Okset come to our aid against Nyro. The armies from Blacksand, Spanbrook, Keepstone, Stoutwall, and Bayfast are gathering in Highgate to make their last stand. Yet we are badly outnumbered. Adding your military might to our own, we might yet prevail. Help us, Prince Kamari, I implore you."

He met her gaze, saying nothing for a few moments. Finally, he cracked a smile, and said, "Leave us."

The others got to their feet and left the council chamber, but Siren said, "Your Highness, I should remain by your side."

"I'll be all right," he told her. "You may go."

She bowed and left the room with the others. The guards stepped into the corridor, closing the doors behind them.

"Please, have a seat," the prince said, sitting down at the head of his table. Allison took the adjacent chair. "How did you appear out of nowhere like that?"

Allison pulled her pyramid out of the void, placing it on the table in front of her. "Using this. It creates a portal to any other place I wish."

"Fascinating," he said. "Where did you acquire such a powerful tool?"

"Nyro and her people used them in ancient times," she told him. "She didn't create them, though, and I don't know where they came from originally."

"You are a sorcerer, then," he said.

"I was. Recently, I became a necromancer." Khaldun had darkened her eyes as part of her transformation, so he wouldn't be able to tell from her irises.

"I seem to recall hearing about you before," he said, furrowing his brow in concentration. "You were the heir apparent in Spanbrook before your metamorphosis, were you not?"

"Yes, that's correct."

"Yet now you're the Princess *Consort*?"

"Forgive me, Your Highness," she said, tucking her pyramid back into the void. "I'm not sure how this is relevant."

He nodded, looking her up and down. "You can summon demons?"

Allison called three of her minor spirits, commanding them to become visible and converge on Kamari. They appeared as dark shadows with burning red eyes and sharp fangs approaching the prince. He jumped to his feet, knocking his chair over and backing away, holding his hands in front of him as if to fend off the demons.

"Send them away!" he said, a quaver in his voice.

Allison banished them, flashing the prince a smile. "The little ones aren't very powerful, but they're quite useful in their own ways."

"I can imagine," he muttered, righting his chair and sitting down again. "Please forgive me, but thus far, Nyro has posed no threat to Okset or any part of Shifar. I see no reason to put our troops in harm's way."

"You must be joking," she said. "Her stated purpose is the extermination of everyone in Anoria. You can count on her invading your princedom once she's wiped out the rest of us."

The prince tapped one finger on the tabletop for a few moments. "How many troops do you each have?"

"Nyro has roughly ninety-five thousand, all elves. We have sixty-five thousand."

"Hmm. Not the best odds, you're right. You must have quite a few sorcerers, though?"

"Eight in addition to myself. Plus forty forty-odd elvish mages, who are each roughly equivalent to one of our sorcerers. And a dozen or two normal human mages. The other side has seven demon mages—deceased human sorcerers whose demons have reanimated elvish bodies. Plus two necromancers, a dozen wraiths, and dozens of elvish mages. Not to mention that every elf can wield the four basic forces."

"I see," Kamari said, taking a deep breath. "Well, I'm sure the battle in Highgate will diminish their numbers to some extent. So if they do attack here, they'll be more manageable."

Allison chuckled derisively. "Don't you understand what you're facing here? Nyro is the most powerful mage in the history of Anoria. When she's finished with us, she *will* come here. And though your own troops may well outnumber hers by then, who do you have for mages? Siren and a handful of witches and wizards? Against the greatest thaumaturgic force Anoria has seen in centuries?"

Kamari shrugged.

"She will destroy you. Our only hope is to join forces now. With the magical forces we've already assembled and our combined military might, we might stand a chance."

The prince considered it, tapping his finger on the table again. Finally, he flashed her a grin. "What would be in it for me if I were to agree?"

"I'm sorry, what?" she said, shaking her head. "Our continued existence as a species is what would be in it for you. The survival of your princedom."

"Yes, yes, but I'm not eager to join this fight prematurely. Perhaps you could provide some extra benefits for me in exchange for my early participation."

She had a bad feeling she knew exactly where he was going with this. "Your Highness, I am married. And I have never had any romantic interest in men."

"You misunderstand me," he said, shaking his head. "I have requested additional sorcerers, but the university has refused."

"They allow no more than one per princedom," she said. "It's not my rule, so I'm afraid I can't help you with that."

"Yet I understand that Spanbrook has three?" he said with a grin. "You could perhaps influence them to, ah, bend the rules for me."

"I can try." If the cost of adding Okset's army to their own was sending him an extra sorcerer, it would be well worth it.

"Good," he said with a nod. "If *you* were to enter my service, I'm quite sure I could be persuaded to assist in your war effort."

"That's impossible. I'm already assigned to Spanbrook. And my family is there—Princess Jezebel and I have *children*."

He shrugged, flashing her that grin she was coming to despise. "We all face difficult decisions in life."

"They could assign one of the others to Okset," she said. She wasn't sure any of them would want to come here, either. But that would be up to them.

"I think they don't have any other necromancers, though."

"That's your price, then? Me or nothing?"

"One person in exchange for a hundred thousand," he said with a shrug. "Sounds like a good bargain to me."

Allison sighed and had to fight back tears. The thought of leaving Jezebel and the girls was too much to bear. Yet if doing so could save

Anoria? She didn't believe they could defeat Nyro without Okset's force of arms. The numbers were simply too overwhelming.

"I'll need to think about this. If I agree, I have your guarantee you'll send your army to Highgate?"

"No, no," he said, waving one hand dismissively. "You would be welcome to bring the others here and add your combined military and thaumaturgic forces to my own. We will fight the enemy in Okset."

Allison doubted very much Salerna would agree to this. But she said, "I'll need to present your offer to the others. Someone will be in touch very soon."

"Very well," he said, standing up with a predatory grin. "I look forward to your decision."

Allison got to her feet. "Thank you, Your Highness. Could someone escort me to your roof?"

"You won't be departing the same way you arrived?" he asked.

"No, I'll be taking my carpet to my next destination," she said. It was a lie. She needed to send Shadow ahead before opening her portal and didn't want to spend another moment in his presence.

The prince led her out of the council chamber and ordered one of his guards to escort her to the roof. Allison followed him through the palace, nearly oblivious to her surroundings. She couldn't stop thinking about his proposal. Leaving Jezebel and the girls to save Anoria.

Long ago, she'd been forced into leaving Spanbrook to go to the university. She'd hated having her fate decided by others. Her future ripped out of her own hands. This would be different, though. Jezebel would never order her to do this. The decision would be hers.

No part of her wanted to make this sacrifice. She loved her life in Spanbrook with her family. Her extended family, which included Khaldun and Mira. Jezebel's parents. Emma. She desperately missed the life they'd made there and she couldn't wait to get it back.

But they were going to lose in Highgate without Kamari's help. Unless they could unearth Nyro's true name before the battle started. But there was no guarantee they'd ever find that.

As much as she dreaded the idea, Allison knew she would make this sacrifice if it were the only way to save Anoria. And at this point, it might very well be that.

Allison reached the roof with the guard, standing there for a moment and taking in the view. She could see the entire city from here, as well as the river and the sea beyond. It was beautiful.

"Did he offer you a deal?" a voice said from behind her.

Turning, Allison spotted Siren approaching. She'd been so lost in her thoughts, she hadn't noticed her standing there. "Oh, he sure did."

"Let me guess. He demanded an additional sorcerer in exchange for sending aid."

"You know him well," she observed.

"The prince isn't a bad ruler. Ambitious, though. I know his requests for additional sorcerers have been denied."

"Yes, well, I'll have to present his offer to Princesses Salerna and Jezebel, and the governors, of course, and see what they say. It's not my decision to make."

"Hmm. Well, let me offer you a little advice. Make sure he fulfills his end of the bargain before you provide him anything—or anyone—in exchange."

"Oh? Does he have a history of reneging on such deals?"

"You could say that," she said with a shrug. "Some princes from Maeda wronged his family long ago, and the Okseti princes have been suspicious of non-Shifari rulers ever since."

"I appreciate the warning," Allison said. There was no way she would throw her life away for nothing. They would have to wait for Kamari to honor his end of the deal first.

"Would you be willing to show me how you do that portal thing again?" Siren said with a grin.

Allison chuckled, removing the pyramid and her carpet from the void. "Give me a moment. I need to send my demon ahead to make sure the coast is clear at my destination first."

"Oh, of course," Siren said. "Take your time!"

Allison summoned Shadow and sent her to Horn. The demon moved through the spirit realm, emerging in the physical world high above the city, giving her a bird's eye view. Like Okset, the buildings were all built from stone. But the city was spread out in a way Allison had never seen before. There were multiple plateaus overlapping each other along the coast like dragon's scales. Each plateau hosted its own cluster of buildings, almost like separate cities. Cliffs separated each level, but structures had been built into many of the cliffsides, linking the urban clusters together. And roads with multiple switchbacks had been carved out of the cliff faces, providing access from one level to the next.

A palace with high towers and golden domes sat atop the highest plateau, and Allison had no doubt that was where they would find Princess Zuri. She didn't want to barge in on her like she had with Kamari, though. Unlike their efforts with Okset, they'd made only their initial overture there.

"I'll be going now," Allison said to Siren. "Thank you again."

"My pleasure," she said. "Please keep me apprised of your progress in the war. Khaldun can reach me with his mirror."

"I will."

Allison opened a portal to Horn, directly in front of the palace gate. Walking through it, she let it close behind her and tucked her pyramid and carpet back into the void. A couple of guards came hurrying out of the gatehouse, weapons drawn, demanding that she identify herself and state her purpose.

"I am Princess Consort Allison Barclay from Spanbrook in the kingdom of Dorshire," she told them, "here to request an audience with Princess Zuri."

One of the guards returned to the gatehouse, while the other remained, sheathing his sword. Several minutes later, the gate opened and a hooded mage emerged.

"Princess Allison?" he said. His dark, golden skin and red eyes meant this could only be Zuri's sorcerer, Davu. Like Khaldun, he'd never bothered taking a new name. He and Sage were the only sorcerers who came from Shifar.

"Yes," she said. "You must be Davu, I presume."

"That is correct, Your Highness. Forgive me, but you don't look like a Dorshirite."

"Ah, yes. I had business in the elven lands, and given their prejudice against humans, we felt it was best to change my appearance," she explained. "Apparently they're more tolerant of Shifari."

"You've been physically transformed?" he said, raising an eyebrow. "Are you a shapeshifter, then?"

"No, one of our other sorcerers has the ability to change others' appearances," she said, growing impatient. "Will it be possible for me to speak with Princess Zuri?"

"Her Highness is very busy. She has asked me to inquire as to the reason for your unexpected visit." Allison told him about the impending battle with Nyro and their need for aid. "Understood. Please excuse me for a moment." He wandered off, producing a mirror and speaking into it for a minute. When he returned, he said, "Her Highness wonders if Prince Kamari of Okset is sending aid."

"He is not," she said.

The sorcerer nodded. "I'm afraid Princess Zuri will be unable to take part in this conflict at this time."

"Why does Okset's participation figure into this decision?" she said. "Nyro will come for your princedom if Highgate falls, regardless of Kamari's involvement."

"Any invading force would have to pass through Okset to reach Horn, Your Highness," he said, and she thought she detected an apologetic tone. His thoughts betrayed a belief that Horn *should* come to their aid, but it was Zuri's decision to make, not his. "Perhaps if Okset does eventually enter this war, you could try again. I believe Her Highness might be more amenable at such a time."

"Let me speak with her now," Allison said. "If she understood how dire—"

"I do apologize, Your Highness, but that will not be possible. Princess Zuri has made her position clear."

Allison nodded. It *would* be possible if she opened a portal into the palace. But she didn't feel this would get her very far. She thanked Davu for his time and moved away from the gates.

Summoning Shadow, Allison sent her to Nyro's old island castle in Drengrvollr. The demon moved through the spirit realm, emerging over the bay. There was no sign of any magic in place over the island—Allison had half-expected to see Nyro's barrier back in place. Shadow moved into the castle, quickly checking all the rooms, but the place was deserted.

Davu was watching her, so she considered flying away on her carpet before going to Drengrvollr. Yet perhaps it would be good for him to realize she could enter the palace anytime she wanted but chose to accept Zuri's wishes. For now.

Pulling her pyramid and carpet out of the void, Allison opened a portal to the castle's dining room, stepping through it and closing it behind her. It was dark here, so she called a small flame to light her way. Tucking her belongings back into the void, she moved through the castle once, checking every area for active spells, but there were none. Shadow could have done that for her, but she preferred to take care of it herself. She hadn't expected to find anything, either. What she was after was any trace of the last magic performed here.

Nyro seemed to spend a lot of her time in the dining room, so Allison returned there. She could sense the echoes of many powerful spells performed in this room. She cast the spell to reveal the last magic Nyro had done. The scene changed. It was still nighttime, but a few of the torches were burning in their sconces. Nyro was here with Emma and Fang, but otherwise, the house seemed empty.

As Allison watched, Nyro held her pyramid in one hand and opened a portal. This was what Allison wanted to see. Gazing through the rift, she tried to glean anything about the area beyond that might help her determine where Nyro had gone. It was an empty room, another dining room, perhaps, with stone walls. She could see a couple of large windows, and it was dark outside there, too. There was no furniture, and the walls were bare. Nothing to betray the place's location. No sounds or scents, either.

Nyro followed the other two through the portal and it closed behind her. The scene around Allison returned to the present time.

"Damn," she muttered. That wasn't very helpful. It looked like Nyro had probably gone to another castle somewhere. On the same side of the world as her old one. It would have been light out if she'd gone to Anoria. Beyond that, it was impossible to say.

Removing the pyramid and her carpet from the void, she opened a portal to Highgate, right in front of her townhouse, and walked through it.

CHAPTER TWENTY-FIVE
TRUE NAME

ucking her things into the void, Allison went up to the castle, entering through the gate and passing into Mira's null. She didn't think she'd ever get used to the sensation of losing her magic. She felt naked without it.

Allison found Jezebel in her chambers with the girls. The two of them sat down at the table by the window, and she told her about her meeting with Prince Kamari—and what Siren had told her.

"He's not dealing in good faith," Jezebel said with a sigh. "What a bastard. Well, I'll bring this up with Salerna, of course, but if we can't take him at his word, what are we supposed to do?"

"We should agree to his terms, but insist that he honor his end of the bargain first," Allison said. "If he lets us take our people there, armies and all, and fights by our side…" She finished with a shrug.

"You'd be willing to enter his service?" Jezebel asked incredulously.

"If it would save Anoria? Jez, what choice would we have? I don't want to leave you and the girls, but if that's what it takes to stop Nyro from exterminating our people, how can I refuse?"

"We can win here without Kamari," Jezebel insisted. "Highgate's impregnable."

"It's not," Allison said. "I could infiltrate it, with or without Mira's null in place, so you'd better believe that Nyro can, too."

"By causing an earthquake," Jezebel said, with a look of dawning comprehension.

"And we're badly outnumbered on the battlefield. Unless we can find her true name, I don't see how we can pull out a victory here."

"So what do we do?" Jezebel said, tears welling up in her eyes.

"We fight," Allison said with a shrug. "And if she defeats us here, we fall back to Bayfast. And if we lose there… you and I take the girls and flee to Ostland."

Jezebel giggled and hugged her tight.

Allison went to find Asmund and Gyda. They had adjoining chambers on the level below Jezebel's. Allison asked if their people had spotted Nyro's new hideout anywhere, but they hadn't. Since leaving her island, Nyro hadn't been seen anywhere in Drengrvollr.

That didn't mean much. It was a massive kingdom, and there were vast tracts of territory with no representation in their resistance movement. She'd gotten her hopes up that maybe someone would know her whereabouts, but it wasn't to be.

Allison left the castle and returned to her townhouse. Sitting on the terrace outside the bedroom, she checked in with her specters in Stoutwall. There was no change. The elvish army was still camped exactly where it had been before, and the spirits hadn't seen anyone enter or leave the camp since their departure.

The demon that had been watching over Castle Stoutwall was gone, though. That was something. Allison summoned another specter and had it check the space above Highgate. Sure enough, there was a powerful demon lurking over the castle. There was no way to know for sure if it was the same one that had been watching Stoutwall. But it hardly mattered. No demon would behave like this on its own. Nyro must have sent it. And that provided further proof that she had survived their spike.

Allison realized suddenly how hungry she was, but didn't feel like moving. The view from the terrace was so beautiful, she just wanted to soak it in. She spotted several dragons roosting on the city walls and had to laugh. She'd wondered where they'd gone—she hadn't seen them since arriving here. The area around the city was pretty arid, though, without any big forests the beasts would normally use for their hunting grounds. She suspected they'd had to venture farther out to find food.

The sunset was breathtaking. Allison could certainly get used to this view. She reflected on all the twists and turns in her life that had brought her to this moment. Growing up an only child, she'd never questioned that she'd inherit her father's princedom. The issues of marriage and children were thorny ones, given that she was attracted only to women. She would have had to take a man to bed eventually to produce an heir. But that was not her fate.

Jezebel had risked life and limb, traveling the continent to find a way to save her from a vicious haunting. Coming to this very city, in fact, not even the farthest point along her journey. In the end, Jezebel had saved her, yet a cruel twist of fate had driven them apart. Allison transformed into a sorcerer. Never had she betrayed the slightest sign of magic, yet there she was. Shipped off to the university against her will.

In hindsight, she was glad it had all unfolded the way it did. She couldn't imagine her life without magic. And she enjoyed the life of a princess consort and court mage far more than she would have that of a ruling princess. Jezebel always included her in major decisions, but the burden of responsibility didn't rest on *her* shoulders. It was a freedom she'd grown to cherish.

Allison had first come to this city a captive of Prince Henry. Those days had been something out of a nightmare. And she'd considered taking her own life more than once to escape it. She was thankful now, of course, that she hadn't chosen that path. Never would she have known the love and joy she shared with Jezebel. Nor would she have known Alanna or Leda or been a mother to them. Or experienced the pride of watching them grow into strong young women. No, Allison wouldn't trade this life of hers for anything.

Yet as she visited this city now, once again in a time of war, the stakes were higher than ever. The enemy threatened to eliminate everything she and Jezebel had built in Spanbrook, everyone they loved, and their very civilization. The last time she was here, she'd had no control over her actions, much less her own life. This time, it couldn't be more different. The odds were against them, but she was here by choice. And as much as it was ever possible for anyone, she had a measure of control. Not over the outcome, perhaps, but certainly in how they responded to this threat. And however it ended, that made all the difference.

She heard someone knocking and went to see who it was. Unlocking and opening the door, she found Jezebel standing there. "I'm sorry—I wouldn't have locked it if I knew you were coming."

"I miss you," Jezebel said, embracing her. "And I'm famished. Have you eaten?"

"No, and I'm so hungry I could eat a horse."

They went to eat at the tavern next door. There was an outdoor patio out back, so they sat there. Jezebel asked the server for water, and she returned a minute later with a full pitcher and two glasses, pouring some for each of them.

"I'm going to stay with you here in the city," Jezebel said, drinking some of her water. "I don't want to be separated from you at a time like this."

"What about the girls?"

"Khaldun and Mira are staying in my chambers. They'll keep an eye on them."

"Fair enough," Allison said, taking a long drink of wine. "I'll enjoy a little time alone together. Despite the circumstances."

They ate dinner and sat up late. Jezebel told her that Alanna had met Sigrid in the courtyard earlier, scaring passersby out of their skin, and confirmed that they'd ventured out to the forest across the river to go hunting.

Jezebel was growing tired, so they returned to the townhouse. Allison stripped out of her armor and helped Jezebel out of her dress. Lying in bed, they kissed passionately and stayed up late into the night making love. Allison never wanted to lose this.

She woke at dawn to the sound of someone knocking on the door. Slipping out of bed, she was about to don her armor, when she spotted a robe hanging on the back of the washroom door, and put that on instead. She opened the door to find Shatter, Imani, and Battleaxe standing there.

"Good morning, Princess," Battleaxe said with a grin. "We're going to train. Care to join us?"

"Yes, definitely," she said. The exercise would do her some good. Get her mind off all the recent developments for a little while. "Come inside while I change into my armor."

They waited for her while she ran upstairs. Jezebel was dead to the world, so Allison let her sleep, doing her best to be quiet as she slipped into the leather. She joined the others, and they headed out of the city. Out on the plain, there was plenty of space for them.

Battleaxe told her that they'd brought Princess Miranda and Beast along with their other mages and their army to Highgate without any trouble. Miranda had insisted on being tucked into the void with her people—she was terrified of flying.

Allison only had her new two-handed sword and the daggers in her leg sheaths. Her other weapons were in Jezebel's chambers in the castle. But she usually fought with the large blade anyway, so that was fine.

It felt good to work up a sweat. She had a couple of turns with each of them and was able to win every bout. Shatter nearly beat her the second time, but she finally managed to disarm him and knock him off his feet.

"I miss the lake," Battleaxe said, gazing around the plain when they were done. "The river's a little far."

"You could fly us there," Imani said, stripping out of her armor. Her squire and Shatter's had both met them by the city gate, carrying their armor out for them.

"What's the current like here?" Battleaxe asked. "It's deadly up near Arthos."

"It's not bad this far south," Shatter said.

"All right," Battleaxe said with a shrug. "Let's do it."

She and Allison stripped out of their leather, and she pulled her carpet out of the void. Once Shatter and Imani had finished taking off their plate and underclothing, Battleaxe flew them over to the river.

The bank was rather steep, and the current seemed pretty strong to Allison, but they climbed down to the water and jumped in. It was cold, and Allison whooped as goosebumps formed on her skin. This was much more invigorating than the lake, and she had to swim continuously to stop from being swept downriver.

When they climbed out of the water, they found Azure standing at the top of the bank. "Now I've seen everything," he said, and though she couldn't see his face through his mask, Allison was pretty sure he had to be grinning from ear to ear.

"You should try it sometime," Allison said, smiling back at him. She didn't think she'd ever seen him out of his leather outfit, facemask, and morion. "Very refreshing."

"I have an image to maintain," he said.

"Yeah, it's hard to inspire fear when people have seen you swimming buck naked in the river," Battleaxe said.

"Indeed," Azure agreed. "Princess Allison, Her Highness wanted to inform you that we've found a name. Saliman's last living descendant. He's here in the city. If you'd care to, ah, get dressed and meet me in the entry hall, I'll be going out to his last known residence after breakfast."

"I'll be there," she said, trying not to get her hopes up too high. This was probably a dead end.

Azure took off on his carpet. Allison went back with the other three to where they'd left the squires. Once the four of them had gotten dressed, they headed up to the castle. Inside the great hall, they sat with Jezebel and the girls, Mira, and Khaldun for breakfast. Allison told them the news as they ate. Khaldun wanted to go with her, so once they'd finished eating, the two of them went out to the entry hall to meet Azure.

"The man we're seeking is named Bartholomew Townsend," the sorcerer told them as he led them through the city. "He's a cobbler if our information is accurate."

They found the man's dwelling on the city's second level. His shop occupied the first floor and it looked like he had an apartment on the upper level. The shop was closed, so Azure knocked on the door to the apartment. There was no answer, so he tried again, louder this time.

Finally, they heard footsteps coming down the stairs inside. A sleepy-eyed man with white hair and a lot of wrinkles opened the door, gazing around at the three of them. His eyes went wide, and he suddenly seemed much more alert. Allison could sense that he was afraid they were there to apprehend him. He was Saliman's heir, all right, and had taken great pains to keep that fact a secret.

"Bartholomew Townsend?" Azure asked.

"Barty, my lord," he said. "I ain't done nothing wrong, I swear. Just a simple cobbler, my lord, trying my best to get by."

"You don't stand accused of any crime," Azure told him. "We just have some questions for you."

"All right," the man said, and Allison could sense his cautious relief. "What about?"

"Might we come inside?" Azure asked.

"The place is a bit of a mess, to be honest, my lord," he said. Allison sensed only embarrassment from him, not anything nefarious. "Could we talk in the shop?"

"That would be fine," Azure said.

"Wait here—I'll open it up for us."

He closed the door, and they heard footsteps moving upstairs. A minute later, he appeared in the shop and invited them inside. As he closed the door behind him, Allison sensed Azure casting the spells to prevent magical observation.

"So, ah, what is it I can do for you, my lord?"

"Our city is once again under imminent threat of attack," Azure told him. "And this time, Nyro herself leads the forces arrayed against us. You've heard of Nyro, haven't you?"

Allison could tell that he'd grown up knowing her history.

"Aye, I seem to recall a story or two from my youth," he said.

"Our people have done some research, Barty," Azure said. "It turns out you're the last living descendant of King Saliman. The one responsible for unleashing Nyro on our world. Did you know about that?"

"No, there must be some mistake," he said. "My family ain't never been related to kings," he said with a chuckle. "Look at this place, my lord! A simple life is all I've ever known. I ain't related to royalty!"

"You're lying," Allison said. "You've always known you were descended from kings, but you've kept that secret, fearing what might happen if people ever found out. Just like your father always had, and his father before him."

The man gaped at her. He was terrified.

"We're not holding your ancestry against you," Azure said. "Your secret is safe with us. And I assure you we are not here to arrest you—if that were the case, we would have done it already."

"We only need information," Allison said.

"I-I'm not sure I'll be much help, my lady," he said. "But I'll assist however I can. I don't want no trouble."

"We are seeking Nyro's true name," Azure told him. "The name holds the power to destroy her. And if we can find it, we may be able to eliminate this threat and save the city. Did your mother or father ever tell you anything about this?"

Barty shifted his gaze between the two of them for a moment, then said, "They never told me no name." He was telling the truth. "But my dad sat me down once, and 'splained where I could find it. I went looking for it after he passed away, though, and I'm sorry to say he was full of shit. Wasn't nothing there."

"Where was it?" Allison asked, her heart pounding in her chest.

"Dad said the name was inscribed on a stone tablet attached to the grave of the last king," he told them. "So I went to the catacombs to see for myself."

"The catacombs have been closed to the public for centuries," Azure said. "How did you get in?"

"I knew someone," he said with a shrug. "Used to be a hidden entrance in the cellar of one of the nearby buildings. That was a long time ago, though. It's been sealed off for years."

Allison could tell Azure was skeptical, but the man was telling the truth.

"Anyway," he continued. "I found the grave of King Verus. And other than his name, the dates of his birth and death, and those of his reign, there weren't nothing written there at all. No tablet of any kind, other than the headstone."

"There could be something hidden," Allison said. If a mage had left the tablet there, it could be tucked into the void. Or even buried with the king.

"Yes, we should investigate," Azure said. "Thank you for your time, Barty."

The man radiated relief, even smiling for the first time.

They left the shop, and Azure led them through the city, up to the third level and the entry to the catacombs. The two guards stationed there stood aside to let them pass. Allison and Khaldun followed Azure through a long tunnel. It grew darker as they moved farther from the entry, and the sorcerer called a flame to light their way.

The tunnel opened into a massive chamber with low ceilings, and the little flame wasn't enough to penetrate the darkness. Azure grew it larger until it illuminated the entire space, and a shiver ran down Allison's spine. Thousands of skulls lined the walls.

"I came here with Jezebel and Raphael," Khaldun said. "My memory of this place doesn't do it justice."

"This is only the antechamber," Azure said. "It's where they buried the common soldiers in the ancient wars. According to legend, they'll rise again in a final battle to protect the city."

"Let's hope that time isn't upon us now," Khaldun said.

Across the chamber, they passed through a stone archway, through a short passage, and into a vast chamber with vaulted ceilings. Giant niches lined the walls, each hosting a stone sarcophagus. Above each of those, carved into the wall, was a different scene.

"These are the ancient kings," Khaldun said. "Raphael told us that the carvings depict an important event from each king's reign."

"Yes, that's right," Azure said.

He led them to the far end of the chamber, where the last sarcophagus appeared to be much newer than the others. "Here lies King Verus," Azure told them. "The last king of Maeda."

Allison examined the grave in the light of Azure's fire. Barty was right. There was nothing inscribed here beyond the headstone, which did not provide Nyro's true name. She wasn't mentioned at all, but Azure told them that the scene carved on the wall represented her killing Verus. She was depicted in the nude, of course, wielding a massive sword with rays shooting out of her head.

"I sense nothing tucked into the void," Allison said. "No active spells of any kind."

"Could there be something inside the sarcophagus?" Khaldun said.

"One way to find out," Azure replied. Holding out one hand, he called air, lifting the massive stone lid and setting it aside.

Allison gazed inside. There was a burial shroud, nothing more. She poked the center section of the shroud, and it collapsed.

"His remains would have long since turned to dust," Azure said. "Nyro's true name is not here." Calling air again, he replaced the lid.

"This is disappointing," Allison said.

"Now, hold on," Khaldun said. "Raphael told us Verus was originally buried in a pauper's grave outside the city. The first prince had him moved here after Nyro's downfall."

"The timing doesn't work out, then," Allison said. "If someone affixed a tablet with Nyro's true name to his grave in Saliman's time, or his immediate heir's, then there's no way it could be *here*."

"I don't suppose there's any record of where Verus's original burial site might be?" Khaldun asked.

"Not that I've ever heard," said Azure. "But I wonder if we've got the right king."

"Was Verus not the last?" Allison asked.

"He was the last king of *Maeda*," Azure said. "To anyone in the early days of Nyro's reign, Saliman would have been considered the first emperor. Making his predecessor the last king of *Pytha*."

"And Saliman was Pythan, of course," said Allison. "So it makes sense that his descendants would have been referring to their Pythan ancestors when referring to the 'last king'."

"According to the history book your people translated for us, that would be King Majid," said Khaldun. "Do we know where he's buried?"

"I'm sure our scholars do," Azure said. "Let's find out."

They returned to the castle, and Azure led them to their library. It was in the rear of the castle and occupied three levels. The only larger one Allison had seen was their own in Castle Barclay.

Azure conferred with one of their scholars, and she led them through the stacks. Searching the shelves, she pulled out an ancient-looking leather-bound tome and took it to a nearby table. After thumbing through its pages for a minute, she found a map of Pytha.

"This was Parthia," she said, pointing to a city two-thirds of the way down the kingdom's eastern coast, roughly equal in latitude to Okset City. "The capital of ancient Pytha."

She turned several more pages, stopping at a sketch. "This is the only known map of Parthia. Here at the top of this hill was where the castle stood. The royal catacombs were accessible from the base of the hill, here by the sea."

"I thought history books about ancient Pytha were lost in the purge," Khaldun said.

"Only those containing information about Nyro," the scholar said. "This book predates her reign by a few centuries. Of course, few texts remain from that era regardless, as most were lost to time. But this has been in our collection for centuries."

Azure thanked the woman, and they left the library.

"Shall we pay a visit to Parthia?" Allison said when they reached the entry hall.

"I must remain here," Azure said, "but the two of you should see what you can find. I'll inform Princess Salerna."

"We should let Jezebel and Mira know where we're going, too," Khaldun said to Allison.

They went up to his chambers, but no one was there. They found the two of them in the great hall with Alanna and Leda having breakfast. Allison was famished, so she and Khaldun sat down to eat with them, telling them about their search for Nyro's true name.

When they were done, Allison left the castle with Khaldun. Inside her townhouse, they went up to the second-floor terrace. The two of them pulled their carpets out of the void, and Allison opened a portal to Parthia. They flew through it, and she tucked the pyramid into the void.

The entire city lay in ruins. It looked like it had been quite large in its day, but not a single structure remained standing. They flew over the hill by the sea, circling the ruins of the ancient castle. The lifelessness here struck Allison. The color green was nowhere to be seen, as if the spells placed upon this land had sucked the life force out of not only its citizens but the plant life, too.

Flying over the sea, they spotted the entrance to the catacombs. They landed on the rocky beach near the cavern, tucking their carpets into the void, and walking the rest of the way. Inside, it was very dark, so Allison called a flame to light their way.

Following a narrow passage, they reached an enormous hall with pillars of stone holding up a vaulted ceiling. Dozens of sarcophagi filled the space, but all of their lids had been removed, many of them lying broken on the ground. Most were missing headstones, too.

"The whole place has been looted," Allison said, crestfallen. "We should still try to find Majid's grave, just to be sure, but how are we supposed to identify it?"

Khaldun gazed around the space for a few moments. "These sarcophagi up front look much older than the ones farther back. It seems like they buried the kings in order. Let's take a look."

They wandered through the crypt, finally locating what was probably the last king's tomb by the rear wall. Like all the others, the lid to his sarcophagus was missing. Behind it, there was a rectangular recess in the wall where his tombstone would have been.

Allison examined the entire area around the grave, but there was nothing inscribed anywhere. "Could it have been on his headstone?"

"That's my guess," Khaldun said with a shrug. "But it appears that's long gone."

All of the newest tombs were missing headstones, and they hadn't detected anything tucked into the void around any of the sarcophagi. "That's it, then," she said with a sigh. "This is the end of the road."

"Perhaps not," he said pensively. "Syllith mentioned in her journal that Kongese antique dealers had plundered this land of ancient artifacts to sell to rich buyers. Chances are that's what happened to Majid's headstone."

"That's not much help," Allison said. "It could be anywhere in Kong by now."

"I'm not so sure. Hido is the one major city in the entire kingdom. And that's where anyone with money lives. The city is enormous—much larger than anything in Maeda or Dorshire. But I have a funny feeling I might know where this particular headstone ended up."

"How could you? If the city's as large as you say, there must be a million people living there."

"It's mostly gang leaders who run the city," Khaldun said. "According to Syllith's journal, the biggest one was one named Krigo. But a woman named Ming helped her out, and in the process, ended up eliminating him and taking over his business. She owned an inn—well, a brothel, from the sounds of it—but also dealt in high-end artifacts."

"What makes you think she would have this particular headstone?" Allison asked skeptically.

"She's a witch," he said. "And she knew who Syllith was and the role she played in Nyro's liberation. She knew Nyro had compromised her, forcing her to do her bidding against her will."

"How could she have known that? To this day, it's hardly common knowledge."

"I know, but Ming had connections with the university," Khaldun told her. "And if anyone would understand the potential significance of Nyro's name showing up on the headstone of the last Pythan king, it would be her."

"All right," Allison said with a shrug. She remained unconvinced, but it couldn't hurt to follow every lead they had. "Let's go to Hido. Do you have any idea where in the city we can find Ming's place?"

"Not exactly," he said. "She said it was close to the mouth of the River Ling, right across from the shore. A four-story building, if memory serves. And she mentioned it being multi-colored—pink, green, and yellow, maybe?"

Allison summoned Shadow and sent her to Hido. The demon hovered over the sea near the river, gazing up and down the shoreline.

There were a handful of four-story buildings and quite a few colorful ones, but only one that fit both descriptions.

Removing her carpet and pyramid from the void, she opened a portal to the space above that building. Khaldun retrieved his carpet, too, and the two of them flew through the portal. Allison closed it behind them, and they landed in front of Ming's building. Tucking their belongings into the void, they went inside.

Most of this level served as a tavern. Despite the early hour, there were quite a few patrons here. A muscular man wearing only a thong approached them, smiling and saying something in Kongese. When Allison shook her head and shrugged, he said in the common tongue, "How might I help the two of you? I do have a room available upstairs if you'd like to accompany me."

"No, thank you," she said with a nervous giggle. "We're looking for Ming."

"You've found her," a voice behind them said. The young man walked away as Allison turned to see a short Kongese woman standing there, holding a staff. "A sorcerer and a Shifari—we don't see very many of either around here. How can I help you?"

Allison was about to explain that she wasn't actually Shifari, but decided not to bother.

"We were friends of Syllith," Khaldun told her. "I'm Khaldun and this is Allison. We're looking for a headstone that was looted from the royal catacombs beneath Parthia. And based on the information Syllith left for us, we thought you might be able to help."

Ming stared at him for a moment, then Allison, before saying, "Come with me."

She led them to the rear of the building and down a corridor. There was an office back there, a wizard standing guard outside the door. The two of them followed Ming inside, and she closed the door behind them.

"Have a seat, please," she said, sitting behind her desk. Allison and Khaldun took the two seats across from her. Holding her staff, Ming cast the spell to prevent sound from escaping the room, before saying, "You said you *were* Syllith's friends. Might I inquire what happened to her?"

Khaldun and Allison took turns giving her a brief account of everything that had happened since Syllith's arrival in Stoutwall.

"I'm sorry to hear that," Ming said when they were done. "I liked her. At least her sacrifice paid dividends. So, whose headstone are you seeking?"

"King Majid of Pytha," Khaldun said.

"Ah, yes," Ming replied with a nod. "My people were some of the first into Parthia after the old spells were lifted. Majid's headstone was in the first shipment of artifacts I received."

"Do you have it here?" Allison asked.

"I'm afraid not. I sold it to a local collector. We brought back the headstones of more than a dozen Pythan kings in that first haul, and they purchased the lot."

"Do you recall what was inscribed on it?" Khaldun asked.

"The usual. Dates of birth and death. Years of his reign. It was the same for all of them."

"There was nothing else?" Allison asked. "On the back, perhaps?"

"No, and I'd remember it if there were," Ming said. "Any oddities like that would have fetched a higher price."

"Damn," Allison said.

"Could you tell us where to find this collector?" Khaldun asked.

"I don't think so," she said. "It's bad business to reveal clients' identities."

"I can understand that," Khaldun said. "But it's possible this stone contains Nyro's true name. And using that, we can destroy her. As we told you, if we fail to defeat her in Highgate, she could very well go on to exterminate everyone in Anoria. Including you and your clients. And that would mean Syllith's sacrifice was for naught."

Ming met his gaze for a moment, then shook her head and chuckled. "You drive a hard bargain, my lord. But I'm telling you, there was nothing interesting about that headstone."

"So it may have appeared," Khaldun said. "But I would need to examine it myself to be sure. There are some things that could be hidden in such a way that only a sorcerer could reveal them."

Ming heaved a sigh and seemed to be debating something with herself. "All right. Here's what I can do for you. You wait in the common room, and I'll go visit my client myself. See if they're willing to let me borrow the headstone in question. If so, I'll bring it to you myself."

"That would be perfect," Khaldun said with a grin. "Thank you."

"Don't thank me," Ming said, getting to her feet. "I'm only doing this to honor Syllith's memory."

They followed her back to the common room, sitting down at a booth in the rear corner. Ming told one of the servers they could have whatever they wanted on the house before heading out. Allison and Khaldun weren't hungry yet but enjoyed a couple of ales while they waited. Several scantily clad men and women stopped by their table offering their services, but they turned them down.

Finally, the wizard who'd been guarding Ming's office showed up at their booth. "Ming will see you now."

He escorted them to her office. They went inside and he closed the door behind them. Ming was standing behind her desk, King Majid's headstone sitting on its surface.

"Make this fast," she said. "I need to get this back to my client within the hour."

Allison could sense that there was something in the void, tethered to the stone. Khaldun cast the spell to release it, and Allison gasped. Sitting on the headstone was a stone tablet. There was a two-line inscription, but it wasn't in the common tongue. Allison flipped it over, but the other side was blank.

"Do you know what this says?" she asked Khaldun.

"I'm pretty sure it's ancient Pythan," he said, examining the inscription. "And I believe this word on the first line is 'Nyro'. This is exactly what we were looking for," he added with a grin.

CHAPTER TWENTY-SIX
THE BATTLE OF HIGHGATE

ing told them they could keep the hidden tablet—her client would never know the difference. Allison and Khaldun thanked her, and she walked them out of the establishment. The two of them pulled their carpets out of the void and shot into the sky. Once they'd flown high above the city, Allison retrieved the pyramid, opening a portal back to Highgate.

Landing in front of her townhouse, they tucked their things into the void—except the tablet—and hurried up to the castle. They found Salerna's steward and requested an audience with Her Highness. Khaldun went off to find Jezebel and Mira. Ten minutes later, Allison, Khaldun, Jezebel, and Mira sat down with Salerna and Azure at the conference table in her council chambers. Allison placed the tablet on the table for Salerna to examine. She handed it to Azure.

"You're right that this is ancient Pythan," the sorcerer said. "And the first word is 'Nyro'. I'll have to take this to our scholars to translate the rest."

"Go now," said Salerna. "We'll await you here."

Azure took the tablet and hurried off.

"If this is her true name, we could end her now," said Jezebel.

"No, I don't think so," said Allison. "We have no idea where she is, so we'd have no way to know if it worked or not. We'll have to find her first. Which may be easier said than done. But if we can locate her, Shadow can keep watch as we invoke her name."

"Has there been any change with her troops?" Mira asked.

"No," Allison said. "They're still camped in Stoutwall—my specters updated me right before we entered the castle."

"If we're unable to locate her, we'll have to proceed with our preparations for battle," Salerna said. "At that point, it would be worth invoking her true name whether we've found her or not."

"I agree, Your Highness," said Allison. "There is also a good chance she will take part in this battle herself. The demon mages she commands now are not loyal to her the way her Sacred Circle was. They are certain to be uncooperative, meaning she must be forcing them to carry out her every order. I doubt she'd trust them to execute her plans here without her."

Azure returned, retaking his seat and placing the tablet on the table. "This says 'Nyro Iron Will' in ancient Pythan." Though he'd spoken the name, he'd done it without intentionality, and without the words of command, "I name thee." Allison knew both were necessary to invoke someone's true name.

"That does sound like a true name," said Jezebel. "Would we have to speak it in ancient Pythan or the common tongue?"

"That's a good question, and we should consult with Allure and Sage," said Azure. "They should know for sure. But my understanding is that it is the meaning of the name that matters. So, either language should work."

"When the time comes, we could do both," Khaldun said. "One way or the other, that should take care of it."

"Do you know how to pronounce this in Pythan?" Allison asked.

"The name 'Nyro' is the same in both languages," Azure said. "The second line in ancient Pythan would be pronounced 'lohee dee ichah'."

"Lohee dee ichah," Allison repeated.

"That's it," Azure said with a nod.

"Princess Allison," said Salerna. "Princess Jezebel and I have discussed Okset's offer at great length. We do not believe it is sincere, especially considering what his sorcerer told you."

"I agree, Your Highness," said Allison.

"However, we would like to expose his duplicity," Salerna continued. "Could you contact the sorcerer and tell her we are prepared to fall back to Okset with our armies and full support staff?"

"And once we have defeated Nyro, we will be happy to reassign your bond to Prince Kamari," Jezebel added with a grin. "We are quite confident he will rescind his offer."

"I'll contact Siren immediately," Allison said.

Allison asked Khaldun if he could link her mirror to Siren's. The two of them left the castle, and Khaldun cast the necessary spells. She went to her townhouse, sitting on the terrace and reaching out to Siren. The woman appeared in the glass, and Allison relayed the princesses' message.

"I'll be sure to let His Highness know," she said with a grin. "And, well done."

Allison summoned Shadow, sending her to Stoutwall. The elvish army was still there and showed no signs of moving out. She checked Castle Barclay and the surrounding area, but as expected, it was empty. And she looked in on Nyro's old island castle, but there were no signs of activity there, either.

She felt someone reaching out to her and pulled out her mirror. It was Siren. Sure enough, Prince Kamari insisted that they'd have to bind Allison to him first before he would allow their people to enter his princedom. Allison returned to the castle and relayed the prince's message.

"As expected," Salerna said. "That's it, then. We shall continue our preparations for battle."

Allison and Jezebel went to bed that night, and Jezebel drifted off right away. Allison lay awake, though, wondering where Nyro could be and what the reason for her prolonged absence might be. Could they be wrong about her having survived the spike? No, she didn't believe so. Her demon still monitored Highgate, for one thing.

Also, if Nyro were gone, that would liberate Emma and Fang. They would be unbound necromancers now. Which would be bad news for Fang—the demons she'd bound were all the animalistic variety, and Allison didn't think she was powerful enough to control them.

Emma's situation would be rather different. *Her* demons were all newly formed and worked against Nyro and her allies in life. If Nyro were gone, there was a very good chance Emma could send one of them here to communicate with Allison. She was outside the null, so there would be nothing to hinder them. And yet that had not happened.

Nyro might have forced one of them to perform the rite to establish her line of succession. Which meant their bonds would have passed to Nyro's heir if she'd been destroyed. Yet somehow Allison couldn't imagine Nyro naming any heirs. Whom would she name? One of her elf mages? That hardly seemed likely.

No, Nyro must have survived. So where could she be?

Allison dozed off eventually. But she woke with a start when Shadow made contact.

"I'm sorry to wake you. But the elvish army has vanished from Stoutwall. We must assume an attack here is imminent."

Dread filled her very soul. War was upon them.

Allison slipped out of bed, moving out to the terrace, not bothering to put on her robe. Staring across the city, she could see their own troops camped on the plain far below. The first light of dawn was cracking the eastern horizon. They didn't have long to prepare.

Waking Jezebel, Allison told her what was happening. The two of them got dressed and headed up to the castle. They sent a messenger to Princess Salerna before going up to Khaldun and Mira's chambers. Once they'd given them the news, they went into the adjoining chamber to wake the girls.

Alanna was always slow to wake up, but Leda sat up the moment Allison sat on the edge of the bed. Once Alanna seemed conscious, Allison and Jezebel told them that the battle was about to be joined.

"The two of you need to remain in the castle, no matter what," Allison told them. "We'll take you down to the great hall with the other families."

"You'll be with us, won't you?" Leda said to Jezebel.

"Yes, my love," she said. "And we'll do our best to stay together. But if for any reason we're separated, you must promise us you will stick to the plan. No flying off with Sigrid, understood?"

"Yes, Mother," they both said, Leda a little more forcefully than Alanna.

Allison escorted them to the great hall. The castle had come alive, and people were hurrying about every which way to prepare their defenses. Allure, Battleaxe, Mist, and Sage found Allison in the great hall, and they left the castle together. They wished each other luck, mounting their carpets and taking off. All four of them went invisible, but they'd cast the spells that allowed them to track each other's carpets.

Racing across the city and out over the plain, Allison could see their armies below—all sixty-five thousand soldiers—already forming lines. It was an impressive sight to behold. She wondered if Nyro's forces were already out there under invisibility spells. Flying toward the river, she went low as she circled the empty plain a couple of times, but sensed no spells.

Allison returned to the city, circling the castle. Salerna and Albert, Mira, Miranda, Leto, Carlo, and Yolanda were gathered on the keep roof, along with Highgate's top military commanders, several guards, and a few non-sorcerer mages. They couldn't cast any spells inside of Mira's null, but if something happened to her, they could defend the royals against magic.

Jezebel had decided to stay inside the keep with the girls because they worried about Alanna doing something impetuous. But they always trusted battle tactics to Amari and Imani anyway, and Amari was on the keep roof with the other commanders, while Imani was leading their forces down on the plain.

Allison spotted Azure and Shatter by the castle gates, taking off on their carpets, and wondered where Khaldun and Beast were. They'd planned on having them down on the battlefield, Khaldun in his dragon-bear form, doing as much damage to the enemy lines as possible, but she hadn't seen them down there.

Asmund, Gyda, and the rest of the elf mages had taken positions on the battlements of the outermost city wall, along with the rest of their non-sorcerer human mages. Except for Camilla. She was on the battlements surrounding the city's uppermost level. They couldn't use mirrors or spirits to send messages between the leaders on the keep roof and the mages out in the field. So instead, they had Kashi and one of the other dragon riders taking care of it. One of them—Allison couldn't tell which—was perched on the battlements near Camilla, the other one on the keep roof. Camilla could use her mirror to communicate with the rest of the mages, and she and the leaders could relay messages to each other via dragon rider.

They still had more than forty dragons flying over the city and the plain, and Magna was leading those. The plan was to keep the dragons assaulting the enemy lines, causing as much destruction as they could. Only a quarter of the dragons had riders, but the entire group would follow Magna's lead. Allison felt they might be their one asset with the ability to win the day for them. Nyro's forces outmatched theirs in every other respect.

This would be a very different battle than the one that had taken place in Henry's final days. Then, she and Mira had been out there on the plain, helping the enemy. Mira had been forced to use her null to protect Fosland's army. They had debated keeping Mira on the battlefield to protect their own forces from thaumaturgic attack. But that would make her too easy a target for Nyro. Added to that, their troops all had armor imbued with spells that repelled the four basic forces. And they needed Mira to protect the castle, keeping it intact in case it came to a siege.

Flying over the plain again, Allison spotted a giant tiger prowling back and forth in front of their army. Beast's animal form was a normal-sized tiger, but this one was about three times larger. Khaldun must have effected this change using his powers—it would explain their late arrival. She heard the cry of a bird, and high above, noticed a giant eagle circling the plain. This had to be Khaldun. He was probably keeping an eye on things until the enemy appeared.

As if on cue, Allison felt a massive spell vibrate the air around her, more powerful than any she'd felt before. And in that instant, she spotted the enemy army appearing out of the void, like a wave moving across the plain. Her heart sank seeing how many more of them there were compared to their own troops. She'd known this, but seeing it was something else. The elves were so much larger that it made the difference in numbers seem even greater than it was.

Ninety-five thousand warriors, if their numbers were accurate. All emerging from the void in one shot, already in their battle lines. Allison couldn't believe Nyro had managed to transport so many on her own—she didn't think she'd be able to handle such a large group herself. But her demon mages had to be here somewhere, and she could have drawn power from them.

A shrieking call sounded across the battlefield, several others answering it, and Allison felt a sense of dread overcome her. The wraiths were here. She hadn't noticed them before, but looking closer, she spotted them scattered around the perimeter of the enemy lines.

Allison summoned Shadow and sent her to look for anyone hiding behind invisibility spells. Sure enough, she found one hovering above the plain just behind the enemy lines. Allison had her cancel the spell, revealing a large, male elf, completely naked, standing on a carpet. Getting a closer look, Allison recognized him—this was Gorm, from Nyro's island castle.

Allison called fire, hitting the elf with lightning. It succeeded only in revealing the shield spell around him. Allison hit it with a fire orb and a twister, but these had no effect, either. Her own magic was far stronger than Gorm's, and taken together, these incantations should have collapsed the shield spell, yet they didn't seem to have had any effect.

"This must be Nyro," Shadow said in her mind. "*We knew she'd reanimate a new elvish body.*"

She had to be right. Allison tried to sense if Nyro had anything tucked into the void, but the shield spell prevented that. A shield wouldn't protect Nyro if someone invoked her true name, though; only Mira's null could do that. Hovering over the enemy army,

Allison cast her own shield spell before speaking the words. "Nyro Iron Will, I name thee!"

Nyro whipped her gaze toward her as if she could see right through her invisibility spell, but nothing else happened. "Nyro lohee dee ichah, I name thee!" Allison yelled.

It had no effect. Except that Nyro could see her now. She hurled fire and lightning spells at her. Allison's shield spell held fast, but she flew off, retreating behind their own army. Nyro threw more spells, but it was clear she'd lost her.

"*Why didn't that work?*" Allison demanded of Shadow.

"*I don't know. My best guess is that reclaiming her own true name in life rendered it powerless for anyone else after she died. No one else has ever accomplished that, though, so it's impossible to know for sure.*"

"Damn," Allison muttered out loud. Pulling out her mirror, she reached Camilla and told her what had happened. The witch told her she'd relay the message to Salerna and the others.

This was it, then. The battle would be joined.

The sound of horns filled the plain, echoing off the city walls, and the elvish army started its advance. Drums joined the horns, adding their rhythmic beats to the footfalls of tens of thousands of soldiers.

A dragon's roar startled Allison as one of the beasts soared over her head, accompanying its cousins and siblings toward the advancing lines. They circled above the elves in a swarm and started diving two or three at a time, breathing jets of fire on the enemy. Dozens of soldiers died before someone canceled the air beneath one of the beasts. He struggled to stay aloft but crashed into the river.

Two more dragons succumbed to the same spell. Allison fired a cancellation spell at the source of one of them, exposing a carpet rider. With her long dark hair streaming behind her, this could only be Cyclone. Allison fought back tears as she hurled fire spells at her old friend. Cyclone had a shield spell in place, so Allison hit her again, this time with lightning, overpowering her and unraveling the magic keeping the shield in place. She canceled the spells keeping the carpet in the air, and Cyclone tumbled out of the sky.

The dragons kept up their barrage of fire on the enemy troops, and the demon mages caused several more of them to crash. With forty of the beasts swarming overhead, this was a losing battle for the elves. But it did reduce the pace of the carnage.

More horns sounded, and the leading regiments of the elvish army charged. They plowed into the lines defending Highgate, and the crash of metal on metal and the cries of their soldiers spread across the plain. Allison spotted Shatter in the middle of the fray, cutting through the enemy soldiers like wheat, using both his weapon and his magic.

Khaldun swooped in from above, landing as an eagle and immediately shifting into his dragon-bear shape. He and Beast, as a tiger, crashed through the enemy lines from opposite ends, cutting down the elvish troops and leaving a trail of corpses in their wake.

The demon mages on their carpets concentrated their attacks on the dragons, so Allison and the four university mages focused on defending them. The demons' spells canceling the beasts' air betrayed their locations, and the sorcerers were able to cancel their invisibility spells. They had shield spells in place, too, though, and Allison alone was able to get through these. She knocked Semblant out of the sky by cancelling the spells keeping his carpet aloft. He hit the ground hard, rolling across the plain several times before regaining his feet and recovering his carpet. Instead of going airborne again, he grew himself to a giant size, turned his carpet into a club, and marched through their army, batting soldiers in every direction.

Mist landed nearby, tucking her carpet into the void and turning to mist. She rolled across the battlefield, engulfing Semblant and hitting him with lightning over and over again. The demon roared, pain and rage in his voice, and finally returned to his normal shape, mounting his carpet and taking off again. After that, Mist moved across the plain, covering the enemy troops in a dense fog instead, and hitting them with fire and lightning spells.

The battle raged on for hours. The Eagle Company and the troops Khaldun had enhanced performed the best. But with their greater size and strength, the elvish soldiers had a significant advantage over most of their own. On top of that, the wraiths focused most of their energy on removing the protective charms from their troops' armor—something most of the elves could not do. With the spells removed, the elvish soldiers were able to hit them with fire spells, incinerating them from within. Yet despite all of that, with the dragons on their side, the enemy lines diminished faster than their own. They were still badly outnumbered, but the difference was getting smaller with every passing hour, as more and more corpses littered the battlefield.

Battleaxe canceled an invisibility spell, revealing her old mentor, Warhammer, on his carpet. She hesitated, and Allison knew the memory of her relationship with him had to be weighing heavy on her. The delay cost her. Warhammer hit her with a barrage of spells, breaking through her shield and igniting her carpet. Battleaxe canceled the fire, but it was too late. The flames had unraveled enough of her spells that the carpet could no longer stay aloft. She managed a controlled landing not far from Shatter. Abandoning the carpet, she pulled her axes out of the void and joined her friend in combat, venting her rage on the enemy forces. Allison knew she kept a spare carpet tucked into the void, but thought she understood her decision. Battleaxe probably wanted to vent her rage after the encounter with Warhammer.

Allison engaged both Vision and Legion, sending both of them crashing earthward only to see them produce spare carpets and rejoin the fight. And Allure knocked Intuit out of the sky one time. But not once did Nyro show up after Allison's initial encounter with her.

Allison located Spring when he hit one of the dragons with his cancellation magic, and she removed his invisibility spell. Before she could do anything else, a shadow passed over her, blotting out the westering sun. Turning, she spotted something enormous moving across the sky. What the hell was this?

Letting Spring go, she raced across the plain to get a better view of the new arrival. It was unlike anything Allison had ever encountered. She'd never seen a jellyfish in person, but she'd seen a sketch, and that was the closest comparison she could make. The creature's body was shaped like an umbrella the size of Castle Highgate, with long tentacles hanging down from it.

The monster floated across the sky, moving over the battle, and catching several of the dragons in its tentacles. This enraged the beasts, and they roared and struggled to free themselves, breathing fire on the tentacles, all to no avail. The tentacles didn't seem to be harming them, but neither could they escape the monster's hold.

Allison had never heard of such a creature. She'd have to consult with the others to be sure, but she suspected Nyro must have brought it here from some other realm using her pyramid. She flew in closer, careful to avoid the tentacles, and detected some sort of magic keeping it aloft. It wasn't any kind of spell she recognized, but she was certain canceling it would rob the creature of its lift.

Flying as close as she dared, Allison focused on the magic, getting a sense of how it worked. Once she was ready, she tried canceling it. It worked, but only on a small section of the magic. She realized the spells had dozens of sources inside the beast. Allison canceled a second source, but the first one sprang back into being. She kept trying, but the spells came back to life faster than she could cancel them.

The tentacles had captured a few more dragons, so she tried freeing one of them instead. She hit one of the tentacles with a fire orb, but this had no effect. Lightning made it twitch, so she used that spell several times in a row until finally it released the dragon.

The monster had gotten additional tentacles around a few of the others. One dragon started screaming, a sound Allison had never heard one of these beasts make before, and it tore her heart out. She started hitting one of the tentacles with lightning, but it was too late. The monster tore the dragon in two, letting its broken corpse fall to the plain.

The rest of the crash retreated, apparently catching on to the danger. Allison got to work trying to free one of the other dragons, and the monster killed another one. Battleaxe and Sage joined her, and before long, they managed to liberate the rest of the beasts.

Moving well away from the tentacles, and hovering close to the other two, Allison said, "Have either of you ever heard of a beast like this before?"

"Never," said Battleaxe. "And I wish I didn't know about it now."

"It must be from one of the elven kingdoms," Sage said. "There's no record of anything like this in Anoria."

"There's another possibility," Allison said. She explained what Gyda had told her about Nyro bringing creatures here from another realm.

"Great," Battleaxe said. "I wonder what other surprises she has in store for us."

Allison reached out to Shadow. *"Can you locate Cyclone or one of the other demon mages for me? I want to get in close and see if I can read them to learn more about these monsters."*

"Let me do this for you," Shadow replied. *"It'll be easier for me to get in close enough for a reading."*

"Very well."

Another shadow blotted out the sun—a second monster had arrived. And this one was moving toward the castle.

CHAPTER TWENTY-SEVEN
TACTICAL WITHDRAWAL

llison produced her mirror as she shot toward the keep. Luckily, the monster wasn't very fast. She told Camilla that Mira needed to increase the size of her null. The jellyfish would need its magic to stay aloft, but its tentacles were long enough to reach through the null at its current size and pluck people off the keep roof or start destroying the castle. It would impale itself on the crystal tower if it kept itself centered above the keep, but Allison was sure it was intelligent enough to avoid that. Lowering itself right next to the tower would allow it to inflict damage on them without injuring itself.

Camilla would need to move out to the wall surrounding the city's top level to continue using her mirror, so Allison told her to stay put—she was almost there. Landing on the battlements next to Camilla, Allison watched the dragon stationed there taking off for the keep. Once Camilla had taken her seat on the carpet, Allison lifted off, taking her to the next wall. The messenger dragon joined them there, and Allison took off again.

The monster had moved over the keep, slowly descending until parts of its underbelly hit Mira's null, which had expanded. It climbed a bit, and its tentacles were too short to reach the keep. Allison breathed a sigh of relief. She didn't know if its appendages would be strong enough to rip stone apart, but after seeing what it had done to the dragons, she had a feeling it probably was. Dragons were incredibly tough, and she'd never heard of anything else being able to cause them physical damage like that.

Shadow reached out to her. *"I made contact with Cyclone. She wouldn't speak to me, but by asking her questions, I was able to read the answers in her mind. Cyclone wants to defy her orders, but Nyro is keeping a tight grip on her and the other demon mages. Nyro used her pyramid to bring these monsters here from some other realm. She searched specifically for a creature that could neutralize the dragons, and it took her a while to find one. That was part of the reason for the delay before her renewed attack. Apparently dragons exist in these monsters' world as well, so they're already familiar with them. Their tentacles can rip apart stone as well, so we should expect her to try using them against the castle."*

"Perfect, thank you." Allison used her mirror to give Camilla that information, who would relay it to the other mages and the leaders on the keep roof.

The first jellyfish had turned its attention to their troops. Dropping low enough to reach the ground with its tentacles, it was grabbing their soldiers and cutting them in half with the force of its grip. Allison tried hitting one of the tentacles with lightning again, but this didn't work the way it had with the dragons. The tentacles weren't holding onto anything this time, so the twitching caused by the lightning accomplished nothing.

Focusing on the monster's body, Allison tried hitting it with fire and lightning, but its skin seemed as tough as dragon hide. She tried calling air to move it away from the battle, but this didn't work, either. Allure, Mist, and Sage joined her in the effort, hitting the monster with everything from fire orbs to cyclones, but nothing in their arsenal seemed to affect the creature.

Meanwhile, it was killing their soldiers in droves. And with the dragons' absence, they'd lost their advantage against the enemy. It was hard to tell for certain, but Allison estimated they'd already lost a third of their troops in this battle, bringing them down to roughly forty thousand. But if this kept up, that number would diminish at a much faster rate.

They could move Mira to the outer wall. Using her null, she could drive the monster away from their troops. Unfortunately, the second one was still hovering high above the keep, and as soon as Mira moved, it could start destroying the castle. Staying where she was, Mira might be able to extend her null as far as the city's perimeter, but not any farther.

Allison grabbed her mirror and reached out to Camilla. "Let Princess Salerna know we need to relocate Mira. If we move her to the wall surrounding the city's third level, she should be able to use her null to drive this monster away from the troops while still protecting the castle."

"Understood," Camilla said, disappearing from the glass.

Allison hovered high above the battle, waiting for the response. Their army was being decimated down on the plain. The dragons were moving in from behind the enemy lines now, taking out as many of their troops as they could, but keeping their distance from the jellyfish was limiting their range.

Allison felt someone reaching out to her through her mirror. It was Camilla. "Her Highness agrees. Can you take care of transporting Mira?"

"It's not ideal," Allison said. "My carpet isn't equipped the way Khaldun's is. But we'll have to make do. Mira will have to extinguish her null temporarily. Have one of their other mages send up sparks when they're ready."

Camilla nodded before disappearing again. Allison flew over the city, circling the keep. She spotted one of the mages shooting red sparks high into the sky, and she sped in closer, landing on the keep roof. Mira hurried over to her, Salerna and Augustine by her side.

"Princess Allison," said Salerna. "With Lady Mira's null in its new position, we will lose our ability to communicate with our people in the field. You know our contingency plans, so we would like you to take command."

"Understood, Your Highness," she said. "Sit right behind me and hold on tight," Allison told Mira.

Once Mira was seated, holding onto Allison for dear life, she lifted off, shooting over to the battlements separating the city's second and third levels. Mira got to her feet.

"Let me get clear of the city walls before you extend your null again," Allison told her. "And be careful—we don't want one of those monsters falling on our troops."

"Hurry," Mira told her, gazing back at the castle. The jellyfish there was descending, its tentacles moving toward the keep. The others who'd been up there had moved inside.

Allison took off, shooting across the city and over the plain. Mira must have expanded her null because both of the jellyfish started listing to one side. The one over the keep moved higher, while the other one moved farther from the city. A little at a time, Mira grew her null large enough to protect both the keep and their troops. The monster over the battlefield was now directly above the elvish army, once again taking the dragons out of play.

The battle raged on as sunset approached. With Mira's null in place, the wraiths and enemy mages were unable to use magic against their soldiers. Allison and the others concentrated their own attacks on the enemy lines while their opponents defended them.

Finally, the pace of the carnage balanced out again, with both sides losing troops at the same rate. But that rate was tragically high. Allison guessed they'd lost close to half of their forces. Maybe thirty thousand troops remained. Meanwhile, the enemy still had double that number on the field.

Massive bonfires erupted all across the plain behind the enemy lines, illuminating the battlefield as the sun slipped below the horizon. This had to be the doing of the enemy mages. Nyro's troops showed no sign of letting up for the night. Would they have an army left come morning? Allison doubted it.

With Mira's null in place, she couldn't reach Imani or any of the others on the ground via mirror. So she landed out on the plain, beyond the southern end of their lines. Tucking her carpet into the void and withdrawing her sword, she took off at a run, moving between the city's outer wall and their army.

Reaching their command post, she sent a messenger to Imani, ordering a tactical retreat. She sent another messenger to the city's primary entrance, ordering them to open the gates once their soldiers reached them. There was only one route from the plain to the gates, a wide path that made its way through several switchbacks.

Hurrying up to the front lines, Allison joined the fighting. She was bigger, stronger, and faster than she'd been the last time she'd faced the elvish soldiers in battle, and as she went into her fighting trance, she found herself cutting down the enemy with greater facility than ever.

Allison became an observer as her body moved on instinct honed by countless hours of training. The soldiers started giving her a wide berth, and before she knew it, she stood in an oasis of calm in the midst of the enemy lines. Their own army had reached the city gates, moving slowly but steadily inside.

Charging toward her own people, Allison entered her battle trance once again, fighting her way through the enemy forces. Moving through the most intense areas of the battle, she had to force her conscious mind back to the forefront lest she start cutting down her own soldiers.

Horns sounded from the other side of the battlefield, and the enemy forces started to withdraw. Allison found Shatter and Battleaxe, and the three of them stood ready to defend their retreating soldiers should this prove to be a ruse. Imani joined them before long, covered in blood and gore, and they waited as the rest of their forces moved up the path toward the city.

"Why are they letting us go?" Imani wondered out loud.

"They can't stop our retreat without magic," Battleaxe said, "and they can't use magic with the null in place. Anyway, they've already cut our numbers in half. Nyro probably figures that's a good day's work."

There were vast caverns behind Castle Highgate's undercroft, and that's where the soldiers were headed. It was the only space in the city large enough to hold so many. Not all of them would go that far, though. Their plan called for leaving a full regiment embedded in each of the city's levels, in addition to the ones already stationed there, as well as archers on the battlements.

The jellyfish monster retreated with the elvish army as it made camp out on the plain. The second one still hovered high above the castle. It took a few hours to get all the troops into the city, and several of the dragons covered them from the air as they moved.

Allure, Sage, Mist, and Azure had landed outside Mira's null, and they joined Allison and the others as they started up the path to the castle. Khaldun showed up with Beast not long after that, and the giant tiger retook his human shape. Naked as always.

Once inside the city, Allison gave the order to close the gates behind them. She and Khaldun went to see Mira atop the battlements surrounding the city's third level.

"I'm so glad you're all right," Mira said, embracing them each in turn. "What the hell are those things with all the tentacles?"

Allison told her Nyro had used her pyramid to bring them here from some other realm.

"I wonder why she didn't bring more than two," Khaldun said.

"I'm not sure I could open a portal big enough for one of them," Allison said. "Or keep it open long enough for the thing to get through. Nyro must have drawn power from all of her demon mages to do it. And even then, it's sure to have cost her."

"Let's hope she doesn't have any other monster surprises in store for us," Khaldun said.

The three of them climbed down from the battlements and headed up to the castle. Mira kept her null expanded to its fullest extent, which reached from the keep to just inside the city's outer wall. They still had the elf mages stationed on those battlements, so they could use their magic against anyone trying to breach the walls.

Allison made her way through the great hall looking for Jezebel and the girls. The hall was packed, and she could hear a minstrel singing about ancient battles as someone played a lute. As she drew closer, she realized Thomas Broadpaunch from the tavern in Stoutwall City was both the singer and the lutist. She had no idea he'd come here to Highgate. Jezebel was sitting at a nearby table with Alanna and Leda, so Allison went to join them.

"Thank the stars you're all right," Jezebel said as Allison bent over to embrace her. She hugged each of the girls before sitting down with them. "What happens now?"

"A siege, most likely," Allison said. "Although I didn't see any siege engines on the plain. I'm sure Salerna will call a council meeting soon. In the meantime, I'm famished."

Battleaxe, Allure, Mist, and Sage joined them for dinner. Battleaxe drank heavily as well. She explained that running into Warhammer in the battle had rattled her, and she needed to get "good and drunk."

"I know how you feel," Allure said. "I'm just glad I didn't have to face Semblant this time."

Sure enough, Salerna called a council meeting. Camilla was sitting nearby with Mira, Khaldun, Shatter, and Azure, so Jezebel asked her to keep an eye on Alanna and Leda. Then the rest of them went to the council chambers.

Once everyone had taken their seats, Salerna said, "We have lived to fight another day. Thank you all for your efforts today. What is our military situation at present?"

"We estimate today's troop losses at thirty-five thousand," her commander said. "Leaving us with thirty thousand or so. Our best estimate of the enemy army puts them at sixty-five thousand."

"I agree with those estimates, Your Highness," Allison said.

"I do not believe we should attempt fielding our troops again," the commander said. "One more day like today, and we wouldn't have an army anymore."

"I agree," Augustine said. "We'll have to dig in for a siege. Were there any signs of engines on the plain today? We couldn't see any from the keep roof."

"No, Your Highness," said Azure. "We saw none from the air, either."

"Nyro could have had them assembled elsewhere," Allison said, "and be planning on bringing them here through a portal. If she could get those jellyfish monsters here that way, I daresay she could move a handful of siege engines."

"I have never seen any that could breach walls so high as these," said Prince Carlo. "A battering ram at the gate, perhaps, but I cannot see how she could hit us here with any other engines."

"Don't underestimate her, Your Highness," said Salerna. "Nyro has been making war for centuries. There's no telling what she might be able to do."

"What is the status of Lady Mira's null?" Leto asked.

"I have it expanded as far as I can, Your Highness," Mira said, "which puts its outer perimeter just inside the city wall."

"One jellyfish monster is holding position directly over the castle," Allison said, "which is reason enough to keep the null intact. The second one is high above the enemy camp out on the plain."

"Nyro could still try taking out the city with an earthquake," Khaldun said. "If she hits the bedrock deep below the surface, the null would provide no protection."

"That she could," Azure said, "but this city has survived numerous earthquakes over the centuries. And Nyro's sure to know that as well."

"Be that as it may, we should consider executing our evacuation plan," said Jezebel. "It's clear we must not field our army again. And one way or another, it's only a matter of time before Nyro comes for us here. The null protects us from thaumaturgic assault, but Nyro wants us all dead. She's sure to find a way."

"I understand that you tried invoking Nyro's true name?" Augustine asked.

Allison told them about her encounter with Nyro earlier that day and Shadow's explanation for the lack of results.

"That's it, then," Salerna said. "We have no way to destroy her. She's already shown us that she can reanimate a new body every time she loses one. The spike didn't work, and her true name holds no power over her."

"Princess Jezebel is probably right," Augustine said. "Nyro is sure to find some way to renew her attack here. I believe, however, we should wait and see what she does next. We can fall back to Bayfast, but the more we know about her tactics before carrying out our evacuation, the better prepared we will be next time."

"I agree," said Princess Miranda. "On top of that, our castle in Bayfast is not nearly so well fortified as Highgate. If we fail to stop Nyro here, it's sure to be a temporary fallback only."

"Very well," Salerna said with a nod. "We shall wait out our enemy here, but remain ready to evacuate at a moment's notice should it be necessary."

The meeting adjourned, and Allison returned to the great hall with Jezebel to collect Alanna and Leda. With the null blanketing the entire city, there was no point in Allison's returning to the townhouse, so she headed up to their chambers with her family. Mira and Khaldun agreed to return to their original chambers.

Allison felt dirty. So once the girls had gone to bed, she filled the washroom tub with hot water, and she and Jezebel bathed together. Once they'd dried off, they went to bed, and Allison started dozing off in Jezebel's arms.

Suddenly, the bed began shaking. Allison started awake, sitting up and trying to determine what was happening. The shaking subsided as quickly as it had started, and she noticed the sky brightening outside their window.

"What the hell is happening?" Jezebel said as the two of them got out of bed.

Gazing out the window, Allison spotted a giant fireball falling from the sky, hitting a nearby structure and reducing it to a pile of flaming rubble.

"Oh, shit!" Jezebel said.

CHAPTER TWENTY-EIGHT
BAYFAST

hey spotted a few more fireballs dropping from above, impacting different spots in the city.

"If one of those hits the keep, we're dead," Allison said.

"How the hell are they throwing fireballs through Mira's null?" Jezebel said.

"They must not be magical," Allison said. "The way they're destroying those buildings, I suspect they're boulders that have been superheated with fire spells. And they're falling straight down—no siege engine could do that. They must be dropping them from carpets."

"From somewhere above Mira's null," Jezebel said. "That makes sense. We need to get everyone out of the upper levels. Perhaps down to the undercroft."

They woke Alanna and Leda, then went to rouse Mira, Khaldun, and everyone else they could find. Hurrying downstairs, Allison found one of Salerna's guards and told him what was happening. He hurried off to evacuate the rest of the upper levels.

"You should extinguish your null for now," Allison told Mira as they entered the great hall. Many of the castle's occupants were gathering there, including all of their sorcerers. "Let us get our carpets in the air to combat our attackers."

Mira nodded, closing her channels of power. Allison felt her magic return. She gathered the rest of the sorcerers and explained what they needed to do.

Just then, Azure hurried into the hall, spotting Allison and the others. "We've just received a messenger from the city gates. The elves have broken camp. They're marching toward the city."

"I'll take a look," Allison said. She told him she was going airborne with the others.

"We should have Mira expand her null again once the carpets are aloft," Azure said. "We've still got those jellyfish monsters out there."

"Yes," Allison said. "There's a good chance they'll target the keep with their fireballs. We've sent one of the guards to get everyone down to the undercroft."

"Good thinking," Azure said. "I'll assist with that," he added before running off.

"We should go out the front gates and take off from there," Allison said to the rest of the sorcerers. "If this goes to hell, we'll proceed with our evacuation plan."

Allison led the way out of the castle, the others following in her wake, including Mira so she'd know when it was safe to expand her null. Once outside, Allison waited till everyone else had taken off first before launching herself. Sure enough, circling the city, she traced the path of a fireball back to its source and exposed a carpet by canceling the rider's invisibility spell. It was too dark to identify them. But as she watched, whoever it was released a flaming rock from the void and dropped it on the city. It landed just outside the castle, and if Allison was right about its point of impact, destroyed the townhouse she'd been using.

Hitting the carpet with a fire orb, Allison discovered there was a shield spell in place, too. She hurled one spell after another until she broke down the shield, then incinerated the carpet. As it went down, she caught a glint of long hair streaming behind the rider's head by the light of the flames now spreading across the city. That had to be Cyclone.

Allison sped away, alarmed at how many fires were springing up below. She had a feeling they had to be dropping oil in the same areas as the fireballs. The entire city was built from stone, so she didn't understand how else the fires could be spreading like this.

Flying high to avoid Mira's null and passing over the city gates, she spotted a long line of soldiers headed up the switchbacks from the plain below. And flying in closer, she realized who was leading the charge in person. A large male elf mage, completely naked. This could only be Nyro.

Allison went invisible and tried hitting her nemesis with a fire orb, but Nyro had a shield in place. She hurled fire orbs at the soldiers following her and managed to take out several dozen that way before someone, probably Nyro, started canceling them. It hardly mattered, though—they had tens of thousands of elves to replace the fallen ones. Allison could've kept up her assault for hours without making much of a difference.

Climbing again, Allison soared high above the city, circling once. Remarkably, the castle remained undamaged. Allison was surprised at first until she realized many of the surrounding buildings had been destroyed. Nyro was sparing Castle Highgate, as she had done with Castle Barclay. She must want it for herself for some reason.

Fireballs continued to fall from the sky, knocking out more and more of the city's buildings and spreading more fires. Allison could see their own sorcerers combating the invaders, and though they'd slowed down the assault, they couldn't stop it.

Returning to the city gates, Allison found Nyro rounding the final switchback, her troops right behind her. She called earth, opening a chasm across their path. Nyro closed it again. Allison hurled a massive fire tornado at them, but Nyro canceled it. Calling air and water, she created a blast of icy cold, forming a wall of ice several feet thick across the final approach to the gates. Nyro shattered it with an earth spell.

The archers stationed on the battlements launched a volley of flaming arrows, targeting Nyro. They bounced off her shield spell, and she called fire, incinerating a dozen archers. They screamed as they tumbled off the wall, the sound cut off as the flames consumed them. Their elf mages kept hurling spells at her from the top of the wall, too, but they weren't strong enough to get through her shield spell.

Nyro stopped a dozen feet from the gates. Allison could feel her summoning her full power. A moment later, she unleashed a massive earth spell. It smashed into the gate, and the surrounding sections of the castle wall shuddered, shedding dust and loose stones. Nyro hit it again, blasting that entire section of wall, gate and all, out of her way.

Marching forward, Nyro entered Highgate City, her legions behind her.

Allison flew to the nearest guard tower, landing briefly on the battlements. She ordered the officer in charge to sound the horns before taking off again. It was time to evacuate the city.

The evacuation plan called for moving as many of the city's people as possible into the castle. From there, they could move down to the undercroft, through the massive caverns behind that, and finally into a tunnel leading to a path into the mountains. They'd have to leave the gates leading to the city's higher levels open as long as possible to allow the maximum number of evacuees through before Nyro arrived.

Mira's null was still in place, and Allison couldn't imagine how Nyro would get through those gates without her magic. Their sorcerers were still airborne, and except for Khaldun, they would protect Highgate's people on their way into the mountains. Allison, Azure, and Khaldun would take care of evacuating their troops and the castle's occupants.

Nyro was about to pass inside Mira's null, so Allison wouldn't be able to follow her on her carpet. Just before crossing the line, Nyro pulled something massive out of the void. Allison realized it was an enormous battering ram on a wheeled frame. Wooden shafts extended from each side, and a dozen elves moved into position behind those to push the ram through the city. That explained Nyro's strategy.

The soldiers embedded in the city's first level arrived to engage the invaders and give the city's people as much time as possible. Landing on the battlements, Allison tucked her carpet into the void, withdrew her sword, and ran along the wall toward the gate for the city's next level. The ram's progress was slow, so she had no trouble getting well ahead of it.

She ran down the next set of steps and made her way through the city to the gate. It was slow going moving through the throng making for the same destination. Reaching the gate, she warned the guards that the battering ram was coming.

The last of the evacuees from the first level passed through the gates, and their soldiers moved into view, Nyro and her engine right behind them. As the battering ram made its final approach, the city's defenders retreated through the gates, and Allison ordered them closed.

Dozens of soldiers stood ready to combat Nyro's forces once they breached the gate. Allison waited with them as the rest of the citizens continued toward the city's next level. The battering ram struck the gate, shaking the entire wall, but the gate held. The ram seemed even heavier than she would have guessed from its enormous size, and she wondered if Nyro had found a way to use magic to increase its mass. She didn't think the gate would hold very long against that thing.

Allison proceeded through the remaining gates as fast as she could, weaving her way between the evacuees and warning the guards at each level that the battering ram was coming. Reaching the castle, she ran inside, finding the great hall empty other than a handful of household guards.

A steady stream of people were making their way down to the undercroft, and Allison joined them. She found Mira, Jezebel, and the girls there with Salerna and the other royals and commanders. Allison updated them on the situation in the city. They agreed to hold out until the last of the city's population made it through the castle, then they could collapse Mira's null and recall the sorcerers. She hurried through the castle, making her way up to the keep roof. She found Azure there, gazing across the city.

"I never thought I would see this day," he said. Highgate was ablaze with fires burning on every level. Allison could hear the clash of arms and spotted their forces trying to repel Nyro and her people as they approached the next gate.

"The crystal tower still stands," she observed. "The princess and Jezebel both saw it fall in the looking glass when it showed Highgate's conquest. Nyro must have hit the city with earthquakes in their visions. Something changed."

"Many things did when Syllith destroyed her Sacred Circle," Azure said. "Somehow, their loss must have created a situation where Nyro would need the castle for some reason."

"I wish we knew what that reason was," Allison muttered.

The last of the city's people moved inside the castle, and Azure ordered a nearby guard to sound the final horns. Moments later, their report echoed across the city. Their remaining troops retreated into the city's third level, closing the gate ahead of the battering ram's arrival. They hurried to the castle, the remaining gates closing behind them.

Allison ran down to the undercroft. The last of Highgate's citizens were making their way down the steps. She followed them through the caverns and out to the passage beyond. Once they'd made it through that, Allison called earth to collapse the tunnel.

Returning to the undercroft, she found Mira, Jezebel, and the others, and said, "It's time."

Mira nodded, collapsing her null. Azure would feel his magic return and contact the other sorcerers via mirror. Sure enough, he came running down the stairs with Khaldun moments later.

Allison embraced Jezebel and the girls, and then Khaldun tucked them into the void along with half of the castle's other occupants. Once Azure had taken care of the rest, Allison drew power from the two of them and cast the spell to move the army into oblivion. The air around her trembled, and the troops vanished.

"Let's get out of here," she said.

Allison, Azure, Mira, and Khaldun ran up to the main level and out of the keep, mounting their carpets in the courtyard. They took off, making themselves invisible. Allison gazed below them in time to see Nyro blast through the castle gates with an earth spell. The city continued burning as her troops moved from one level to the next, and Nyro entered the keep. Highgate was hers.

Battleaxe, Sage, Mist, and Allure had gone to defend the people fleeing into the mountains. Other than the tunnel from the undercroft, the only way to reach that path from the castle was by carpet, and

Allison didn't see any of Nyro's demon mages heading that way. She used her mirror to contact Allure, and the sorcerer reported that all was well.

Allison summoned Shadow and sent her to keep an eye on Nyro, keeping herself hidden. Then she headed south with Azure, Khaldun, and Shatter. They caught up with the dragons before long, flying together to Bayfast.

The city came into view as the first light of dawn cracked the eastern horizon. Allison checked in with Allure one more time, and she reported that there continued to be no pursuit from the city. They were planning to stay with the evacuees for the rest of that day, then they'd join the others in Bayfast.

Allison landed in a field east of the city and liberated the army from the void. They started making camp, and she flew to the castle. Azure had landed in the courtyard, and the people he'd transported were making their way into the keep. Once there was room, Khaldun liberated his passengers from the void.

Once she'd found Jezebel and the girls, Allison accompanied them into the castle. They went to the great hall, where Miranda's people were serving breakfast. Mira and Khaldun joined them and they sat down to eat.

Castle Bayfast was much smaller than Highgate, and there wasn't enough room for all the new arrivals. Princess Miranda's people provided chambers for as many as they could, but more than half of them had to take lodging in the city. They'd prioritized the royals from the other princedoms, though, so Jezebel and the girls ended up with connected rooms on the topmost level. Mira and Khaldun took the chambers right next to theirs. Nyro still had her pyramid, so Mira expanded her null to protect the castle.

Allison hated confining the girls to the castle again, but there was no choice. It was the only way to keep Alanna safe. She needed to stay in contact with her demons, though, so she stayed in a small house in the city.

Shadow kept an eye on Highgate. Nyro and her people were settling into the city and the castle as if for an extended stay. Most of their army remained camped out on the plain, the two jellyfish monsters nearby, but they had regiments stationed in the city's every level. Nyro had taken Salerna's chambers for her own. She spent most of the day consulting with her mages and commanders in the council chambers but put spells in place to keep Shadow out.

Allison summoned a few of her lesser spirits to monitor the area around Bayfast. One of them reported a demon watching the castle from above. Nyro must know where they'd gone, then. She ordered that spirit to continue watching the demon while keeping itself hidden.

Kashi and the other riders had taken the dragons into the forest west of the city, near the coast. The beasts had plenty of room to fly and hunt there.

Allison contacted Siren in Okset and told her that they'd lost Highgate, and were regrouping in Bayfast. Once again, she pleaded for Okset's aid, and Siren told her she would relay her message to Prince Kamari. Predictably, she got back to her later that day to let her know the prince forbade them from entering his territory.

That evening, Nyro went to the library. After pulling several books from the shelves, she sat at one of the tables pouring over them. Shadow couldn't get too close, lest she alert Nyro to her presence, so she couldn't identify the books. Allison found this extremely curious. Nyro was researching *something*, but what could it be?

Allure reached Allison by mirror as she was getting ready for bed. She told them Highgate's people had settled in camps far from the city, without any sign of pursuit. She was setting out for Bayfast with Sage, Battleaxe, and Mist, and they were taking one carpet so they could all call air and get there faster.

They arrived in the middle of the night. There was no more housing available in the city, so they stayed with Allison. The house had only two bedrooms, so Allure slept with Allison in her bed, Mist and Sage shared the second bed, and Battleaxe slept on the floor in the main room.

The next morning, they held a council meeting in Princess Miranda's private dining room. Allison and Jezebel attended, along with Mira and Khaldun, the rest of the university sorcerers, the mages and rulers from the other princedoms, and their top military commanders.

Allison didn't see Commandant Bishop from the Bastion and asked Prince Leto about his absence.

"I'm sorry to report that Bishop fell in the battle outside of Highgate," Leto said. "He will be missed."

"You have our deepest condolences," Miranda said. "We knew him only by reputation, but our father always spoke highly of the man."

"Thank you, Your Highness," Leto said with a nod.

"We must decide this morning how to proceed," Miranda said. "Highgate has fallen for the first time since Saliman's rise to power. It seems Nyro has suspended her campaign against us for the time being, though we don't understand the reason for it. Princess Allison tells us she has ensconced herself in the library. Researching something, though we don't know what."

"I have spoken to our scholars," Azure said. "Princess Allison was able to identify the section of the library Nyro is using, and they tell me that's where we keep our texts on the healing arts."

"The healing arts?" Augustine repeated.

"Highgate's collection on the subject is the largest in Anoria," Salerna told them, "exceeding even the university's."

"What could she want with that?" Leto asked.

"Perhaps capturing her in our spike in Stoutwall did more damage than we thought," Allure said. "She could be having trouble using her new elvish body the way she did the previous one."

"I suggested as much to our scholars," Azure said. "And they tell me there are a few texts about elvish anatomy and physiology in our library."

"There are?" Sage said.

"Yes, apparently a couple of healers from Highgate came to the aid of some injured elves after Nyro's defeat," Azure explained. "I had no idea the information was there. The texts don't touch upon anything pertaining to magic or history, so they survived the purge.

"The trouble, however, is that we have only a small number of volumes on the subject. According to Princess Allison, Nyro has already included several dozen books in her research. I fear this is leading to something more nefarious than healing herself."

"Might we send Princess Allison's demon closer to identify the specific materials Nyro is examining?" Prince Carlo asked.

"I don't think it would help," Allison said. "She's pulled so many volumes, it would be impossible to tell exactly what she's seeking. And once alerted to Shadow's presence, she could banish her from the library."

"So we know Nyro has taken up residence in Castle Highgate," Khaldun said. "Do we know if Emma and Fang are there with her?"

"Shadow has seen no sign of them," Allison said. "At this point, I'm inclined to believe Nyro left them behind in her new castle in Drengrvollr or wherever it is."

"That's too bad," Allure said. "Had we been able to rescue them, we could have severed Nyro's ties to her demon mages, at least."

"Once Nyro finds whatever it is she's looking for, she's sure to resume her campaign against us," Jezebel said. "She knows we're here—Allison's demons have confirmed that. We must decide how best to defend ourselves."

"We will lose if we make a stand here," Miranda said. "They defeated us in Highgate, and as you can see, our fortifications here pale in comparison to the ancient capital. Not to mention their greater strength in numbers. Our only hope is to convince Prince Kamari to allow us to come to Okset. Perhaps there, with his greater defenses and standing army, combined with our thaumaturgic resources, we could emerge victorious."

"Yet Princess Allison tells us that Kamari continues to refuse us," Salerna said. "We have no leverage against him. Nothing with which to bargain."

"Not only that," said Augustine, "but even if we were to defeat Nyro's army in Okset, it would only buy us time. Only when we have destroyed Nyro—body *and* spirit—can we claim ultimate victory."

"This is true," Leto said. "As long as she survives, I believe she will continue pursuing her goal of exterminating our people. Yet without an army, how could she hope to accomplish this? Surely the citizens of the elvish kingdoms will not be willing to continue sacrificing their own people indefinitely in pursuit of our annihilation."

"Nyro maintains an iron grip on our lands," Gyda said. "She's eliminated all resistance in the Drengrvollri senate. But you are right that our resources are limited. She left enough mages and military units in all of our major cities to stay in control, and beyond those, I'm not sure where else she could raise another army."

"With Okset's help, we could defeat her existing forces," Allison said. "We must find a way to change Kamari's mind. And the means to destroy Nyro."

Chapter Twenty-Nine
Plague

llison wanted to spend some time with Jezebel and the girls. It seemed they were getting a bit of a respite from the war, so why not take full advantage of it? But first, she needed to check in with her demons. So she left the castle with Battleaxe, Allure, Mist, and Sage and went to their house in the city.

The lesser spirits around Bayfast had nothing to report. No strange activity and no sign of Nyro or her forces anywhere near the city. Shadow told her that Nyro had left the library, leaving most of her books strewn about, and relocated to Azure's workshop. She'd ordered more than a dozen human prisoners brought to her. Allison hadn't realized they had any prisoners, but Shadow checked the army camp out on the plain and found a tent concealing a pen with a couple of hundred people inside. Allison had to assume these were stragglers from Stoutwall or Highgate.

Allison had a bad feeling about this.

Once the humans were brought to her, Nyro had sealed the chamber against magical observation and cast spells Shadow could not penetrate. So there was no way to know what was going on inside. The demon did check Nyro's library books, though. They covered a wide variety of topics related to the healing arts, and Allison could tease out no clear connection between them.

Allison used her mirror to contact Siren again, pleading with her to do anything she could to convince Kamari to join the fight. The sorcerer said she had been doing exactly that, but the prince refused to listen.

"We could go there and assassinate him," Battleaxe said when she told the others about her conversation. "You can use that pyramid to open a portal right up his asshole if you wanted, right?"

Allison had to laugh, but Allure said, "After Nyro's escape from Pytha, the governors approved a resolution stating we would openly work against any Anorian regime aiding Nyro in any way. It allows for extreme measures such as assassination. After what Henry did, we refuse to make the same mistake again. Had we stood against him sooner, Nyro's return might have been prevented."

"You were serious, then," Allison said to Battleaxe.

"Hell yes, I was serious," she said. "About the assassination, not going up his asshole."

"My understanding is that Kamari has produced no heirs but has three younger siblings," Allison said. "One of them would inherit the princedom were we to assassinate the prince, and there's no way of knowing if they'd be any more helpful than he is."

"We could ask Siren," Mist said with a shrug.

"Not wise," said Sage. "A question like that would make it obvious what we were considering. Siren is an old-timer, and none of us know her well at all. She might have helped us a bit in our recent negotiations, but there's no telling where her loyalties truly lie. If she reports our questions to Kamari, it could do more harm than good."

"Fuck 'em all, then," said Battleaxe. "If his siblings take the same position he has, we eliminate all of them and take control of the princedom ourselves."

"Surely their military commanders' loyalty lies with the royal family," said Allison. "Overthrowing the rightful rulers isn't going to win them over."

"Could Kamari have made an alliance with Nyro?" Battleaxe said. "She could have promised to leave his princedom out of her plans in exchange for his refusal to support us. There's no doubt she'd renege on that promise, but he does seem to consider himself quite the dealmaker."

"I don't think so," Allison said. "I sensed nothing like this when I met him."

"So we take out Kamari when no one else is around and one of us assumes his identity," Mist said. "Siren would sense an illusion spell, but Khaldun could transform one of us into the prince. No one would ever know."

"I'll do it," Battleaxe said with a grin. "I've always wondered what it would be like to have a cock."

Normally, Allison would never consider something so underhanded and blatantly wrong. That she might find this an acceptable solution was a reflection of just how dire their situation had become.

"Let's think about this for a while before we bring it to the ruling princes and princesses," she said. "This may be our only way forward. But it's not a step we should take lightly." She told them about Nyro's activities inside Castle Highgate.

"Nyro wasn't interested in healing *anyone*," Allure said when she was done. "She must be experimenting with plague magic."

"Plague magic?" Battleaxe repeated with a frown. "I guess that would explain some things. Plague was the one member of the Sacred Circle she kept out of the fighting. Other than Reaper, of course, but he was crazy."

"This must be why," Sage said. "Nyro could have used him to unleash a disease that would wipe out everyone in Anoria."

"Why didn't she, then?" said Mist. "Why go to the trouble of sending so many troops here and waging a war when she could have exterminated us with a spell?"

"Because we can cancel plague magic," Allure said. "As long as we have sorcerers on our side, we could prevent such a disease from spreading fast enough to achieve her desired result."

"Not only that, she wanted us to suffer," Allison said. "To bring us to our knees and know she was the one who had done it. No disease would have quite that same effect."

"And she only brought Plague here after the dragons arrived in Stoutwall," Sage said. "She was crushing us until then, so she could afford to wait until she'd eliminated more of us. But once we turned the tide, she decided to accelerate her plans."

"That could be," Allure said. "And once Syllith destroyed the Sacred Circle, we took away the weapon she needed to complete her plans."

"That makes sense," Allison said. "Shadow confirmed that Nyro had never acquired Plague's unique abilities. This would explain what she's doing in Highgate. She needed their library to help her research ways to duplicate Plague's magic."

"And now she must be testing her spells on those prisoners," Battleaxe said. "Well, this is going to be fun!"

"Can you go there using the pyramid and stop her somehow?" Mist said.

"I don't see how," Allison said. "Even if I were to kill her, she could reanimate another body. There's no way to take away her knowledge."

"That's the crux of the problem," Sage said. "Even if we defeat her in battle, we have no way to destroy her."

Allure met Allison's gaze for a moment, but didn't say anything.

Allison went up to the castle and found Jezebel in their chambers with Alanna and Leda. Alanna was desperate to see Sigrid, but there was no good place for him to land in the castle—the courtyard here was too small. She could probably land there, but wouldn't have enough room to take off again. She would have to climb up the castle and take off from the battlements and might damage the building on the way up.

"What about the keep?" Alanna said. "She could land *and* take off from the roof." Allison gave her a skeptical look. "*Please*, Mother! Sigrid is dying without me!"

"We'll need to get Princess Miranda's permission first," Jezebel said.

"Let's go ask her now!" Alanna said.

Allison went to find the princess. She was in her council chambers with Beast and her advisers. Allison apologized for the interruption and asked about the dragon. Much to her surprise, Miranda not only granted her permission but asked if she could meet Sigrid. So Allison went to get Jezebel and the girls, and they joined Princess Miranda and Beast on the keep roof.

Alanna summoned Sigrid, and moments later, they saw his winged form rising above the forest to the west. The dragon reached the city, swooping around the castle once before landing near the roof's edge. She lowered her head as Alanna approached, and the girl pressed her forehead to her snout.

Miranda gasped. "How majestic! I've never seen one this close before!"

"You can pet her if you want," Jezebel said. "She's very friendly as long as Alanna is around."

"No, no, I think this is close enough," Miranda said. "Thank you, though."

Allison moved toward the dragon. She knew Alanna was probably communicating with her, but she couldn't tell what they were saying. She could, however, sense the dragon's feelings and her love for Alanna. It went beyond just love, though. It was devotion. A loyalty that would never waver. Sigrid would sacrifice herself for Alanna should it ever be necessary. It was, Allison realized, something akin to a mother's love for her daughter. She'd never known the dragons were capable of such powerful emotions.

"Mother, could I take Sigrid for a ride?" Alanna asked.

"Out of the question, I'm afraid," Allison said, wiping a tear from her cheek. "Nyro's demon is watching us from above, and she still has her pyramid."

Alanna looked up as if expecting to see the demon floating there. It was keeping itself hidden, however. "Sigrid says you could ride with us. That would be safer, wouldn't it?"

"On my carpet, you mean," Allison said.

"No—Sigrid says you could ride her with me. You'd have to hold on to me as tight as you can—as long as we're together, she can protect us both. But if we separate, she might drop one of us, and unfortunately, it would be you."

She was so earnest, Allison had to giggle. Yet she found she was a little scared of riding the dragon. Which was foolish—she'd been flying for years. And once outside the null, she could pull her carpet out of the void and fly on her own if anything happened.

"Please?" Alanna said, bouncing on the balls of her feet.

"Wait here," Allison said. "I'll be right back."

She hurried out of the castle, and once clear of Mira's null, checked with Shadow. She reported Nyro had not left Azure's workshop. That might change in an instant, of course, if the demon alerted her to Alanna leaving the null. Allison told Shadow to let her know immediately if Nyro emerged.

Hurrying back to the keep roof, she told Alanna she would ride Sigrid with her. She let Jezebel know what she was doing as the dragon lowered her head and wing and Alanna climbed onto her back. Allison followed her up, sitting right behind her and holding on for dear life.

Sigrid ran across the roof, extending her wings and catching air as she leaped off the far end. They soared once around the city before flying off toward the forest. One of the other dragons gave chase as they passed the rest of the crash and Sigrid headed out over the sea. She went into a dive, tucking in her wings, and Allison felt weightless. Alanna screamed for joy, Allison for terror. She'd pulled maneuvers like this on her carpet, but she'd been in control then. This was completely different.

Sigrid pulled up before they hit the water, somehow managing to get behind the other dragon. Allison realized it had a rider, too, and figured this had to be Soren. The two beasts chased each other around for a while before landing in the field with the rest of the crash.

Allison and Alanna climbed down, and Alanna ran off to embrace Soren, who'd landed right behind them. Allison checked with Shadow again, but Nyro was still locked inside her chamber. She pretended not to be watching as Alanna kissed Soren, even though part of her wanted to pull her away from him. Alanna wasn't a little girl anymore and would be making her own way in the world soon enough. Assuming any of them survived.

Despite Shadow's repeated assurances that Nyro had shown no sign of leaving Highgate, Allison remained nervous the whole time they were out with Sigrid. Not for herself, but for Alanna. She breathed a sigh of relief when the dragon returned them to the keep roof and she climbed off, Alanna right behind her.

Allison wanted to spend more time with her family, but inside the null, she'd be cut off from her demons. So she left the castle and found Allure and Sage in their house. Battleaxe and Mist had gone off to explore the city. Allison let them know she'd be staying in the castle for a while and would have Shadow alert them if anything happened with Nyro. Once she'd let Shadow know, she returned to the castle.

She stayed with Jezebel and the girls until dinner and went with them to the great hall to eat. They sat with Mira and Khaldun, and as the others chatted, Allison paid attention to something that had been in the back of her mind since the battle in Highgate. Maybe longer. They did actually have a way to destroy Nyro. It was obvious once she'd thought of it. And though it would require her to make the ultimate sacrifice, that would be a small price to pay, given the stakes.

Allison decided to keep this realization to herself for now. She hoped to avoid this path. And it was something she would do only as a last resort. Yet she could think of no other way.

For the next few days, very little happened. The bulk of Nyro's forces remained camped on the plain outside Highgate. The two jellyfish monsters hovered nearby. Nyro left Azure's workshop only briefly to eat or nap. Every now and then, her people would bring her more human prisoners. None of them had left that chamber. Allison had to assume they were right about Nyro experimenting on them with plague magic.

Allison spoke to Siren in Okset a couple of more times, but it was clear Kamari wouldn't budge. She and the university sorcerers had several more discussions about the idea of forcibly removing him and replacing him with Battleaxe transformed to look like the prince. Allison wasn't comfortable with this idea but was willing to do it if they could find no other way of getting Kamari to cooperate. Battleaxe and Mist wanted to do it right away so they could move their people to Okset and prepare to face Nyro again. And Allure and Sage felt this course of action was morally wrong, but wouldn't stop anyone else from carrying it out.

In the end, they decided to present the idea to the ruling princes and princesses at the council meeting the next morning. Allison revealed the plan to Jezebel at breakfast, and she hated the idea but given the circumstances, supported it wholeheartedly. And together with Battleaxe and Mist, they were planning on trying to convince the other rulers.

Allison asked Camilla to wait outside the castle during the council meeting and let her know if there were any reports from Shadow. She let her into her house and told Shadow what she was doing. After that, she returned to the castle and met Jezebel and the others in the private dining room.

Once all of the usual participants had taken their seats, Princess Miranda asked for any updates. Allison told them that nothing had changed with Okset or in Highgate, and explained their plan to replace Prince Kamari.

"No, we cannot do this," Prince Augustine said with a frown. "We must not. It is wrong to supplant a ruling prince or princess in their sovereign territory. There must be some pressure we can exert on Kamari to get him to change his stance."

"With all due respect, Your Highness," said Prince Leto, "I must disagree. What you say does apply in a time of peace. But we will know no peace until we vanquish Nyro. The very survival of our people depends on this."

"I do not relish this choice," Princess Salerna said. "And if it comes to it, I must agree with Prince Leto. However, might there not be another way? Could one of you sorcerers use a spell of compliance on Prince Kamari? If I understand the magic correctly, that would bend him to our will without the necessity of assassinating him."

"His sorcerer, Siren, would sense such a spell, Your Highness," said Allison. "Battleaxe's transformation, on the other hand, would not be detectable. She would be physically changed, so there would be no spell for Siren to sense."

"Siren would know something was afoot when the prince suddenly reverses course on his decision not to join forces," Imani pointed out.

"We could place Siren under a compliance spell, too," said Azure. "Most of us here lack the power, but you could do it, Your Highness," he added to Allison.

"That's not a bad idea," Jezebel said pensively. "We could put Kamari under the spell first, then let Siren know what we've done. Who knows—she might support us. If not, then we could put her under the same spell."

Camilla burst into the room at that moment and let Allison know that Shadow had reached out with important news. Allison left the castle with her to take Shadow's report.

Nyro just emerged from her workshop. Cyclone and Warhammer were waiting for her in the undercroft with their carpets unfurled on the floor. They went into the chamber, and I lost sight of them for several moments. Nyro's spells prevent me from seeing inside. Cyclone returned to the undercroft, using magic to move four large sacks onto her carpet. Nyro opened a portal for her. Cyclone flew through it and disappeared.

"Could you tell where she was going?"

"*I saw nothing but blue sky on the other side. And now Warhammer has gone through another portal, also with four sacks. I could see the sky and the sea beyond his portal.*"

Allison was about to check in with her lesser spirits when one of them reported that a carpet had appeared above their army camp outside the city. The rider dropped three sacks over the side before flying over the keep and dropping a fourth one there. Then the carpet took off again, disappearing through another portal. Nyro must have created it remotely.

"Oh, no," Allison said out loud, her eyes going wide. She ran back inside, returning to the private dining room.

"What is it, Your Highness?" Princess Miranda asked.

Allison told them what had happened.

"We have to get word to the soldiers *not* to approach the sacks," Allure said, getting to her feet.

Allison left the castle with Allure and Battleaxe. She summoned Shadow and sent her out to the camp. A moment later, she met Allure's gaze. "We're too late."

CHAPTER THIRTY
LEVERAGE

he soldiers near the fallen sacks had already moved in close, opening them to reveal there were people inside. Two women and a man who seemed like they'd been very close to death even before they fell from the carpet. Through Shadow, Allison told the soldiers to clear an area around each of the fallen victims and not to let anyone else approach them. Next, she relayed orders to the commanders not to let anyone enter or leave the camp.

Allison and Battleaxe hurried up to the keep roof with Allure. Another sack had landed there. Without moving too close, they could hear someone moaning and coughing inside of it. Allison called fire, carefully burning away the material without letting the flames touch the man within.

She'd revealed a heartbreaking sight. The man was only in his twenties, naked, emaciated, and filthy—covered in his own feces from the smell of him. He coughed up a puddle of blood before saying, "Kill me, please," his voice raspy.

"This must be the result of Nyro's plague magic," Battleaxe said.

"I should give him a reading," Allure said, "but I'll need to get closer."

"Allure, no," Allison said. "If you touch him, you could get sick, too."

"I require close proximity but not physical contact," she said. "And we're inside Mira's null, so the magic can't spread here."

"Why would they drop him here, then?" Battleaxe asked. "They must know the null is intact. Why not drop him somewhere in the city?"

"It was Cyclone," Allison said. "Shadow told me she wants to resist Nyro's commands. Maybe this was her way of helping us out—it's probably the most she could do."

Allure moved in closer, stopping only a couple of feet away from the sick man. Closing her eyes and reaching toward him with one hand, she said, "His body is consuming itself. The internal damage has progressed too far to save him." Backing away from him, she added, "I feel this sickness must be the result of Nyro's plague magic, but it's impossible to tell inside the null."

"We should go to the army camp," Allison said. "That's well beyond the null, so we should get a better idea of what we're facing."

"Yes," Allure agreed. "We should take care of him first. Can Mira shrink her null long enough to fly him out of here?"

"I'll let her know," Battleaxe said, hurrying inside the keep.

Once Allison felt her magic return, she pulled her carpet out of the void, unfurling it on the rooftop. Calling air, she moved the sick man to the center of her carpet. Allure sat down by the rear edge, Allison up front.

They flew to the seashore, landing on a sandy beach. Allison called air again, moving the man onto the sand, well away from her carpet. Allure let the man know what she was going to do, and he begged her to hurry. Closing her eyes, she called the magical force, putting him to sleep. She kept going, though, putting him further and further under until his heart and brain stopped functioning.

"It's done," Allure said, wiping a tear from her cheek.

"We should incinerate the body just to be safe," Allison said.

Allure nodded. Calling fire, she burned the corpse until nothing remained but ash.

Boarding Allison's carpet, they flew to the army camp. It was easy to find the other three victims from the large spaces the soldiers had left around them. Allison landed near the first one.

The victim was lying naked on the ground, her condition even worse than the man on top of the keep. She was only semi-conscious and seemed to be hallucinating—she was screaming about being eaten alive by scorpions. Allison stayed back as Allure moved closer, shutting her eyes and holding out one hand toward the woman.

"This is plague magic for sure," Allure said. "It's still active inside of her. I believe I can cancel it, but it's already too late for her. The sickness is consuming her from the inside out."

Allure canceled the spell. She tried explaining to the woman what was happening to her, but she was too far gone to understand her words.

"There's nothing else we can do for her," Allison said. "Ending her life would be an act of mercy at this point."

Allure nodded. She cast the spell to put the woman to sleep, pushing her further under until she breathed her last breath. Allison called fire, incinerating the body.

They were about to fly to the next victim when one of the soldiers approached them. His nose was bleeding. "Your Highness and my lady," he said, bowing to them. "Some of us who got close to that poor woman when she first hit the ground aren't feeling too well. Most of us have got nosebleeds. Is there anything you can do for us?"

"We can help," Allure said. "But we should take care of the last two dropped from the sky, first. They're the source of the sickness. Round up anyone experiencing symptoms of any kind and isolate them from the rest of the camp. We'll be there as soon as we can."

The soldier thanked them and hurried off.

Allison and Allure took care of Nyro's last two victims. The soldiers had moved the sick among them to a separate area of the field, so they went there next. As they rose from Allison's carpet, she realized that Allure was bleeding from the nose.

"The magic must be moving through the air, carrying the sickness from one person to the next," she said. "It enters the body through the mouth or nose and goes to work immediately. Can you sense the magic in me?"

Allison focused on her, and sure enough, she could detect the spell doing its work. She examined it for a minute to understand how it worked, then canceled it. And then Allure pointed out that her nose had started bleeding, too. Allure canceled the spell for her.

The two of them got to work helping the sick soldiers. They all had Nyro's plague magic inside of them. Allison and Allure canceled the spells and assured the afflicted that they should be fine. The magic worked very fast but still needed time to spread through the body before doing enough damage to be fatal.

A steady stream of victims arrived as they worked, and once they'd treated the last of them, they waited a while longer to see if anyone else would show up. Several more did, but after another hour, it seemed like they'd managed to contain the outbreak.

Allison and Allure flew back to the city, landing outside the castle. They were about to go inside when Allison sensed someone contacting her by mirror. It was Siren, and she looked awful. She was bleeding from the nose *and* eyes.

"Your Highness," she said, "the prince doesn't know I'm reaching out to you. Something has happened here that I cannot explain. Four people fell from the sky—I have to assume one of Nyro's people dropped them from their carpet."

Allison stopped her, explaining what was going on. "Where did they drop the victims?"

"One in the middle of the courtyard and the other three outside the city in the midst of our army. They were on death's doorstep anyway, so I stopped their hearts and we incinerated the bodies."

"How many of your people are sick so far?"

"Only a few of the prince's advisers and me inside the castle," she said. "Perhaps two hundred soldiers. It seems to be spreading very fast—I've never seen anything like this."

"What about Prince Kamari?"

"His nose has started bleeding but he says he feels healthy other than that."

"He's not. Unless someone cancels the magic soon, everyone in your city is going to die."

"I'm the only sorcerer here," she said, her eyes going wide. "And this illness is affecting my magic. I can't sense active spells anymore. And as you know, I can't cancel this if I can't get a sense of how it works first. Can you help us?"

"Let me speak with the ruling council. I'll contact you as soon as I can."

Allison and Allure moved into the castle. They found the rest of the council still assembled, anxiously awaiting their report. The two of them took their seats, and Allure recounted their efforts to counteract Nyro's plague. Allison told them about the situation in Okset.

"How the tables have turned," Battleaxe said with a grin.

"We should help them, of course," said Allison, "but make sure Kamari joins the fight against Nyro in return."

"Yes, definitely," Miranda said. "How do we guarantee Prince Kamari will honor his side of the bargain?"

"Let Allure and me go to his palace," said Allison. "We'll cure the prince and his sorcerer. At the rate this sickness seems to spread, it's already too late for us to help his army—the two of us would never be able to outpace this thing.

"Mira could, however. If she were to engulf their entire army within her null, that should cancel the active magic. We'll tell Kamari that if he lets us come to Okset—all of us, including our army—and agrees to join the fight against Nyro, we'll cure his soldiers."

"By the time we get there, many of them could be beyond saving," Allure said. "But we'll do the best we can, of course."

"To hell with that," said Battleaxe. "Let him die. We'll deal with his next-in-line."

"Bad idea," said Imani. "He or she could be worse. At least you know where you stand with Kamari."

"Now, wait a minute," said Augustine. "Are we sure we've eradicated this sickness here? Among our own people?"

"Allison and I acted fast enough to stop it in its tracks," Allure said. "I've never heard of a disease spreading anywhere near this fast, but it's the magic itself that's carrying it from one person to the next. That's what makes this different from a normal plague."

"That makes sense," Khaldun said. "Nyro needn't have bothered sending armies here if this disease spread the normal way. She could have released it in a few major population centers and been done with us. This way, she knows she needs to take out our sorcerers first."

"At this rate of transmission, it may well spread too fast to move beyond the initial target zone," Sage said. "If we declined to intervene in Okset, for example, it might kill everyone there before it has an opportunity to spread anywhere else."

"Nyro knows two major forces stand in her way," Allure said. "Okset and us. She has to take out our mages and Okset's army before she can proceed with the rest of her plans. This disease has a greater chance than most of eliminating both of those groups. With us out of the way, she could unleash a more traditional plague that would be virulent enough to take out the rest of the population, while spreading slow enough to reach every corner of Anoria."

"With Shadow's help, we anticipated this move," said Battleaxe. "Were it not for that, Nyro might well have succeeded. Or at least incapacitated our sorcerers enough to keep us from stopping the spread."

The council agreed with Allison's proposal unanimously. Allison and Allure left the castle together, and Allison reached out to Siren with her mirror. The sorcerer's condition appeared to have worsened just in the short time since their last communication. Siren told them they'd have to come there and propose their agreement to Kamari directly. She agreed to meet them in the entry hall.

Allison used her pyramid to open a portal to Kamari's castle and walked through it with Allure. Siren was waiting for them, leaning on a cane. She looked worse in person than she had through the mirror.

"We should cure you now before it's too late," Allure said.

Siren nodded. "His Highness won't like it, but he'll like it even less if I die. Please, proceed."

Holding out one hand, Allure canceled the plague magic. "The sickness has already spread into your lungs and heart. It may take a day or two before your symptoms resolve."

"Thank you," Siren said. "Now, if you'll come with me?"

The sorcerer led them into the throne room. They found Prince Kamari slouching in his seat, his scepter drooping in his hand, and his crown tilted to one side. Blood was oozing from his nose, and he seemed unaware of their presence.

Siren cleared her throat. "Your Highness, may I present Princess Allison and Lady Allure."

Kamari sat up with a start. "My apologies, I was lost in thought for a moment. My sorcerer tells me you have a new offer for me?"

"Your Highness, you are not well," Allison said. "Please, let us help you, then we can proceed with our negotiations."

Kamari nodded. "Yes, perhaps that would be for the best."

Allison focused on the prince, sensing the magic that had invaded his body. She canceled it with a wave of her hand. "The disease spread into your lungs, but not any further. It may take a while before you feel better, but you should be out of danger."

"Thank you," the prince said. He coughed once, then added, "Now tell me about your proposal."

"It's quite simple. You allow us to come here with our army and the rest of our people, and together, we will fight Nyro and her forces. In exchange, we will cure anyone in your castle who's become sick and as many of your soldiers as we can. Please realize, however, that for some of them, it may already be too late."

"If you can rid my people of this plague, I shall gladly consider joining forces with you," he said with a smile.

"I'm sorry, Your Highness, but that's not how this is going to work," Allison said. "We'll need to bring all of our people here first and have your guarantee that you will join us in this fight before we help your people."

Kamari chuckled. "If you let my army die, there will be no one left to come to your aid."

"So be it," Allison said, turning and striding away, Allure right behind her. She half expected the prince to call them back, but he said nothing.

They left the throne room, and Allison opened a portal back to Bayfast. They stepped through it, and she let it collapse. But before they'd entered the castle, Allison felt someone reaching out to her through her mirror. She pulled it out to find Siren staring up from the glass.

"Your Highness, Prince Kamari would like a word," she said.

Allison nodded and she handed the mirror to the prince.

"Please forgive me, Princess Allison," he said. "You came here to cure me without requiring anything from me in return, and it was rude of me to be so ungrateful."

"Yes, it was," she said.

"My father taught me from a young age to put Okset first in all things," he said, taking a deep breath and coughing. "Our people have always been suspicious of anyone not from Shifar and this has led to our isolationist tendencies. My father told me that the princedoms in Maeda often took advantage of our forebears and it was best to go our own way. But your actions have shown you to be honorable. Even selfless, perhaps."

"I wouldn't go that far," Allison said with a grin. "We *need* you if we're going to defeat Nyro. You could say saving you was an act of self-interest."

Kamari chuckled. "I like your honesty, Princess Allison. You win. Bring your people here. On my honor, together, we will defend Anoria."

Allison wasn't about to take him at his word, and her sympathetic magic didn't work through the mirrors. She opened a portal back to Okset and insisted that the prince repeat his pledge in person. He did, and she sensed no duplicity in him. This time, he intended to uphold his end of their agreement.

Allison returned to Bayfast. She entered the castle with Allure, and they gave the council the good news. After discussing the situation, they decided it would be best to leave for Okset immediately. Miranda sent her people to assemble all of the various royals now occupying Bayfast in the castle courtyard, along with their mages, commanders, and advisers.

Heading back outside, Allison had Shadow give her an aerial view of Okset. It was a much bigger city than Bayfast or even Highgate. Kamari's army was camped outside the city walls, which was quite far from the castle. The city was sprawling like Arthos, but unlike the free city, the vast majority of the structures were built from stone instead of wood, with gleaming towers and domed structures throughout. There were many gardens and public squares, too, giving the city's populace plenty of space to gather and stretch their legs. The castle sat on a hill, with thick, high walls. Despite its size, most of the city was walled as well.

Shadow told her that Okset had grown tremendously over the centuries, and every time it overgrew its walls, the ruler at the time had new ones built. Each wall had several gates, all of which were usually kept open, but could be closed in time of war. Castle Okset was also much larger than its counterparts in Highgate and Stoutwall.

Once everyone had gathered in the courtyard, Mira collapsed her null. Khaldun and Allure each tucked half of their people into the void and took off on their carpets. Mira, Sage, and Battleaxe rode with Khaldun, while Mist and Beast rode with Allure. They'd reach their destination much faster with extra mages calling air.

Allison took care of their combined armies. Once she'd tucked them into the void, she took off on her carpet. Shatter and Azure rode with her and they caught up with the other carpets in no time, heading south for Okset. She worried that a significant percentage of Kamari's army would be beyond saving by the time they arrived, but there was no faster way to get Mira there. And Siren had assured her they were doing their best to isolate the troops who were already displaying symptoms from the healthy ones.

Even with multiple mages calling air, it still took the entire day to reach Okset; the dragons were coming, too, but it would take them longer to get there. Once Khaldun and Allure had landed in the castle courtyard, Allison doubled back, landing in an open field by the sea. She released their armies from the void and returned to the castle. Allure and Khaldun had already liberated their passengers, and Allison reunited with Jezebel, Alanna, and Leda. She was going to keep the girls with her until Mira could return to the castle and establish her null there.

Khaldun and Mira took off again, and Allison followed, Alanna sitting in front of her, and Leda behind. They flew to the Okseti army camp, and Khaldun landed right in the center. Allison stayed aloft, far enough out to avoid losing her magic. Mira expanded her null to its fullest extent, easily encompassing the entire army, including those who'd been isolated. She left it in place for a minute before collapsing it again. That should be enough to cancel Nyro's plague magic.

Siren was waiting for Mira to establish her null over the castle, then she'd send their healers to help as many of the sick soldiers as they could. It was possible some of the healers could be infected with the plague magic and not know it yet, so they wanted to take every precaution. Mira's null would eliminate the spells whether they were symptomatic or not.

Allison's best estimate was that ten thousand of Okset's standing army of seventy thousand had been isolated from the rest. So even if they lost all ten thousand, they'd still have sixty thousand healthy soldiers. Combined with their own armies, that would give them roughly ninety thousand troops, even before Kamari called in his levies.

Allison and Khaldun flew back to the castle with Mira and the girls. Once they'd landed and tucked their carpets into the void, Mira expanded her null to include the entire castle. Certain now that the healers would be plague-free, Siren sent them out to the army camp.

For the first time since the Battle of Stoutwall, it seemed like they stood a good chance of defeating the enemy forces. Yet Allison still felt uneasy about their prospects.

CHAPTER THIRTY-ONE
CHANGE OF PLANS

nlike Bayfast, Castle Okset had more than enough room to house all the extra people. Allison stayed with Jezebel and the girls, and they had adjoining rooms, each with its own washroom. The accommodations were nothing short of opulent, with walls and floors of marble, four-poster beds large enough for four people each, and rich tapestries hanging from the walls. The four of them ate together in the great hall, and the food was some of the best Allison had ever tasted.

Shadow was still monitoring the situation in Highgate, and she had her lesser spirits take positions around Okset to keep an eye on things there. They wouldn't be able to reach her inside the null, so she stationed several of their guards outside the castle. The lesser spirits would report to Shadow if anything was amiss, and Shadow could alert the guards. One of them could relay any message to Allison inside the castle.

The next morning, Prince Kamari held a council meeting. His usual council chambers were too small to accommodate everyone, but there was a separate meeting hall with more than enough space. All the various rulers, mages, and military commanders were present.

"Good morning, everyone, and thank you for attending," the prince said, smiling around at them from the head of the table. Gone were his crown and scepter, and he wore simple leather armor, not unlike Allison's. "We stand united here in the ancient capital of Shifar to face the greatest enemy Anoria has ever known. And this morning, we must lay our plans to ensure the most glorious victory in the history of the continent.

"We know Nyro will send her army here, along with her mages and these jellyfish monsters I have heard so much about. With the city nestled between the river and the sea, she will have no choice but to attack from the northeast. There is no other approach an army so large could use."

"Nyro will tuck her army into the void and transport them here by carpet," Allison said. "But that is where she will have to release them for sure."

"Our latest estimate puts the enemy force at sixty-five thousand," Kamari continued. "Okset lost roughly five thousand to Nyro's plague, and another three thousand or so will not make a full recovery in time to join the battle. This leaves us with a little over sixty thousand, combined with the thirty thousand the rest of you have brought here. I have called in the levies from our holdings, which should give us another thirty thousand, for a total of one hundred twenty thousand."

"Almost two-to-one in our favor," Battleaxe said, nodding appreciatively. "It's nice to be the dominant force for once."

"Yes, and yet from what the rest of you have told me after your previous battles, it will still be a difficult fight," Kamari said. "So why not increase our numbers as much as we possibly can? Face Nyro with *overwhelming* force."

"That would be ideal, of course," said Prince Carlo, "but where would we find more soldiers?"

"Horn," Allison said simply.

"Horn indeed," Kamari agreed with a smile. "Princess Zuri has a standing army of forty thousand. If your sorcerers can bring them here the same way you did your own people, we could go into this battle with the largest army Shifar has ever seen."

"Zuri's sorcerer did suggest that the princess would be more inclined to send aid if Okset joined the fight," Allison said. "I can go to Horn when we're done here and make our request."

"I shall accompany you," Kamari said. "Zuri will not turn me down. Tell me where we stand thaumaturgically."

"We're facing Nyro, of course, the greatest mage in the history of Anoria, and based on recent experience, it's likely she will come here in person," Allison said. "Now that she's added plague magic to her repertoire, we can expect her to use it in battle. She still has seven demon mages, twelve wraiths, and dozens of elf mages in her service. And, of course, she's sure to bring her two jellyfish creatures as well."

"Your Highness, your city does present a unique challenge when it comes to using my null," Mira said. "It's too large for me to protect the castle and the army at the same time. If I position myself halfway between the two, my null won't extend far enough to protect either."

"Not a good situation," said Shatter. "Without the null, the jellyfish could destroy the castle. We'd have nowhere to retreat if we're overwhelmed on the field. Yet without the null protecting our troops in the battle, Nyro could wipe them out with plague magic."

"This isn't like Highgate," Battleaxe said, shaking her head. "This time, there is nowhere else to fall back. If it came to that, retreating to the castle for a siege would only prolong the inevitable. No, this is our final battle. We leave it all on the field. Everything we have."

"And if they overwhelm us again?" Salerna said. "If we reach the same point we did in Highgate, where our destruction becomes certain? Surely retreating to the castle would improve our chances."

"Yet if we keep Lady Mira here to protect the castle, then we could lose our entire army to Nyro's plague," Augustine said. "And if she protects the army, we lose the castle. There is no third option."

"Maybe there is," Battleaxe said. "Years ago, we fought one of Henry's armies in Arthos. Unlike Okset, Arthos has no city walls. It has no fortified gates or battlements. We drew the enemy force into the city, with soldiers embedded in every building along the route to the central square. By the time the army reached our remaining forces there, we'd whittled them down to more manageable numbers.

"We could use a similar ploy here, only it would be far stronger. Close the outermost city gates, and make Nyro fight to breach that wall. Once she does, her army would have to fight its way to the next wall. Have companies waiting in every garden and square along their route. Soldiers embedded in every structure and archers on every rooftop.

Wear them down and reduce their numbers the entire way. The largest square in the city is right outside this very castle. So we keep our best soldiers waiting there and draw the enemy toward them.

"The problem in Highgate was that with our entire army outside the city walls, they were easy pickings for the jellyfish. This way, with the troops spread out, and many of them hidden inside various buildings, it'll be much tougher for the monsters to get to them. We'll still lose some, but nowhere near the numbers we did in Highgate. And that will allow us to keep Mira in the castle."

"Yes, I believe you are right," said Kamari. "We have already begun evacuating our people from the city. With them safely removed to the countryside, the buildings you need will be empty."

"We should still field a force outside the city walls," Shatter said. "A sizable one, I think. Let Nyro think we are engaging her in a traditional battle. Once her forces begin to overwhelm ours, then we retreat into the city, drawing her army in after us."

"Maybe, but that's going to mean greater losses to the jellyfish," Battleaxe said.

"We can keep our sorcerers near the fighting," Allure said. "Perhaps by working together, we can overcome the monster's defenses. It seems like its outer shell is impervious to magic, but perhaps with all of us attacking its underside, we can take it down."

They spent another hour debating the details of their plan, and finally, Kamari adjourned the meeting. Allison left the castle with the prince. She removed her carpet and the pyramid from the void and opened a portal to Zuri's palace in Horn. Kamari felt it would be best to show her the proper respect, so they arrived outside the palace gate. Allison tucked her carpet and pyramid back into the void as two of the guards hurried over to them from the gatehouse.

The guards didn't draw their weapons this time. Allison remembered one of them from last time, and it seemed he recognized her, too. "Your Highness," he said with a bow. "What brings you to Horn?"

"We need to speak with Princess Zuri," she said.

"Let her know Prince Kamari from Okset requests an audience," he added with a grin.

The guard's eyes went wide. "Yes, Your Highness, right away."

He hurried off while the second guard waited with them. Only moments later, he returned, saying, "The princess will see you immediately."

"I told you so," Kamari said to Allison.

They opened the gates, and the guard led them inside. The palace equaled Castle Okset in opulence without any of the fortifications. Allison figured they must have a separate building they used in time of war like Stoutwall had. They followed the guard into the throne room, where they found Princess Zuri waiting for them.

"Your Highness," Kamari said as he approached the dais.

"Prince Kamari," she said with a smile. Zuri appeared to be about the same age as Kamari, with a keen look in her eyes. Her demeanor alone indicated she was not someone to be trifled with. Allison sensed an energy between them that suggested an intimate history. She'd heard that Kamari was quite the rakehell when it came to women, but this seemed like something more serious.

Kamari spoke to her in a different language, and Allison suspected it was ancient Shifari. She didn't know what he was saying, but Zuri's expression grew suspicious, then determined. She responded in the same tongue, and judging by the prince's body language, he was satisfied with what she said.

"Princess Zuri has agreed to join us in our fight against Nyro," the prince told Allison, shooting her a wink; Allison failed to stifle a grin.

The princess sent her steward to gather her sorcerer, Davu, and her three other mages, as well as her military commanders and advisers. It ended up being a group of roughly twenty. Allure tucked them into the void, except for Davu.

The sorcerer led them out of the castle, and he, Kamari, and Zuri each took a seat on Allison's carpet. She flew them farther inland, where the army had its barracks. Davu went to speak to the commanders while the others waited. Once they'd notified their soldiers what was happening, Allison tucked the entire army into the void, the air around them vibrating as if from a giant gong.

They mounted the carpet again, taking off for Okset. With Allison and Davu both calling air, they made it to the city well before sunset. Allison landed out in the fields near their own armies. Getting to her feet, she released the Hornish army from the void. Flying into the city, she landed again right outside the castle and released the rest of Zuri's people.

Allison tucked her things into the void, and they headed inside. She reached her chambers to find Jezebel and the girls trying on dresses.

"What's going on here?" she asked with an amused smile.

"Kamari didn't tell you?" Jezebel said. "He's holding a feast in the great hall tonight. The master of wardrobe has sent formal wear for the members of all the royal households."

"This hardly seems appropriate with the threat of war upon us," Allison said.

"His castle, his rules," Jezebel said with a shrug. "It might be the last celebration of our lives, so we might as well enjoy it!"

Allison had to admit she had a point. Someone had told the master of wardrobe about their tradition of wearing matching gowns in white and black. So they chose their favorites, and the four of them got dressed. Allison wore white to contrast against her dark skin.

They made their way down to the great hall, where they found Soren waiting for Alanna, dressed in formal wear. Scarlett from Stoutwall's household guard was there, too, and she greeted Leda with a kiss.

Prince Kamari and Princess Zuri were sitting at the head table, along with Siren, Davu, and their other mages. There were tables just below that for the royal households from Blacksand, Keepstone, Stoutwall, Highgate, Bayfast, and Spanbrook, and a separate table for the university. Hanging from the wall behind the head table were the banners of the five ancient kingdoms, Dorshire, Maeda, Kong, Shifar, and Pytha.

The staff served wine as the guests continued to arrive. Battleaxe wore her armor, which made Allison chuckle. But Mist and Sage wore gowns, and Allure a dress that left very little to the imagination.

Khaldun and Mira arrived wearing their mage's robes and sat with Allison and her family.

"No formal wear for you?" Jezebel said.

"They did provide us with several options to choose from," Mira said with a shrug. "But we always dress like this for formal occasions back home. Why break with tradition?"

Once everyone had arrived and taken their seats, Kamari got to his feet, clinking his glass with his fork to get everyone's attention. "Your Highnesses, lords and ladies, people of Anoria. We are gathered here tonight on the eve of the most important battle in the history of the five kingdoms. Our ancient nemesis seeks to annihilate us, yet in the face of that threat, we have united. And together, we shall bask in the glory of the greatest victory the continent has ever seen!"

"Or die trying," Battleaxe shouted.

Many chuckled as Kamari raised his glass and yelled, "To Anoria!"

"To Anoria!" the guests responded, everyone taking a drink of their wine.

Kamari's staff served a feast fit for a king, with a seemingly endless number of courses. Halfway through the meal, Allison was so full she couldn't eat another bite, but the food kept coming.

After the last course, a group of musicians started playing, and many people got up to dance—Prince Kamari with Princess Zuri, and Battleaxe with Shatter, Allison noted with a smile. Alanna and Soren danced together, as did Leda and Scarlett. Allison didn't feel much like dancing, but Jezebel insisted, so she went with her, and Mira and Khaldun joined them as well.

The feast continued late into the night, but the longer it went, the less festive Allison felt. Despite their newfound strength in numbers, there was a good chance that most of these people—along with tens of thousands of soldiers—would be dead within days.

Allison could prevent it. She'd been hoping to avoid this, trying her best not to consider it as a serious option. But seeing everyone gathered here, she finally realized what that would cost them. Even if they somehow won the battle, it would only delay the inevitable. The price of waiting was far too high. There was only one way to destroy Nyro, and only she could do it. Why let so many people die first? What would be the point? Their deaths would be senseless.

Jezebel went to chat with some of the other royals, and Allison returned to their table. When she thought no one was looking, she slipped out of the hall and left the castle. Sitting on a bench along the edge of the square, she checked in with Shadow, who reported no change in Highgate. Nyro was still ensconced in her workshop. Allison realized that not only was there but one course of action she could take, it needed to happen soon. If not immediately. They could lose this opportunity at any time.

"*Your plan is sound,*" Shadow told her when she explained what she was thinking. "*The sheer audacity of it is its greatest strength. Nyro will never expect this. She believes herself to be too powerful.*"

"You're certain? I must know beyond any doubt this will not be like the spike." She could see no reason it would be. The method was more fundamental than the spike. More absolute—not even Nyro could protect herself against it. But she wanted reassurance.

"*The spells keeping me out of Nyro's chamber will die the moment Mira expands her null. That could put the others at risk. But I can teach you those.*"

"Good, I hadn't thought of that. What about the rest?"

"*There is no way to prevent or counteract the first rite.*"

"That we're aware of," Allison said. "But it's Nyro, so could she have devised some method of protecting herself against it?"

"*It shouldn't be possible. But if she has, then there would be no reason to carry out the second rite.*"

"True enough," Allison said with a sigh.

"*As long as the first step goes according to plan, then your success is assured if you carry it to the end. The timing will be critical, however, especially for that first step. Trapping Nyro inside her workshop will help, but it buys you seconds only.*"

"After that, it will be out of my hands."

"*Not entirely. You'll be the only thing standing between Nyro and the others. It will be a contest of wills until the final step is completed.*"

"Yes. This course of action will end you, too. You assist me willingly?"

"It seems fitting, somehow, does it not?"

"That it does."

Shadow taught her the magic to repel demons. The spells were complex but not difficult. Allison cast a protective barrier around herself, and Shadow could neither penetrate nor see inside of it. Like the barrier spell protecting the university, it could not be canceled from the outside.

Next, Allison cast the same spells around Shadow and herself. The demon could see through the magic from the inside, but couldn't escape. It was possible to cancel the spell from the inside, but Allison could stop her.

Allison sat quietly after that, gazing across the empty square. Kamari had evacuated the city, otherwise she was sure there would be people out and about. Staring up at the night sky, she wondered what her father, Prince Aldo, would think about the decision she was making. He'd taken his own life out of despair. Allison was going to do it to ensure their people had a future.

"Your Highness," a voice said.

Allison turned to see Allure approaching. The sorcerer sat down next to her, gazing into her eyes. She stroked her cheek with one hand, and tears came to Allison's eyes. "I know what you're going to do. I've known for years."

"Your prophecy," Allison said, fighting back a sob. "I didn't realize it until after the spike failed. I thought I was supposed to be *stronger* than Nyro, but I'm not. I can end her, but only by ending myself."

"That's precisely what makes you stronger," Allure said. "Nyro would never sacrifice herself for the ones she loves."

"Of course not. She doesn't love anyone."

"Exactly," Allure said with a smile.

Allison broke down, unable to hold back the tears any longer. Allure embraced her, and she cried on her shoulder, sobbing uncontrollably.

"I'll n-never see Alanna or L-Leda grow up and get m-married," she said, releasing Allure, and taking a deep breath. "Never meet our unborn child, or see Jezebel unite Dorshire, or Mira take the dragons to Spanbrook."

"Yet they will do all of those things because of you," Allure said. "*Only* because of you. Your sacrifice will allow people all over Anoria to keep living and loving and fulfilling their dreams. Without you, we all die. This is what you were born to do, Allison Barclay. And history will remember you as the greatest mage who ever lived."

Allison broke down again, and Allure held her tight.

CHAPTER THIRTY-TWO
SACRIFICE

eturning to the great hall, Allison found Jezebel sitting at their table with Khaldun and Mira.

"Here you are," Jezebel said, smiling as she took her hand. "We were wondering where you'd gone."

"We need to talk," she told them. "Privately."

Alanna and Leda were still dancing with Soren and Scarlett. That was good. She would want to say goodbye before leaving, but let them enjoy this evening while they could.

Allison went up to her chambers with Jezebel, Khaldun, and Mira. She sat down on the edge of the bed with Jezebel, holding her hand, and Khaldun and Mira sat at the table facing them. Allison explained her plan in great detail. Jezebel squeezed her hand tighter and tighter as she went, tears streaming down her cheeks.

"There must be some other way," Jezebel said, her voice cracking. "What is the point of doing this if it takes you away from us?"

"There is no other way," Allison told her, stroking her cheek and wiping away a tear. "We have to do this. You saved me long ago, now let me save you."

Mira sobbed, and Khaldun held her tight. "I don't believe there is any other way, either," he said. "Nyro took steps to protect herself against the spike, and her true name no longer holds any power over her. But are we certain this will work? I see no reason it shouldn't, but we must be sure your sacrifice won't be in vain."

"As long as the initial rite works, then nothing can stop us," Allison said, taking a deep breath. "If Nyro's found some way to prevent that, then there would be no reason to continue. And the second rite will act on *me*, so there's nothing Nyro can do about it.

"This will be extremely dangerous, though. Perhaps more so than what we attempted with the spike. All four of us will have a role to play to ensure its success, and our timing must be perfect. But who better to carry this out? We have been working together for years."

"Why wouldn't the initial rite be enough?" Jezebel said. "As long as Mira continues living in Castle Barclay with us and keeps her null expanded around the clock, that would protect you."

"It would protect everyone inside the castle but not the rest of Anoria," Allison said. "Nyro is far too strong to be controlled. She could continue carrying out our extermination and I would be powerless to stop her. I'm sorry, my love, but this is the only way. We *must* destroy her."

Jezebel held her tight, crying on her chest. Allison couldn't hold back her own tears.

"We should let the other rulers know what we're planning," Khaldun said.

"No, I can't bear to belabor this any further," Allison said. "I need to tell the girls before we go. But we should get underway as soon as possible."

"At the very least, you should consult with Salerna," Mira said. "You said the castle is under heavy guard, and Nyro still has an entire army under her command, as well as dozens of mages. Your plan itself is dangerous enough, but that's a moot point if we can't get into the undercroft."

"That's fair," Allison said with a nod.

"We'll lose Mira's null when we leave," Jezebel said. "We should have Allure or one of the others sneak the girls out of the castle and take them somewhere safe."

"Yes," Allison agreed. "And she should keep the destination secret from us to ensure Nyro can't read it in our minds."

"I would also suggest we take the elf mage, Gyda, with us," Khaldun said. "With Nyro gone, who knows what her lieutenants might do? Gyda was a respected figure in their society long before

Nyro's rise. Perhaps she can lift the veil from their eyes and make them understand how Nyro deceived them."

"Excellent point," Allison said.

"So, we'll need Gyda, Salerna, Kamari, and Allure," Jezebel said. "We'll tell them what we're planning and let them relay it to the others."

Mira and Khaldun left to return to their chambers and change into their armor. Allison and Jezebel did the same, then headed down to the entry hall. Jezebel went to fetch the others from the great hall, and a few minutes later, they all sat down at the table in the prince's council chambers. Salerna gasped when they explained what they were going to do and why it was necessary.

"None of us can ask this of you, but I see the wisdom in it," Salerna said. "The entire continent will owe you a debt of gratitude we can never repay."

"Thank you, Your Highness," Allison said.

"As far as getting inside the castle, I should be able to help. Do you know the disposition of Nyro's forces?"

"Yes, thanks to Shadow," Allison said. "There is a heavy troop presence on every level of the city and throughout the castle, including a half dozen guards on the keep roof. Only two soldiers in the undercroft, though, standing guard by the bottom of the stairs. Periodically, others arrive to take more prisoners to Nyro. But she is mostly isolated down there."

"She hasn't put a barrier around the castle?" Khaldun said.

"No," Allison confirmed. "Which makes me believe she did leave Fang and Emma behind somewhere in Drengrvollr. She established the barrier around her first island to protect them, not her."

"The tunnel we used to evacuate Highgate's people would have been the ideal entry point," Jezebel said.

"There is another hidden entrance that leads to the undercroft," Salerna told them. She explained how to find it.

"That should work," Khaldun said when she was done. "As long as we stay invisible on our way into the city, we should have no trouble accessing that. Does Nyro have any demons watching over the city?"

"None that Shadow has seen," Allison said. "She does have one keeping an eye on Okset, but none in Highgate."

"We'll need to get the girls out of the city before we depart," Jezebel said. "Prince Kamari, if you have any hidden passages out of the castle, we would like to ask Allure to take them somewhere safe, without divulging her destination to us. Nyro can't read it in our minds if we don't know it ourselves."

"Yes, of course," Kamari said. "I have the perfect route in mind. It will let you out by the seashore."

"I'd be happy to take the girls," Allure said.

"We should go the same way," Allison said. "Once Allure has left with the girls, I can send Shadow to confuse Nyro's demon, and then we can slip out."

Gyda agreed to accompany them. They didn't know how many of Nyro's top people were with her by choice, but the elf believed at least some of them would have been brought into the fold against their will. She would appeal to them, and hopefully, they could sway the others to abandon Nyro's cause.

Salerna bade them farewell and wished them luck, embracing Allison and thanking her for her sacrifice. Kamari told them where to meet, and then Allison and Jezebel returned to the great hall to collect the girls. They were reluctant to leave their partners but understood that something serious was happening.

"Why are you two wearing your armor?" Alanna asked once they'd reached their chambers. She'd sat down in the bed next to Leda, and Allison and Jezebel had pulled two chairs from the table closer to them.

Allison took one of their hands in each of hers and explained what they were going to do. Her throat burned the whole time, and she had trouble holding back the tears, but she got through it. Leda and Alanna cried their eyes out but listened intently.

"I don't want you to g-go," Leda said, hugging her and sobbing when she was done. "P-please stay with us. We can go somewhere f-far away where Nyro will never find us. As long as we're together, I don't care."

"I'm sorry, I'm so sorry," Allison said, holding her tight and crying freely. "There's nowhere Nyro wouldn't find us in time."

"You're the bravest person I know," Alanna said, embracing them both. "I want to be just like you someday."

"You can be whoever you want to be," Allison said. "Both of you. There is nothing you can't do. Being your mother has made my life worth living, and I wouldn't trade the time we've had for anything. Now it will be your time, and knowing that makes me happier than I ever imagined I could be."

Jezebel stood beside them, squeezing the three of them to her. Allison wished this moment could last forever, and in her heart, it would. But it was time to go.

Alanna and Leda changed into their armor, and the four of them made their way down to the castle's main level. Moving into the library, they met Mira and Khaldun, Gyda, Allure, and Kamari by the rear wall.

"This is it," Kamari said. Pushing a section of the bookshelves, it receded into the wall and he slid it aside, revealing a hidden passage beyond. Moving inside, he took the flint and steel set from a niche in the wall, using it to light the torch in the nearby sconce.

"My pride and joy," Allison said, gathering Alanna and Leda to her and hugging them one last time. "Never forget how much I love you."

The girls held her tight, both of them sobbing, before moving into the passage.

"Good hunting, all of you," Allure said, embracing Allison, Khaldun, and Jezebel in turn. "We will never forget your sacrifice," she added to Allison before moving into the passage. She took the torch from its sconce, leading Alanna and Leda away.

Jezebel held Allison as she sobbed quietly, knowing that was the last time she'd ever see her daughters.

"It will take them about thirty minutes to reach the other end," Kamari told them, handing Jezebel an hourglass. "Two turns should do it. I will leave you now. Good luck to you all. You carry the hopes of every Anorian with you."

The five of them waited until the time was up. Mira collapsed her null, and Allison reached out to Shadow.

"Nyro's demon continues to watch over Okset. I have not seen any sign of Allure or the girls."

Allison told her to confuse the watching demon. Producing her mirror, she contacted Allure.

"We're airborne and invisible," the sorcerer told her, "a minute or two outside the city."

"Perfect, thank you for everything," Allison said, putting away the mirror. "It's time," she said to the others.

Allison took the lead, moving into the passage and calling a flame to light their way. Khaldun brought up the rear, sliding the bookshelf back into place behind them. They moved through the passage, down several flights of stairs, and then through another tunnel, finally emerging in a cavern near the sea.

Once they'd reached the beach, Khaldun pulled his carpet out of the void. Mira sat down in the center and strapped herself in, as Khaldun, Allison, Jezebel, and Gyda each took a seat by one of the corners. Allison checked in with Shadow once more, and she confirmed Nyro's demon had drifted away from the city. Khaldun made them invisible and took off, flying north.

Even with four of them calling air, it would take until the following evening to reach Highgate. They made a few stops to get up and stretch their legs but didn't stay anywhere very long. Allison kept checking the situation in Highgate with Shadow. Nyro left her workshop at one point in the middle of the day, going up to Salerna's former chambers. Allison started to worry that they'd lost their chance, but Nyro only napped for a few hours before returning to the undercroft. Her soldiers brought her another dozen prisoners, so hopefully, she'd be busy with them long enough for Allison to strike.

They reached the city just before sunset. The fires had finally died, leaving many of the building exteriors blackened. Companies of elvish soldiers filled the city's every level, with the majority of the army camped out on the plain. Khaldun took them into the catacombs, still on the carpet. There were no guards stationed at the entrance; Nyro had no interest in such places.

Once beyond the antechamber, Khaldun called a flame to light their way. They landed by the sarcophagus Salerna had told them about, getting to their feet as Khaldun tucked the carpet into the void. Sure enough, the panel behind the tomb gave way when Allison pushed on it. She moved it far enough to create a space for them to pass, and they made their way into the hidden tunnel. Once everyone was through, she pushed the stone back into place. Before they went any farther, Gyda cast an invisibility spell around the five of them. Khaldun's was still in place, but he and Allison would have to separate from the rest of the group soon, and they didn't want to cast any spells once they entered the castle.

After climbing a narrow staircase, they emerged into a short passage with a dim light at its far end. Khaldun canceled his flame and they proceeded through the tunnel. There were iron rungs embedded in the far wall, leading to a metal grate at the top. The light was coming from the openings in the grate.

Allison climbed the rungs, moving the grate out of the opening as quietly as she could. Casting the spell to contain sounds would be far too dangerous—Nyro was sure to detect it. The two invisibility spells should keep them hidden. Nyro was unlikely to detect the magic if she wasn't looking for it—only the casting of a new spell would attract her attention. Poking her head out of the opening, Allison saw the castle undercroft extending in every direction. The two soldiers were standing sentinel by the bottom of the stairs, and it didn't seem like they'd heard the grate moving.

Nyro's workshop was on the other side of the undercroft, and there was nothing to indicate she was aware of their presence. Allison breathed a sigh of relief as she climbed the rest of the way into the vast chamber. Jezebel, Khaldun, Mira, and Gyda followed her in.

Allison embraced Jezebel, crying silent tears. This was goodbye. Jezebel kissed her, and Allison wiped the tears from her cheeks. She hugged Mira and Gyda, then hurried off with Khaldun. They reached Nyro's chamber, stopping beside the door. Once they opened it, the others would be able to see inside. The spells Nyro had put in place prevented Shadow from getting a look in there but wouldn't have any effect on living beings. And those spells would die when Mira expanded her null.

This was it. Allison pulled her sword out of the void, and Khaldun canceled his invisibility spell and transformed into his octopus form. Nyro was sure to sense their magic, but it didn't matter now. As planned, Mira expanded her null when Khaldun transformed, and Allison felt her magic die. They stormed through the door, and the sight and smells that greeted them made Allison gasp. Dozens of people lay on the floor, most of them long since dead, the rest not far behind. Feces and blood covered nearly every surface, and Allison had to fight back an urge to vomit.

Nyro faced them from across the chamber, a dying woman on the work table behind her. She was in Gorm's body, naked and bloody, sword in hand. Khaldun bolted across the chamber toward her. She tried hacking off his tentacles as he reached for her but it was no good. Within seconds, he'd immobilized her, wrapping up her arms and legs.

Something had changed, though. Nyro was far stronger now. She freed first one hand from Khaldun's grasp and then the other. Allison remembered that battering ram she'd used to break down the city gates and wondered if she'd acquired the ability to transform her own body as well as other objects like Khaldun could. Freeing her legs, Nyro turned, punching Khaldun in the head.

The octopus made a noise approximating a scream. Its legs spasmed, and the beast wilted over, no longer moving at all.

"NO!" Allison screamed. She rushed in, swinging her blade, but Nyro sidestepped, moving toward the door. Allison hooked her leg with one foot, and Nyro went sprawling on the floor. She rolled away before Allison could follow up, but she managed to get herself between Nyro and the doorway.

Nyro regained her feet, her sword at the ready. "You cannot stop me. Anoria will die and there's nothing you can do to prevent it." She rushed in with an overhead cut. Allison evaded, countering with a swing of her own.

Back and forth the two struggled, slashing, cutting, and stabbing faster than the eye could see. Allison cut her wrist one time but failed to disarm her. Nyro caught Allison in the ribs after that, but her armor held true.

Nyro's strength had increased dramatically since their last encounter. Perhaps it was simply the difference between Estrid's body and Gorm's, but Allison didn't think so. Khaldun wasn't as strong in this form as he was as a dragon-bear, but it must have taken incredible force to break his grip. She was swinging her blade fast and strong enough to cut Allison in half.

Allison kicked Nyro in the ribs, knocking her into the work table, and she thought she had her. But Nyro recovered almost instantly, pressing her own attack in return. She drove Allison back and nearly disarmed her. Allison punched her in the throat, giving herself a moment to regain her balance.

Nyro tried circling her, but Allison moved to stop her progress. There was no way she was letting her through that door. Nyro feinted with an attack to her left, but Allison was ready for it. When Nyro charged the other way, Allison swung her blade, the force of it shattering Nyro's sword. The blade severed her arm at the elbow.

Nyro screamed, blood gushing from her limb, and retreated, searching for another weapon. Allison rushed in, swinging her blade and removing Nyro's head. "Mira, now!"

Allison felt her magic return as the corpse hit the floor and cast the spells to prevent demons from entering or exiting the chamber. Nyro's spirit rose from the body, taking the shadowy form of a human. It tried fleeing from the workshop, but the spells prevented her from leaving. Allison invoked the rite of binding to merge her soul with Nyro before she could remove those spells. If she made it to the spirit realm, it was all over—Allison lacked the power to force her to return.

The demon screamed as Nyro realized what Allison was doing. She unleashed a barrage of spells, hitting Allison with fire and lightning. Allison smashed into the wall, bouncing off of it and dropping her sword. She hit the floor, struggling to remain conscious.

But it was too late—the rite of binding was complete. As Allison regained her feet, she spotted Jezebel standing in the doorway.

"*YOU BITCH!*" the demon screamed as it charged toward Jezebel. She backed away a few steps and cowered, but was never in any danger. Nyro couldn't leave this chamber.

"Jezebel, *NOW!*" Allison yelled.

Jezebel stared at her wide-eyed, sobs wracking her body. Now that the time had come, she didn't have it in her—she couldn't invoke her true name. The demon came for Allison, and as hard as she fought, she couldn't stop her from possessing her body. Nyro took over completely, saying, "Fang Gentle Heart, I name thee!"

Allison hadn't realized until that moment she shared a connection with the Kongese necromancer, but it died then as Fang ceased to exist.

"*Free me and I'll let the girl live,*" Nyro told her in her mind.

Allison sensed Nyro getting ready to invoke Emma's true name and put every ounce of her power into reasserting control of her own body.

"Jezebel, you have to do it *now*! She's going to kill Emma!"

Jezebel wailed, dropping to her knees. "*ALLISON LIFE GIVER, I NAME THEE!*"

"I love you," Allison said, then gasped as flames consumed her, body and soul. She felt Nyro screaming in her mind, and then she knew no more.

Chapter Thirty-Three
Going Home

Searing pain wracked Khaldun's entire body, agony beyond anything he had experienced before. His head was broken. He had no bones in this form, but something was badly damaged. Summoning his magic, he repaired himself. It took a little time, but finally, the pain receded, and he could think clearly.

He retook his human shape, gazing around the chamber. Allison was gone. Was Nyro? He was vaguely aware of her possessing Allison's body before Jezebel invoked the true name. There was no sign that Nyro had survived, but no proof that she was destroyed, either.

Khaldun left the chamber. Jezebel was on her knees, hands covering her face, sobbing uncontrollably. Mira kneeled next to her, holding her tight. She gazed up at Khaldun, tears streaming down her cheeks.

The sound of dozens of footsteps echoed off the walls as elvish soldiers ran down the steps, moving into the undercroft. Their leader approached, the others staying behind. Gyda spoke to him in elvish for a minute. He kept looking through the doorway to Nyro's workshop. Gorm's body was still lying on the floor but not visible from this angle.

"The commander is demanding to see Gorm," Gyda told Khaldun as the elf summoned one of his underlings. "They have strict orders not to enter the workshop unless they're delivering more prisoners. I've tried to explain that Gorm wasn't Gorm anymore and that Nyro was behind Estrid's rise to power. He doesn't seem to understand."

"So now what do we do?" Khaldun said, eyeing the troops still coming down the stairs.

"He's only in charge of the company assigned to the castle," Gyda said. "He's sending this other one to fetch someone higher up the chain of command. They'll decide what to do with us."

There was a commotion by the stairs. The elvish soldiers moved aside to let someone pass, and Khaldun spotted Cyclone coming down the steps. Vision was right behind her. Followed by Intuit, Spring, Semblant, Warhammer, and Legion. Cyclone approached Khaldun and Gyda while the others stood behind her.

"Emma sends her regards," Cyclone said with a smile. "She awoke from a sleep spell and freed herself from the void. While she still commands us, we no longer feel Nyro's will through our connection to her."

Khaldun explained what they'd done. "So Nyro's truly gone, then?"

"She must be. We've felt her unyielding will every moment since Emma bound us. Until now."

"Where is Emma?" Jezebel asked. She and Mira had gotten to their feet.

"In a castle on a small island off the coast of northern Drengrvollr," Cyclone told them. "She is stuck there for now, I'm afraid, with no carpet or ship to take her elsewhere."

"I have people I can send to rescue her," Gyda said. "They'll put her on a ship for Anoria. It will take weeks to get her home, but she should be safe."

"Nyro must have a barrier spell in place around the island," Khaldun said. "How will Emma escape?"

"The barrier is gone," Cyclone said. "With our help, she was able to take it down from the inside."

Cyclone told Gyda exactly where to find the island, and she went off to use her mirror.

"We will take care of sending the elvish army home," Cyclone said. "Nyro's generals will defer to us in her absence."

"They didn't know her as Nyro, though, did they?" Khaldun asked.

"No. Estrid was their leader. When she took Gorm's body instead, their understanding was that Estrid had placed him in command of all her forces in Anoria. With him gone, they'll accept our orders.

"Most of Nyro's top generals served her willingly," Cyclone continued. "Some of them had to be kept in line using armor imbued with compliance spells. We will execute those whose loyalty was true."

"How will you get the army back to Drengrvollr?" Jezebel asked. "There are so many of them."

"Their ships have remained anchored off the coast near Northcoast," Cyclone said. "The others and I can transport them to the port five thousand at a time by tucking them into the void and flying our carpets."

"What will happen with the jellyfish monsters?" Khaldun asked.

"We have no way to send them back to their own realm," Cyclone said. "They live over the ocean in their home world, feeding on fish. They've left Highgate, heading north, so I suspect they're making for the North Sea."

"What about the wraiths?" Mira asked.

"We will round them up and destroy them," Cyclone said. "They were bound directly to Nyro and now they're free. We'll need to deal with them first, then we'll take care of the army. Once the ships have set sail for Drengrvollr, we will release each other from these bodies and return to the spirit realm."

"You're still bound to Emma, though," Jezebel said. "What will happen to her? She's not strong enough to command all of you on her own, is she?"

"Nyro used spells to help us retain our sense of ourselves," Cyclone explained. "The magic changed us, and her demise will not affect that. And we have an understanding with Emma. We will not attempt to take her over as long as she does not force us to wage war. Otherwise, we will remain under her command for the rest of her life."

"Sounds like a fair bargain to me," Khaldun said.

"We will vacate the castle before we round up the wraiths," Cyclone said. "You are welcome to spend the night here."

"Thank you," Khaldun said. "And farewell."

Gyda told them she should set sail for Drengrvollr with the rest of the elves. Without anyone left who could use the pyramids, that would be her only way home. She bade them farewell and headed out with Cyclone and the other demon mages. The rest of the elves went with them, too, leaving the undercroft empty except for Khaldun, Jezebel, and Mira.

"I'm exhausted, but I do not wish to stay here," Jezebel said. "Let's leave for Okset, and once we've put some distance behind us, we can sleep under the stars tonight."

"Yes, I would like to get underway as well," Khaldun said.

Khaldun reached out to Allure by mirror to let her know what happened and that it was safe to take the girls back to Okset. He let Azure know the situation, too, and the sorcerer told him he'd relay the message to Salerna and the others.

"One of us will need to take Asmund and the rest of the elf mages to Northcoast," Khaldun said to Azure. "If they miss those ships, they'll have no way back to Drengrvollr."

"I will make the arrangements," the sorcerer said. "But Asmund will not be going with them."

"Oh? Why not?"

"Let's just say there have been some developments here in your absence. I won't spoil the surprise, though. You'll find out soon enough."

"Nothing bad, I hope," Khaldun said.

"Not at all. Safe travels, my friend."

Moving into the workshop, Khaldun checked on the remaining prisoners, but they were dead. He suspected Nyro must have been keeping them alive with magic. They looked like they'd been deprived of nourishment for quite some time. He worried for a moment that whatever new plague she'd been working on might infect them, but Mira's null would have snuffed out any such spells.

Khaldun retrieved Allison's sword and sensed other items tucked into the void. He removed Allison's carpet and pyramid. They'd been tethered to her, but in her absence, remained tethered in place. He found Nyro's carpet and pyramid, too. Incinerating the carpet, he tucked the pyramids, sword, and Allison's carpet into the void.

Khaldun left the undercroft with Jezebel and Mira. They made their way up to the keep roof, looking out over the city and the plain beyond. In the twilight, they could see the elvish army already breaking camp, and one of the demon mages had started a pyre for the wraiths. Khaldun spotted one of the monsters racing north on his horse, a carpet in pursuit. The rider called air, lifting the wraith out of the saddle and throwing him to the ground. The carpet rider landed, producing a sword and decapitating his foe. Moving the corpse and its head onto his carpet, he took off again, heading toward the pyre.

Khaldun, Mira, and Jezebel took off on his carpet, heading south. Once out of sight of the city, they landed by a small river. Khaldun told Jezebel and Mira he'd take the first watch, and they lay down. He was planning on letting them sleep until morning, but Jezebel woke with a start in the middle of the night. Sitting up, she gazed around and said, "Allison?"

After that, Khaldun heard her crying. She must have been having a dream, and it took a few moments for reality to set in. He sat next to her, embracing her and rubbing her back.

"What have I done?" she asked between her sobs.

"The only thing you could," he said, a tear slipping down his cheek. "There was no other choice."

"I miss her so m-much…"

Mira woke up and sat on Jezebel's other side. After a few minutes, she convinced her to go back to sleep. Khaldun told Mira he would keep watch for the rest of the night, but she insisted on taking over for him. He *was* exhausted, so he agreed, lying down and drifting off within minutes.

The next morning, they rose at dawn, flying that whole day and the next with only a handful of short stops, finally reaching Okset late in the afternoon. They landed in the square in front of the castle, getting to their feet and stretching. Jezebel had let Allure know they were almost there, so as Khaldun tucked his carpet into the void, Alanna and Leda ran out to meet them. Jezebel held her girls, all three of them crying freely.

Prince Kamari had recalled the city's population from the countryside, and they were starting to return. That evening, he held a feast in the great hall to celebrate their victory and honor Allison's sacrifice. The seating arrangements were much the same as last time, and Khaldun and Mira sat at the Spanbrook table with Jezebel, Alanna, and Leda. Shatter and Azure were absent—Khaldun learned that they'd left to take the elf mages to Northcoast. Once everyone had taken their seats, Kamari invited the minstrel, Thomas Broadpaunch, to the front of the hall.

Kamari's steward escorted the man to the space in front of the head table, setting down a chair for him to use. Broadpaunch sat down with his lute, playing and singing the song he'd written in Allison's honor. He sang about her rise to power as a princess and mage, her devotion to her friends and family, and her courage in the face of unthinkable horrors. Her acts of bravery in the war against Nyro and her sacrifice to save them all.

Everyone got to their feet and clapped for the minstrel when he was done. Jezebel went to speak to him and invited him to sit with them for the feast.

"That was truly lovely," Jezebel said with a sniffle once they'd taken their seats.

"You honor me, Your Highness, but I cannot take all the credit. Battleaxe came to see me and asked me to write it."

"There are other stories I'd love to hear told in song," Jezebel said.

"I would be happy to accept the commission," he said.

"How would you feel about making the arrangement permanent?" she asked. "Come to Spanbrook as our court minstrel. It pays well, I promise."

"It would be my pleasure, Your Highness," he said with a nod. "As for pay, keep me stocked in victuals and drink, and I'll be yours forevermore."

"You have yourself a deal," Jezebel said with a chuckle.

The feast began, and Broadpaunch entertained them with stories of his travels throughout Maeda and Dorshire. When the meal was finished, Prince Kamari and Princess Zuri got to their feet, and the prince clinked his glass to get everyone's attention.

"Honored guests," he said, smiling around at them. "On the occasion of our bittersweet victory over our mortal foe, Princess Zuri and I have an announcement to make. Princess?"

She smiled at him, then turned to face the room. "Prince Kamari and I have long discussed joining forces to unite the ancient kingdom of Shifar. I am thrilled to announce tonight that the prince has asked for my hand in marriage, and I have agreed."

There was a moment of stunned silence before everyone got to their feet again, clapping and cheering in response to this news.

"We will be uniting Shifar as king and queen," Zuri continued. "And we invite all of you to the wedding to take place here in Okset one week hence."

Everyone cheered again. Siren raised her glass and made a toast to the royal couple, and everyone drank in their honor. After that, the court musicians began playing, and many people got up to dance. Alanna and Leda ran off to find Soren and Scarlett, but Khaldun and Mira stayed with Jezebel and Broadpaunch.

"Azure told us there had been developments while we were away," Khaldun said with a grin. "I guess this must be what he meant. But I'm not sure what it has to do with Asmund."

"The elf mage from Drengrvollr?" Broadpaunch asked. Khaldun nodded. "I've heard the prince invited him to stay in Okset as his court mage, and he accepted."

"That would explain it," said Mira.

Khaldun knew Kamari had been trying to get the university to assign him another sorcerer for years, so he was sure he'd be happy with this new arrangement.

The feast ran very late into the night. Khaldun had asked Jezebel if she wanted to retire to her chambers, but she told him she wanted to be around people to stave off the loneliness. It was well after midnight by the time they all returned to their chambers.

Three mornings later, the leaders from the various princedoms, their mages, and the university governors held a meeting in Kamari's council chambers. Azure and Shatter were in attendance, having returned safely from Northcoast. Khaldun and Mira attended with Jezebel, and it felt sad and strange to be there without Allison.

"We have heard from the elf mage, Gyda," Allure told them. "The demon mages finished transporting Nyro's army to Northcoast, and all of the ships have set sail for Drengrvollr."

"This is truly it, then," Prince Carlo said. "Anoria has prevailed. And now we can return to our princedoms and rebuild what we have lost."

"Not just yet," Augustine said with a smile. "We have a royal wedding to attend first. Will the rest of you be staying?"

"My people and I will remain here for this historic occasion," Jezebel said.

"As will we," said Salerna.

The others all agreed they would remain until after the wedding.

"Princess Miranda and I have been talking," Augustine said, "and we would like to propose reuniting the old kingdom of Maeda as well. As long as Princess Salerna would consent to becoming our queen, of course."

Khaldun knew Salerna well enough to tell this was not coming as a surprise.

"It would be my honor," Salerna said.

"We would also like to see Dorshire unified once more," said Leto. Khaldun knew Prince Carlo had been lobbying for this, but was skeptical about Leto agreeing to it. "Princess Jezebel has proven herself a strong and capable leader, and though Keepstone was the traditional seat of power in the kingdom, we would like to nominate her as our queen."

"Blacksand seconds the motion," Prince Carlo said with a grin.

"Princess Jelena of Rockport regrets she could not be here in person," Khaldun said, "but asked me to inform you that she lends her support to this proposal as well."

"I proudly accept," Jezebel said with tears in her eyes.

"Governor Allure has agreed to officiate our coronation as part of our wedding ceremony," Kamari said.

"It would normally be a separate event," Zuri said, "but we wanted all of you to be present for it."

"We could hold Princess Salerna's coronation next," Allure said. "It will fall to the rest of the governors and me to transport everyone to their home princedoms anyway, so we could make a stop in Highgate."

The others agreed.

"I would like to wait until my sister, Emma, returns from Drengrvollr before holding my own event in Spanbrook," Jezebel said. "So you are all invited, of course, but I don't expect you to attend. I daresay most of us will be sick of traveling by then."

For the next few days, Mira and Khaldun spent most of their time with Jezebel and the girls. With the threat of Nyro finally removed, Alanna left the castle often to fly with Sigrid. Mira joined her a few times, flying Magna. But Alanna wanted some time alone with Soren, too, so Mira gave them their space. They didn't see much of Kamari or Zuri after their council meeting, and Khaldun figured they were busy with preparations for their ceremony.

The big day finally came, and Okset's citizens and all of the visiting dignitaries gathered in the square outside the castle. Kamari's people had decorated the surrounding buildings with various banners, including those of the five ancient kingdoms, Shifar's hanging from the castle. As the most senior governor, Allure presided over both the wedding and the coronation. They held a giant feast in the great hall after that, celebrating late into the night.

The next day, Khaldun, Azure, and Shatter assisted the university mages in transporting all of the non-Shifari to Highgate. They stopped in Bayfast to drop off Miranda's people, but the princess continued to Highgate. King Kamari and Queen Zuri delayed their honeymoon to join them, but the rest of their household stayed behind.

They waited a few days to give the city's residents time to return from the countryside. By the time they held Salerna's coronation in the castle courtyard, the dragons had arrived, many of them perching on the castle walls as if in approval. Once again, Allure officiated, and they held a celebratory feast in the great hall in honor of their new queen.

The next morning, Azure came to see Khaldun and Mira in their chambers. He pulled a carpet out of the void, lying it on the floor. "This is for Her Highness's sister, Emma. You'll have to teach her how to use it, but as a necromancer, she shouldn't have any trouble."

"Thank you," Khaldun said. "She'll be thrilled, I'm sure."

"I'm surprised this survived," Mira said. "Nyro pretty well destroyed your workshop."

"Luckily, I keep the extra carpets locked away in a separate storage room," he said. "I don't think Nyro bothered looking for them."

It took a few days to return everyone to their proper princedoms. Azure flew Miranda back to Bayfast, and Kamari and Zuri to Okset. Khaldun, Shatter, and the university sorcerers took care of transporting people to Stoutwall first, and hence to Keepstone, Spanbrook, and Blacksand. Khaldun took care of transporting Jelena's children, Susan and James, to Rockport—they'd returned to Spanbrook with Jezebel's parents. Once that was done, Jezebel invited Allure, Battleaxe, Sage, and Mist to stay the night in Spanbrook, and they accepted. Kashi and the other dragon riders were returning to their aeries in the Anthar mountains, where they'd collect the rest of the crash before moving to Spanbrook. Mira was their leader now, so they'd decided to relocate.

Jezebel had sent word to their people in the countryside that it was safe to return to the city, and they had started arriving by the time Khaldun returned from Rockport, including most of Jezebel's household staff. Both the castle and the town still seemed empty, though. Especially with Emma and Allison missing.

Jezebel and the girls went to bed right after dinner. But Khaldun and Mira sat up late with the university sorcerers and Imani, drinking in the private dining room. Khaldun had talked to Jezebel about the two pyramids, and they agreed it would be best to send them to the university for safekeeping. So Khaldun removed them from the void and gave them to Allure.

"Do we know where these came from?" Khaldun asked. "I always assumed the elves made them, but apparently that's not the case. Allison asked Gyda, and she thought Nyro made them."

"I've looked into it, and I'm afraid I can't say for sure," Sage said. "I can give you my educated guess, though."

"Your guesses are usually as good as other people's facts," Khaldun said with a grin. "Please, go ahead."

Sage took a deep breath. "Keep in mind that records from the time of Nyro's rise and reign are extremely hard to come by because of the purge. Legends and oral tradition provide the bulk of my information. That being said, I can find no mention of the pyramids from any time before Nyro's rise. I believe she took them from those beings in that other realm you sensed when you encountered those monks at that temple."

"The old gods?" Mira asked. "The ones Nyro allegedly cast down from heaven?"

"The very same," Sage said. "I believe they came to our world from some other realm, much like those jellyfish monsters. I don't know if they created the pyramids, but I think they used them to come here. And Nyro took them before sending them wherever they are now."

"They do seem rather ancient," Allure said, holding the artifacts. She tucked Allison's into the void but examined the other for a moment. "As I would have expected," she said, before sending it to oblivion.

"What did you expect?" Mist said.

"Nyro's pyramid used to be locked to her," Allure said with a shrug. "Now it's not. It's just like Allison's."

"Well, of course that would be the case," Battleaxe said. "Nyro must have unlocked it before she started using the thing herself, right?"

"Yes, I just wanted to be sure," she said with a sigh. "She was such a huge threat for so long, it's hard to believe she's actually gone."

"Believe it, sister," Sage said with a grin. "We never have to worry about that bitch again."

"Thank the stars for that," Mira said.

"A toast," Battleaxe said, raising her glass. "To Princess Allison. The greatest mage who ever lived."

"And the greatest fighter," Imani added.

"And our dearest friend," Mira said.

"To Princess Allison," the others said, clinking their glasses together, and finishing their drinks.

CHAPTER THIRTY-FOUR
THE RETURN OF THE QUEEN

ife in Spanbrook and Castle Barclay in particular slowly returned to normal. Yet in many ways, it would never be the same. Khaldun was grateful beyond words that Mira, Jezebel, Alanna, and Leda had survived the war. But their army had suffered massive losses. And Allison's absence was palpable in a million little ways. Grief hung over them like a cloak, none of them more so than Jezebel. Khaldun and Mira worried about her and the girls and spent as much time with them as they could.

In Emma's absence, Mira had taken on the duties of steward. Jezebel didn't know if Emma would want to resume her post or not, so was reluctant to give the job to anyone else. Scarlett from Stoutwall had requested and received Augustine's permission to resign from his castle guard and had made the move with them to Spanbrook. With Jezebel's permission, she was living in the castle with Leda now. The princess was considering her for the position of steward if Emma didn't want it, so Mira had taken her under her wing, teaching her about the inner workings of the castle.

Prince Leto of Keepstone had invited Amari to come to the Bastion and take over as the Commandant in Bishop's place. Amari agreed, and Jezebel approved the transfer. Imani continued to serve as the master-at-arms, and Jezebel appointed her Captain of the Eagle Company, too.

The dragons had arrived from the aeries—the entire crash this time. Mira reported that Lavinia, the former leader, had grudgingly accepted this new order. The beasts hunted mostly in the forest north of the city, sleeping along the banks of the River Ember. And the riders made their camp in the same area. But many of the beasts roosted on Castle Barclay's ramparts at night, including Alanna's dragon, Sigrid, which was causing an issue with their waste piling up by the moat. And some of the local farmers had complained about livestock going missing. Though Alanna insisted Sigrid understood not to hunt in the fields, it seemed obvious some of the others had to be the culprits. Jezebel was searching for a better solution, including somewhere permanent for the riders to reside, but so far, had come up empty.

Jezebel commissioned a local artisan to craft a sarcophagus for Allison and had them place it in Castle Barclay's courtyard, right in front of the keep. Allison's likeness was carved into the stone lid, and they placed her carpet, sword, and other weapons inside. A few days later, they held a memorial service for their fallen princess, and the townspeople and surrounding landowners crowded into the courtyard to pay their last respects. Many of the dragons perched on the battlements, and Thomas Broadpaunch performed the song he'd written for her. When he was done, the dragons raised their heads to the sky and howled, something Khaldun had never witnessed before. He asked Mira about it, and she said it was the tune they sang to honor a fallen brother or sister.

Gyda had told them that Emma's ship would land in Hido, in the kingdom of Kong. Once Emma was underway, she sent Cyclone to keep them apprised of her progress across the ocean. The demon had liberated herself from her elf body and could travel anywhere in the world by moving through the spirit realm. When the time came, Khaldun set out from Castle Barclay on his carpet. He spent that night in an inn in Northcoast, then flew the rest of the way to Hido the next day.

Once he'd landed, he tucked his carpet into the void and found the inn he'd visited with Allison. Heading inside, he asked to see the owner, Ming. One of the servers escorted him back to her office.

"I never thought I'd see you again," she said, inviting him to have a seat. "What brings you back to Kong?"

"Princess Jezebel's sister is on her way from Drengrvollr," he said. "She should arrive in the next day or two, but I don't know precisely when, so I figured I'd stay here while I wait."

"Understood," she said. "I heard about Nyro's demise and Princess Allison's sacrifice. I'm sorry for your loss. We all owe her our lives."

"Thank you," he said, his throat burning. "Do you keep track of ships entering the harbor? I'm sure you don't get many from Drengrvollr, and I was wondering if someone could alert me if one arrives."

"I can make that happen," she said. "You're welcome to stay upstairs while you wait. On the house, of course. And, ah, avail yourself of our other services as much as you like."

"I will pay for the room," Khaldun said with a chuckle. "Princess Jezebel sends her regards and has provided enough coin for an extended stay. I shall enjoy some hot meals and ale, but must decline the rest."

"As you wish," she said with a nod.

Khaldun linked his mirror to hers and went to eat in the tavern. After that, he retired to his room and used his mirror to speak with Mira.

He spent the next day exploring the city without any sign of a Drengrvollri ship entering the harbor. Finally, on the third day, he woke before dawn when someone tried to reach him by mirror. Sitting up in bed, he found Ming staring back at him.

"An elvish ship has arrived," she told him. "It's docking now."

She told him exactly where to find it. Once Khaldun had donned his robes, he hurried out, making his way to the docks. The city was already busy despite the early hour, so it was slow going moving through the crowd. But he made it just as they lay down the gangplank.

Emma disembarked, looking just how he remembered, except for her white eyes and translucent skin—and something more. It was subtle, but there was a wariness about her that hadn't existed before. She spotted Khaldun as she reached the dock and ran over to him, hugging him tight and sobbing.

"Welcome home," he said, patting her on the back.

It was a few minutes before she calmed down enough to speak. "I never thought I would see you again. And I didn't know how I was going to get home to Spanbrook. Thank you so much for meeting me here!"

"It's my pleasure," he said. "I'm staying at an inn nearby. Would you care for some breakfast?"

"That's perfect, I'm famished," she said with a grin.

They went to Ming's and sat down in the tavern. The two of them chatted as they ate, catching each other up on everything they'd endured since Emma's abduction from Stoutwall. Nyro had never named any line of succession, so her demise meant that Emma was now an unbound necromancer. Khaldun explained that they'd need to stop at the university to have her bound to Jezebel.

"Yes, the sooner, the better," Emma said. "I worried they'd force me into service somewhere else."

"It is unheard of for them to allow more than one mage to be bound to a single ruler," Khaldun said, "but these are not exactly normal times. In a sense, I suppose you'll be taking Allison's place."

Emma didn't want to wait, so after breakfast, they set out for the university. With the two of them calling air, they had no trouble making it there before nightfall. They went to see Allure when they arrived, and she invited them to stay with her. It was safest to fast for seven days before the right of binding, and with the threat of war removed, there was no longer any reason to rush the process.

Emma wasn't thrilled with the prospect of consuming nothing but water for so long. And Khaldun felt bad—she already looked like she hadn't eaten well in quite some time. But in the end, they agreed to abide by the precautions.

Khaldun *did* enjoy spending time with Allure, Battleaxe, Mist, and Sage with the stress of the invasion behind them. They ate and drank together every night, and he wished only that Mira could have been there with them. It wouldn't take long for him to return to Spanbrook by carpet and bring her to the university, but they didn't want to leave Jezebel alone.

They had a lot of time on their hands, and Khaldun had brought the carpet Azure made for Emma. So they went out to the quad one morning, and he taught her how to fly it. She was a little uneasy at first, and it took a few tries for her to get the hang of it. But once she did, she was soaring around the campus at top speed and racing Khaldun out to the river and back.

Allure told Khaldun one night that they'd discussed inviting him and Mira to join the university as governors. Khaldun was honored but he declined. He and Mira had already discussed their plans and wanted to remain in Spanbrook and continue serving the Barclay family.

"We figured as much," Allure said with a knowing smile. "And that's the only reason we decided not to extend the formal invitation. But know that if anything should ever change, you'll always have a home here."

"I appreciate it," he said, squeezing her hand. "And I know Mira does, too."

The day finally came, and Allure performed Emma's rite of binding. It went perfectly, and she bound Emma to Jezebel. Once Emma had recovered, she and Khaldun bade the governors farewell and returned to Spanbrook.

Emma shared a tearful reunion with Jezebel, Alanna, and Leda when they reached the castle. Khaldun left them alone and went to see Mira. Lord Arthur Asterly came to visit Emma the next morning, and later that day, Jezebel announced that they'd finally be getting married in two weeks' time.

They held the ceremony in the great hall, and all of the local lords and ladies attended. Jezebel gave the new couple the villa in the northern hills as a wedding present, and they went there for their honeymoon.

Soon after, Jezebel told Mira and Khaldun that Emma had agreed to retire as steward and take the role of court mage instead. Now that she had a carpet, it would be easy for her to live in her new estate with her husband and fly to the castle each day to fulfill her duties there. Scarlett had agreed to take on the role of steward in her place. Khaldun was thrilled for them both.

Mira pointed out that it was time to schedule Jezebel's coronation as Queen of Dorshire. Khaldun had the feeling she was dragging her feet for some reason. And when Jezebel broke down in tears at Mira's suggestion, she finally revealed the reason for it.

"Allison and I had talked about uniting the old kingdom for a long time," she said with a sniffle. "And I always imagined doing it with her by my side. But now I'm alone, and… it just d-doesn't seem the same…"

Mira held her, and Jezebel sobbed into her shoulder. But once she'd calmed down, she agreed that it was indeed time to schedule the coronation.

Scarlett got to work preparing for the event, and Mira assisted her every step of the way. The following month, dignitaries from across Dorshire and the other kingdoms started arriving, including Prince Leto and Commandant Amari, Prince Carlo and his daughter, Yolanda, and Princess Jelena and her children.

Queen Salerna let them know she was not up to the journey but would be sending her son, Albert, in her place. And as much as Jezebel didn't expect it, King Kamari and Queen Zuri accepted their invitation. They arrived by carpet with Siren two days before the event. Prince Augustine and his family made the trip from Stoutwall with Shatter, and, of course, the governors flew in from the university.

The day arrived, and the courtyard was decorated with the ancient banner of Dorshire and the Barclay family crest. The people of Spanbrook packed the castle courtyard in addition to the visiting dignitaries, and the dragons took their positions on the battlements.

Governor Allure performed the ceremony, crowning Jezebel the Queen of Dorshire, and Governor Sage gave her the royal scepter, a gift from King Kamari and Queen Zuri. Jezebel spoke to her people and their guests, thanking them for their support and promising to work tirelessly for the people of Dorshire. After the ceremony, they held a feast in the great hall, celebrating their new queen.

After the festivities had ended, and the honored guests had all departed for the night or retired to their chambers, Jezebel invited Alanna, Leda, and Scarlett, Emma, Khaldun, and Mira, Imani, and the university governors to the private dining room. They sat down at the table, and members of the staff served them wine—and water for Jezebel.

Getting to her feet and holding up her glass, Jezebel said, "I want to thank all of you for your support, your friendship, and your love over the years. As you all know, I grew up on a farm and never imagined I'd become a princess, much less a queen. But I couldn't have done it without all of you."

"Mother's a little drunk," Alanna said in a stage whisper, and the others chuckled.

"I am not," Jezebel said, giving her a stern look. "I've had nothing but water." She took a deep, steadying breath before continuing. "I know Allison felt the same way I do. While she *was* born a princess, circumstances conspired to take that away from her. And for a time, her future remained uncertain. But in the end, she returned to Spanbrook and we ruled side by side.

"Those years we reigned together will always be the happiest of my life. Allison would have made a great queen. Yet even though she's not with us anymore, it was her sacrifice that made this possible. Her sacrifice that ensured we all had a future." Her voice had remained steady, but it started cracking as she continued, and tears streamed down her cheeks. "She loved you all as much as I do. And in your presence, I feel like she's still here with us. So thank you all for being here today. As queen, I will do everything in my power to repay the devotion you have always shown Allison and me."

Imani got to her feet. Holding up her glass, she said, "Long live Queen Jezebel!"

The others stood up as well, repeating, "Long Live Queen Jezebel!"

Khaldun drank his wine, swelling with pride for his queen. It had been a long and winding road getting to this point, and he was eager to see where it would lead them next.

EPILOGUE

lanna woke at dawn, quickly getting dressed and hurrying down to the courtyard. Sigrid wanted to show her something. She didn't know what, but the dragon was extremely insistent about it. The beast swooped over the castle, landing in the courtyard. She lowered her head and one wing, and Alanna climbed onto her back. Moments later, they were airborne, flying north.

Not long after the coronation, Alanna had asked if she could stay with the riders in their camp for a while. Mother had refused, insisting that she stay in the castle. Alanna had pointed out the inherent inequity in her decision—Scarlett was living in the castle with Leda, after all—and at first, she'd denied it. She said it wasn't safe for Alanna to live outside the castle.

Alanna had reminded her that she'd have an entire crash of dragons protecting her, and finally Mother had relented. She confessed that she worried about Alanna taking Soren to bed and getting pregnant. Alanna had told her she still had the potion Shatter had made for her and would honor her promise to take that.

In the end, Alanna decided not to go stay with the riders after all. For her, it was the principle of the thing. She'd wanted Mother's permission more than she'd wanted to live with the riders.

Her situation with Soren was completely different than Leda's with Scarlett. Leda was in love, for one thing. As much as Alanna enjoyed kissing and flirting with Soren, it was only for fun. She had no delusions about her feelings for him. And while she was curious about taking someone to bed, she wanted to be in love first.

Leda had taken Scarlett to bed, but of course, Leda couldn't get pregnant that way.

Mother Allison had given her the potion to make sure she could stay in control. That she could make love to someone if she wanted, without the fear of an unwanted pregnancy. And by sacrificing herself, she'd given all of them *life* and all the limitless potential that went along with it. Alanna would always love her for that, knowing that every moment she continued to breathe was because of her.

There was something more, though. Thanks to Allure's reading, Alanna knew she had the transformation in her. She'd always wanted to be a sorcerer one day and she was thrilled that it was possible. But now was not the time. She'd have to go off to the university when that happened and she wanted to explore other possibilities first. Taking Soren to bed might trigger that transformation, and that was another reason to put it off. She might have done it anyway, just for curiosity's sake, despite not being in love. But her desire to avoid the metamorphosis had made up her mind.

And besides, not long after she'd told Soren she wouldn't take him to bed, she'd caught him kissing one of the other riders. And she found out he'd been taking *her* to bed all along. So to hell with him. Alanna would wait until she found someone loyal.

Mother Allison had told her she could do anything she wanted in life, and she liked that. Neither of her mothers had ever tried to force her into marriage the way Allison's father had done to her. And with the transformation in her, Alanna would probably never ascend to the throne anyway. That would fall to Leda or perhaps their unborn sibling. Probably Leda. And that was all right with Alanna. She was eager to explore possibilities but she was pretty sure she had no interest in becoming a ruling princess, or worse yet, a queen. Those positions carried far too much responsibility, and Alanna enjoyed her freedom.

Sigrid took them far into the northern hills, following the River Ember. Alanna started to wonder if she'd take them all the way to the sea, when finally, the dragon dove, following a tributary into the forest. They reached a little waterfall with a large basin at the bottom, and Sigrid circled it once before landing on an outcropping of rock. Dense vegetation covered the surrounding hills.

"This is beautiful," Alanna said. It wasn't as high or large as the falls in Stoutwall but it was pretty nonetheless. "But why were you so insistent on showing me this?"

Sigrid shared a vision of the crash making a home here. Alanna had trouble seeing how it would suit their needs. The waterfall was nice, and the lake at the bottom could serve as a watering hole, but there weren't many places for them to perch.

Sigrid's vision changed. Much of the vegetation disappeared, revealing craggy hills with a complex cave system inside. The dragon was trying to show her that another crash had lived here long ago, the riders making their homes in the caves. If they could clear the plant growth, this place could serve that purpose again. Alanna knew dragons had once flourished all over Anoria but had never imagined a crash living right here in Spanbrook.

"You're right, Sigrid," she said, grinning from ear to ear. "I think we've found our new home."

The End

Milton Keynes UK
Ingram Content Group UK Ltd.
UKHW041836171124
451242UK00011B/187/J